THE WIZARD OF HOPE

THE ALASKAN ADVENTURES OF PERCY HOPE

BOOK FOUR

NEIL PERRY GORDON

ISBN: 979-8-9875632-8-1

To the people of Hope, Alaska—
a town that has lived up to its name in every sense.

For nearly twenty summers, I have found in your valley a refuge of
friendship, laughter, and inspiration.
To my dear friends Tom and Barbara Miller, whose hospitality and
warmth have made Hope my home away from home, and to their sons,
Sam and Jack, whose good nature and adventurous spirits embody the
very heart of this place—thank you for sharing your lives and memories
with me.

And to the wonderful, open-hearted people who call this valley home—
thank you for welcoming me into your community and stories.

This book is dedicated to you—
the true wizards of Hope,
who remind me, year after year,
that magic is real, and it is found in community.

Contents

PROLOGUE: AUGUST 1915 1

CHAPTER ONE: MURDER IN TENT CITY 5

CHAPTER TWO: TROUBLE 15

CHAPTER THREE: THE ANCHORAGE HOTEL 27

CHAPTER FOUR: SEWARD 33

CHAPTER FIVE: FIRST RAIL 37

CHAPTER SIX: THE REVEREND 44

CHAPTER SEVEN: THE SHAMAN'S CALL 58

CHAPTER EIGHT: FIRE ISLAND 64

CHAPTER NINE: THE CAVES 72

CHAPTER TEN: A WHISPER 81

CHAPTER ELEVEN: THE FLATS 89

CHAPTER TWELVE: MATANUSKA 101

CHAPTER THIRTEEN: ELI 111

CHAPTER FOURTEEN: PEGGY 117

CHAPTER FIFTEEN: SUSITNA 125

CHAPTER SIXTEEN: BROAD PASS 137

CHAPTER SEVENTEEN: THE WIZARD OF HOPE 149

CHAPTER EIGHTEEN: CAVE OF THE SOUL 163

CHAPTER NINETEEN: SABOTAGE 170

CHAPTER TWENTY: CUTTER 181

CHAPTER TWENTY-ONE: HELL OF A STORY 195

CHAPTER TWENTY-TWO: THE FROZEN EARTH 203

CHAPTER TWENTY-THREE: REFLECTION 213

CHAPTER TWENTY-FOUR: FREDERICK MEARS 219

CAHPTER TWENTY-FIVE: AN OATH 226

CHAPTER TWENTY-SIX: UNION STATION 232

CHAPTER TWENTY-SEVEN: BUTTE 242

CHAPTER TWENTY-EIGHT: TRAP 253

CHAPTER TWENTY-NINE: CAGED 260

CHAPTER THIRTY: CLARK 266

CHAPTER THIRTY-ONE: HOME 279

CHAPTER THIRTY-TWO: FAMILY 285

CHAPTER THIRTY-THREE: LOOKING HOPEFUL 292

CHAPTER THIRTY-FOUR: ONE MONTH LATER 299

CHAPTER THIRTY-FIVE: FAREWELL 310

CHAPTER THIRTY-SIX: HURRICANE GULCH 319

CHAPTER THIRTY-SEVEN: A WIRE 332

CHAPTER THIRTY-EIGHT: THE HUNT....................................339

CHAPTER THIRTY-NINE: HOME 351

CHAPTER FORTY: A SIGN 357

CHAPTER FORTY-ONE: THE RETURN 364

CHAPTER FORTY-TWO: WALTER 371

CHAPTER FORTY-THREE: THE GOLDEN SPIKE............................377

EPILOGUE: RAILS OF HOPE 383

About the Author...389

PROLOGUE
AUGUST 1915

They call me Percy Hope.

But the name on my birth certificate—buried in a box beneath my mother's faded papers and letters—says otherwise: Samuel Rothman, born January 19, 1880, San Francisco, California.

I was born under sunlit skies and the tang of salt fog drifting in from the bay—or so my mother always told me. She never let me forget it, as if the weather itself might shield me. "Clear skies, Samuel," she'd say, "the day you arrived. Fog at the edges, but the light broke through." I was her only child. She told the story like scripture.

Even as a boy, I felt the restless drumbeat of distant places. And my parents feared what that restlessness might cost a Jewish son in a world that still read names like warnings. In San Francisco, they were safe, known, and buffered by community. But out there, in the rougher reaches of the world, that was another story. Rothman was a flag, they believed, waved in a country that liked its Jews quiet, grateful, and preferably somewhere else. Especially if that son ever wandered into Alaska's wild heart.

So they gave me another—Percy Hope—a made-up name polished smooth to help me slip through a world where names can be doors or traps.

We have kept the certificate filed away. Not out of shame, but remembrance. Because who we are and who we must become—those are not always the same.

It was under the name Percy Hope that in the summer of 1898, I stepped off Cap Lathrop's steamer, the *LJ Perry*, the salt wind off Turnagain Arm snapping my coat like a battle flag. Beside me was my best friend, Liam Kampen, steadfast as bedrock.

On the dock stood Magnus Vega—a man with eyes like black ice and a grin that could mean gold or graves.

He wasted no time. He stepped closer, looking me up and down.

"What's your name, kid?" he asked, although he was not much older than me.

"Percy Hope."

Magnus jabbed a finger at me, then at the raw sprawl of log cabins and muddy streets behind him, and barked: "Hope. We'll call this place Hope City. Hell, we've got ourselves a name!"

And just like that, Alaska claimed me for its legend.

In its first year bearing the name, it struggled to keep itself righteous under the watchful eyes of Reverend O'Hara, a man who thundered against whiskey and sin with the same fiery zeal he used to preach salvation. Yet sixteen miles away, Sunrise City glittered like temptation in silk stockings. There, Magnus opened the Gold Digger Saloon, where the Seven Deadly Sins weren't whispered—they were staged nightly, under velvet lamps and the shimmer of sequins, accompanied by the hush of dealt cards and the soft chime of gold dust spilling into waiting palms.

I learned quickly that Alaska's true currency wasn't gold—it was secrets, slick as summer rain and just as treacherous. Ella Carson, with eyes shimmering warm as mink, wrapped me in her love spell until I found myself drawn into an ancient Asatru ritual, my blood nearly spilled beneath towering spruce. I remember the resin-scented heat of the forest, the whisper of leaves overhead, and the crack of Magnus's pistol saving my life with less than a moment to spare.

But Alaska's shadows run deeper than any man's greed. It was Sha-e-dah-kla, a Tyonek shaman, who first opened my ears to how the land itself speaks, its voice hidden beneath the roar of wind and ice.

"The earth remembers, Percy. Walk gently, or it will answer."

And so I began listening for the rustle beneath the drifts, the whisper riding the aurora's green glow.

From the churned mud streets of Hope City to the storm-lashed goldfields of Cape Nome, I chased stories alongside legends like Wyatt Earp—yes, *that* Wyatt Earp, and his indomitable wife, Josephine. I crossed frozen rivers under skies so clear they appeared as if carved from crystal, journeying toward Denali's towering crown. There, under a cathedral of blue ice, I traced the secrets buried in Magnus Vega's journal, secrets older than any claim staked in the Territory.

And somewhere along that winding trail, I collided with Peggy Greenburg—a woman with fire in her veins and lightning in her voice.

Our beginning crackled with sparks, sharp words traded like pistol shots, but somehow, from that storm, love took root. She became my wife, the iron anchor to my drifting soul, and the mother of our son, Walter. Thirteen years old now, Walter stands as a curious hybrid of us both—Peggy's fierce determination blazing behind eyes that scan the world with my same restless hunger for truth.

Today, the *San Francisco Examiner* has engaged with me to chronicle the forging of the Alaska Railroad—a steel spine meant to stitch this vast land into one. Some call it progress; others whisper that it's a wound the mountains and forests will never forgive.

As I stand on the dock, the salt wind off the Arm stinging my face, Peggy's last words toll through me like a distant bell:

"Don't wait for this story to find you, Percy. You go out and take it."

So I lean into the wind, caught between duty and the wild ache of discovery. Ahead stretch rails gleaming like a promise beneath the northern sun, mountains waiting to test every man's resolve, and secrets buried deep in lands that remember every boot step.

Come with me, reader. Let's chase the clang of hammers and the whisper of spruce needles. Let's follow these tracks into Alaska's vastness, where each mile holds a mystery—and sometimes, the truth comes howling on the wind.

— Percy Hope

CHAPTER ONE
MURDER IN TENT CITY

"Ladies and gentlemen, esteemed guests, and fellow Alaskans," Governor John Strong began, his voice rising above the crowd. "Today marks a monumental occasion that will forever be etched in Alaskan history. We gather to witness the groundbreaking of the Alaska Railroad, a project symbolizing progress, unity, and the limitless potential of this great land."

As the governor's words resonated in the crisp morning air, I couldn't help but feel the significance of the moment. I stood on the brink of history, about to witness the transformation of this untamed frontier by a ribbon of steel that would carve through its rugged heart.

Tucked in my coat pocket was an advertisement, its ink smudged from the cold, calling for pioneers of every stripe—lumberjacks to fell timber for ties and trestles; sawyers and tie-cutters to shape the wood; teamsters to haul supplies through snow and mud; blacksmiths to forge tools and mend rails; dynamiters to blast paths through mountains; and laborers, strong-backed and willing, to lay track across bogs and river crossings.

It promised years of steady work and fair wages—a lifeline for some, an adventure for others. And as I gazed at the gathering of men in wool coats and fur hats, their faces weathered by wind and ambition, I knew we were standing at the threshold of a new era, poised to tame both wilderness and distance with hammer and spike.

But for me, this journey was more than just another assignment; it was an opportunity to document the heartbeat of this ambitious venture. This railway would connect Alaska's isolated communities and draw this remote territory into the embrace of the modern world.

"It's an honor to stand before you," Governor Strong continued, "among men and women who share the vision of a connected Alaska, where steel tracks and dreams bridge distant lands. This railway is more than just a transportation system—it represents our steadfast commitment to the future."

As quickly as my hand could manage, I furiously scribbled notes, determined to capture the essence of his words for the article I would later wire through the telegraph to my editor at the *San Francisco Examiner*. This was my chance to do more than report on the progress— I wanted to bring to life the spirit of the endeavor, one that echoed the same ambition I witnessed in these lands years ago during the great Alaskan gold-rush days.

When the governor explained why Anchorage had been chosen as the hub for the Alaska Railroad, I glanced up, curious.

"With its strategic coastal location," the governor said, pointing toward the dock where sunlight danced on the waters of Cook Inlet, "Anchorage provides access to the inlet and a central position within the Territory. Its flat terrain and rail connections make it the ideal choice for receiving and distributing the construction materials required for this grand project."

I couldn't help but reflect on how much the landscape had changed since my earliest travels. Years ago, my best friend Liam and I sailed north on the steamship *Bertha* as two naïve dreamers into a chaotic frontier—miners shouting over one another, chasing gold and glory in the raw wilderness surrounding Turnagain Arm. Anchorage didn't exist back then—not even as a whisper. But with the arrival of the railway project, that whisper had become a roar—a thriving settlement poised to become the gateway to Alaska's future.

"The railway will stretch through the breathtaking landscapes," the governor's voice continued, "from Seward, winding through the majestic Kenai Peninsula, past the serene beauty of Moose Pass, and into this burgeoning city of Anchorage. This route will open a new frontier of opportunity and growth, connecting the southern coast with the heart of the interior."

He paused, letting the vision sink in, his gaze sweeping over the gathered crowd. A crisp breeze carried the scent of spruce and salt.

"Beyond Anchorage, the railway will continue its ambitious journey, traversing the rugged terrain of the Susitna River Valley and advancing northward toward the rich coalfields of Matanuska. Eventually, it will arrive at the banks of the Tanana River, culminating in Fairbanks. This plan will create a lifeline, a steel thread that binds together the scattered communities of Alaska. It will pave the way for commerce, settlement, and the dream of a united and prosperous future in the vast northern frontier."

As I furiously jotted down his words, my mind conjured images of the train's path—a vital artery cutting through the rugged beauty of Alaska's wilderness. I imagined its whistle piercing the crisp air as it passed the towering peaks of Denali and rolled through valleys shaped by glaciers and rivers, places I had once traversed in search of the truth. Each destination along the railway was soon tied together, stitching a network of steel through the heart of America's last frontier.

But then, a blood-curdling scream shattered the governor's speech. The crowd swiveled toward the city of tents, where hundreds of laborers were crammed into makeshift shelters, braving the bitter conditions in hopes of working on the railway. From the maze of canvas tents emerged a woman, disheveled and covered in blood, her voice choking with anguish.

"Someone killed my husband!" she screamed.

Without hesitation, I bolted toward the chaos, clutching my notepad in one hand and pushing through the throng of onlookers with the other.

Even in the light of day, Tent City was a grim place. The canvas shelters sagged under the weight of grime, and the stench of damp earth and unwashed bodies hung thick in the air.

This wasn't the first time I'd seen men gathered in such desperate conditions, but something about this place appeared more sinister. In Nome, at least, there had been the hope of gold to buoy spirits. Here, it felt as though the very earth had sucked away any trace of optimism, leaving only the bitter reality of survival.

When I reached the scene, the woman wept over her husband's lifeless form, though now her cries were softer, resigned to the fact that no one would bring him back. The man lay sprawled on the ground, his body rigid, his face contorted in what seemed to be a final moment of agony. His clothes were rugged and worn, suited for a man used to hard labor. A tattered wool shirt rolled at the sleeves revealed forearms etched with scars—testaments to a life of toil and struggle. His hands were calloused, fingers frozen mid-clench, as though he had fought against his fate until the very end.

As I examined the body, the sharp scent of iron hung in the air, mingling with the damp earth beneath him—his blood still fresh, soaking into the mud and gravel where it pooled. A jagged wound along his side testified to the violence that had claimed his life. Then something caught my eye—a glint of light, a flicker against the mud just beyond the reach of his outstretched arm. I got closer and wiped away the wet dirt, revealing a crude silver medallion, half-buried as if torn from his neck in the final moments of struggle. It lay there, silent and gleaming, as though waiting for the right hands to find it.

The medallion was circular, its surface tarnished yet still catching the fading light. On the front, a simple etching of a raven in mid-flight stood out, its eye marked with a tiny dark stone. The symbol was unfamiliar, yet something about it stirred a memory.

Claiming it as evidence, I tucked it into my coat pocket, unaware of what significance, if any, it might hold. Was this a random act of violence, or was something more at play? The dead man didn't seem like just another unfortunate soul lost to the chaos of Tent City. Perhaps he was a casualty of something larger, a piece of a puzzle yet to be understood. And the medallion—was it merely a trinket, or could it be a clue? Maybe even a motive?

The construction of the railway attracted all sorts: honest laborers seeking a fresh start, opportunists eager to profit from the chaos, and men desperate to escape the shadows of their pasts. Any of them could have been responsible for this murder—or perhaps it wasn't the work of a single hand but rather the unseen forces of greed, fear, and power clashing within this rough, chaotic settlement. Whatever the truth, the medallion's presence suggested that this death was only the beginning.

I crouched beside him, studying his face and the faint outline of his features. His furrowed brow hinted at years of hardship, perhaps even the suspicion that had followed him through life. Deep lines etched the corners of his eyes, and a faint scar traced his left cheekbone—a pale slash beneath days of stubble. This wasn't just a senseless act of violence but a consequence of the dangerous currents swirling in Tent City. I was determined to discover who had done this and, more importantly, why.

I rose slowly; the widow's soft sobs still filled the tent, providing a heartbreaking counterpoint to the silence of her dead husband. I turned to her, her eyes red and swollen, her hands trembling as they clutched his lifeless arm.

"Ma'am…" I began gently. "Did you see who did this?"

She stared at me, eyes glassy, as though the question took a moment to reach her through the fog of grief. Then she gave a tiny shake of her head, her lower lip quivering.

"Do you recognize this?" I asked softly, pulling the medallion from my pocket and offering it for her to see.

She glanced at it for a moment, then shook her head, her voice barely above a whisper. "I've never seen it before."

But there was a flicker—a split second where her eyes widened just enough to betray her.

She knew more than she was letting on. Since she made no claim, I slipped it back into my coat pocket, masking my suspicion.

I crouched down again, my voice gentle. "Ma'am… what's your name?"

She wiped her eyes with trembling fingers. "Margaret. Margaret Morse."

I nodded, pulling a small notebook from my coat pocket. "And… your husband? What was his name?"

Her lips quivered as she glanced at the man beside her. "Harlan."

I jotted it down carefully, the scratch of my pencil loud in the hush of the tent.

There was nothing more to be learned here, not now. The answers wouldn't be found in his lifeless form but in the living souls outside—the ones who had seen, heard, or perhaps even caused this.

Stepping from the tent, I scanned the makeshift camp. A nearby cluster of workers stood huddled under the muted light of the gray sky, their faces shadowed with suspicion as they watched me. Their voices were low, a murmur of unease threading through the group. I approached them, brushing the dirt from my hands, my footsteps deliberate.

"Does anyone know what happened here?" I asked, my voice slicing through the soft hum of conversation.

One man, taller than the rest, with a sunken, haggard face, spoke first. "No one saw nothin'. Fights happen all the time 'round here. Ain't no one gonna risk their neck to stop it."

His words held a bleak finality. The lawlessness of Tent City was evident—this was a place where the strong preyed on the weak, and survival depended on how well you could fend for yourself.

I returned to the scene of the crime and turned my attention back to the ground, catching the faint traces of disturbance in the dirt. Near the entrance, among the chaos of overlapping prints, I noticed a set of footprints—fresher than the rest. The edges were crisp, not yet softened by time or wind. They led away from the tent, cutting a clear path toward the outskirts of the camp.

"Someone left here not too long ago," I muttered, my curiosity piqued. I followed the trail, my footsteps steady and purposeful. The prints led me through the rough terrain, past clusters of tents and cautious eyes, until I reached the riverbank. The gentle murmur of water was the only sound concealing my approach.

There, standing by the water's edge, was a man. His back was to me, his hands submerged in the current. But it wasn't just mud he was scrubbing away—the tension in his shoulders, the frantic movements of his arms, told me he was trying to wash away something far more incriminating.

I called out to him, "Hey! What are you doing?"

He stiffened but didn't turn around. My instincts told me he was involved, but I needed more than a gut feeling to link him to the crime.

"Just cleaning up," he said, his voice rough as if caught off guard.

"Cleaning up, are you?" I took a step closer. "Funny timing, considering there's a dead man back there."

His head turned, and for an instant his eyes met mine—wide, guilty, and filled with unmistakable fear. His beard was meticulously trimmed, its edges crisp along his jaw, an unusual sight in a place where most men, myself included, wore theirs untamed. Mine had become unruly over the past few weeks, something Peggy never failed to scold me about. But beyond the neat beard, there was something else—a flash of recognition, as if he knew exactly who I was. Before I could press him further, he turned and tore off down the riverbank, vanishing into the thick brush.

I cursed under my breath and gave chase, but the man had the advantage. Within minutes, he was swallowed by the wilderness beyond the camp. I stopped, panting, frustrated. Whoever he was, he at least knew something about the murder, and his flight only confirmed my suspicions.

My instinct told me that this murder wasn't merely an isolated act of violence. It marked the beginning of something far more sinister, and my mission as a journalist would be to uncover it. With renewed determination, I returned to the camp, my mind already assembling the clues, prepared to face the harsh realities of life in Alaska's new frontier.

CHAPTER TWO
TROUBLE

The day's chaos lingered like smoke in the night air, stubborn and oppressive. The widow's anguished scream and the image of her husband's lifeless body haunted my every step, like shadows cast by the flickering campfires dotting Tent City. It was around eight, but the sky still blazed with the lingering sun, casting long, restless shadows as the campfire's glow danced across the weathered tents and the hollow-eyed faces of the workers.

The questions wouldn't let up as I picked my way across the uneven ground. Who was the man by the river? And what had he been scrubbing from his hands—mud or the guilt of something far more sinister?

The camp was quieter now, subdued after a day marred by violence, yet the tension still lingered, coiling through the whispered conversations around the fires. Men huddled in small groups, their voices low and cautious. The atmosphere was brittle, poised to crack under the burden of the unknown killer among them.

I pulled my jacket closer against the chill, the faint scent of pine and smoke swirling on the breeze. My wife's words echoed in my mind. *"You're a hunter, Percy. Not of game, but of truth. Go find it."* Peggy always had a knack for pushing me into situations where most would turn away. And here I was, in the thick of it, with more questions than answers and a growing sense that I was chasing something much bigger than a headline.

I passed a group of men unloading crates from a wagon, their faces smeared with dirt and weariness. No one met my eye. Here, people knew when not to ask questions. But if the murder I'd stumbled upon was just the beginning, someone had to speak up.

Near the center of camp, I spotted a tall man with a stern demeanor and the kind of voice that could cut through the din of the day. "Excuse me," I called, stepping toward him. "You in charge here?"

He turned, his eyes narrowing as they sized me up. "Depends on who's asking," he said, his tone wary.

"Percy Hope. Reporter for the *San Francisco Examiner.* I'm covering the railway project, and for information regarding the murder."

The man folded his muscular arms, his expression unreadable. "You're here for the railroad, not for what goes on in camp. Leave that to the law."

"There's no law here," I said evenly. "Just a dead man and a lot of questions."

His jaw tightened, but he said nothing. Around us, the noise of the camp seemed to dim, as though the workers themselves were straining to hear.

I pressed on. "A man fled when I tried to question him by the river. I don't believe in coincidences, so I'm asking you: Who's gone missing today?"

The man's lips pressed into a thin line. "I don't keep tabs on every soul in this place, and I don't plan to start now. People come, people go."

"Even murderers?" I challenged, stepping closer.

His eyes flicked to the workers around us, then back to me. "If you've got questions, try Raynor. He's been here longer than most."

"Where can I find him?" I asked.

His gaze shifted toward a thin column of smoke curling upward through the trees. "Mess tent," he said tersely. Then, with a hint of weariness, he added, "But don't stir up trouble, Mr. Hope. This camp's hanging by a thread as it is."

I nodded, though his warning fell on deaf ears. Trouble wasn't something I needed to stir—it was already steeped into every corner of this place. All I had to do was follow the trail to its source.

The moonlight illuminated Tent City as it wound its way past the camp, a rare moment of beauty in a harsh and unforgiving landscape. The air carried a pungent cocktail of pine sap, freshly sawn wood, and the smoke of a kitchen fire. Following the foreman's directions, I wound my way toward the smoke, each step pulling me closer to the heart of the camp and, with it, whatever secrets it was struggling to contain.

The mess tent loomed ahead, its canvas walls stretched and stitched with patchwork repairs. As I stepped inside, the scent of charred wood and lingering grease greeted me. A few men sat hunched over tin plates, their conversation muted and their faces lined with exhaustion.

At the back of the tent, a man stood at a battered counter, his thick arms plunging into a basin of soapy water as though scrubbing the pots could rid them—and him—of more than just grime. His apron bore the stains of a long day's work, and his movements carried the deliberate haste of someone who didn't welcome distractions.

"We're closed," he barked without looking up, his voice gravelly but firm. Wiping his hands on his apron, he finally glanced my way, his sharp eyes narrowing with suspicion.

I took a step forward, undeterred. "I'm not here for food. At least not now," I said. "I'm here for answers."

The moment I stepped closer, recognition flickered in his eyes. "Hey, aren't you Percy Hope?" he asked, pointing a soapy finger toward me.

Caught off guard, I smiled. "Yes, that's me. Have we met before?"

A wide grin spread across his face. "I saw you fight Paddy Ryan at the Northern!"

"You were in Nome?" I asked, surprised. "That was fifteen years ago."

"Indeed, I was," he chuckled. "I ran an outdoor eatery there until the big storm nearly wiped the whole town off the map. I'm John Raynor," he said, extending his wet hand.

We shook, and I looked closer at the man's sun-weathered face. "I'm sorry, sir, I don't recall meeting back then."

"That's because we never did," John admitted, "but I was in the crowd that night you took down the Trojan Giant in that bare-knuckle boxing match. Should have placed a bet on you instead," he added with a hearty laugh.

I joined in, remembering the wild chaos of Nome. "I might've done the same."

John wiped his hands on his apron and looked around. "What brings Percy Hope to Tent City, then?"

"I'm on assignment," I explained, "covering the construction of the Alaska Railway for the *San Francisco Examiner*."

John raised his eyebrows, clearly impressed. "That's quite a task."

"And you? What brought you here?" I asked, gesturing to the bustling camp around us.

"After Nome, I took a job with Thomas Riggs, cooking for his bank in Juneau. Then he asked me to head up here and keep the workers fed," John said, his hands resuming their work, scrubbing a pot with the same vigor he'd likely bring to a wrestling match.

"Oh, yes, Riggs, the president of the Alaska Central Railway," I said, leaning against the counter.

"Good man." John nodded, his voice carrying a tone of quiet respect. "Knows how to keep things running, even out here in the wild."

"Hey, John," I said casually, adjusting my stance and lowering my voice to indicate I was probing for something deeper, "you've been around here for a while. Have you noticed anything unusual lately? Any trouble among the guys? Maybe someone acting strangely?"

John set the pot down with a dull thud, his brow furrowing as he wiped his hands on his apron. "Percy, this place is nothing but trouble," he said. "You've got men working themselves to the bone for scraps, tempers flaring left and right. What kind of strange are you talking about?"

I hesitated for a moment, letting my question settle in. "Strange enough that it might lead to a man being killed. Heard anything about that?"

His eyes darkened, and for a brief moment, I thought I'd hit a nerve. But he shook his head, his lips pressed tight. "I heard about the murder, sure. Words like that spread faster than fires in these parts. But no, I don't know anything. And if I did…" He trailed off, glancing around the tent, his voice dropping. "Well, I wouldn't be shouting it for everyone to hear."

I nodded, allowing his words to linger between us. Tent City was chaotic, filled with swirling dust and restless energy, yet it was also where everything had begun. If the answers to the murder could be found anywhere, they were buried in the shifting sands of its transient chaos.

I left John's mess hall with a nod of farewell, the warmth of the conversation still lingering in my mind as I stepped back into the chaos. The camp grew louder as the sun sank, casting long shadows over the makeshift settlement. Each sound—the creak of wagons, the shouts of men, the distant clang of hammers—felt sharper, as if the energy of the place was reaching a fever pitch. Tent City was raw and untamed, a jumble of desperation and hope, and I felt myself being pulled deeper into its fierce heart.

As I walked along the muddy pathways, a group of men gathered around a barrel fire caught my eye. The rich, smoky scent of roasting meat drifted toward me, and my stomach tightened with hunger. I hesitated, then approached, feeling the heat from the flames on my face.

"Got an extra plate?" I asked, forcing a friendly smile.

One of the men, a burly fellow with a thick beard and a battered cap, looked me up and down. "Depends," he said slowly, his gaze lingering on my relatively clean clothes. "You got a story worth tellin'?"

I chuckled, sensing the test in his words. "I've got a few, but none half as good as the ones you boys must have," I said, easing myself down onto a log beside the fire. "How about I listen first and see where things take us?"

The tension eased, and the bearded man handed me a tin plate with a hunk of greasy meat. "Name's Bill Sullivan," he said, extending a rough hand. "Been here since the first batch of men arrived. You're new. What brings you?"

"Percy Hope," I said, shaking his hand firmly. "I'm covering the railway for the *San Francisco Examiner*."

Sullivan snorted. "A newspaperman. Well, you're in for a hell of a story, that's for sure."

A younger man sitting across the fire, barely out of his teens, laughed bitterly. "A story? More like a damn nightmare," he said, staring into the flames.

I took a bite of the meat, chewing thoughtfully before speaking. "What makes you say that?"

The young man's eyes remained fixed on the fire. "Supplies are running thin, and what little we get costs a fortune. There's talk of strikes—rumors that some foremen are pocketing the difference, lining their pockets while we scrape by."

Sullivan shot the boy a stern look. "Mind your words, Robbie. You don't know who's listening."

I leaned in, curiosity piqued. "Is it that bad?"

Sullivan's face tightened. "Worse. Prices are high now, but if the next shipment's delayed or stolen, they'll be through the roof. Every man here's on edge, and it won't take much to set things off."

I glanced around at the other faces around the fire—hard men with wary eyes, weariness etched into their features. They weren't just workers but survivors, each carrying their hopes and grievances. I lingered longer, listening to their stories, soaking in the uneasy camaraderie that held the camp together.

I said my goodbyes and wandered deeper into Tent City. The sun finally sank below the mountaintops, though daylight still lingered, while a chill settled. Near the edge of the camp, I came across a boisterous group of men gathered around a makeshift card game. Their laughter pierced through the noise of the camp. I stood at the fringe, watching until one of them spotted me.

"Care to join?" he asked, dealing the cards with a quick, practiced motion.

"Just watching for now," I said with a polite nod. "I've got an eye for cheaters."

That earned a few chuckles, and they made space for me on an overturned crate. I settled in, watching the game unfold with practiced patience. Back in Nome, Wyatt Earp had taught me how the smallest gestures—a flick of the wrist, a glance too quick to catch—could reveal a cheat. I noticed it here as well, in how some players handled their cards a little too smoothly, their eyes betraying more than they realized.

Between rounds, I asked a few casual questions, probing about supplies and the rising tensions. The cards told one story, but the men around the table might tell another.

One of the men, swaying slightly with drink, leaned close and whispered, "You'll hear things around here. But if you're smart, you'll keep your mouth shut."

"Who's behind it all?" I asked, trying to sound casual.

He only grinned, taking another swig of whiskey. "Figure it out for yourself. But watch your back."

As the night deepened, I moved from fire to fire, joining in the singing of old folk songs that echoed across the camp. Among the laughter and music, I caught the first whispers of genuine trouble. Men spoke of missing comrades who had disappeared without a trace—vanishings that the foremen dismissed as desertions. However, the way they conversed, with their voices low and eyes darting nervously, revealed a different story.

I found myself drifting toward a large campfire where a group of men sat warming their hands, the flames casting long shadows across their faces. "Mind if I join?" I asked, feeling the cold seeping into my bones.

A tall, thin man with a long nose nodded, scooting over to make room. "Pull up a log, stranger," he said. "Name's Tom, and this here's George and Lenny." He gestured to two others, one burly and bearded, the other wiry with a nervous energy that made him look like he might spring to his feet at any moment.

"Percy Hope," I said, settling in. "I'm covering the railway for Hearst's newspapers."

"A press man," George said with a grunt. "I hope you're ready for what you're about to see. It's not all optimism and progress out here."

Lenny, who had been staring silently into the fire, spoke up. "They say we'll work through the winter," he said, his voice low. "But have you seen an Alaskan winter, Mr. Hope? There's talk of men freezing to death."

Tom shook his head. "If the weather doesn't get us, the prices will. The cost of supplies has doubled since the first ship arrived, and if we don't see another delivery soon, we'll be lucky to eat through the end of the month."

I listened, absorbing the bitterness in their voices, the restless edge of men who'd arrived weeks ago, hoping for work that hadn't yet come. The camaraderie was genuine, but so was the growing unease. They were bound together by shared hopes, yet divided by the gnawing fear that Tent City held only empty promises and dwindling chances.

As night fell, the camp's fires multiplied, and laughter and shouting filled the air. Men gathered around makeshift tables for card games, their faces lit by the flickering flames. I lingered at the edges of these gatherings, listening for rumors and searching for any signs of the tensions brewing beneath the surface. There were talks of thefts, missing supplies, and whispers of discontent among the laborers.

Later that night, I sat with a group of men around a fire, their faces grim as they spoke of the rising costs. "Five dollars for a sack of flour," a grizzled old man spat, his fists clenched around a dented tin cup. "It's robbery, plain and simple."

I filed away the information, adding it to the growing list of mysteries surrounding Tent City. As the temperature dropped, the fire's warmth became a comfort, and I listened to the stories that filled the night—the legends of miners who had struck it rich, the tales of lost fortunes, and the promises of a better future that seemed as elusive as the Northern Lights.

It wasn't all gloom and hardship. There were moments of laughter, too, such as when a group of men, half-drunk and warmed by the fire, began singing old folk songs, their voices rising into the cold night air. "The Old Oaken Bucket" came first, its nostalgic melody stirring memories of home, followed by a rousing rendition of "Hot Time in the Old Town Tonight," which had us clapping along, the rhythm infectious even in the biting cold. I joined in, and for a brief moment, it felt like the weight of the world had lifted. But as the last notes faded, the reality of Tent City swept over us like a frigid, sharp, and unforgiving wind.

Though summer reigned for the moment, the shadow of winter was never far from thought in Alaska, and those in charge steadfastly vowed that the work would endure, unbroken by the seasons. The challenge could break a man or forge him into something stronger. As I moved from one conversation to another, from one fire to another, I knew I was only scratching the surface of the truth. Whatever was happening here, whatever darkness lurked in the shadows of the camp, I was determined to find it.

CHAPTER THREE
THE ANCHORAGE HOTEL

The lobby of the Anchorage Hotel breathed with the steady murmur of maps and men, the kind of quiet that settles only when stakes are high and words matter. Its timber walls, stained deep with pipe smoke and oil heat, seemed to lean in, listening. Light from the lamps caught in the resinous grain, flickering like memories across the faces of those gathered there—men whose decisions were carving a new artery through the frozen heart of Alaska.

The floor creaked under worn leather soles. Rugs once rich with pattern had faded to the color of old blood, threadbare from seasons of boots and mud. But nothing about the place felt tired. It held the charge of a telegraph wire, taut with the hum of intent.

Colonel Frederick Mears stood by the hearth, back straight as a rail spike, blue eyes alert beneath the shadow of his brim. A West Point man and seasoned officer, he carried his military bearing into every calculation of grade, cost, labor, and time. Every delay pressed against his ribs like a steel plate. He wasn't just building a railway; he was defying wilderness with math and muscle. A colonel without a battlefield—unless you counted the mountains, rivers, and icefields in his path.

To his left, Thomas Riggs sketched something in the soot on the stone mantel with the tip of his gloved finger, explaining a reroute around unstable tundra near Broad Pass. His voice clipped and precise, gestures sharp as surveying stakes. Riggs had walked every miserable mile of the interior—his confidence wasn't born of theory, but of frostbitten boots and frostbitten men.

Otto Ohlson, leaning back in a chair with arms folded, said nothing. He had the posture of a man who knew the money better than the soil, but he listened like he meant to remember every word. His future with the railroad would come later, when it was built and was bleeding money. That's when men like Ohlson got to work, squeezing profit from steam and schedule. For now, he watched, calculating the cost of every pause in conversation.

In the corner, cradling a cup of coffee that had gone cold long ago, John Ballaine watched the others with something unreadable in his expression. Maybe satisfaction. Maybe resentment. Maybe both. Two decades earlier, he'd tried to build a line from Seward northward—had financed it, preached it, nearly gone broke for it. The Alaska Central had collapsed under snow and ambition, but some of its bones still lay beneath what Mears was building now. He didn't speak, not yet. Just watched the men picking up where he'd left off, the way a ghost might watch its old house being rebuilt.

Outside, a gust swept down Fourth Avenue, rattling the windows in their frames. No one flinched. The winter was always trying to get in.

But inside, around that hearth, the real storm was already underway—a convergence of engineers, visionaries, pragmatists, and ghosts. And from their silence rose the shape of something vast, steel-boned and steam-hearted, waiting to be laid into the land.

The Alaska Railroad wasn't just being built. It was being decided.

These were men wrestling steel into wilderness, and though they stood together, the tension between ambition and peril lay coiled around them like a live wire.

I was there to tell their story, but I sensed even then that the story might be far bigger—and far darker—than any headline could hold.

"Mr. Hope?"

The voice belonged to Mears. He moved toward me, offering his hand with a firmness that left no doubt he'd hauled his share of timber and iron in younger years.

"Mr. Mears," I said, taking his hand.

"Call me Frederick," he replied, his face cracking into a fleeting smile. "I hear you're chronicling our progress for my old friend Mr. Hearst."

"And you can call me Percy," I answered. "Yes, I'm here to capture it all—the triumphs, the failures, and the people making it happen. Have you a few moments to share your thoughts?"

He cast a glance back at Riggs and Ohlson, then inclined his head. "Walk with me."

Outside, the night air bit cold against my cheeks. Campfires flickered on the far edge of Tent City, painting wavering constellations against the violet sky. The wind carried the scents of spruce smoke, damp earth, and distant coal dust. Hammers rang faintly through the darkness, a metallic heartbeat pulsing out of the wilderness.

"You've spent time in Tent City?" Frederick asked as we strode along the boardwalk.

"I have," I said, tucking my notebook into my coat. "The place has the same look as Nome did in the old days—hunger behind every eye, men sleeping two to a cot, tempers set to flash. How long can that hold before something gives way?"

Frederick slowed, his eyes fixed on the line of campfires in the distance. "What you've seen in Tent City is only the beginning. These men are still close to town. There's still warmth, supplies, the sense that civilization is just over their shoulders. Wait until they're carving grades through mountain passes buried under forty feet of snow. Wait until the rivers freeze solid, cutting them off for weeks at a time. That's when Alaska shows her true teeth."

I studied his face as he spoke, the harsh lines cut deeper by the pale moonlight. "And the men?" I asked. "Will they hold?"

Frederick let out a low breath, as though testing the chill of the night air. "Some will. Many won't. The cold breaks bones, but it's the silence that breaks minds. Three dollars a day won't keep a man out here if he believes he's dying for nothing."

"And the leadership?" I pressed. "Is Riggs doing enough to keep them from breaking?"

Mears paused, glancing over his shoulder as though deciding how far he could trust me.

"Riggs is a good man. So's Ohlson. But we're building this on a shoestring. Every dollar spent on comforts is a dollar not spent on rail or blasting powder. And there's something else…"

He fell silent for a few paces, boots thudding on the wooden planks.

Finally, he spoke. "Not everyone wants this railroad to be finished."

I blinked. "Who in their right mind would want it to fail?"

He gave a short, humorless laugh. "Men with plenty to lose, Percy. Steamship owners who've controlled freight prices for decades. Private syndicates sitting on mineral claims who'd rather keep the Territory cut off. And there's… other interests. Interests that go deeper than copper and coal. Some would rather see this wilderness stay closed, no matter the cost."

"Why?" I said. "What's so bad about building a railway?"

Frederick's eyes gleamed as they caught the shimmer of firelight from Tent City.

"Because the railway will open everything. And some things buried in this land were never meant to be unearthed. Some fortunes, some secrets… the sort of secrets that could turn powerful men into enemies."

A chill crept down my spine that had nothing to do with the wind. "Is the murder in Tent City tied to this?"

His face turned flint-hard. "Hard to say. But I'd wager it wasn't just a drunken quarrel. Too much is at stake. And the way the pieces are shifting… I'd advise you, Percy—tread carefully."

I flipped open my notebook again, suddenly aware of the weight it carried. "Frederick, I came here for the truth. The people deserve it."

He held my gaze, his eyes steely and resolute. "The truth is a dangerous thing. It's a blade, Percy. Handle it without caution, or you'll bleed more than ink."

We'd come to the edge of the boardwalk. Beyond lay the black expanse of the tundra, dotted with orange firelight and restless shadows. Somewhere out there, men laughed and sang over cheap whiskey, while others plotted or prayed for survival.

Frederick turned back toward the hotel's glow. He paused, looking over his shoulder one last time. "Remember—Alaska doesn't forgive mistakes. And not everyone who smiles at you is your ally."

Then he disappeared into the hotel's warmth, leaving me alone beneath the stars. I stood there a while, staring toward the flickering fires of Tent City, my breath ghosting in the cold.

Alaska was going to test all of us. And the deeper I dug for the truth, the more certain I became that the real battle wasn't only against ice and granite, but against men who'd kill to keep certain secrets buried.

And I feared I was already too close to finding them.

CHAPTER FOUR
SEWARD

The *Admiral Evans* pitched and rolled through the choppy waters of Resurrection Bay, the early morning mist curling like ghostly fingers along the coastline. Seward lay ahead, emerging from the thinning fog— its wooden buildings clustered at the base of towering, forested peaks, with smoke rising from chimneys as the town stirred to life. Beyond it, the railway's promise stretched northward, its steel and timber set to carve a fragile pathway into the wilderness.

I gripped the railing, the sea spray cold against my face, and let my gaze linger on the shoreline ahead, marking the first step into the railway's great gamble. As I took in the scene, my thoughts drifted back to the men who had boarded the steamship back in Anchorage, carrying with them the weight of exhaustion and expectation.

Eighteen hours earlier, Tent City had emptied onto the docks, hundreds of men crowding forward, clutching their meager possessions. They had moved with a mixture of weariness and hunger, their faces lined with the scars of hardship, their eyes clouded with unspoken histories.

The ship's deck was thick with sweat, damp wool, and salt air as they packed in, claiming whatever space they could find—some by the railings, others near the cargo hold where the engine's warmth could fend off the Alaskan cold. They spoke in low voices, a mix of tongues—Scandinavian, Irish, German, Russian—all blended in the pursuit of survival.

Tent City had served as their waiting ground, a realm of mud-slicked walkways, flickering campfires, and endless promises of work. Some had arrived with hope in their hearts, while others had come with nothing left to lose. Yet, all of them had sought something—a second chance, a future, or perhaps just another paycheck to keep the past from engulfing them.

And perhaps, one of them had come with murder on his hands.

The first lights of Seward flickered through the thinning mist, reflecting off the bay as the *Admiral Evans* groaned against the waves. Smoke rose from chimneys, blending with the sharp scents of salt, spruce, and coal dust.

Next to me, Thomas Riggs, president of the Alaska Engineering Commission, exhaled slowly.

"Seward is where this all begins," he murmured. "A deep-water port, the key to opening the interior. Without it, the railway would be nothing more than a dream."

A dream, I thought—or a gamble, depending on who you asked.

The railway's construction had drawn hundreds of men to this land—ambitious, desperate men with nowhere else to go.

As the ship docked, the men began filing off, boots hitting the damp planks of the pier, their breath rising in the crisp morning air. Supplies were offloaded—timber, iron rails, crates of dynamite—the lifeblood of the railway, stacked in neat rows along the waterfront. Horses and wagons bustled down the muddy streets, stirring up the scent of wet earth, sweat, and something metallic in the air.

A few yards away, railway laborers stood in line for rations. Faces hollow. Hands calloused. Some were fresh arrivals, their eyes still filled with the illusion of opportunity. Others had seen too many winters and buried too many friends beneath the tundra.

And then I saw him.

A man with sharp, deep-set eyes stood with his collar turned high against the cold, the crisp lines of his meticulously trimmed beard cutting a precise silhouette amid the chaos. A jolt shot through me—it was him. The same immaculate jawline I'd glimpsed in Tent City the night of the murder, when I'd caught him by the stream, scrubbing his hands as though trying to wash away a sin.

His gaze speared into mine for an instant, taut with unspoken recognition. Then, like smoke, he vanished into the crowd.

"Not the gold rush you expected, eh, Hope?"

The voice snapped me out of my thoughts. I turned to see John Ballaine, the businessman who had initially championed the railway. His sharp blue eyes reflected the burden of a man who had fought for his vision—and almost lost.

"You'd think after Nome, I'd know better than to expect easy fortunes," I said with a smirk.

Ballaine laughed. "That's what reporters do—chase stories. But I'll tell you this—more than just iron and timber is being laid here. The railway is reshaping Alaska—who holds the power, who reaps the rewards, and who gets left out in the cold."

I glanced back toward the ration line.

The murderer was gone.

As we stepped into the muddy streets of Seward, the crisp morning air was filled with the sound of iron striking steel.

A new frontier was being built.

CHAPTER FIVE
FIRST RAIL

The scent of fresh-cut timber and damp earth clung to the crisp air as crews hacked away at the dense forest lining Resurrection Bay, clearing a path for the first stretch of railway. Massive Sitka spruces, their trunks as thick as a man was tall, groaned as they were felled, their branches crashing into the underbrush below. The men worked tirelessly—axes swung, saws bit through stubborn wood, and horse-drawn carts creaked beneath the weight of cut logs—all in preparation for the first ceremonial rail to be laid in Seward.

I stood at the edge of it all, notebook in hand, preparing to return my first report to the *Examiner.* The Alaska Railroad was no longer just a plan drawn on maps—it was a reality.

But reality in Alaska was never easy.

The land fought back at every turn. The coastal terrain was unforgiving—thick with roots, hidden sinkholes, and jagged granite outcroppings that made excavation nearly impossible. Workers would have to rely on muscle, grit, and luck to clear the path for the tracks.

"We're not just building a railway," one foreman muttered, wiping the sweat from his brow despite the chill in the air. *"We're carving it out of the damn wilderness."*

Indeed, progress won't come easily. Every foot of track will be won inch by inch, not in sweeping advances. Dynamite crews must blast through stubborn rock faces, sending tremors through the valley as the land resists every effort to tame it. Teams of horses will strain against the burden of uprooted trees and overturned soil, their muscles rippling with the sheer force needed to clear a path forward.

Workers will push on in silence, their determination forged by necessity rather than choice. This land has no patience for weakness, and those who falter will be left behind in one form or another.

But it won't just be the workers who have come to Seward. Others are here, too—watching, waiting—drawn by something more than steel and progress.

By midday, a crowd had gathered at mile zero—railway officials in their heavy woolen coats, businessmen in tailored suits and bowler hats, engineers with their surveying instruments slung over their shoulders, and the countless workers who would carve the memories of this moment from the wilderness itself. They had all come, drawn by the gravity of history about to unfold, by the knowledge that this moment, the laying of the first rail, would mark the beginning of something that would reshape the Alaskan frontier forever.

The first steel rail lay ready on its wooden ties, its polished surface catching the weak sunlight straining through the cloud-laden sky. It was simple and unassuming, yet it carried the weight of thousands of miles, countless hours of labor, and an untamed land that would soon feel the bite of steel.

At the center of it all stood Thomas Riggs, the man charged with bringing Washington's grand vision into reality. The embodiment of power and purpose, he surveyed the crowd, his posture firm, his gaze unwavering. Even in the brisk wind from Resurrection Bay, he remained steady, knowing that this moment belonged to him and to every man who had gambled his fate on this railway's success.

He cleared his throat, his voice rising above the wind, carrying through the expectant hush.

"Greetings to you all," he called. "This marks the first step in opening the vast Alaskan frontier: a railway to connect the coast to the north, uniting this wild land and bringing opportunity where there was once only isolation."

A murmur rippled through the crowd, some nodding, others standing stiffly as the meaning of his words settled over them. For the officials, it was a political and economic milestone. For the workers, it was another day of backbreaking labor, a gamble for survival. And for some—myself included—it was something else entirely.

A moment that felt larger than itself. A threshold between past and future.

Riggs lifted the silver-plated spike, its surface gleaming as he positioned it above the waiting rail.

The hammer came down once—a sharp ring against the steel, cutting through the air like the first note of an anthem.

Then, twice—a sound that seemed to reverberate beyond the physical world.

There was only silence as the wilderness held its breath, waiting to see if the blow had truly landed.

Then, like a wave crashing against the shore, a cheer rose from the crowd.

Workers tossed their hats in the air, engineers clapped each other on the back, and the distant howl of a wolf echoed from the mountains beyond the bay as the wild issued its own acknowledgment, or warning.

Standing among them, the notebook in my hand suddenly felt heavier, as if I had recorded something not just for the *San Francisco Examiner*, but for something beyond myself.

A story not yet written. A future not yet seen.

But as the voices swelled around me, something strange unfurled at the edges of my perception.

It was as though the air itself thickened, pressing closer, carrying a weight I couldn't explain. The sky darkened imperceptibly, its color sinking into a deeper gray. The scent of timber and iron sharpened until it nearly stung my nose, vivid and metallic.

A sudden stillness pooled around me, though the shouts and laughter of the men continued unabated. For an instant, I felt caught in a space between heartbeats, my senses heightened, every sound and texture brighter and more immediate.

Then a pulse of heat flared against my chest where the medallion lay hidden beneath my shirt. It was subtle but unmistakable—a quick, deliberate throb, as though the metal itself was alive and reacting to forces unseen.

I drew a breath, my lungs oddly tight, aware of nothing except the strange, electric hush inside my skin.

A heartbeat later, the world snapped back into motion. The workers' voices crashed in around me again, and I blinked as though emerging from deep water, my hands trembling with an energy I couldn't name.

I turned, scanning the crowd, half expecting to find someone staring back—someone else who had felt it and seen what I had just seen.

But no one did.

I blinked, and the feeling was gone.

The crowd continued cheering. No one else had noticed.

I inhaled sharply, steadying myself against the pull of something I could not name.

Was it exhaustion? The bite of cold mixed with too little sleep? Or had I just touched something beyond the five senses buried within the land? But now, I couldn't shake the feeling that I was standing at a threshold, peering into something more significant than a railway project.

There was something here—something older than the steel being laid, older than the men carving their way through the wild.

Alaska was not just a land of physical trials and brutal winters. It was a place where the veil between worlds had worn thin. Where the past, the present, and something else entirely bled together.

I needed grounding—something ordinary, something tethered to the world of ink and deadlines. The rail camp's telegraph shack stood just beyond the last string of surveyor flags, smoke curling from its chimney like a whisper of connection. I pushed open the door, letting the dry heat and scent of singed wires wrap around me.

Behind the counter sat a lean man with sun-reddened cheeks and sleeves rolled to the elbows. He glanced up from his logbook as I stepped in.

"Afternoon," I said, brushing off the chill. "Name's Percy Hope. I need to send a wire to the *San Francisco Examiner*."

The operator straightened slightly, eyebrows knitting. "Percy Hope, you said?"

"That's right."

He turned, rummaged through a small rack of envelopes, and plucked one free with two fingers. "Well, you're in luck. This came through less than an hour ago." He held out the folded slip like it might sting.

I took it slowly, my name staring back in blocky type across the front. My pulse ticked up.

No one should've known I was here, except, of course, Peggy.

I broke the seal and unfolded the telegram.

It was a wire from Hope.

The words seemed to blur and shimmer under the sputtering lamplight, as though refusing to settle into meaning. But the message was plain enough, each letter pressing into my chest like the weight of a hammer blow:

REV. O'HARA DEAD. COME HOME. — PEGGY

I read it again, lips forming the shape of each word. Then once more, though the meaning had already carved itself into my bones.

Reverend O'Hara was gone.

CHAPTER SIX
THE REVEREND

The steamer cut through the rising tide of Turnagain Arm, its flat hull gliding toward the distant cluster of wooden buildings nestled against the wilderness. Hope. The town that bore my name, the town that had once welcomed me as something greater than I was. But as I neared the dock, the tightness in my chest told me this wasn't a homecoming—it was a reckoning.

Reverend O'Hara was dead.

The wire had been brief, Peggy's words stark and cold. Gone. The same man who, upon my arrival all those years ago, had placed me on a pedestal, calling me the savior of Hope, the town's good fortune made flesh. The same man who had stood before the congregation in the Hope Social Hall in 1902, pronouncing Peggy and me husband and wife.

I stepped off the ship, gripping my satchel tighter as my boots struck the damp wooden planks of the dock. The town was quieter than usual, and the murmur of daily life dulled beneath a solemn weight. Faces turned toward me, and grief and something unspoken shadowed their eyes. Some nodded in acknowledgment, while others averted their gazes entirely.

And then, there she was.

Peggy stood on the porch, arms crossed, shoulders stiff. The exhaustion of the past few days had settled into the lines around her eyes. Her blonde hair, usually pulled back in a neat twist, hung loose around her face, dulled by the strain of sleepless nights. Once bright and full of life, her blue eyes now carried a distant, hollow look—like the reflection of an overcast sky before a storm.

Beside her, Walter, my boy, watched me with an expression carefully schooled into indifference. But I knew better. I saw it in the way he shifted his weight, in the way his fingers curled inside his pockets—the uncertainty of a child too young to bear such grief. He was the very image of his mother. The same sandy-blond hair and piercing blue eyes, though his held a sharper edge, not yet softened by years of life's wear. Looking at him was like seeing Peggy at thirteen, caught between childhood and something far heavier.

I climbed the steps, my throat tightening. Peggy didn't speak right away, just reached out, resting a hand on my arm—a silent anchor.

"He's gone, Percy," she finally said, her voice barely above a whisper.

I nodded, though the words still didn't feel real. "What happened?"

She sighed, glancing toward the hills beyond town, where Turnagain Arm stretched like a silver serpent beneath the afternoon sky. "He collapsed outside the church. By the time someone found him, it was too late."

I exhaled sharply. "Just like that?"

Peggy pressed her lips into a thin line. "No signs of illness. No warnings."

I frowned, but Peggy spoke again before I could press further. "You're just in time. The service is in a few hours."

Though my thoughts were already unraveling, I nodded, tangled in something I couldn't yet name.

Hope hadn't changed much in seventeen years. The muddy, chaotic outpost I first set foot in had become something sturdier, something lasting. But it had never shaken the shadow of those early days—the wild ambition, the desperation that turned men into ghosts before their time.

Sixteen miles down the Arm, Sunrise City was something entirely different. While Hope clung to restraint, Sunrise indulged in a lifestyle built on gold, whiskey, and fleeting pleasures.

Until leaving for Nome in the summer of 1900, Magnus Vega ruled there with a gangster's grin, his Gold Diggers Saloon an empire of temptation where the Seven Deadly Sins were not just whispered about—they were celebrated. Night after night, the glow of gas lamps flickered against smoke-filled walls as fortunes were won, bodies were sold, and men lost themselves to drink and desire.

But by 1915, Sunrise was a ghost town—its gold veins depleted, its streets emptied, its once-thriving saloons now hollow shells of their former glory. The revelry had faded, the music had stopped, and all that remained were the echoes of a town that had burned too brightly to last.

By the time we arrived, the church was packed, the wooden pews filled with men and women, most of whom called Hope home for as long as I had. The building itself was sturdy yet unadorned—no stained glass, no elaborate carvings, just simple timber and faith, built by hands that had known struggle. In its earliest days, it was constructed from the proceeds of the first and only nugget of gold I ever found.

The Reverend had been its heart, the town's steady voice in the storms of fortune and folly. Now, that voice was silent.

With no immediate replacement for the Reverend, Mr. Russel Jones, owner of the Hope General Store, stood at the podium, his usually reserved demeanor carrying the strain of unexpected responsibility. Clearing his throat, he surveyed the overflowing congregation before offering a solemn nod.

"We gather today to honor a man who gave this town more than just sermons—he gave it purpose," Russel began, his voice steady despite the emotion in his eyes. "Many of you knew him as our spiritual guide, the man who stood at this very pulpit, offering wisdom, comfort, and faith. But if not for Percy Hope, the Reverend would have passed many years ago."

A murmur rippled through the crowd, and I felt every gaze fasten on me.

Russel let the moment linger before continuing. "Some of you may not know the full story, but it's been told time and time again, passed down like a legend. Back in '98, Reverend O'Hara nearly drowned in the icy waters of Cook Inlet. When the current dragged him under, it should've been the end of him. But fate had other plans. He was pulled from the water and taken to a Tyonek shaman, clinging to life by a thread. And it was there, in that sacred place, that Percy Hope was said to have saved him—not with his hands or medicine, but with something greater. A miracle, they called it."

The murmurs grew louder, heads nodding, memories stirring.

"He never spoke much about that night within the caves, but I know what it meant to him. He believed he was saved so he could serve. So he could bring faith, guidance, and strength to this town. And he did."

I shared a look with Peggy, who offered a subtle smile.

"This was his place." His voice caught slightly as he looked out over the gathered crowd. He let the silence linger long enough for memory to rise like smoke in the air. Then, with measured reverence, he added, "And now… it's Percy's turn to honor the man who built more than a church—he built a legacy."

I swallowed. The knot in my throat tightened as I rose. A hundred pairs of eyes watched, but it was the unseen ones—the ghosts of memory—that I felt most.

I stepped forward, each footfall echoing like a drumbeat of destiny. The memory and expectation settled across my shoulders like a heavy mantle. As I climbed the steps to the podium, where the Reverend had once stood so many times before, I ran my fingers along the worn wooden edges, tracing the grooves where his hands had rested—

steadying himself, calling forth grace, speaking words that shaped this town.

Now, it was my turn.

I faced the congregation. Miners, merchants, mothers, fathers—the very people who had built Hope from the mud and the cold, just as I had. Many had been here since the beginning, watching this town rise from nothing, shaping it with their hands and will.

And yet, none of us had built it alone.

Hope had a heart; for as long as I could remember, that heart was Reverend O'Hara.

When I arrived here as a young man—barely more than a boy chasing gold—I didn't come looking for salvation. That word belonged to preachers and promises, not to boys like me, born with names that sounded foreign in every mouth but our own.

I was the son of Jewish immigrants, raised on stories of wandering, of exile and return, though I barely grasped their meaning then. Faith was something my parents carried like an heirloom—precious, fragile, tucked away. I carried ambition. I came north because I thought this land held fortune, a future carved out of rivers and rock.

I came under a different name, wearing a different identity, believing I could shape myself into someone new. Someone who didn't have to explain where he came from or what Rothman meant. Someone who belonged.

But Alaska doesn't let you hide for long. The land knows what you are—even when you don't.

But the Reverend saw through that.

He called me Percy Hope, not just because it was the name Magnus Vega had stamped upon this town, but because he believed that's what I would bring to it—hope. He believed it so deeply that he spoke it from the pulpit, raising me up as something greater than I was, something I could never become. I didn't deserve it and certainly didn't understand it, but that's who he was. He saw in people not what they were but what they *could be*. And sometimes, his belief alone was enough to make it true.

The church in which we now gathered was built on that same belief. It was never about gold or wealth, never about status or power—it was built on faith, on the idea that something stronger than men's ambition and greed could take root here. And he was right. I know that because I was here when it was nothing more than an idea, when its walls were barely more than a dream rising from the earth. I was here when I handed that golden nugget that I pulled from the creek—not to a prospector or a saloon—but to this man because I believed in what he was building more than I believed in any fortune.

And he repaid that faith by standing at the altar when Peggy and I were married, binding our lives together in the heart of this town, the very one he helped shape. That was the kind of man he was. He wasn't just our preacher. He was our guide, our witness, our conscience when the world around us felt lawless and untamed.

I took a slow breath, my gaze sweeping over the congregation, their faces a mosaic of grief, reverence, and quiet remembrance. These were the people who had built Hope—the same people Reverend O'Hara had guided, counseled, and stood beside through life's trials and triumphs.

I steadied myself and began.

"I cannot stand here and say that he is gone. Not truly."

A few heads lifted, some nodding slightly as if they, too, had felt the lingering presence of the man who had once stood where I now stood.

"Because Reverend O'Hara was never just a man of the pulpit. He was the voice that reminded us who we are, the hands that lifted us when we stumbled, the presence that steadied us when we doubted."

My eyes landed on Russel, who dabbed at his eyes with a wrinkled handkerchief, and on Mrs. Whitmore, whose children had been baptized in this very church.

"And as long as we carry forward what he built—this town, this church, this hope—he will never truly leave us."

A hush fell over the room, the presence of memory pressing against us all.

I drew a slow breath, my voice steady.

"And yet, I cannot forget when we thought we had lost him."

A murmur rippled through the congregation.

"But his story wasn't meant to end. I know because I was there, deep in the caves where shadows stretched long and silence pressed in. I stood alongside Sha-e-dah-kla, the shaman of the Tyonek, as he called him back from the edge of death."

Some in the crowd shifted uneasily, exchanging glances. The mention of the shaman and the caves still unsettled people.

But I carried on.

"Many of you know this story because Reverend O'Hara himself told it. He called it a miracle. He called it *my* doing. However, the truth is that I did not perform a miracle. I did what any of us would have done—I fought for him, how he had always fought for this town, our faith, and each of us."

A pause.

"Because of that, we were gifted more time—time to hear his words, walk beside him, and carry his lessons forward. That was the true miracle."

Silence followed—not of doubt, but of understanding.

"I know because I saw what no man should see—I saw the thin veil between this world and the next, and I walked its border to bring him home."

Silence.

Then, a quiet voice whispered from somewhere in the pews, "A miracle."

I let the word settle before continuing.

"He once told me that hope is not merely something we hold onto but must fight for. And on that day, I fought for him."

A few nods. Many tears.

"He returned to us not just as a man, but as a testament to what is possible. To the mysteries we may never fully understand. To the faith that does not falter, even in the face of death."

I met Peggy's gaze, her hand resting over Walter's, steadying our son as emotion flickered across his young face.

I straightened.

"So as we stand here today, mourning the loss of a man who shaped this town, who shaped me, let us not fall into despair. Let us not forget the lessons he left behind."

A deep breath.

"Because Hope is not gone."

It wasn't just a name. It wasn't just a place.

"It is here—in these walls, in these people, in the lives he touched and the faith he instilled."

I gripped the edges of the pulpit.

"And if we hold onto that, then Reverend O'Hara will never truly leave us."

Silence followed—not of doubt, but of understanding.

As the service concluded and the congregation slowly filed out, I greeted the mourners, shaking hands and offering quiet words of comfort. Faces passed in a blur—men and women who had built this town alongside me, their grief mirroring my own. But one face stood out among them, standing just beyond the church doors.

Mother.

Not my mother, she had passed ten years ago, but the spiritual leader of the Dena'ina tribe's summer fishing camp on Fire Island. It had been years since I had last seen her, yet she remained a striking figure, even as time had worn its mark upon her. Her long hair had turned silver, her deep wrinkles seemed deeper, but the wisdom in her dark eyes remained unchanged. She did not step forward or beckon me—she waited.

I turned to Peggy and Walter, touching my son's shoulder. "I need to speak with her. Alone."

Peggy studied Mother for a moment before nodding. "We'll be home."

I stepped outside, blinking into the pale blaze of the Alaskan evening. Though the hour was late, the summer sun still hovered above the spruce tops, casting the yard in molten gold. The air was sharp with pine and the distant scent of river silt.

Mother stood just beyond the porch, half veiled in the gentle fade of sunlight, as though she belonged to the land more than to the hour.

"Mother," I said quietly, my voice catching in the hush.

She turned toward me, eyes steady, ancient in their knowing, as though they carried the hush of snow falling in forgotten valleys.

"Percy," she said, her voice gentle yet carrying a resonance that seemed to rise from beneath the earth itself.

A silence opened between us, so vast and deep that even the breeze seemed to hold its breath. Then, as though speaking a sacred truth, she murmured, "You've been summoned."

I blinked, her words striking me like a hammer on steel. "Summoned?"

Mother held my gaze, her expression as immovable as bedrock.

A frown creased my brow. "Mother… who has summoned me?"

She didn't look away. "You must hear it from him."

A flicker of unease passed through me. "From who?"

She drew in a slow breath, and the light seemed to shimmer on the silver in her hair. "Sha-e-dah-kla."

The name hovered in the golden air, weighty and electric, sending an involuntary shiver through me.

I stared at her, my heart pounding like rails under a speeding train. "But… the shaman… he's dead," I said, though my voice faltered, crumbling under the strain of disbelief.

Mother tilted her head, a quiet sorrow threading through her words. "Not all who vanish are gone, Percy. Some stand just beyond the veil, waiting for the right moment to step through again."

A breeze rustled the spruce needles, whispering secrets in a tongue older than words.

She stepped closer, her eyes narrowing in quiet insistence. "Has he given you something?"

I opened my mouth to say no, but hesitated, the denial freezing on my tongue.

Slowly, almost without meaning to, I reached beneath my shirt. My fingers closed around the cool circle of silver resting against my chest. I pulled it free and held it out, the medallion swinging gently from its thin chain, catching shards of sunlight in the etched raven's wings.

Mother's eyes glistened, a mix of pride and sorrow. "There. You see? It was never just a gift, Percy. It was meant for you. A mark. A key. A summons."

I stared down at the medallion, the metal cold and impossibly heavy in my palm. The raven seemed alive in the slanting light, its wings poised mid-flight.

My voice came out raw. "And what if I don't want to know what he has to say?"

Mother's eyes softened, though a steely glint remained beneath the sorrow. "Wanting has nothing to do with it. The land remembers you. And Sha-e-dah-kla waits. There are truths only you can hear—and burdens only you can carry."

The sun shone bright and endless over the clearing, but the world tilted beneath me, opening into depths I could neither measure nor name.

I closed my eyes, feeling the medallion's weight press into my palm like a promise—and a command. In that moment, I knew my path no longer followed steel rails or printed maps. It led somewhere older and stranger—where time curved back on itself, where spirits whispered in the hush between heartbeats, and where the dead were never truly gone.

Dead or not, Sha-e-dah-kla was waiting.

And whether I was ready or not, I knew I had to go.

CHAPTER SEVEN
THE SHAMAN'S CALL

Later that evening, after Walter had gone to bed and the house had fallen into that hush unique to deep Alaska nights, I stood near the window, staring at the tree line beyond our home. The medallion sat in my palm, its coolness pulling me back again and again to what Mother had said.

Peggy entered the room, her arms crossed, eyes searching mine.

"You've been pacing for over an hour," she said gently. "Is it something Mother said?"

I nodded.

She waited, not pressing—just watching. Always patient, always more perceptive than I gave her credit for.

I drew in a breath and held out the medallion.

"This," I said, "I found next to a murdered man in Tent City. I didn't think much of it at first. It seemed… strange, yes, but not significant."

She stepped closer and took it from me, holding it beneath the lamp's light. "The raven," she murmured, tracing the engraving with her fingertip. "It looks old."

"It seems so," I said.

Her brow furrowed. "You think it means something?"

I exhaled, feeling everything pressing in at once. "I didn't give it much thought," I said. "But Mother does. She said I'd been summoned."

Peggy blinked. "Summoned? By whom?"

"Sha-e-dah-kla."

I watched her reaction carefully, saw the flicker in her eyes.

"But, Percy—he's dead."

I nodded slowly, the truth unfurling in me like a scroll. "I know. But Mother believes not all who vanish are truly gone. And maybe this medallion is proof."

Peggy's eyes widened. "Proof? That he's trying to reach you?"

"That he already has," I said, closing my fingers around the cool silver once more. "This isn't just some trinket, Peggy. It's a summons. He's waiting for me."

A hush fell between us, the lamplight flickering as if caught in a breath of unseen wind.

I ran my thumb along the rim. "She told me he has a message for me. I need to go to the Tyonek village. Beyond it. Into the caves."

A long silence settled between us, and in its depth, the memory returned with startling clarity. I could see the caves again and their stone walls flickering with the light of a small fire, shadows dancing like spirits in the dim. Reverend O'Hara lay on a stone bed, barely breathing.

The shaman poised beside us, his hands moving with ancient precision, murmuring words older than scripture. The air had been thick with the scent of smoke and earth, and a stillness hung there—not empty, but watchful, as if the cave itself were listening.

"I never told you," I said, my voice roughened by time and truth, "what I saw in those caves. When I found the Reverend… something else was there too. I can't explain it—not in a way that makes sense. It wasn't just a cave. It was… a portal."

Peggy stepped back slightly, her brows knitting as she searched my face.

"A portal?" she repeated.

"Yes. Between worlds. Or realities. I don't know. But I felt it—like the walls of the world had thinned. One more step and I might've fallen through." I looked past her, as if the memory were painted on the dark beyond. "There was no wind, no sound but the fire, and yet the space around us breathed. The shaman didn't speak—not in words—but he sang, and the air shimmered. I swear it. I watched the Reverend—lifeless one moment, and then stirred by something I couldn't see. Not magic. Not faith. Something older."

I swallowed hard, the memory too clear now to ignore. "It was as if the cave itself had opened to another realm—a place beneath or behind this one. I saw flickers—shapes made of light. I felt them moving just beyond the fire's reach, and I knew, somehow, that Reverend O'Hara had been brought back."

A silence settled again, but it was heavier now, freighted with the truth of what I'd finally spoken aloud.

Peggy's voice broke it—soft, but precise.

"And you think this medallion is connected to that?"

"I…" I hesitated, the words stirring from some deeper place. "I think it's more than that," I said slowly. "I think the railroad—what they're building, the ground they're tearing open—it's disturbing something. And someone doesn't want me to see what that is."

Peggy's eyes didn't leave mine. "Percy… what exactly happened in Tent City?"

The question cut clean through the haze of memory. I drew in a breath, felt the chill of the medallion pressing into my palm. For a moment, I just stared at it—cold, ancient, watching me as much as I was watching it.

"There was a murder," I said finally. "In broad daylight. A woman came screaming through the camp—her husband had been killed in their tent."

I turned the medallion over in my hand, the etched raven catching the firelight.

"His body was still warm. Stabbed clean through the side. The person who did it wanted it done quickly and without a chance to speak. But he must've known something—because half-buried in the mud beside him was this."

Peggy leaned forward, eyes narrowing at the metal. "That's where you found it?"

I nodded. "At first, I thought it was nothing. A keepsake. A charm. But it had this strange… pull. Not like gold. Not like anything I've ever held. It felt *alive*. Not warm—but watching. And then…"

I looked past her, to the fire, to the memory that still clung like smoke.

"I spotted a man at the river. Scrubbing his hands like he was trying to wash off more than blood. When I called to him, he froze. He looked at me—really looked—and there was recognition in his face. Not just guilt. *Recognition.* Then he ran. Fast. Vanished into the brush before I could follow."

"And you think he killed that man?" Peggy asked.

"Yes. To stop him from reaching me. Because I think the man who died… was trying to deliver this to me. A message. A warning. Something."

She folded her arms tightly, her voice now a whisper. "Something someone didn't want you to know."

"Exactly," I said. "Tent City was a boiling pot—tension, desperation, corruption. But this felt different. I've seen violence born from greed. This wasn't that. This was silence. Engineered silence. That man wasn't just killed—he was erased."

Peggy stared at the medallion again, her expression unreadable.

"And now you're holding what they tried to bury," she said. "And it brought you back here. Back to him."

I nodded slowly. "To Sha-e-dah-kla."

Her eyes softened. She reached out and gently closed my fingers around the medallion. "Then you need to find out what it is you were meant to receive."

"I think he was trying to give me something, a message, a warning, maybe even a truth too heavy for the waking world. Something bound to this." I lifted the medallion slightly.

Peggy looked down, arms folded tightly against her chest. "So… you're going back."

"I have to," I said. "He may be gone, but he's not finished. Not in that place."

I moved to the hearth and knelt, placing the medallion on the stone. "This isn't just about a story anymore. It's something else. Something I can't ignore."

Peggy knelt beside me. "Then promise me one thing."

I looked at her.

"When you go into those caves again," she said, her voice shaking just slightly, "don't forget the way out."

I reached for her hand. "I won't."

But deep down, I already knew—if what waited beyond the village was truly calling me, I might not come back the same.

CHAPTER EIGHT
FIRE ISLAND

The morning air bit at my cheeks as I stood on the dock, while behind me the flat-bottom skiff hissed in the cold, its little boiler sending up steam in slow, serpentine coils, like breath from some slumbering sea creature. Walter, growing into his lanky frame, stood beside Peggy, his shoulders stiff beneath the heavy coat. His eyes were wide, flicking between the skiff and me, a storm of questions swirling behind them.

I laid a hand on his shoulder and gave it a gentle squeeze. "Look after your mother, all right?" I said, my voice rougher than I meant it to be. "She'll be counting on you."

Walter nodded, swallowing hard. "I will, Pops."

And in that small moment, he looked older than his years, and it left me both proud and aching.

He nodded, and I could see he was fighting tears. So was I.

I looked at Peggy. She was doing her best to stay composed, but I knew that look—stone on the outside, fire underneath. We'd been through too much for her to fall apart now. She just stared at me, waiting. Not for an explanation. Not for apologies. For something else.

"I won't promise when I'll be back," I said, my voice low. "I don't know how long this will take."

"Then don't make promises you can't keep," she replied.

I nodded. "I'll try to get word through when I can. But…"

She cut me off with a glance. "Don't say it. Just go, if you're going."

We embraced. Her lips brushed mine. I kissed Walter's cheek, ran a hand through his thick blond hair, then turned before I could talk myself out of it.

The gangplank groaned beneath my boots. I stepped aboard and didn't look back.

The whistle cried out, long and mournful, and the skiff pushed off into the Arm. The dock grew smaller, the shoreline blurring into fog and memory. I watched until I couldn't make out Hope anymore—just smoke and trees and the shape of a life I was leaving behind, if only for a while.

Cook Inlet stretched ahead, restless and silver beneath a cautious sunrise. I stood at the rail, coat collar high against the salt wind, as Fire Island slid by off the starboard bow—a dark silhouette half-lost in mist. Mother's summer home.

I'd only set foot there once, August of '98, when Liam and I left Knik village in the company of Nicholai, our Dena'ina friend. We waited for the tide to turn, then paddled out in his birch-bark canoe, each stroke deliberate, the blade angled to slip through the wind's grip. Eagles wheeled overhead, and the inlet's cold breath stung our faces. Somewhere between the hush of paddles and the surge of current, I realized how swiftly gold fever could be drowned by sheer water and sky.

When Fire Island lifted itself from the fog, it shattered any illusion of a pristine dreamscape. Fish huts perched on stilts above slick mudflats, while racks of drying strips of salmon caught the wet light. Nets, cork floats, and canoes lay strewn along the shoreline like the aftermath of some quiet storm.

Above it all stood Major Austin Lawrence—a red-bearded giant wrapped in a fur robe, newly transferred from Fort Egbert to oversee the Army Signal Corps' Morse-code relay station that kept this corner of Alaska connected to the wider world. From the bluff he waved, his figure carved in sharp relief against the cloud-thick sky. Then he turned and led us up a driftwood ladder into the village, where alder smoke coiled sweetly through the damp air.

That evening, we feasted on bannock speckled with blueberries plucked from fiery bushes nestled among the spruce. Rain whispered on cedar shingles, and then she emerged—Mother, or Shunkda as the Dena'ina called her. Her hair was still dark then, eyes glinting with the same calm that could hush an entire room. She spoke of tides and spirit nets, and shadows gathering. Her voice was soft as falling snow, yet carried the weight of mountains. It felt as though the island itself leaned closer to listen.

Now, as Fire Island slipped once more behind a veil of fog, that same hush stirred in my chest. The land remembers—and so do I.

Cook Inlet opened like a great gray mouth, swallowing the boat whole. I pressed my hand to the inside of my coat where the medallion lay against my chest. It was heavier than metal should be, not just in mass, but in meaning.

This wasn't about a news column. Sure, my editor wanted updates—stories about track-laying, steel, and grit. But I wasn't after such mundane details. I was following something older. Something that felt like it had been waiting for me long before I stumbled on that body in Tent City.

By dusk, the outline of Tyonek came into view—low hills, scattered cabins, and behind it all, a mountain of dark spruce trees. The place looked half-asleep.

The inlet narrowed as the skiff slowed its approach. The coastline thickened with spruce and alder, and soon the familiar slope of the Tyonek bluff came into view—low-slung cabins nestled against the trees, smoke curling from chimneys into the pale sky. It looked much as I remembered it.

We docked in silence. I stepped off the boat, boots sinking into the muddy shore, the cold wind rolling in from the water. A few villagers paused their work to watch me. One of them—a boy with a salmon net slung over his shoulder—stared hard at the medallion that rested on my chest, visible beneath the open flap of my coat.

I had thought, more than once, to keep it tucked away—safe beneath my shirt, unseen. But as the shoreline neared, something in me shifted. I couldn't explain it, only that hiding it felt like hiding from the very thing

I'd come seeking. So upon our approach, I exposed the medallion for them to see. Let it speak before I do.

And it had.

The boy's gaze was not just one of curiosity—it was recognition. Reverence, even.

"I need to speak with the shaman," I said to no one in particular, lifting my voice just enough to carry. "Sha-e-dah-kla."

A silence fell, not hostile, but thick with expectation. The boy looked at an elder man beside him. The elder stepped forward slowly, his eyes never leaving mine.

"You've come late," the elder said, his voice worn and deep as river stone. "Sha-e-dah-kla left his body many winters ago."

"I know," I said, lowering my head.

He regarded me in silence, eyes narrowing slightly. Then said, "But you are remembered, Percy Hope."

I looked up, startled. "You… know who I am?"

He nodded once. "Your name is still spoken here. The one who stood between death and the Reverend. The one who entered the sacred cave and returned."

I hesitated, the past rising unbidden like a scent on the wind. "I remember," I murmured, "but sometimes, in my dreams, I'm still there."

The elder gave the faintest nod, as if he understood. Then he turned without another word. "Come."

I followed him through the village. Children watched from doorways. Women paused in their weaving. I saw in their eyes not suspicion, but something closer to reverence, like I had walked out of the very stories they'd been told around firelight. And maybe I had.

I was brought to a cabin where five elders sat in a half-circle near the hearth. Smoke twisted above them into a hole in the roof. They did not rise. They only looked at me, and in their eyes I saw time itself—measured not in hours, but in memory.

One of the elders sat slightly forward from the others, his shoulders draped in a robe of raven feathers, his face lined like riverstone—ancient, watchful. I knew without needing to ask that he was the eldest. The firelight clung to him as though it had known him the longest.

He raised a hand, thin and steady, and spoke in a voice like dry wind through cedar, low, brittle, and solemn. "You carry something with weight. Speak."

I stepped forward and drew the edges of my coat aside, letting the medallion swing free. It hung against my chest, worn smooth with time, unadorned save for the meaning it carried. For a moment, it caught the firelight and flickered like an ember. I held it out, not as a challenge, but as a memory made visible. The room stilled around it, the elders leaning in—not with movement, but with silence.

"I was summoned," I said, my voice steady but low. "Not by letter. Not by messenger. But by something older."

I paused, feeling the gravity of memory settle over me.

"I found this buried in mud at Tent City," I continued. "It was next to a murdered man—one I believe had come to find me. He never had the chance to speak, but this was left behind. I didn't know what it meant. Still, I took it."

I let the silence speak for a breath, then went on.

"And then, after the Reverend passed away, Shunkda came to see me in Hope. She knew of the medallion. She said it was time. That it was not hers to explain, but I had been summoned… by Sha-e-dah-kla himself."

The circle of elders did not speak, but the shift in the air was palpable. It was as though the walls of the cabin itself had taken notice.

"She told me I would know what to do when the moment came," I said. "I didn't. Not at first. But I know now. That's why I'm here. To understand why he called me. And what is it I'm meant to do?"

An elder nodded, his eyes deep wells of memory. "Sha-e-dah-kla spoke of you before his passing. He knew your journey would bring you back. Though his body has long returned to the earth, his spirit walks still within the sacred caves."

Another elder spoke, his voice hushed but firm. "You may enter. But understand—this is not a path beneath branches and sky. It is a passage carved through earth and memory, a winding descent through the old tunnels that lead to the sacred chamber. The shaman's spirit will not greet you with words. He will come through what you feel… and what you are ready to remember."

I bowed my head. "Then I'll go now."

The medallion felt heavier than it ever had, but no longer as a burden. As a key.

Outside, the dusk was falling, painting the village in cool blue shadow. A raven cried once from the treetops, as if to mark my steps. I turned toward the edge of the forest, where the earth opened its mouth in stone and shadow, and walked toward the place where breath and silence meet.

CHAPTER NINE
THE CAVES

I struck a match and touched it to the pitch-soaked rag, shielding the flame with my hand until it caught and flared into a smoky glow. The bitter scent of burning tar coiled upward as light spilled over the bluff, revealing the cave's entrance—a narrow, jagged slit in the limestone, half-hidden behind drapes of moss and tangled alder roots. I was shown this place once, years ago, whispering of spirits and secrets sealed beneath the earth.

Now, standing before it, I felt that same tightening in my chest. The opening yawned no wider than a coffin lid, slick with beads of moisture that caught the torchlight like a scatter of tiny stars. I bent low, shouldering through the stone jaws, the walls scraping at my coat as though trying to keep me out—or swallow me whole.

Inside, the air grew colder, dense with the scent of wet stone and something older still—a sharp tang of iron, like old blood rusting in a forgotten wound. The tunnel squeezed tighter around me, forcing me to shuffle sideways, the torch spitting and hissing in the constant draft. Water dripped from above, each droplet ringing off stone, counting out centuries in patient beats.

When the light brushed the ceiling, it caught a forest of stalactites, thick as musket barrels, glistening with meltwater. Beneath them rose stalagmites like white-fanged beasts reaching up from the floor, frozen mid-surge. In the shifting glow, quartz veins glittered in the rock like lightning trapped in stone.

A low rumble tremored through the cave, subtle as a giant rolling over in its sleep. Tiny stones rattled across the floor, and the darkness leaned closer, listening. I paused, breath held, heart hammering so loud it felt like it might crack a rib.

Then, all at once, the cave exhaled—a burp of icy air that snuffed the torch, plunging me into a darkness thick as velvet. For a single, breathless moment, I was nowhere. No sky, no earth, only the memory of stone pressing cold and close.

And then, farther in, a pulse of flickering gold lit the tunnel—a glint of firelight bouncing off hidden pools, just as I'd seen the night Sha-e-dah-kla called me deeper.

The cave breathed again, this time with a hollow roar, and dust spiraled upward in ghostly tendrils. I realized I was no longer merely exploring. I was being pulled by something buried in time, waiting for me to return.

As I pushed farther in, the chill of the cave wrapped around me like an old cloak, and memories rose with every step. Seventeen years had passed since I first crawled through these limestone jaws, torch in hand, chasing the trail of Reverend O'Hara. He'd vanished without a trace, and though my pockets were empty of weapons, my mind bristled with questions.

Back then, all I knew was that Tommy—Chief Ephanasy's son from the Knik tribe—had spirited the Reverend away. Beyond that, it was shadows and rumors, whispers of a plot woven by men with more gold than scruples.

It wasn't until later that the truth crystallized like ice forming on the inlet. Magnus Vega had been the spider at the center of the web, determined to clear Hope City of its moral sentinel. The Reverend had stood firmly against Magnus's plan to open a saloon, and for that, Magnus meant to send him to the Southlands, far from the flock he guarded.

Tommy, swayed by the glint of a gold nugget, played his part—at least until the Reverend refused to board the steamship. Instead, the holy man hurled himself into the iron-gray waters of Cook Inlet, a feeble attempt at escape. It was Tommy who dove in after him, seized by conscience, and hauled the half-drowned preacher back to the boat. The tide carried them south until Tyonek's wooden pilings loomed out of the fog like the ribs of a shipwreck.

It was there that Sha-e-dah-kla, the Tyonek shaman, took the Reverend into his care, hiding him in this very labyrinth of stone. I remember how the walls closed in as I was led through, the torchlight revealing quartz veins that flashed like lightning, frozen mid-strike. The air was heavy with the sharp scent of wet stone and pitch smoke, every breath tasting of secrets.

Inside these walls, I'd knelt beside the Reverend's fevered body while Sha-e-dah-kla pressed a bitter potion into my hands, urging me to sleep and follow the Reverend's spirit into the hidden corridors between life and death.

Now, as the cave exhales around me, cool and deep, I know I'm not merely retracing my steps. I'm revisiting the crucible where hope, betrayal, and redemption fused into something stronger than gold. And still, somewhere in the hush, I hear the echo of the Reverend's vow—that Hope City would not be sold for whiskey, not under his watch.

That night lives in me like a second soul. I remember the flicker of the firelight as I found them—the Reverend lying pale and near death, the shaman standing watchful beside him. I remember the cup pressed into my hands, the bitter taste of the herbal brew, and the moment I surrendered to sleep. But it was not sleep. It was a journey into the spirit world, where I found the Reverend's soul teetering on the threshold. Somehow, I led him back to the living.

And now, the caves received me again.

I emerged into the great cavern, breath catching in my throat. The fire at the center burned, though no one stoked it. In the stillness, I felt it—not nostalgia, not fear—but recognition. The place knew me. And I had returned, not as a boy chasing miracles, but as a man seeking truth.

I stepped deeper into the chamber, my breath rising in visible clouds. Though the fire at the center burned low, the air felt warmer—charged. My eyes swept the stone alcove where Reverend O'Hara had once hovered between life and death. The shelf was there, carved smooth by time and prayer. I stepped toward it, heart pounding.

Nothing stirred.

No voice, no figure, no confirmation that I had not come all this way for a memory.

I brushed away the fine layer of dust as if peeling back time itself before settling onto the cold stone. It seemed to groan faintly beneath my weight as I lay down, the cave embracing me like a familiar story. The medallion stayed flat against my chest, its warmth pulsing—subtle, rhythmic, like a heartbeat not my own.

The ceiling above blurred as my eyelids grew heavy. The firelight flickered against the stone, leaping like shadows of forgotten sentinels, and then—

—silence.

Darkness.

But it was not empty.

The wind.

The wilderness.

I stood at the edge of a vast tundra, the Alaskan wild stretching in all directions. Peaks rose like sleeping gods. The sun hung low, casting a light that was neither dawn nor dusk. The scent of spruce and glacier drifted in the air. And silence—deep, sacred silence—pressed against me.

Somewhere in that hush, I felt him.

Sha-e-dah-kla.

Not seen, but known.

"You have come," said a voice—not spoken, but impressed upon my spirit, as if the land itself spoke through root and wind.

I turned slowly, but saw nothing—only vastness, yet threaded with presence.

"I don't understand," I said aloud, or perhaps only thought. "I thought you were gone."

"I am," came the reply. "And I am not. I do not vanish—I linger where needed, reaching through the veil to stir those still walking the earth. I am the thread that binds memory to the living."

The ground beneath me shimmered, then lifted, until I was standing atop a ridgeline overlooking a vast and living map. Below, I saw the winding snake of the railroad—raw, new, defiant. It pierced the forest like an iron spear. But in some places, the earth writhed beneath it. Trees bled sap like tears. Spirits of the land—blurred and sorrowful—gathered at points of rupture.

Then I saw it: the medallion floating before me, glowing amber. Etched symbols moved like breath—raven feathers, mountain spines, rails becoming roots.

And then came the visions.

A rail collapse in a narrow gorge. A bridge, half-built, swaying as thunder cracked above. Magnus Vega, clad in fur, his grin melting into bone, then vanishing into blackness. A child crying out beneath splintered timbers. And through it all, me. Not watching from afar. *There*. At the heart of the chaos. Standing. Failing. Or—standing, and *turning the tide*.

"What must I do?" I asked, my voice a little more than a breath.

"Use it," the voice said. "Use what was given to you."

The medallion lifted before me, burning now with a fierce, molten light. It pulsed with something ancient—not memory, but *force*. Not merely symbolic—*real*. Then, like a spark drawn to kindling, it dropped into my chest, passing through flesh as if it knew the way.

I gasped—not from pain, but from recognition. Heat flooded my limbs. My vision flared. And for a moment, I knew things I could not possibly know.

Where it came from.

It was no charm, no trinket—it was forged in the old world, long before rail or rifle, shaped by those who once moved with the earth instead of against it. It was handed down through generations in secret, meant to awaken only when the balance of the land tipped too far.

The man who died in Tent City had not wandered into that moment by chance. He was coming to find me. A messenger. A guardian, perhaps. He had crossed great distances, driven by purpose, or by the command of someone who knew the medallion was meant for my hands.

But he was murdered before he could speak the truth.

By whom?

A scream tore through the camp—a cry of anguish that froze me in place. I ran toward it, weaving through the rows of tents until I saw her. A woman, disheveled and wild-eyed, was standing over where he had fallen. She looked up, and our eyes met.

"He was my husband!" she cried. Her voice cracked with pain and something else—fear, maybe.

But then she was gone—swallowed by the crowd, or the night itself.

I must find her.

Because the others are still out there. Watching. Waiting. They know what the medallion is. They know what it can do.

It's more than a talisman. It doesn't just illuminate—it alters. Steel softens. Timber strengthens. Bridges hold against the storm. Tunnels carve through stone like water. In the right hands, it paves the impossible path.

But in the wrong hands…

It could unravel everything.

I jolted upright on the stone shelf, breath rushing in. The cave flickered back to life around me. The fire still burned low. My skin was damp with sweat. But my chest—where the medallion lay—was warm, steady, and alive.

I sat in the silence.

The medallion was still mine. But it would not be mine alone for long. The game had already begun. The messenger was silenced, but the message had reached its mark.

They will come for it.

But I won't run.

I've been given this for a reason—not to hide it, but to *use* it.

And the railway must succeed.

Not just for commerce. For something deeper.

Something no one else yet sees.

But I do now.

CHAPTER TEN
A WHISPER

Tent City was not as I remembered.

Gone was the frenzy of makeshift commerce and drunken ambition, yet the place still pulsed with a quieter kind of energy—one born not of gold-rush fever, but of grit and necessity. The clapboard taverns still stood, though now subdued, their windows half-boarded and their doorways shadowed by men who no longer roared with dreams, but waited—quietly, grimly—for work, or for something unnamed to end.

Supply wagons creaked through the rutted streets, loaded with iron spikes, crates of beans, and coils of telegraph wire. Mules huffed, their breath pluming in the chill. A crew of foreigners rolled a wheelbarrow past, one singing low and tunelessly in his mother tongue. A few children darted between cook tents, chasing a dog with three legs. A woman stirred a pot over a smoky fire, her eyes hollow, her motions mechanical.

There was life here still—weathered, worn, but enduring. A new city built on canvas and willpower, in motion not upward, but forward.

I passed through the muddy thoroughfare with a strange pull in my chest. This was where the murdered man had died, his blood mixing with rain and muck, soaking into the earth beneath a sagging tent. The medallion had lain just inches from his outstretched hand; left for me, I now knew.

I hoped to find his wife—the woman who had cried out, who had called him her husband before vanishing into the crowd—but no one seemed to know her. Or if they did, they weren't telling.

"She was seen heading along the shoreline toward Knik Arm," a railman offered with a shrug, wiping soot from his brow. "But that was weeks ago."

Another said she wore a blue shawl. Another swore she never existed at all.

I searched anyway. I wandered past the depot where laborers lined up for day assignments, past the rear alleys of boarding tents where slumped shoulders whispered over tin cups, past the infirmary where a nurse wrung out bloody linens in a wooden basin. I asked after her in hushed tones, describing her face to anyone who would listen. But her trail dissolved like morning frost—there, and then gone.

And still, the medallion burned faintly draped under my shirt, as though aware of our nearness to something it recognized. A silent sentinel. Or a compass.

Somewhere in this shifting city of tents and wheels and half-spoken truths, a thread had been cut. But the rest of the fabric was still in motion.

And so was I.

Meanwhile, news of the railroad's progress had swept through the camps like wildfire.

The line had crossed into the heart of the Kenai Peninsula, carving its way through spruce forest and sheer granite. Near Moose Pass, they'd blasted through solid rock to clear the Bear Creek tunnel. Bridges now spanned creeks fed by recent rains, their currents swift and muddied. All along the line, men drove spikes with rhythmic precision, racing not just time, but the wet earth's growing resistance.

The mood across the line was one of gritty optimism—each mile laid down felt like a small triumph over nature's stubborn grip. In the evenings, around mess tents and campfires, men swapped stories of close calls and near disasters, but the tone had shifted from fear to pride. They were pushing boundaries, taming the wild inch by inch.

I was halfway through my second cup of coffee when the flap of the mess tent flew open and John Raynor barreled inside like a storm wind, apron flapping around his waist.

"Percy?" John blurted, blinking at me like he was seeing a ghost. "I thought you were long gone—off to Hope, weren't you?"

"I was," I said, setting my mug down. "Made it there, all right. Then followed a lead toward the Tyonek village."

John stared a beat longer, then let out a low whistle. "Well, you picked a hell of a time to show up."

I raised an eyebrow. "What's going on?"

"It's bad, Percy," he said, voice low and tight. "Real bad. The railway crews hit the Placer River Flats. That whole stretch's gone soft—swallowed up the line like it was never laid. Ties, track, everything—just gone."

I stared at him, trying to wrap my head around the image. "The whole line?"

"Like it never existed," he said, wiping a bead of sweat from his temple. "They'll have to start over—or find a way around. Either way, it will take weeks. Maybe more."

I leaned back, the coffee suddenly bitter on my tongue. If the line was sunk, the whole push north could stall.

I stepped out of the mess tent and into the sharp afternoon air. For a long moment, I just stood there, staring out over the sprawl of Tent City—half-built dreams and mud-choked ambition.

The trail had gone cold. The widow, wherever she was, had slipped through my fingers.

For now.

Down by the docks, I found a grizzled captain named William Smith, whose beard looked like it had soaked up every storm between here and the Aleutians. He was loading crates onto a shallow-draft steamer—*The Chinook Belle*.

"You're looking to ride the tide?" he asked, sizing me up as I approached.

"I am. Bound for Placer Flats, where the river spills into the Arm."

Smith spat into the harbor mud and gave a grunt that passed for agreement. "We shove off in an hour. Tides are in our favor—for now. But those Flats will take a man if he sets foot wrong."

"Noted," I said.

He eyed me again. "Two dollars gets you space on deck—four if you want to keep your boots dry."

I handed him three. "I'll take my chances with the spray."

He nodded, pocketing the coins with a calloused thumb. "Then welcome aboard, Mister…?"

"Hope," I said. "Percy Hope."

The Chinook Belle nosed out of the harbor just as the sun settled behind a peak, its hull groaning like it knew what lay ahead. We followed the curve of the shoreline as the inlet narrowed into the claw-like Turnagain Arm—a stretch of water that coiled and struck like a startled snake.

The tides surged beneath us with a force that felt alive. Twice a day, they came barreling in like a stampede—said to be one of the fastest tide changes on Earth. The water foamed and twisted in strange currents, sweeping past in long, snaking rips that made the rudder shudder.

To the north, the Chugach Mountains loomed, spotted with late summer snow and draped in low-hanging clouds. Southward, the Kenai Range rose like a silent wall, its dark green flanks lying in shadow. It was wild country—primeval, untouched. The kind of place where a man could vanish and never be found, intentionally or not.

We passed a pod of belugas about halfway down the Arm, their pale backs breaking the gray surface like fleeting ghosts. The deckhands leaned on the rail to watch, one of them calling out that the sight meant good luck. I wanted to believe him, but the moment stirred something deeper than luck. There was a quiet holiness in their passage, as if the whales carried with them a memory older than the tides, a reminder that the Arm was not ours to command but to cross with humility. Their breath rose like small prayers, vanishing into the cold air, and for an instant I felt as though they were escorting us, guardians of the water's hidden spirit.

As we traced the shoreline, Hope appeared through the mist—alive and working, wood smoke curling from chimneys, the chatter of hammers and laughter drifting faintly across the water. I turned my eyes toward it, heart tightening.

Just four weeks ago, I'd kissed Peggy at the edge of the dock, our son Walter waving with his mother's strength in his eyes and, perhaps, too much of my own wandering in his blood. Leaving them never came easily. But the trail had called again, as it always seemed to do.

Still, it brought me comfort to know they were there. Hope wasn't just a town anymore—it was the anchor I returned to, the center of a life I never thought I'd have.

Soon, the shoreline fell away into emptiness, and the ruins of Sunrise emerged from the mist like the bones of a giant, half-buried and forgotten. Charred beams bowed beneath moss, sluice-boxes lay splintered and half-swallowed by alder. The place was hollow now, a silence where once there had been shouts and the ringing of picks. It should've been nothing more than another ruin—but a shiver ran through me. A name surfaced like a warning bell.

Magnus Vega.

We'd started as enemies. In the fevered days of '98, when Hope and Sunrise were still raw cuts in the wilderness, Magnus stood at the heart of the chaos. Gold dust sparkled in his beard, a Colt rode his hip, and men circled him like gulls drawn to a carcass. He dealt in promises, sometimes kept, often broken. I wanted nothing to do with the shadows that clung to him.

But Alaska rarely cares what a man wants.

When Ella Carson's Asatrus swept into Hope—chanting the old tongues of Odin and blood sacrifice—Magnus stepped between me and the blade. I can still see Ella's eyes blazing like blue flame as she raised her knife over me, words of the Old World on her tongue, ready to carve out secrets in flesh. I was seconds from dying beneath the Northern Lights when Magnus pulled the trigger. Ella fell without a cry. He hadn't done it for me. Not out of loyalty. Not out of friendship. But out of something older. A reckoning, perhaps. The first spark of redemption.

Two years later, I found him again on the wind-scoured beaches of Cape Nome. The gold rush was roaring like a hot fever, tents sprouting overnight, fortunes rising and falling with every shovelful of gravel. There, Magnus and I stood shoulder to shoulder, exposing a phantom-claim swindle on Anvil Creek. We burned ledgers. We freed stampeders who'd been held hostage by blackmail and fear. For a short season, we moved like comrades—two men battered by ambition, finally weary of chasing ghosts.

But Alaska doesn't let debts go unpaid.

A late-season gale came screaming off the Bering Sea, capsizing our canvas raft off Sledge Island. I dove in after Magnus and dragged him back to the raft. But the spark was gone from his eyes. The sea had claimed him.

Yet death didn't finish the story of Magnus Vega.

In 1902, beneath Denali's towering ice walls, I found him again—not in flesh, but as spirit. His soul was caught in a chamber of glacial stone. It is believed the mountain binds the restless until someone speaks their truth. So I knelt there on ice hard as iron, and I told his story—the bullet that saved me, the moments he tried to be more than the man the world believed him to be. I offered him what he never dared ask for: remembrance, and the promise that he would not be forgotten.

Now, as Sunrise's weathered remains slip behind me into the ship's wake, I feel his presence, faint as breath. A reminder that even the darkest soul can arc toward the light—if someone is willing to bear witness.

Magnus Vega. My rival. My friend. A soul released.

And yet, what stirred in me wasn't yearning. It was worry—a quiet, coiled unease I couldn't name. Why should I fear him? He was gone. Freed. At peace.

But something in the wind suggested otherwise.

CHAPTER ELEVEN
THE FLATS

The Chinook Belle hissed into the shallows. As the steamer slowed, the smell hit first—wet earth, coal smoke, and something sour beneath it, like old blood. The Placer River Flats sprawled before us, gray and heaving. Nothing about it was still.

Rails twisted like eels through the muck. Freight cars leaned at strange angles, their bellies half-swallowed by the trembling bog. Spikes, cross ties, tools—all strewn like the wreckage of a battle long lost. Telegraph wires sagged into pools of black water, snapping faintly in the wind. The land shivered, as if trying to expel everything man had pressed upon it.

Laborers moved cautiously through the ruin, their steps tentative, as if the flats might open wider at any moment and take them too. A few worked shovels listlessly; most just stood.

Waiting, maybe. Or mourning.

I disembarked and made my way into the mire, notebook in hand, boots sinking deeper with each step. My first thought was the article. Readers would want scale, drama, loss. They craved calamity packaged with precision, and I could provide it to them. But first, I needed the bones of the story. I needed facts.

Near the edge of the last intact trestle stood a man who looked like he belonged to the land itself—barrel-chested, wind-chapped, arms folded like the whole disaster had personally wronged him. He watched the sunken rail with a glare, jaw working side to side.

I approached slowly, lifting a hand. "Excuse me, sir—are you the foreman?"

He turned, eyes narrowing beneath a thick brow. "Who's asking?"

"Percy Hope. Journalist. *San Francisco Examiner*," I said, stepping closer. "I'm reporting on the railroad's progress, but…" I nodded toward the sunken rail line, its twisted remnants half-swallowed by the bog, "this looks like a very different kind of story."

The man didn't move. Just squinted at me like I'd stepped out of the fog with bad timing.

"Dray," he said finally, voice rough as gravel. "Foreman."

He looked me over, then at the notebook in my hand.

"Well, Hope—unless that pencil of yours can lay timber or charm the marsh into drying up, you're too late." He thumbed toward the wreckage. "The land made its choice."

He turned back to the Flats, arms crossed, jaw tight. I gripped my notebook anyway. Sometimes stories waited for you. Sometimes, like this one, they were still unfolding—slowly, bitterly, in mud and silence.

"Maybe so," I said, flipping open my notebook. "Still, I'd appreciate whatever you can tell me."

We walked the edge together, him pointing out where the line had gone in, how quickly it happened. "Middle of the night," he said. "Sounded like thunder, only lower. Like something underneath was shifting. By morning, half the line was under." He shook his head. "There's no bottom here. Just layers of muck going down to hell."

"What's the plan?" I asked.

He laughed, short and bitter. "There isn't one. Not yet. They want to shift the line east, but that adds weeks. Maybe months. Others think we should lay gravel by the ton and try to rebuild on top of it."

"And you?"

"I think we're screwed," he said.

I scribbled notes, watched the way the water pooled, the rhythm of how it moved—like breath through lungs. And somewhere, quietly, thoughts began to arrange themselves in my mind. I couldn't say how or why, but connections formed. Not ideas, exactly, but patterns. I found myself muttering them under my breath as I walked: "Too much weight in the center… wrong kind of timber… bank reinforcement…"

"What was that?" Dray said, looking up.

I hesitated. "Nothing. Just thinking out loud."

"No, say it again."

So I did. I mentioned the grade angle, the weight distribution of the loaded freight cars, and how they might reposition the ties to prevent lateral drag. It sounded absurd coming from my own mouth—technical, confident, even practiced. I didn't know these things.

A silence followed.

Dray narrowed his eyes. "You an engineer, Hope?"

"Hardly."

"Well, hell. Maybe you should be."

I laughed it off, but inside, I wasn't. I was wondering. Not about the flats. About me. I'd come here to write a story. But suddenly I was part of one. Not because I tried to be—but because something in me... had sharpened.

Dray didn't say much after that. He just studied me, jaw working as if chewing on something tougher than jerky. Then he cocked his head. "Come on," he said. "There's someone you need to talk to."

We wove through the skeletal remains of the worksite—collapsed trestles, shattered crates, timber sunk like gravestones—until we found a knot of men standing near a tall figure in a wool coat and oilskin boots. He was older than Dray, clean-shaven, with a polished silver walking stick and eyes like cold flint.

"Mr. Camden," Dray called out, raising a hand as we approached. "This here's Percy Hope. Reporter, *San Francisco Examiner.*"

Camden turned at the sound of his name. Tall, lean, and sharpened by years of command, he looked at me like I was another problem needing a quick solution-or better yet, dismissal.

"A journalist," he said flatly. "Of course."

"I'm here to cover the line," I offered, trying not to bristle. "Though it seems the line's decided to cover itself."

Dray snorted behind me, but Camden's expression didn't flicker.

"You'll get your story," Camden said. "Disaster's good copy. Just stay out of the way while we salvage what's left of this mess."

I nodded, notebook still in hand. "Understood."

But I couldn't help it—my eyes scanned the terrain again. The deep pooling where it shouldn't be, the angle of the fallen ties, the line of tension where the earth had torn. I stepped closer to the edge of the mud, thinking aloud more than speaking to anyone in particular.

"You're losing integrity through the center," I said. "The water's feeding in from that rise to the south—see that? And with the weight this concentrated, you'll get another collapse if you shift the line too close."

Camden turned. "Come again?"

I blinked, caught off guard. "Just something I noticed."

Dray stepped forward. "He said something earlier, too. About grade angles. Weight distribution. Seemed to make sense."

Camden studied me now, for real. "You have experience in rail construction, Mr. Hope?"

"Ah, no," I said slowly. "Not at all."

"Then where the hell is all that coming from?"

I hesitated. "I wish I could tell you."

But even as I said it, the words were already forming—clear, complete, and oddly certain. I didn't feel like I was inventing them so much as uncovering something already there.

"I'd say shifting east won't help. The ground's no better there—same bog, different angle. You'd just be buying time until the whole thing sinks again."

Camden folded his arms. "Go on."

I blinked. The words came before I could stop them. "You'd need to create a floating base—layers of interwoven timber and brush, something flexible. Distribute the weight outward, not down. Raise the line above the most unstable veins and anchor the pilings on the periphery, near the higher rock shelf. That channel there"—I pointed toward a meandering run of black water—"it's feeding an underground flow that's destabilizing the center. Divert that, and you cut the heart out of the collapse."

A long silence followed. Even the wind seemed to pause.

Camden slowly turned to Dray. "Where'd you say this man was from?"

"San Francisco. Reporter."

He narrowed his eyes. "And he just knows this?"

Dray shrugged. "Apparently."

I felt every pair of eyes on me, but all I could hear was the strange quiet in my own head like something had taken over—not possession, but precision. I hadn't studied hydrology. I'd never built a rail line. Yet the concepts had risen out of me with the certainty of memory. It was as if the land had whispered its secrets and I'd somehow spoken them aloud.

"I'm not sure how I know," I admitted. "Only that I do."

Camden stared a moment longer, then gave the barest nod. "Come with me."

I followed, heart thudding, the press of the medallion pressing warm against my chest like a second heartbeat. I didn't look down. I didn't touch it.

But I felt it.

And it was speaking.

The bunkhouse stood at the edge of the Flats, where the marsh gave way to gravel and the wind picked up the scent of woodsmoke and iron. It was little more than a long timber box, crooked with age and hastily expanded—half shelter, half afterthought. One side was given over to the living: men sprawled across straw mattresses or hunched over chipped enamel mugs. The other side… belonged to those not quite on either side of the veil.

Dray showed me in with a nod and a grunt. "Take any empty cot."

Inside, the air was thick with tobacco smoke and the ripe stench of unwashed bodies. But there was camaraderie too—a low, rusting sort, forged not in joy but survival. Laughter barked from the far corner over a game of cards, while someone strummed a broken banjo, its missing strings filled in by the rhythm of boots on planks. The men looked up at me without interest. Another stranger in boots and a coat, that's all.

I found a cot near the back wall, between a crate of salted meat and a young Irishman muttering feverishly in his sleep. I dropped my satchel, pulled out my notebook, and got to work. The words came fast now—tight, muscular sentences, coiling into something more than reportage. The Flats weren't just a story. They were an unraveling, a reckoning. I described the land as wounded, the men as its splinters, and the railroad as both promise and punishment.

But I couldn't ignore what lay beyond the partition. A thin canvas sheet marked off the infirmary, though "infirmary" was generous. I'd peeked behind it when I passed: bandaged limbs, fevered eyes, two men coughing blood, and a nurse with sleeves rolled to the elbow and eyes like riverstone. Outside the bunkhouse, beneath a tarp weighed down with rocks, sat six pine coffins stacked like cordwood. The names, if there were any, had already smudged in the rain.

Sleep came slowly. I wrote until the lines blurred, until the lamplight burned low and the voices quieted to murmurs and snores. Somewhere in the distance, an owl called once, then again. I slipped into uneasy dreams, where the medallion pulsed softly beneath my coat and the earth itself whispered in a tongue I almost understood.

Morning came with the clang of a bell—sharp, metallic, and final. I followed the men outside, boots crunching frost-hardened mud. A small crowd gathered near the coffins, where a reverend, a man with soot-streaked hands and a Bible held like a ledger, recited prayers in a low, steady voice. There were no hymns, only the wind, and the occasional sniffling of a man trying his best not to grieve.

One by one, the coffins were lowered into the shallow trench. No eulogies. Just names spoken once and a shovelful of earth to follow. A railroad was being carved through wilderness, but this too was part of the cost—measured not just in timber and steel, but in breath.

I stood at the edge, hat in hand, and wondered not just how I would write about this, but how I would carry it.

The Flats were not finished with me yet.

*

That night, after the funeral service, I returned to the bunkhouse and lit a stub of candle beside my cot. Most of the men had already turned in, their snores rising and falling like the tide beyond the walls. The infirmary on the far end was quiet now, too, save for the occasional groan or cough behind the canvas partition. Outside, the wind sighed low over the graves, and somewhere in the night, a wolf howled a lament.

I sat there with my notebook open, pen in hand—but the words I wrote weren't just for the *Examiner*. They came through me as if channeled. I'd spoken of grade angles and weight distribution, of creating a floating base from interwoven timber and brush to distribute the load outward, not down. I'd pointed to the underground flow feeding the collapse and suggested diverting it to stabilize the center. None of it came from any education I'd had. The thoughts had simply... arrived. Observations too precise, too practiced.

My fingers brushed the medallion. I hesitated, then lifted it off and laid it on the blanket. It sat heavy in the candlelight, the engraved raven catching the flicker of flame. I stared at it, and slowly, a strange truth unfurled in the back of my mind—not with logic, but with knowing. The way an image appears in a dream, and you understand its meaning without needing explanation.

I hadn't learned those things I said today about weight distribution, grade angles, timber reinforcement. They had come from nowhere—and yet, I'd spoken with the authority of a man who'd studied the science all his life. It wasn't guessing.

The shaman's presence returned to me—Sha-e-dah-kla, not as a memory but as something still alive in the marrow of the land. I had met him again in that sacred cave, lying on the same stone shelf where Reverend O'Hara once hovered between worlds. The warmth of the medallion had pulled me into a vision, not a dream, but a communion. In that otherworldly Alaskan wilderness, Sha-e-dah-kla had spoken not in words, but in knowing. He showed me that the railroad was disturbing something ancient, something alive. That I was chosen not just to observe, but to act. The medallion wasn't just a relic. It was a tool of transformation—meant to strengthen, to reveal, to align progress with purpose. And now, sitting in a bunkhouse thick with grief and the scent of mud and sweat, I could feel the truth of his warning. The knowledge I had spoken today—about floating timber beds, weight distribution, underground water veins—it hadn't come from me. It had come *through* me. The medallion had begun to awaken. And I was no longer just writing history. I was being written into it.

The medallion didn't glow or hum. It simply was—still, silent, ancient. But it had changed something in me. Or perhaps it had amplified something that was already there. Like an unseen hand nudging my thoughts toward clarity. Like I was a vessel—and something, or someone, had poured knowledge into me.

I looked again at the lines I'd written. They were good. Too good. The kind of prose that editors usually sent back with praise and suspicion. But I hadn't labored over them. They had come in a rush, like water through a broken dam.

It frightened me because it felt too easy. Too fluid. Too… *perfect*.

And yet it wasn't just the writing. It was the understanding. The way I had spoken to Camden and Dray about rail work, engineering, hydrology—fields I had never studied. I knew it hadn't come from books. It had come from something older.

The medallion.

I didn't know what it was yet, or what it wanted. But it had chosen me.

As I lay back, the candle flickering low beside me, I whispered aloud, barely above breath, "Sha-e-dah-kla… is this what you meant? Is this the path I'm meant to follow?"

No answer came.

Just the wind curling around the bunkhouse walls, and the steady, quiet thrum of something old and waiting, deep beneath the surface.

I drifted to sleep with the medallion clutched in my palm, not knowing whether I had just crossed a threshold or been led to it.

CHAPTER TWELVE
MATANUSKA

The time that passed since Placer River was not without meaning.

I continued to track the railroad's relentless push north—documenting the birth of camps and the death of illusions, the carving of steel through the glacier-carved silence. My dispatches traveled farther than I did, picked up by papers in Seattle, Chicago, and even New York. Editors began to recognize my name. A few called my reporting essential.

But the praise that meant the most came in a handwritten letter—from a man who had once changed the course of my life.

Jack London.

It was Jack London who'd spoken at our high school graduation—mine and Liam's—when we were still two wide-eyed dreamers clinging to a world of possibilities. It was Jack London who stoked the fire that led us to Alaska. And it was Jack London who later mentored me, edited my first novel—*A Summer of Hope*, and kicked down the door to the *San Francisco Examiner* newsroom so I could walk in.

We stayed friends after all these years, then he turned inward. A few months before he died, he sent me a letter. Just one line, scribbled on battered stationery: *"You've got the eye—don't let the work make you blind to it.* " That was Jack: blunt, brilliant, and cutting through sentiment like a blade through bark.

He died in agony. Dysentery, uremia, and the bottle took him piece by piece. Toward the end, I heard he was dosing heavily on morphine and opium—ironically, both you could buy at the druggist between toothpaste and soap. But even those comforts couldn't dull the pain that chased him. You could hear it in his last essays—each word like a man gasping through smoke.

I miss him.

Walter was writing too—slowly, methodically, chasing the truth like a boy chasing fireflies. At fourteen, he was beginning to find his voice—not loud or boastful, but careful and clear, shaped by observation and a quiet hunger to be known.

When I was away, he would write to me. Long letters tucked into bulging envelopes. His words weren't just updates—they were offerings. Bits of himself folded neatly into paragraphs. Descriptions of the mountain light on frostbitten mornings. A fox he saw moving like smoke through the birch.

Sometimes, he'd slip in pieces of prose—little essays he called "dispatches," written in the style he imagined I used in the field. He never asked for praise, but I knew he was hoping I'd read them like a fellow writer, not just a father.

Every sentence was another attempt to say: *See me. Understand me.*

Walter was never chasing fame. He was chasing *recognition.* Not in the way headlines offer it, but in the way a boy watches his father, waiting for the faintest nod.

And Peggy? With all the savvy she'd honed selling women's clothing at Goldberg's Clothier in Nome, she'd claimed a corner of the Hope General Store for herself, arranging dresses and delicate accessories as though she were tending orchids. It wasn't much of a market in Hope—silk and lace had little place among mining dust and spruce sap—but the locals did their best to support her, stopping by to finger the fabrics and dream of finer days.

We saw each other from time to time—letters passed between us like secret messages, and the occasional visit when the weather allowed. And yes, we spoke of the cave. Of the medallion. Of that one shattering moment at Placer, when a tide of visions and symbols had poured into me, flooding my mind with truths that defied any schooling I'd ever received.

Peggy had been the only one who truly understood what I meant— what it felt like. Not merely to glimpse something uncanny, like a flash of light at the edge of vision, but to be drawn into it so completely that it reshaped who you were. To have your mind carried beyond itself, into something ancient and immense, as if the universe had borrowed your eyes for a moment to look back at its reflection.

She knew how it left a person trembling and thrilled at the same time. How, afterward, nothing ordinary felt quite the same. How colors seemed brighter, shadows deeper, and every silence buzzed with secrets waiting to be spoken.

We never found the perfect words for it. But when Peggy looked at me with that knowing glint, I knew she'd been touched by something similar—that we were both marked, in some hidden way, by mysteries too big for the world we lived in.

We didn't dwell on it often, but when we did, there was no need for embellishment. The experience was its own kind of scripture, etched into our lives. What lingered after those conversations wasn't silence but reverence—a quiet knowing that whatever had moved through me in that flooded valley hadn't yet finished its work.

Life moved on, as it tends to do when wonder is forced to make room for Alaskan weather and work. But something had changed in me after Placer—subtle, persistent. The shaman's words had taken root in my mind, strange and resonant: *"The medallion is not yours to possess, but to remember. It awakens what once was forgotten."* At the time, I hadn't known what to make of it. But after what happened at Placer, I couldn't ignore it.

I had stood beside the engineers, watching them debate how to span the Flats. And then, almost as if from outside myself, I had spoken—describing a method, a solution they hadn't considered. It was detailed, technical. Too precise to be guessed. Yet it worked. I had no training to justify it, no blueprint in hand. It was as if the knowledge had arrived fully formed, bypassing thought and memory alike.

There were other moments too—quiet, almost unnoticeable—when knowledge surfaced unbidden. It also didn't feel like something I had learned. It felt remembered. As if some ancient part of me, stirred by the medallion, was awakening. A former life rising through the seams of my present one.

I still wrote my articles, still followed the slow march of progress as the line stretched northbound. Yet beneath the daily tasks and deadlines, a quiet watchfulness had taken root. I was waiting. Waiting for the current to stir again. For the veil to lift. For whatever had touched me once—through the medallion, through the earth itself—to reach through time and snow and summon me forward.

The railroad had opened a reliable line stretching from Seward through Anchorage to the newest front of construction. It was one of the few luxuries the project afforded—movement, in the dead of winter.

I boarded the train north, following steel into the heart of trouble, where the rivers had risen, and the ground had turned against us. I rode north with the men, the ones who swung the hammers, drove the spikes, cleared the land inch by inch. There were no seats, no stoves, no comforts. These were freight cars—open-topped gondolas and makeshift boxcars meant for hauling timber, rails, and sacks of cement, not passengers, not yet. Someone had spread a layer of straw across the floorboards, but the wind still sliced through the cracks in the planks, and every jolt sent cold air whistling up through the iron ribs of the car. We huddled under wool blankets, shoulder to shoulder with pickaxes, crates, and the stink of oilskins. The metal walls groaned with each curve, and the scent of coal smoke seeped in from the engine, mingling with the sharp tang of frost and damp wood.

Around me were men with stories carved into their hands and faces—immigrants, drifters, war veterans, and debtors—each of us bound to the same steel trail, heading into a wilderness both geographic and unseen. They shivered beside me, not knowing I carried something different, not just in my coat pocket, but in the marrow of my bones. A question that wouldn't let go—a whisper just beneath the wind.

Yet the ride offered a sweeping view of the Territory—raw, untamed, and scarred. I watched as the engine carved its way through ancient rock, the cuts still fresh and jagged where dynamite had bitten through mountainsides. Trees had been felled by the thousands, their stumps like broken teeth jutting from frozen soil. There were places where the land looked flayed open—but I knew, in time, nature would return. Snow would soften the wounds. Moss would creep back. Spruce and alder would reclaim what was theirs, inch by inch.

And in between those bruises, there was majesty.

White-dusted peaks rose like cathedral spires. Valleys opened wide and hushed, cradling frozen rivers that shimmered like braided glass. Caribou trails stitched through drifts, and every so often, a fox darted across the tracks, a flicker of red against the white. The stillness was not silence—it was breath held. Watching. Waiting.

The Matanuska Valley was cold, not just in temperature, but in temperament. The cold here didn't sting—it settled. Into lungs, into joints, into the silences between men. The mountains loomed on every side, glacier-scored and watching.

When I arrived, the camps were already falling apart. Canvas tents leaned drunkenly into the wind, their ropes iced over and flapping like the broken wings of birds. Snow crept in through seams, and seams gave way—some tents had half-collapsed, swallowed at the base by drifts. Firewood was so scarce that the men burned splintered crates, their fires crackling low and blue in the brittle air. Shovels snapped like brittle bones in the iron ground, and the usual curses were spoken with a kind of hollow resignation, like the men weren't angry, just tired of pretending they weren't losing.

Daylight was a brief guest—four, maybe five hours of gray-tinged light that slanted low across the valley and disappeared by midafternoon. The rest belonged to shadow. Men worked by lantern glow and firelight, setting up carbide lamps at the trackline, their bluish flames flickering like ghost-lights against the snow. In the camps, oil lamps dangled from ridgepoles or perched on crates, hissing quietly as they threw weak halos against the canvas walls. The darkness wasn't just outside—it pressed inward, making every task harder, every silence heavier. And still they worked. They had to. Steel doesn't wait for spring.

I stepped off the train into a silence that felt deeper than the cold. It wasn't the air—it was underneath it, like the earth itself was holding its breath. Something was wrong. Not loudly. Just insistently.

It didn't take long to understand what was holding things up.

Permafrost.

They'd lay down track, and by morning it was as if the rails had been toyed with by a giant child—bent, bowed, sometimes sunken a foot or more into the muck. The ground heaved like something dreaming fitfully beneath it. The engineers were in a kind of fevered war—dumping gravel by the ton, sinking piles into the frost like stakes into a vampire, trying to outthink something that didn't think at all. It just reacted. Patient. Inevitable.

I walked the edge of the site where the work had been halted. The tracks twisted like serpents fleeing the light, their steel warped and buckled by the whims of the frozen earth. Frost clung to every bolt like lichen on bone. The silence was unnatural—thick, expectant.

I stared at a length of rail bent into a slow, sad arc—and something seized me.

My breath caught. My chest tightened. A strange clarity surged up my spine, and the words spilled out, not thought but spoken, simultaneous with the jolt that passed through me.

"Try timber cribbing," I said, eyes wide, like I'd just heard someone else speak through my own mouth. "Stacked pine boxes, filled with rock. Float the rails above the frost line."

A foreman nearby lifted his head. "What was that?"

I turned toward him slowly, heart still pounding, and repeated it—firmer this time. He scribbled it down. Nobody questioned it. But I stood there, unsettled.

It was happening again—words, images, entire solutions rising whole, without origin. A door had opened inside me, and something old had stepped through. A current of knowing surged from the ground through my bones, the land itself whispering the answer into my blood. My mouth had simply given it shape.

There was no thinking. No weighing of options. Just the words, already on my tongue—as if they'd been waiting. Not memory. Not intuition. Something older. Something ancient, stirred awake in the frost and speaking through me.

And then, just as quickly, it was gone. The silence returned. The wind picked up. Men moved past me, hauling timber. But I remained where I stood, shivering—not from the cold, but from the echo of having been used. Not harmed. Not chosen. Just… opened.

And somewhere, just beyond the reach of my senses, I could feel that presence again, watching. Waiting.

I lingered while the crews moved into motion. Word of the solution passed from foreman to foreman like steam through the cold, subtle but rising. Some men looked at me differently. Most didn't look at all. They just got to work, cutting pine, hauling stone. The sound of tools resumed—axes biting into frozen trunks, sledges cracking gravel—and with it came the illusion of progress. But I could still feel something beneath it all. A presence. Not men or earth. Something watching.

I was still standing near the twisted rails when the shouts began.

A boy was missing.

CHAPTER THIRTEEN
ELI

Eli Brandt—junior surveyor, barely seventeen. He'd gone out with a team that morning to flag the next milepost. Midday came and went. The others returned. He didn't.

At first, no one panicked. Maybe he'd lost his way. Maybe he'd stopped to relieve himself and doubled back on another trail. But when early night began to drift in like smoke through the trees, worry hardened into something heavier.

They found his tracks before sundown—clear and deliberate, leading into the spruce. And then they just… ended. No sign of a struggle. No drag marks. No boot prints veering off. Just a single trail that vanished like a wick snuffed in snow.

They called his name. Fired into the air. Someone brought a dog from a crew down in Anchorage—but the animal whined, turned in circles, and lay down without a sound.

I followed the trail myself, heart steady but cold. The light was dying, silver and sharp as a blade. The woods didn't move. Not even the wind dared speak. I found the last marker he'd planted, its orange flag fluttering with an eerie cheerfulness. A few paces beyond, his final footprint pressed into the crusted snow like a signature.

And there, snagged on a low branch, hung a torn scrap of bluish wool.

I held the scrap between my fingers. Coarse. Torn clean. Still warm from a boy who should've been too far gone to leave warmth behind. The medallion at my chest flared—not in heat, but in pressure, like a heartbeat outside time. I slipped the fabric into my pocket and stepped beyond the last footprint.

The woods didn't want me.

I don't mean in some poetic sense. I mean it physically—viscerally. The moment my boot crossed the invisible threshold, the air thickened. My lungs strained. The trees, still and bare a moment before, now leaned ever so slightly inward. Closing. Narrowing.

Snow swallowed sound. Light twisted.

Each step felt like wading through something unseen—resistance thickening with every movement. A sensation like walking upstream in a river you couldn't see. I pressed on.

Then the cold changed.

It wasn't colder, just… older. Deeper. As if I'd stepped beneath the crust of the world and into something that hadn't been touched by man in centuries.

A branch snapped—sharp and close—and I spun.

Nothing.

No wind. No animal. But still, that pressure. It was no longer resisting me. It was watching.

The medallion pulsed again. Not a warning—an alert. Like a dog stiffening before a quake.

I closed my eyes, heart thundering low. "Who's there?" I asked aloud, though I already knew no voice would answer. Not with words.

Instead, the presence pressed in.

Not malevolent.

Not kind.

Just deliberate.

Just known.

It filled every hollow in the air around me, like breath exhaled by the earth itself—ancient, familiar, inescapable. I didn't need to see it. I had felt it before.

Under Denali, in the Cave of the Soul.

Where I once found Magnus, not as a man, but as a presence caught between worlds.

And now here again.

Not Magnus's voice. Not his form. But the essence of him. The sorrow of him. The will of him.

The same force that once whispered through ice and shadow, begging not for forgiveness, but for release.

It crowded close—like gravity reversing course—pulling instead of grounding. I gritted my teeth. My vision blurred.

And then I knew.

Magnus.

"Is it you?" I whispered.

No answer came. But a memory did—of that long night in the cave, when I told his spirit form he was loved, when I spoke of Suzie, and his parents waiting beyond.

I thought I had freed him.

I thought I'd done enough.

But here he was again. Not in torment. Not in peace. Simply *present*—like unfinished music.

It wanted me to turn back.

Not because it feared me. Because it feared what lay ahead.

I reached for the medallion again, and this time, I didn't just hold it—I *asked* it.

Not with words. With intention.

Let me see. Let me *through*.

And just like that, the pressure eased.

Not entirely. Just enough.

As if the force had made its point—and now, reluctantly, was letting me pass.

I stumbled forward. The snow thinned. A break in the spruce appeared like a wound in the forest's skin.

And there—curled beneath a tree, his blue plaid scarf drawn up to his chin—was Eli.

His eyes were open. Alive. Dazed.

I dropped to my knees beside him. "Eli," I said softly, my breath hanging in the cold between us. "My name is Percy. I've come to bring you back."

His gaze latched onto mine, confused. "You're not from my crew."

"I'm not. But I've been looking. The whole camp's been looking."

He blinked, like it took effort to understand. Then, almost to himself: "I didn't think anyone would come." He swallowed. "Especially not someone I didn't know."

I tried to smile, but the heaviness of the place pressed in around us. "Sometimes it takes a stranger."

Eli pushed himself upright with trembling arms. "I tried to turn around. I did. But something… something kept pulling."

He turned toward the woods behind him, eyes narrowing. "I didn't want to go further. But I couldn't stop."

"You weren't walking alone," I said.

He looked at me, startled.

"I felt it too," I added. "Whatever it was. Like walking into a tide. A will that wasn't ours."

Eli's lips parted slightly, but no words came. His eyes—wide, ice-blue, ringed with exhaustion—searched mine as if to confirm he hadn't imagined it all. The boy was young, with a freckled face that still clung to childhood. His scarf had unraveled at the neck, and his breath fogged in quick, shallow bursts.

"We've been calling for you since sundown."

I helped Eli to his feet. His legs were stiff, but he could stand.

"You're alright now," I said. "We're going back to camp."

As we stepped back toward the break in the trees, the pressure around us thinned, like a current releasing its grip. Still, I didn't look back. I didn't need to.

Magnus was there.

Not chasing.

Not retreating.

Watching.

Not to punish.

But to protect something. Maybe Eli. Maybe me. Maybe something older than both of us.

And as the boy leaned into my side, quiet and shivering but safe, I began to understand—

Magnus hadn't tried to stop me out of anger.

He had done it out of fear.

But not for Eli.

For what finding him might awaken.

CHAPTER FOURTEEN
PEGGY

The freight train rumbled south through the sleeping wilderness. Cold seeped into our bones as we sat wedged between crates and bundled cargo, the darkness outside broken only by fleeting sparks from the rails.

Eli sat across from me on a plank of timber, knees drawn up beneath a wool coat two sizes too large. He hadn't said much since we left the Matanuska Valley. The wind whistled through a gap in the slats, stinging our faces and frosting the edges of a cracked window high on the wall.

But as the rhythm of the rails stretched into silence, he finally spoke.

"My life didn't start in Alaska," he said, his voice nearly lost to the clatter. "We came from Spokane. Mother died when I was eight. My father remarried fast. Mary tried with me. Just… not very hard."

I gave him space. Sometimes boys his age talk like frost forms—quietly, and only when the air is still enough.

"We moved to Sunrise after that," Eli said quietly. "My father—Captain Gerhardus Brandt—wasn't chasing gold like the rest of them. He ran a steamer across the Arm, hauling prospectors and freight from the steamships in the Inlet to Sunrise. Said the town was the future, that the Arm would make us rich."

His breath curled in the cold. "But in 1909, he didn't come back. He died on one of those crossings, and the crew buried him on the bluff west of Sixmile Creek, looking down at the tide. I was ten."

He pressed his hands deeper into his coat sleeves. "After that, it was Mary—my stepmother. Like I said, she tried. Just… not very hard. And when she was gone, there wasn't much left to hold on to."

He turned back toward the slit of forest racing past the slats, his breath hanging in the cold. "After that, it was just me. Then I got this job with the railroad and met you."

I looked at him—really looked—and saw the same flicker I'd once carried. Not fear. Not even loss. Just that strange, searching fire that makes a boy walk toward the unknown and not turn back.

"Have you ever been to Hope?" I asked.

He shifted on the plank, eyes dropping to the scuffed toes of his boots. "Sure, I've heard of it," he mumbled. "But no, never been."

"It's not much. But I've got an extra bunk and a stove that mostly works, and a son, a few years younger than you, who could use someone to throw snowballs at."

He cracked the faintest smile. "You sure?"

I nodded. "I'm sure."

He didn't say anything else. Just leaned his shoulder against the crate behind him and closed his eyes. And I knew, without needing words, that he'd accepted the invitation.

Sometimes that's all it takes. A place. A pause. A second chance.

We sat in silence after that, the mountains rolling past like frozen waves. Somewhere in the dark between settlements, the boy drifted to sleep, and I kept watch, thinking how the land has a way of sending us back to ourselves—only sometimes, if we're lucky, it sends someone with us.

*

By the time we reached Hope, winter had closed its fist around the land. The creek coiled beneath its sheath of ice, still and watchful like a serpent in hibernation. Snow swallowed the trails overnight, and the air didn't bite so much as settle—slow and marrow-deep—dragging even our thoughts into stillness.

I brought Eli into the house and introduced him to Walter. The boys stood across from each other like two wild creatures caught in one another's shadow—silent, curious, uncertain.

Walter crossed his arms; Eli hunched into his oversized coat. But boys don't stay strangers long. Within hours, they were sledding behind the smithy, shouting into the wind, trading secrets over firewood runs. Their laughter cracked the silence like a spring thaw.

Peggy stood on the porch with her arms folded tight against the cold, her smile barely more than a shadow. From a distance, she looked content—maybe even proud—but I'd come to recognize the quiet drift in her eyes, the way her gaze lingered too long on the trees or the trail or nothing at all. She moved through the house like a woman whose bags were already half-packed in her mind.

Most nights, she sat alone beneath the kerosene lamp, poring over ledgers from Nome—shipping manifests, old sales slips, brittle letters from Greenburg's Clothier. That place had been her stand, her stake in the world. I still remember the day she opened it—bunting across the awning, Peggy beaming in a dress she'd sewn with her own hands. She'd made something then. Something hers.

But now her dreams hung on a single pegboard in the corner of the Hope General Store. Three dresses, two blouses, and not one had sold. Price tags yellowing, numbers rubbed faint from being marked down too many times. Townsfolk passed them by without pause. Russel had tried to soften the truth—"Not much call for fashion here."

Each unsold garment was more than lost coin. It was a kind of erasure. A quiet unraveling of who she thought she might be. And so she sat at the table with those ledgers, watching her past speak louder than her present. In the hush of this town, in the corners no one looked, even failure had a voice. And it was speaking now, soft and steady, through the silence she carried like a second skin.

There was Izzy, her first husband, who'd breathed mercury and madness, dying a suspicious death.

There was Hummel, the crazed gold miner who swore Peggy slipped poison into his coffee, his eyes darting like he expected demons to crawl out of the steam.

There was Sheriff Baker, who took a pull from Peggy's silver flask one bitter night and never woke up again.

And there were the children. Olaf Lindblom, just eight, vanished while digging holes in the dunes, leaving behind nothing but his velvet cap tangled in a patch of eerie, glowing seaweed. Before the town could finish saying one prayer for him, another boy was gone before dawn, and Hummel's talk of "more lost boys" didn't sound so crazy anymore.

She'd always had her explanations—always. But now, she wasn't running from those memories. She was listening to them.

One night, with the wind curling through the shutters and the boys asleep upstairs, she finally said it.

"I want to go back."

I looked up from my notebook. "Back where?"

"San Francisco."

The words hit hard. "You hated it there," I said.

She nodded slowly. "I hated who I had to be. But I've lost track of who I am now. Hope is too quiet. I can't hear myself in it."

She wasn't running from me. That much she made clear. "I'm not leaving for someone else," she said. "I just need to remember who I was before survival became the whole story. And Walter will come with me."

That hit harder than anything else. I'd quickly imagined if she left, Walter would stay—that I would guide him through the years ahead, steady as the forge. But she looked at me with the same resolve I saw on the train to Cheyenne back in '03, when she read *The Wonderful Wizard of Oz* like it was scripture and praised Dorothy's grit as if it were her own. I remembered the girl who had survived the massacre of her family at twelve, then been taken in by her Aunt Josie and Uncle Wyatt. Her life had been carved out of catastrophe, stitched back together with stubborn thread. She had always moved forward—whether toward Nome's gold, a freight car's gamble, or a new storefront dream.

"I want our son to see a world that's louder than sled tracks," she said. "He needs to look out windows that open onto boulevards, not spruce forests."

I said nothing, not at first. I wanted to argue that there was magic here, too—that spruce sap and silence could teach a boy as much about the world as any avenue ever could. But I saw the clarity in her eyes, and I knew the decision had already taken root. She would go. And Walter would go with her.

*

She didn't leave right away. These departures are quiet things. A green cloth-bound book vanished from the shelf. Her old boots—unworn since Nome—were cleaned and placed by the door. She began writing letters without return addresses. I never asked who they were for.

By March, she was still here, but not really. Her body moved through the house, folding linens, ladling soup, brushing snow off the porch rail. But her spirit had already stepped beyond Hope, bound for something she couldn't name but needed to find.

The morning they left was pale and still. Peggy tightened Walter's scarf, then looked back at me with eyes bright but steady.

"You're steadier than I am," she said. "But steadiness won't teach him to dream."

I wanted to tell her she was wrong. That dreams lived here, too—in the hush of the trees, in the crackle of firewood, in the calm of silence well-held. But I didn't. Instead, I placed a small black spruce whistle in Walter's mittened hand and told him to use it when he missed the sound of the wind.

They boarded the freight sled bound for Portage, the nearest rail station, hugging the far side of Turnagain Arm. It was the first leg of a long journey south—a winding trail through spruce-shadowed valleys and over ice-clad ridges.

From there, they'd catch the passenger train to Seward—still so new that some folks spoke of it like a miracle, iron rails finally linking the coast to the interior. Not like the north, where tracks were still being laid mile by mile through rock and snow.

In Seward, a steamship waited to carry them down the Pacific and into the gray sprawl of San Francisco. I'd arranged it all quietly, without ceremony, knowing it was the last thing I could offer her, the last thread I could tie before letting go.

The dogs strained against their harnesses, paws digging into the packed snow, breath steaming into the morning air. The sled groaned, then surged forward. Snow flurried beneath the runners, and the brass bell rang once—sharp, clean, final—before the forest swallowed it. I stood there long after they disappeared down the ridge, the stillness pressing inward like a hand on the chest. The air still carried her scent—citrus, pine, and that trace of forge-warmed copper that always followed her, even through winter. It lingered like a final breath—a memory. A goodbye, I never found the courage to speak.

Eli came and stood beside me. "They'll come back, won't they?"

I didn't answer right away. My voice felt like it would break under the truth. Finally, I said, "Hope doesn't hold people forever. It's a place to remember. Or forget."

The whistle's faint trill echoed back over the ridge. I closed my eyes. The winter remained, and I with it.

But the house would feel emptier now.

Not because of the cold.

Because of the absence of what I'd dared to hope might stay.

CHAPTER FIFTEEN
SUSITNA

The river stayed locked in ice longer than expected. We followed the line north through a land still gripped by winter's hand, the ground firm beneath our boots, and the trees rimmed in frost that hadn't yet surrendered to the sun. The Susitna lay frozen in silence—its broad white surface gleaming like glass under the pale sky—offering a rare moment of advantage to the men trying to tame this wilderness with steel.

In most parts of the country, winter meant pause. Here, it meant progress.

The Alaska Engineering Commission had learned to use the cold. With the muskeg frozen solid and the wetlands sealed tight, they could haul tons of steel, timber, and fuel to places no wheeled freight could reach in summer. Horse-drawn sleds moved like shadows through the timber, and dog teams slipped across the river's back, carrying food, coal oil, and iron to camps that would otherwise be unreachable until the dry season.

The Susitna crossing—one of the line's more ambitious undertakings—had advanced precisely because of the freeze. Pile drivers worked through the ice, sinking timbers into the firm bed below. Crews had rigged scaffolds over the ice, and with the river low and its banks hardened, steel trusses began to take shape in the brittle light. This was winter's gift: a road made of ice, soil firm underfoot, and rivers that stopped moving long enough for bridges to catch up.

I arrived with Eli in tow—he'd taken to calling himself my assistant, and I didn't correct him. He carried my satchel, kept the stove packed tight, and tucked inside his coat was the latest issue of the *San Francisco Examiner*.

My piece on "The Quicksand of Ice—Permafrost Perils on the Alaska Line" had splashed across the Western Digest's front page. It told how whole lengths of rail in the Matanuska Valley had curled like fiddle-strings overnight, the steel sucked a foot into the earth, and how a desperate crew—prodded by an offhand notion I'd blurted out—stacked pine cribbing, filled it with rock, and let the track float safely above the frost line. The article praised the men who worked by carbide lamp in twenty-below cold, and it shamed the Commission into rushing seasoned timber and fresh gravel north before another thaw could undo the fix.

Eli had underlined my byline twice in red, then a third time for luck. He didn't say a word, but I caught him laying the paper just so on a mess-table barrel—headline up, angled toward the path most of the men took to their bunks. When a brakeman jabbed a finger at the masthead and asked, "That you?" Eli didn't answer. He just gave a slight shrug, but I saw the way his back straightened, his shoulders lifting like he'd grown an inch in the span of a breath.

It wasn't vanity over knowing the writer—it was pride in being part of something that mattered. He'd fetched hot water while I scribbled by lantern light, and stood beside me when the newsprint hit the hands of men who finally saw themselves on the page. For the first time in his seventeen years, Eli wasn't just watching the world turn around him. He'd helped shape it—and he knew it.

A week earlier, a telegram had found me in Hope—delivered by a boy no older than Walter, his boots soaked and his gloves too thin. The message was short, all uppercase, and bristling with urgency: *REPORT TO SUSITNA CROSSING. SPEAK TO TIERNEY. – ACRC.* No signature, but the initials told me everything I needed to know. The Alaska Central Rail Commission wasn't in the habit of sending pleasantries. They were either calling in a favor or cashing one. I thought I was coming to write. Now I wasn't so sure.

By the time Eli and I reached the crossing, the air was thick with sawdust, wet bark, and nerves. A loose gathering of men stood just beyond the supply wagons, clustered around a cookstove barrel burning low. Most had the same posture—arms crossed, faces tight, too worn out to talk but too restless to rest. They looked like they'd been chiseled from the same stump: broad-shouldered lumberjacks in red flannel and suspenders, their cork boots crusted with sap and river silt. Beards hung like frost-heavy moss, some braided with twine, others wild as the woods. A few wore fur caps pulled low over their brows, their breath ghosting in the chill. They turned as I approached, eyes scanning me with the weary curiosity of men who'd seen too many strangers come and go—some buried by the work, others swallowed by the wilderness.

I tipped my hat to the group. "I'm looking for Tierney."

"You found him," came a voice from the far side.

A man stepped forward—barrel-chested, his cheeks wind-burnt and his knuckles raw from frost and friction. He studied me for half a breath, then stuck out a hand rough as bark.

"Figured you'd be taller," he said.

"Percy Hope," I replied, returning the shake. "The Commission said you needed a hand."

Tierney gave a nod. "Glad you're here. I asked for you."

"You did?" I asked, caught off guard.

"They say you made track float at Placer River," he said. "Kept the rails from sinking into frost at Matanuska." His voice carried a tone that wasn't exactly admiration—more like desperate expectation. "You've got men saying you hear things—solutions, I mean. Like the land talks and you listen."

I blinked. "They say all that?"

He grunted. "They do. And if even half of it's true, I'll take it. Things are going sideways out here, and fast."

He turned without another word, and I followed him toward the trestle, Eli at my heels. As we walked, Tierney gave a terse update.

"Crews are working twelve-hour shifts," he said. "Up and down that scaffold like ants on a birch limb. Every step's a prayer the boards hold."

Tierney led us to a broken crate, its side collapsed like a cracked rib, tools scattered in the mud. He kicked it hard. The metal clanged with finality.

"Camp's gone sour," he said. "First, the rations—barrels of pork turned green in the center. Then someone slit the flour sacks clean across. By morning, half the shipment was mush."

I frowned. "Storm damage? Animals?"

Tierney didn't answer. He pulled something from his coat and held it up so we could see.

A bolt, silver and spotless.

"Axle bolt," he said. "For a handcar."

Eli frowned. "Shouldn't that be holding the wheels on?"

Tierney nodded. "Exactly. Without it, the whole car could jump the track. I found it tucked under a foreman's seat—never even been used."

A cold weight settled in my gut. "You think someone left it there on purpose?"

Tierney's jaw tightened. "I think someone's showing us how easy it would be to kill us. And listen to this—three sticks of dynamite are missing from the powder shack."

That stopped us.

"No signs of forced entry," he went on. "Lock's intact. No footprints. No broken latch. Just… gone."

Eli blinked. "Who would even—"

"Someone sending a message," Tierney said, voice low. "First the food. Then the bolt. Now the powder. They're not trying to hurt us. Not yet. They're trying to make us wonder when they will."

A gust of wind stirred the trees. Somewhere up the grade, a hammer stopped mid-strike.

"What do we do?" I asked.

Tierney tossed the bolt back into the crate. "We keep building. And we watch our backs."

His meaning settled over us like snowfall—quiet, cold, and heavy with what might come next.

*

That night, just after dusk, it began.

I was crouched by the fire, pouring water into the cook pot, when a strange stillness settled over the camp—too sudden, too complete.

Then the ground gave a sharp, deliberate shudder. A few seconds passed—just long enough for every man nearby to glance up, eyes searching, breath caught.

Then came the shouting—sharp, scattered, rising like sparks in dry grass.

And then the blast.

The crack of explosives split the air, raw and thunderous, followed by the groan of splintering timber.

From the far end of the trestle, a bloom of smoke surged upward, curling into the cobalt sky. The scaffold there folded in on itself and dropped, vanishing into the black churn of the river below.

Timbers snapped like dry bones. The echoes rolled back across the frozen river, long and hollow.

Three weeks of labor—gone in seconds.

By dumb luck alone, the crew hadn't yet taken the line. No one was lost. But luck, I knew, was a currency with a short shelf life.

Tierney burst in half a minute later, jaw locked and fists clenched, already shouting for the men to be roused, interrogated, searched.

"Strip their tents. Turn out their gear. If a single man's hiding something, I want to know before sunup."

"You start swinging accusations like that," I told him, "and the men will lock up worse than the river ever did. Let me try something first."

He didn't like it. But he gave me the night.

Later, I nailed a fresh ledger to the post inside the mess tent—blank pages, spine cracked wide—a place for grievances, anonymous and unfiltered. If someone had lit a fuse out of fury, maybe they'd be bold enough to scrawl something more.

But that wasn't where it would end. Not for me.

At first light, I'd begin walking the line—pick-and-shovel men first, dynamite crew last—listening not just to their words, but to what lived between them. The stammer in a timeline. The flicker of the eyes. The shake in a hand that should've been steady.

Because this bolt, this missing powder—this wasn't an accident. It was sabotage. And it felt deliberate, staged, as if someone wanted someone to notice.

Back in Tent City, a man was stabbed before pressing the raven-marked medallion into my hand. His killer vanished into the night. That was murder.

Now this—railroad sabotage. Same shadow, different weapon. I was beginning to wonder if the reason I'd been drawn north had less to do with the railroad—and more to do with whatever lay buried beneath it.

Whoever was behind it was guiding me, fuse by fuse.

Tomorrow, I'd take their trail the only way I knew how—face-to-face, name by name, until the mask slipped. If they wanted me here, then I was here—awake, watching, and ready to return the favor.

*

The stove died just after midnight, frost seaming the canvas walls. I drifted into a dream and found myself back on the splintered trestle, fog curling between the beams. From that swirling pale stepped Magnus Vega, yet nothing about him matched the man I'd known. Not my savior from Hope, nor the drowned companion I lifted from the freezing waters off Nome. This figure was drained of warmth, midnight eyes set in glacial skin.

He opened his mouth, but no words reached me; instead, impressions flooded in—splintered beams bleeding dark sap, rail spikes sinking into living flesh, the river below pulsing like a wounded vein. The meanings tangled together: warning, accusation, grief. I tried to speak, to justify steel and progress, but my own voice sounded distant, swallowed by the mist rising off the water.

Magnus raised a hand—whether to bless or to condemn, I couldn't tell—and the fog swallowed him whole. I jolted awake, breath clouding in the frozen air. On the tent wall, hoarfrost had traced a shape—so faint I nearly missed it—a crooked line intersecting a circle, with three short marks beneath like falling steps. It melted the moment I reached for it, leaving behind only damp canvas and an unease I couldn't name.

By morning, the crews were back to work. The cold was sharper, the air brittle with tension. No one spoke of the blast directly, but it hung in the periphery—every glance over a shoulder, every hammer strike paused a second too long. The dynamite hadn't just broken timber—it had cracked the illusion that this was just another job.

Anchorage offered no apology. No inquiry. Only a terse wire pinned to the post beside the commissary door:

REBUILD IMMEDIATELY. NO EXCUSES.

By nightfall, the first shipment of timber had arrived—fresh-hewn and sap-slick, as if lumber alone could mend what had been broken. The men unloaded it in silence. Not the usual grumbling or foul jokes, just the steady thump of boots on frost and the creak of splinters finding ground.

But the camp wasn't quiet everywhere.

The ledger I'd left in the mess tent—blank when I'd posted it—was now a map of frustration. Page after page filled overnight with grievances long kept under tongue: spoiled rations, stolen wages, busted tools gone unreplaced. Men had written what they wouldn't dare speak aloud. Not to Tierney. Not to one another. But the mark, I've found, invites truth that voices cannot.

I turned each page slowly, hoping to spot a thread—a clue buried in complaint. But there was no smoking gun—only a rising pressure, the kind that builds beneath snowpack before an avalanche.

Tierney glanced at the pages, snorted, and walked off. "You'll find nothing in that mess but bellyaching," he said. "Half the men wouldn't know sabotage from snowfall."

Maybe. But someone had rigged that trestle. Someone had waited until the crew cleared out. Someone had known just when to strike.

And someone was watching still.

Perhaps the real story wasn't in the words—it was in the hands that hadn't written. The eyes that looked away. The way certain men moved too quickly to fetch a tool or stepped too wide around the wreckage.

That was where I'd start.

I'd talk to every crew—from sawyers to shovel men to the powder gang. Not as a foreman. Not as a reporter. As a man with questions that needed answers.

This wasn't just sabotage.

It was a message.

And I intended to answer it.

But even as I closed the ledger and stepped back into the cold, Magnus lingered in the edges of my mind. His midnight eyes, the mist that swallowed him—it all clung to me like a scent I couldn't scrub away.

I kept thinking how in the dream the beams of the trestle bled sap like open wounds. And I wondered if we were truly building something grand, or were we driving iron into the bones of a land that had never wanted taming? Each rail spike felt less like progress and more like an intrusion.

The explosion didn't just tear through timber. It reverberated with something deeper—the echo of Magnus from my dream, carried up through stone and frost, as if the earth itself had borrowed his voice to cry out. The trestle screamed in protest at the burden we forced upon it, and the ledger of grievances rose like a chorus to that cry. Spoiled meat, broken picks, weary bones—all of it swelled into one question: how long before the land itself, or the men bound to it, struck back?

I couldn't shake the notion that Magnus hadn't come back to torment me, but to remind me. He wasn't merely the shade of a man lost to grievance—he was the earth's memory speaking through him, demanding to know why I was helping drive a steel spine across mountains that had stood unbroken since the first glaciers drew back their breath.

Once, I'd believed in the poetry of railways. Rails gleaming in the sun, chasing horizons. Locomotives roaring like modern beasts of destiny. Steel and steam binding the world together. It had seemed noble—linking places, linking people, forging futures out of wilderness. The kind of work you could look back on and say: *I was part of that.*

But standing there beneath that pale moon, the wreck of the last blast still smoldering in my thoughts, I realized how brittle those convictions had become. The explosion had stolen more than timber and time. It had taken something I hadn't known I carried—faith. Faith that progress was worth any price. Faith that the future we were building was brighter than the silence we were breaking.

Now, doubt pressed harder than the cold. Was Magnus right to resist? Was the earth itself resisting through him?

When he raised his hand in the dream, perhaps it wasn't a curse to bind me, or a blessing to absolve me. Perhaps it was a question. A demand that I reckon with the cost of each rail we drove into this land.

And I owed him an answer—not in words, but in the quiet reckonings of my own heart. For each step forward would shape not only the rails ahead, but the soul I would carry with me.

CHAPTER SIXTEEN
BROAD PASS

We left Susitna as dawn struggled to be born, dragging a thin band of light across a sky the color of old pewter. The Susitna River lay behind us like a silver scar locked in ice. Ahead waited Broad Pass—a name that sounded gentle enough on a map, but whispered of avalanches and white silence deep enough to swallow men whole.

Somewhere beyond those ridgelines, Denali stood, though we couldn't see it. On a clear day, it would rise over the horizon like a white altar, casting its shadow across half the interior. I found myself searching the cloud cover for even a hint of its summit.

The sleds groaned as they climbed the grade. Chains creaked. Leather traces snapped taut. Snow squeaked beneath the iron runners. Even the horses moved quietly now, heads low, breath drifting in ragged clouds. Their flanks were crusted with ice, steam rising as if the earth itself were exhaling. Behind them, the long sled train crept forward, laden with rails and timbers destined for the line inching north through the wilderness.

Eli rode beside me on the first sled, his scarf pulled so high only his eyes showed.

"Percy," he said, voice muffled, "the trees are gone."

I looked around. He was right. The spruce and birch that had flanked our trail for miles fell away, leaving nothing but white slopes rolling toward the mountains.

"This is timberline," I told him. "Beyond this, the wind and cold scrape everything off the rock. Trees can't hold on."

Eli kept staring at the pale ridges. "Feels like we're crossing into someplace we're not meant to be."

I didn't argue.

As we climbed higher, the trail narrowed into a throat between towering walls. Loose snow hissed down with every gust. The mountains leaned closer, as if listening. Somewhere above those pewter skies, Denali waited—silent and unseen—a reminder that the land remembers every man who dares to pass through its hush, and every debt left unpaid.

A foreman on snowshoes slogged over and slapped a folded envelope into my hand.

"Came in on the dog run," he grunted.

He stomped off before I could say thank you.

I peeled off my glove and broke the seal, recognizing Peggy's careful handwriting. Her letter carried the damp chill of the San Francisco winter, full of small details about home—and about Walter, who'd been spending long hours hunched over his notebook, determined to write stories like his hero Jack London.

Tucked behind her page was a thin sheet, the edges soft from handling. Across it ran Walter's tight, earnest script—the title scrawled at the top:

Spirits in the Ice

There were spirits dancing in walls of ice, flickering like firelight, singing without words. They showed a sign to a man traveling far from home—a sign that belonged to the land and somehow to him as well. The man knew he had to be careful because the spirits were watching.

In the margin, as though the story itself refused to remain only words, Walter had sketched a circle, split by a jagged line. Below it, three short marks descended like steps into darkness.

I flipped open my reporter's notepad, its pages crowded with half-formed thoughts and hurried jottings, until I found the crude sketch I had made from memory. The frost-mark had melted almost as soon as I'd seen it, but I'd drawn it quickly before it faded from memory: a circle split by a jagged line, with three short marks descending beneath like steps into shadow.

I set it beside Walter's story. In the margin of his page, he had drawn the same figure, sharper than mine, as though his pencil had been guided by something more than chance. Line for line, the two matched. My notepad, Walter's notebook—two hands sketching the same mark, though only one of us had ever stood before that frozen wall.

The proof chilled me more than the mountain air. Whatever message was etched in that symbol, it had passed from ice into ink, binding us both to it.

But now, staring at it on paper, something else stirred in my memory. It looked almost like a map. Or part of one. A scribble I'd glimpsed before—on an old survey chart, perhaps, or tucked into the corner of an engineer's blueprint. I couldn't place it, but it scraped at the edges of my mind, demanding to be remembered.

The frost-damp wind tugged at the paper, eager to steal the secret back into the mist.

I felt a chill crawl along my spine.

I didn't know what it meant, only that it kept circling back to me like a question I wasn't ready to answer. And deep down, I couldn't shake the feeling it wasn't about me at all, but about the places we were tearing open, the veins of the land we were slicing mile by mile. As if the railroad itself was tracing lines across a hidden map, pulling us toward something buried and waiting.

Out here, nothing stays hidden for long. And in Alaska, the land always knows.

*

Broad Pass opened before us like the floor of a giant cathedral, flanked by pale mountain walls whose peaks were lost in ragged veils of cloud. The valley stretched wide and white, an endless sweep of wind-scoured snow broken only by boulders crusted in ice and the stunted skeletons of willow and alder half-buried in drifts.

The wind never let up. It screamed across the flats, lifting sheets of powder and hurling them into low whirlwinds that vanished as quickly as they appeared. Beneath my boots, the snow was packed so hard it rang like stone. In places, old snow had hardened into sharp, frozen ridges that snagged the runners of the sleds and threatened to tip us over.

By the time Eli and I finally pulled in, the horses were lathered with frost and their breath, sides heaving. Men were scattered across the basin, dark figures moving against the relentless white.

Some swung axes into the frozen ground, chopping at willow roots that would foul future ties. Others wrestled with saws and shovels, carving a path wide enough for rails and embankments yet to come. Steam rose off their shoulders like spirits fleeing into the cold.

I paused beside Eli, sweeping my eyes over the pass. It felt impossibly vast, yet the mountains leaned inward, as though the land was closing in to reclaim what we dared to trespass.

Every sound felt sharper up here—the scrape of steel on ice, the distant crack of shifting rock, the low mutter of men cursing the cold.

This was the railroad's rooftop—Broad Pass, the highest point along the line between Seward and Fairbanks. On a clear day, Denali would have been watching us from the horizon, white and implacable. But clouds hung low, hiding even the mountain's memory.

They called this place avalanche country. Storms blew in from every direction, dumping snow that clung to the slopes until a breath of wind—or a passing train—could send it roaring down. The workers never stopped glancing at the ridgelines, half expecting the white walls to break loose at any moment.

Eli lowered his scarf, breath coiling into white plumes. "This place feels wrong," he said. "Like we're standing in the middle of something we're not supposed to see."

I nodded slowly, feeling it too—the presence beneath the wind, the sense we were intruders in a place that tolerated us only by a thin and temporary mercy.

Ahead, a foreman was barking orders while two men struggled to dig out a sled half-buried in a drift. The wind kept burying their gear almost as fast as they uncovered it.

Above us, snow hissed down the slopes, whispering secrets only the mountains seemed to understand.

That night, we bunked in a rough cabin thrown together from green spruce logs and tar paper, the wind clawing at the gaps, rattling the walls like a beast trying to get in. I lay on a mattress of spruce boughs, staring up at the rafters while the stove ticked and popped, sounding too much like rifle shots echoing off ice.

When sleep finally came, it did not settle gently. It gathered me in like a riptide and carried me north.

I drifted over a plain of ice, sled runners hissing, though I saw no sled, no reins in my hands—only the blur of seven shadows pacing ahead, their breaths spilling like phantoms into the air. Above, Denali loomed, not mountain so much as silhouette, black and silver against a sky hammered from tin. Beneath its shadow glowed an opening, pale blue as gaslight, a wound in the ice I somehow knew as Du Daashagoon—the Cave of the Body.

Crossing the threshold, light seeped through cracks in the walls, veins of turquoise and green pulsing like blood beneath glass. The air stung but did not choke, as if it wished to test me rather than drive me out. My footfalls echoed in ways that seemed less sound than memory.

I followed into a chamber vast and vaulted, and there a figure shimmered, no more than outline at first: a man swathed in caribou hide, hair white as hoarfrost, eyes obsidian pools that swallowed their own light. I felt him see me, though his lips did not move.

A vibration filled the cave—words or wind, I could not tell. *The mountain remembers... names swallowed in snow.* I thought of Sha-e-dah-kla, though I could not swear he stood before me. Before I could speak, the vision fractured, scattering like sparks of frost in darkness.

The ice split underfoot, and a tunnel yawned, deeper, black as the inside of an eyelid. I felt myself drawn into Du Toowu—the Cave of the Mind. Silence clothed me, heavy and soft, as if sound itself had been locked away. My breath lingered before me, a ghost reluctant to leave.

The stillness pressed against my chest until I thought I might vanish with it, reduced to nothing but memory. A shape flickered in the dark, but before I could reach it, the ground broke open again.

I fell, weightless, and the silence fractured into a corridor of jagged light. When I rose, I stood within a chamber vast and terrible, its walls bending into angles that seemed to fold thought itself into knots. This was Du Yahaayí—the Cave of the Soul.

Here, there was no air, no sound, no time, only presence.

And then he was there.

Not flesh and bone, but a current coiled from the shadows—Magnus Vega. His voice came not as words but as resonance, striking along my ribs, trembling in my skull.

"Percy…"

My throat closed. "Magnus. What are you?"

"Not what, but where. This is where I remain." His form rippled like smoke, the outline of his grin etched in darkness. "The Spirit Cave holds what the mountain cannot bury. It holds me."

The medallion at my chest throbbed once, heat and cold all at once, and Magnus's presence swelled until it filled the chamber, pressing against me from every side.

"You carry the key," he said. "But every key turns both ways. You can open the way forward—or lock yourself in the past."

The cave shuddered, shards of ice raining down in silent cascades. I could not tell if it was the mountain's wrath or Magnus's laughter.

Then the vision burst apart in a blinding flare, and I was cast upward, gasping, as though the mountain itself had spat me back into the world of breath and light.

From the shadows came a voice, so thin it might have been the groan of the glacier. *Percy… is it you?*

I whispered the name that rose unbidden: "Magnus."

No shape answered, only presence—urgent, aching. Fragments reached me like words half-remembered in a dream: *Help me. I cannot move on.*

I spoke to the darkness, telling it of parents waiting, of Suzie's love beyond the veil, of how a man's wrongs did not weigh heavier than his whole life. Each word rang like iron striking ice, shivering through the cavern.

Then a cry pierced the silence—not wholly pain, not wholly release. The walls trembled as if some hidden door had been forced open.

I woke with a start, the cabin pressing back around me. My skin slick with sweat, the stove reduced to a single ember glow, and the wind rattling the logs like bones in a shaken cup.

Eli was crouched beside me, eyes bleary. "You were yelling. I thought an avalanche was coming down on us."

I sat up slowly, dragging air into my lungs like a man hauled from beneath ice. My pulse thudded against my ribs.

"It wasn't an avalanche, Eli. It was Denali—the caves under the ice. And Magnus Vega."

Eli blinked at me. "Magnus who?"

I stared into the stove's glow, shadows jumping like spirits on the walls.

"He was my friend. But before I knew him—back in '96—Judge Wickersham hired Magnus for something no one else would touch. Word was that Denali didn't want to be climbed. Too many vanished without a trace. The judge, practical man though he was, had started to wonder if spirits were guarding the summit. He needed proof before he made his ascent. So he paid Magnus to slip inside Denali's ice caves and find out if the mountain was under a spell—if something ancient was stirring in its depths."

Eli's eyes widened. He let out a long, low whistle, then shook his head slowly, as if trying to dislodge the image. For a moment, he just stared at the flames, lips parted, the lines on his face caught between disbelief and reverence. Finally, he muttered, almost to himself, "Damn…"—like the word had to climb out of someplace deep.

"Magnus took a Tlingit guide and crawled into those caves. The first chamber—the Cave of the Body—was all green and turquoise ice, beautiful enough to steal your senses. The second was the Cave of the Mind, twisted like lightning, where Magnus nearly lost himself."

I drew a sharp breath. "But it was the third cave—the Cave of the Soul—that broke him. Total darkness swallowed him up. The Dark Spirit asked why he'd come, then demanded a pledge: that after he died, Magnus would belong to the caves. He agreed. When he came out, he had seven star-shaped burns on his skin—marks of the Seven Deadly Sins."

Eli jerked back like the words had burned him. "Seven burns?" he rasped. "Star-shaped?" His voice cracked around the edges. "God help us… that's old magic."

"After that, Magnus changed. Turned hard, driven by gold and power, like he was trying to outrun whatever he'd seen in the dark. Four years later, he drowned off Nome in the Bering Sea—but that wasn't the end of him, at least not his spirit on earth."

Eli narrowed his eyes. "Are you saying his ghost is still out there?"

"I am." I kept my voice low. "Many years ago, I followed his journal north and found those same caves. In the Cave of the Mind, I met the spirit of Sha-e-dah-kla, a Tyonek shaman who told me Magnus's soul was trapped, bound by that old bargain. And in the Cave of the Soul, I heard Magnus himself—just a voice, afraid to move on. I told him about his parents. About his love, Suzie, who is waiting for him. The ice came crashing down around us, but before I escaped, Magnus promised he'd repay me in this lifetime. He's still trying to cross over, Eli."

I paused, staring at the flicker of firelight. "And there's something else. I can't shake the feeling this all ties back to the medallion—and the railroad we're laying across Alaska. It's like Denali, Magnus, the railway, and the medallion I carry… they're threads of the same story. And if I don't see this through, we might be laying rails across a land we don't truly understand."

Eli pulled on his mittens, shaking his head slowly. "So… thirty miles of blizzards and crevasses for a man with no body left—and maybe the fate of the railroad hanging in the balance?"

I met his gaze, steady. "Not just a ghost. A friend. And maybe the answer to why we're here at all."

Eli let out a rough sigh. "Well, hell. If you're going, I'm going. Someone's gotta drag you back alive."

By dawn we were out in the pale light, breath fogging in the bitter air as we lashed the sled and harnessed the dogs. Behind us, Broad Pass disappeared into a swirl of wind and drifting snow. Ahead, Denali loomed unseen behind its veil of cloud, its hidden halls breathing, and deep within, Magnus still waited. And somewhere in the hush between gusts, I felt the weight of the medallion pressing against my chest, as though it, too, wanted answers.

CHAPTER SEVENTEEN
THE WIZARD OF HOPE

The dogs waited, six huskies shifting their stance, breath coiling upward like smoke signals in the cold. I handed the lead rope to Eli and turned toward the quartermaster's shack, the snow squeaking under my boots.

The quartermaster stood just inside the doorway, coat half-buttoned, eyes sharp even in the gloom.

"Help you with something?" he asked.

"I'm Percy Hope," I said, stamping snow from my boots. "I've come to—"

His brows lifted, cutting me off. "Hope, you say?" A grin tugged at the corner of his mouth. "Well, I'll be damned. If it isn't the Wizard of Hope himself." He gave a short laugh and shook his head as if the name amused even him. "They're talking about you from Broad Pass clear back to the Placers. The men say you've performed miracles with nothing but a pencil."

I froze at the words, the title striking me like a stone hurled out of nowhere. *Wizard of Hope?* My chest tightened, breath catching in the cold air.

"Wait," I said slowly. "Where did you hear that?"

He chuckled, leaning his shoulder against the doorframe. "Where didn't I? The name's everywhere—spread faster than the flu through a bunkhouse. Some swear it started at Broad Pass when you redrew the maps. Others say it came from Curry, after the business with the bridge footing. But the stories have a way of growing. Men say you see farther than any surveyor, that storms break around you as if you willed the skies to clear, that iron bends easier when you're near. Some even whisper you carry luck itself in your pocket, enough to turn disaster aside. Doesn't matter where it began. Once a name like that gets loose, it runs on its own. Men repeat it because they want to believe it. Gives them something to hold onto."

I shook my head, heat rising despite the cold. "Trust me, I'm no wizard."

"Maybe not," he said, his grin softening, "but that's not how stories work. Out here, hope's rarer than gold. You give men a scrap of it—even without meaning to—and they'll pass your name around like it's gospel. You can't call it back."

Heat climbed into my face despite the cold. Wizard of Hope. The name felt like a burden laid across my shoulders, heavy with expectation I never asked for. I drew in a sharp breath, my voice rough. "You give me too much credit."

The quartermaster only shrugged and pushed the door wider. "Maybe. But a name like that doesn't care what you think. Once it's loosed, it runs on its own. Now—what brings you here, Wizard?"

I hesitated, glancing at the stacks of gear lining the walls. "I need rope. Blasting cord. Two crates of carbide lamps. I know it's meant for the crews, and I wouldn't ask if it weren't—"

He held up a hand. "You don't have to explain. If there's something up that mountain worth finding, I'd rather it be *you* finding it. Consider it borrowed on behalf of the Alaska Railroad."

I blinked, grateful. "That's generous of you. Truly. I'll bring back what I don't use."

He started pulling items off the shelves. "I'll mark it as advanced survey materials. That's not a lie, is it?"

"No," I said with a chuckle. "Not a lie at all."

He paused, holding a coil of fuse. "This isn't just about surveying, is it?"

I hesitated. "No. There's something under Denali. I've seen the signs. And I've got to know what it means."

He studied me for a long moment, then set the fuse beside the crates. "Then I'd say the mountain's lucky to have the Wizard of Hope on its trail."

I ran a hand through my hair, embarrassed. "Please don't call me that. Wizards pull rabbits out of hats. I'm just trying to make sense of the pieces in front of me."

"Well," he said, leaning in close, voice lowered, "just promise me you'll come back with all your pieces in one place. That's all I care about."

I clasped his arm. "I'll try my damnedest."

"See that you do," he said, pressing the manifest into my hand. "And, Percy—if you find what you're looking for… don't let it stay buried."

*

By morning, we pressed north out of Broad Pass, the huskies driving hard into a wind that refused to ease. I did my best to keep them in line, but my hands on the handlebars were clumsy, my commands rough and uneven. More than once, the sled skidded sideways, the dogs bunching into confusion before surging forward again in a ragged pull. Years ago, Jack London tried to teach me the ways of a musher, but little of his hard-won wisdom had stuck. I could manage enough to keep us moving, but no more.

Then Eli stepped up beside me on the runners. He leaned into the gale, his voice carrying in a cadence I hadn't heard before—half English, half singsong dog talk. *"Gee. Haw. Easy now. Hike."*

At once, the team steadied. The huskies dropped their haunches, shoulders rising and falling in unison, their rhythm smoothing into a powerful glide I hadn't been able to coax from them. The sled leapt forward as though the trail itself had loosened under their paws.

I glanced at Eli, startled. "Didn't know you'd run a team before."

He kept his eyes on the trail, breath fogging. "After my father died, I worked for my uncle in Kotzebue. He kept dogs, hauled wood, mail, and even fish for the cannery. He taught me everything—how to harness them up, feel the tension in the gangline, and know when to hold back or let them run. But mostly, he taught me to listen. Said the dogs always knew more than the man on the runners."

The huskies leaned into the traces as if to prove him right, shoulders bunching, claws biting for purchase in the drifts. I bit down a smile, surprised at how the boy I'd taken for a green hand moved with the ease of a seasoned musher.

By midday, the land began to change. The ridgelines sharpened, drawing closer until the trail funneled between them like a throat narrowing. The air grew restless, gusts whipping through unseen corridors and rattling the sled as though warning us back.

Toward afternoon, the sound reached us first—a low, constant roar that grew louder with every bend of the trail. Then the snow-thick horizon fell away, and we came to the precipice.

The canyon yawned beneath us, more than three hundred feet down, sheer walls plunging to a river locked in ice, its frozen surface split by ribbons of dark water that thundered like an angry throat.

Eli steadied himself on the runners, eyes fixed on the abyss. "God help the men who think they can bridge this."

So this was Hurricane Gulch—the place the surveyors spoke of in hushed tones, as though naming it alone could measure its depth. The wind funneled through the chasm, tearing at our parkas and snapping the traces until the dogs whined. I felt the medallion heavy at my chest, thrumming faintly—as if the earth itself anticipated the strain of steel daring to span such emptiness. I shuddered, thinking of the men who would one day dangle from beams above that void, one slip away from eternity.

We did not linger. There was no path across, not for us. Instead, we turned westward, the gulch falling away behind like a swallowed breath, and drove on into the greater shadow of Denali.

As the morning ground on, the terrain bucked and heaved under the sled. Snowdrifts hid sudden hollows that lurched the sled sideways. The dogs dug in, claws scraping for purchase, chests heaving with effort.

Once the trail vanished beneath a white dune, Eli leapt off without hesitation, plunging thigh-deep into snow, probing with his boot for the packed crust underneath.

"Hold, boys! Easy—easy now." His voice cut through the wind, low and steady. The team froze, haunches quivering, eager to run but trusting his voice.

When he clambered back up beside me, snow cascading off his parka, he shot me a grin. "Snow's no different from a tide. You just have to feel which way it's pulling."

The day stretched on, hour folding into hour. My legs stiffened, toes numb despite wool and fur. My fingers ached on the handlebars, even inside thick mittens. The dogs worked tirelessly, though their breath now came in ragged clouds, flecks of ice crusting their whiskers.

As the sled hissed over wind-packed drifts, I let my mind drift too. Journeying deeper into this snowbound wilderness, I felt the thin line between man's ambition and nature's raw power. It wasn't just mountains and storms out here. It was something older.

Shadows from the past kept rising behind my eyes—Magnus's voice, threading through memory like a whispered warning; Reverend O'Hara's booming sermons echoing over rows of bowed heads; and Jack London slamming his palm on the podium, and insisting that in the end, we'll be gone from the world like a squashed mosquito.

And through it all pulsed the silent gravity of the medallion.

I reached for it beneath my coat, feeling its chill press into my fingertips, dense as a stone. Just a piece of metal… or perhaps the key to doors I didn't yet know existed.

Out here, with the wind clawing at me and the railroad stretching into whiteness, I couldn't shake the question: Was I the master of my fate—or merely a passenger, bound to rails laid by forces older and deeper than any man's will?

By midafternoon, the wind began to ease, dropping into a hush so profound I could hear only the panting of the team and the distant, eerie groan of ice settling deep beneath us.

Then the sky cracked open like a shell, and there it was—Denali, rearing sheer and silver against a backdrop of blue so pure it strained the eyes. The mountain soared into the heavens, its summit shrouded in veils of wind-blown snow that shimmered like powdered diamonds in the sky. Vast ramparts of ice and granite fell away in staggering sweeps, ridges standing black-edged like hammered steel, shadows poured into every crease as if an entire night was hiding there. The sheer scale of it dwarfed everything around us, and we were specks crawling across a world forged for giants. The air was thinner, crisper, as if we were inhaling the breath of the gods.

Eli fell silent beside me, jaw slack in wonder.

"Looks like it could swallow the whole world," he murmured.

"That it could," I said, my voice barely more than a breath.

And in that instant, I felt certain of two things: the mountain was waiting for me, and so was whatever lay hidden beneath it.

We made camp in the lee of a jagged wall of shattered ice, its towering ramparts shielding us from the wind that shrieked like some starving beast across the glacier. While Eli worked in silence, stacking blocks of snow into a windbreak, I sparked the carbide lamp and swept its glow over the icy face behind us.

That's when I saw it—a shape glimmering faintly where frost clung to the wall: a circle, cleaved by a lightning-bolt crack, with three short lines dropping beneath it like steps into darkness.

I froze. It was the very same mark I had once scratched into my reporter's notepad after seeing it in frost on the tent wall. And it was the same Walter had drawn, unbidden, in the margin of his story.

With trembling hands, I fumbled for my journal and pulled out his sketch. Side by side, there was no mistaking it—every line, every angle matched, as precise as an architect's tracing.

"It's a map," I whispered. "Walter wasn't just doodling—he was charting an entrance."

Eli turned toward me, breath fogging in the dark. "Entrance to what? And how would Walter even know about a map like this?"

I shook my head, feeling a chill deeper than the glacier's cold. "I don't think he knows. Not really. It's like… it came through him. Like he was drawing something he didn't even understand."

Eli frowned. "You mean—like a dream?"

"Or something deeper."

I laid my gloved palm against the frosted circle. Chips of ice splintered away under my touch, revealing a thin, dark slit in the glacier. When I leaned closer, I felt a breath of cold air seeping out, as though the mountain itself had stirred to whisper secrets.

A hidden tunnel.

"We found the way in," I said, my voice low but trembling with urgency.

Eli stared into the black crack, jaw tight. "Percy… this could bury us alive."

"Or it could be the way to everything we've been chasing," I shot back, my voice echoing sharper than I intended. "Magnus, the medallion, all of it—it's tied to this."

Eli's head jerked toward me. His eyes narrowed. "The what? Percy, what in God's name are you talking about?"

For a moment, I faltered, the weight of silence pressing on my chest. Then, with a trembling hand, I reached beneath my coat and drew it out. The tarnished silver glinted in the dim light, the raven etched upon it seeming to stir as though alive.

"I found this in Tent City," I said, my voice thick with memory. "Beside a murdered man, lying in the mud, like it was waiting for me. I should've left it—but the moment I touched it, I knew it wasn't just a trinket. It's been with me ever since. Sometimes it burns hot as fire, sometimes it hums like a heartbeat, and every time I think I might walk away from this cursed road, it reminds me that I can't."

Eli stared, frost clinging to his beard, his expression torn between disbelief and awe. "And you never thought to tell me?"

I shook my head. "Because I didn't understand it myself. Still don't. But it's shown me things, Eli—visions, warnings. It's pulled me deeper into all of this, as if the railroad, Magnus's voice, and this piece of silver are bound together in ways I can't explain. Whatever lies ahead, this medallion is the key."

Eli's eyes flicked from me to the medallion and back to the crack yawning in the ice. His breath came in slow, ragged clouds. "So we stake our lives on a murder trinket and a ghost's whisper?"

I closed my fist around the medallion, feeling its steady thrum against my palm. "No. We stake them on the truth—and this is the only trail that leads to it."

I met his eyes, feeling the bite of the cold pressing in. "I'm not leaving without knowing what's in there."

Eli looked away, breathing hard, then nodded. "All right. But we do it smart. We tie off, mark our trail, and if it goes bad, we come back up."

"Agreed," I said. "We'll keep it slow."

He clapped my shoulder once, firm as a hammer blow. "Then let's see what the mountain's hiding."

But before we could vanish into the glacier, Eli jerked his thumb toward the sleds. "What about the dogs?"

The huskies stood nearby in the snow, ears pricked, breath steaming into the frigid air. Their blue eyes glowed under the aurora's faint wash of green, as though they sensed we were about to step someplace no man or beast belonged. One of them—a gray male named Taku—let out a low, uneasy whine.

Eli pointed. "We'll stake them with a double hitch and leave a blanket roll for each. Give them a fighting chance if the weather turns."

Together, we moved through the sled traces, working quickly. Eli drove steel pickets into the snow and lashed the dogs' lines, giving them enough slack to lie down but not run off. I draped heavy wool blankets over each dog's back and tucked the edges close, my fingers stiff and clumsy in the cold. The dogs pressed against my legs for warmth, tails drooping low.

Taku licked a line of frost off my glove, his eyes searching mine. "We'll be back," I murmured, though the promise felt like a lie whispered to both of us.

At last, Eli moved down the line, giving each dog a firm pat and a quiet word. One by one, they sank into quiet, watchful heaps around the sleds, their bodies relaxing under his steady touch.

We tied ourselves together, roped the crates to a belay line, and approached the narrow slit yawning in the glacier's side. I took a deep breath that tasted of steel and snow, feeling the pressure of ice and secrets pressing in from all sides.

Then I swung my legs over the lip and eased myself into the darkness.

At once, cold swallowed me whole. My breath billowed back in shimmering clouds, each exhale turning the close air to diamonds. The rope creaked against my harness as I inched downward, boots bouncing off glassy walls that shivered beneath my weight. Ice flakes tinkled like breaking glass, spiraling past my cheeks into blackness below.

The light from above grew smaller, dimming to a pale star as the walls pressed in, slick and veined with ribbons of milky frost. Water dripped somewhere out of sight, each drop echoing like a distant drum. My gloved fingers, rigid with cold, clenched around the rope as the chill crept through my bones, sinking into marrow.

Then, suddenly, the shaft widened.

Thirty feet down, the passage flared into a vault of turquoise glass. The rope slackened, and I dropped the last few feet, boots crunching onto a floor that shone like polished crystal as they found solid ice beneath me.

Eli landed beside me with a grunt, the sound echoing off the frozen walls.

We stood there, catching our breath, lantern light flickering over the icy chamber. Sha-e-dah-kla's words came back to me: Du Daashagoon—the Cave of the Body.

Green veins pulsed faintly through the walls like blood beneath translucent skin. The ice under our boots glittered like starlight caught and frozen mid-fall. A hush filled the space, as if the glacier itself were holding its breath, waiting for us to move deeper into its secrets.

At the center of the chamber, the frost-mark reappeared—etched in white rime on the ice. The jagged line pointed toward a low archway, the first of the "steps" in Walter's symbol. I felt the medallion thrum beneath my parka like a second heartbeat.

"First marker," I said. "Stay close."

The next tunnel coiled like a lightning bolt caught in ice, reflecting our lamplight into a thousand shifting corridors. Every sound twisted back at us in distorted echoes. More than once, I could have sworn I heard Magnus's voice whispering my name from the walls.

We crept forward, testing each passage, only to circle back again and again to the same turquoise vault. Walls of glassy ice rose at identical angles, concealing dead ends and icefalls behind illusions of depth. The cold thickened the deeper we went, pressing into our chests until even breathing felt like inhaling shards of glass.

Eli slammed his fist against the ice. "We'll freeze in here before we find a way through." His voice bounced around us, repeating itself in icy mockery.

I fumbled inside my coat and pulled out Walter's story. My fingers trembled as I traced the jagged line and the three short strokes beneath it.

"Wait… the 'steps.' They're not steps. They're distances."

Eli peered at me, blinking frost from his lashes. "Distances?"

I pointed to the sketch. "Each stroke is a measure. Left, then right, then straight. It's a path. These are instructions."

Slowly, I retraced our steps and counted off paces, adjusting our course where the ice slanted underfoot. At the end of the last measure, I swung the lamp in an arc—and there it was: a narrow fissure hidden in shadow, just wide enough for a man to squeeze through.

Eli exhaled a plume of mist. "I'll be damned."

I pressed my gloved hand against the cold wall, feeling the medallion's pulse quicken like a drum. "This way."

CHAPTER EIGHTEEN
CAVE OF THE SOUL

We walked single file, boots crunching over frost-ribbed stone into the tunnel of ice. The air grew colder with every step. Walls of frozen blue pressed in on either side, throwing back our breath in clouds and our lamplight in fractured halos.

The passage twisted like a wound vein, slick and silent. Water dripped somewhere far off, the sound stretched and warped by the cold. Neither of us spoke. Eli moved with caution, his eyes darting to every strange glint in the ice.

At one point, I reached out to steady myself and felt the smooth, translucent surface pulse beneath my glove, not like melting, but like breath. Alive, almost.

We rounded a bend where the ceiling dipped low, and that's when I saw it: a seam in the rock floor, half-buried under rime and shadow. I scraped it clear with the toe of my boot.

A shaft.

Narrow, ancient, vertical.

I turned to Eli. "This is the way."

He nodded once, jaw tight, and we went to work. I lowered our gear first, the rope whispering through my gloves, then followed it down, the walls closing in until I could feel stone brushing my shoulders.

When my boots touched bottom, silence thickened around me, deep as the hush between two heartbeats.

Ahead, a faint gold glow pulsed—a light with no visible source. The tunnel sloped a few more yards, then leveled out before spilling into a chamber so black it seemed to drink the lamplight whole.

These ice caves under Denali weren't fixed like bedrock. They melted away with the spring thaw and reformed each winter, never in the same place twice. No map could hold them. No memory could guarantee their return. It was as if the mountain carved new secrets for each season, then buried them again beneath the snow.

"Du Yahaayí," I whispered. "Cave of the Soul."

Eli's voice quavered behind me. "And Magnus?"

"If the mountain remembers," I said, stepping forward, "we're about to find out."

I moved cautiously, one gloved hand skimming the stone wall to keep my balance as the tunnel curved deeper into the mountain's gut. The cold sharpened with each step, burrowing into my bones.

Eli shuffled close behind me, silent except for the hitch in his breath.

A few dozen paces deeper, Eli faltered. I turned, lifting my lamp just in time to catch his eyes glazing over, fixed on some distant point far beyond me.

"Percy… I'm so tired," he murmured, his voice drifting off like smoke dissolving into mountain air.

Before I could speak, Eli's knees buckled. He crumpled beside a spur of stone, folding his arms around himself as though to keep in the last of his warmth, and slipped into a still, fathomless sleep.

"Eli!" I hissed, dropping beside him. I shook his shoulder, but he lay limp, breath rising and falling in slow, even measure, lost to depths I couldn't touch.

A shiver carved its way down my spine. This was no simple fatigue. The mountain—or something older still—was folding Eli into silence, just as it had with my guide, Emile Joseph, the last time I crossed the threshold of the Cave of the Soul in Denali over ten years ago. I remembered how Emile sank into that same deep, unreachable sleep, as if the cavern itself had gently set him aside and sealed the path behind me.

Now, I felt it again: the cave had chosen me, and me alone. Whatever truths waited in the dark, they would open themselves only to my eyes and speak their secrets into no other ears.

I lingered, torn between the press of the unknown ahead and the boy who lay silent beside me. Then I laid my gloved hand on his hair and whispered, "Wait for me, Eli. I'll come back for you."

The tunnel remained in silence as I continued, until even the scrape of my boots seemed stolen away. The cold grew sharper, each breath slicing into me like glass. Darkness gathered thick as ink, pressing close, until it felt as though I was creeping through the marrow of the mountain itself.

Then, without warning, the walls dissolved. I felt, rather than saw, that I'd stepped into a chamber vast enough to cradle a city, its edges swallowed by silence and shadow. My breath curled outward in pale ribbons, fading into endless black.

I stood frozen, listening for any sign of life, when a voice rolled through the dark.

"Percy."

It wasn't sound in the ordinary sense. It resonated inside me, humming along my bones. Gentle. Grave. Unmistakable. Magnus Vega.

"Magnus?" My voice quivered, instantly consumed by the darkness. "Is it truly you?"

"There is no 'me' to see," came his reply, echoing a whisper he'd once left me in the Soul Cave. "But we speak all the same."

My hand flew to the medallion beneath my coat. It pulsed warm against my chest.

"It's the medallion, isn't it? That's how I'm hearing you?"

"The medallion is old," the voice murmured, his words gliding through me like water beneath ice. "Forged as a bridge between worlds. It carries memory. And memory warns."

A shiver rippled over me. My breath hung suspended, catching a faint glow that bled from nowhere.

"But why me, Magnus? Why now?"

His tone deepened, heavier than stone. "Because the railroad you build is not only iron and timber. It is a scar. A wound cut into living earth. And through that wound will come powers that do not belong among men."

Images flashed behind my eyes: mountains flayed open, rivers choked with ash, the iron road stretching northward like a vein gone black.

Magnus's voice swelled, the cavern shaking with it. "They will tell you it is progress. They will speak of unity and wealth. But every spike you drive pierces deeper into the land's flesh. And through those wounds, the old darkness seeps back. It feeds on greed, on division, on the blindness of men who think they own what cannot be owned."

The medallion grew hot beneath my palm, but this time it steadied nothing. It only burned.

"You mean…" My throat tightened. "The railroad could damn us?"

"The railroad is not salvation," Magnus thundered. "It is a net. A cage. Those who dwell beyond the veil—beings who whisper into the dreams of kings—use such roads to bind humanity tighter to their yoke. They thrive when men forget the wild, when they forget they are kin to river and rock. You do not build a bridge, Percy. You build chains."

My knees weakened, dread coiling around my ribs like iron bands.

"And these forces," I whispered. "They're trying to stop me?"

Magnus's voice turned grave, almost mournful. "No, Percy. They are not trying to stop you. They are using you. You carry the medallion because it suits their purpose. It drips truths into your mind so that you believe you are chosen, when in truth, you are only their vessel. And when the final spike is driven, when the road is sealed, you will see what it was meant for all along."

I clutched the medallion until my knuckles whitened, but its warmth felt alien now, like the breath of a predator at my throat.

"Magnus… what happens when it's finished?"

For a long moment, silence thickened, heavy as snow burying the world. When Magnus spoke again, sorrow and shadow filled his words.

"When the last rail is laid, the road will belong not to you, nor to men. It will belong to them. And by then, Percy, it will be too late to turn back."

A cold wind coiled through the cavern as though the mountain exhaled a secret. The glow ebbed away. The medallion cooled beneath my palm. And Magnus was gone.

Yet a gnawing question clung to me: why was he still here? Years ago, in this very cave, I believed I had set his soul free. I had carried that certainty like a torch through dark winters. But now… if Magnus still lingered beneath Denali, had I been wrong all along? Or had something stronger bound him here, deeper than death itself?

I turned and retraced my shallow footprints through frost. As I reached Eli, he stirred, blinking as if waking from a nightmare.

"Percy?" he whispered. "I… I dreamed someone was talking to you."

I helped him sit up, brushing ice crystals from his hair.

"Come on," I murmured, forcing the tremor from my voice. "There's work waiting aboveground. And a railroad yet to build."

But as we climbed from the shadows, Magnus's warning echoed in my bones, colder than the cave itself: *the iron road is a chain, and you are the one forging it.*

And still, the medallion burned steadily against my chest, as if daring me to choose. My gut hardened into resolve. *No, Magnus. I'll prove you wrong. This road will not bind men in chains. It will set them free.*

CHAPTER NINETEEN
SABOTAGE

We tore out of Denali as though the mountain might rear up and swallow us whole. The sled careened over the trail, the runners screaming over ice, the dogs lunging forward until their breath smoked the air in ragged, white gusts.

I kept my eyes locked on the snow-streaked horizon, but my mind was still deep in the caverns under Denali, where a golden light had pulsed like a heartbeat, and Magnus's voice had coiled around my name, pressing secrets into my veins I wasn't ready to bleed out.

Even now, over the thunder of the dogs and the whip of wind, I heard him.

Every spike you drive pierces the earth's flesh.

The iron road will bind, not free.

You are the hand they've chosen, Percy—and when the final spike falls, the chain will close.

The medallion burned against my chest, as if to remind me it was listening too. I pressed my glove against it through the layers of wool and fur, trying to smother the heat.

Eli hunkered low on the sled behind me, silent but watchful. He hadn't asked what I'd seen in the caves—what I'd heard—but I felt his eyes on my back, heavy as stone.

I wanted to believe Magnus was wrong, that his words were only the raving of a soul never set free. Hadn't I released him years ago, in those very caves? Sha-e-dah-kla had said Magnus lingered, fearful of moving on, bound to the earth even in death. And now here he was again, his voice bleeding through ice and darkness, proof that my mercy had never been enough.

But another thought gnawed at me—what if it wasn't only Magnus speaking? What if his voice had been twisted, borrowed by something older, darker, using his sorrow as a mask? Was it my failure that left him shackled here, or had the shadows claimed him long ago?

His warning clung like the taste of iron in my mouth, bitter and unshakable. The wind knifed across my face, yet it was his voice that made me shiver.

Build your road, Percy, he had said. *But know what you build. Know who waits at its end.*

Eli stood behind me on the runners, silent, his hands tight on the backbow like he'd fall off the world if he let go. I hunkered low in the sled's basket, the snow hissing beneath us and the dogs panting hard against the wind.

Finally, Eli's voice cracked through the cold like a tree limb snapping under ice.

"Percy... we gotta stop. The dogs can't keep this pace."

I nodded, my voice lost in the wind. "Yeah... you're right."

Eli hauled the brake, and the sled skidded, snow spraying up in a glittering arc. The dogs dropped where they stood, trembling and gasping.

He drove the hook deep into the snow, the iron biting with a dull *chock*. Only then did the team settle, the lines slack, steam rising from their backs.

I stood there a moment, my breath fogging around me, half expecting Magnus to emerge from the shadows, eyes glowing with secrets I didn't dare name.

Eli stumbled forward, dropping beside the lead dog and rubbing its ears.

"Hell, Percy," he muttered, shaking his head. "We didn't even look back. Just ran."

All I could offer in reply was a forced smile. I crouched by the sled, tugged the canvas tarp free, and found the small tin of firestarter and a bundle of birch bark. My hands shook—not from the cold, but from everything else still clinging to me.

Eli cast me a wary glance but said nothing more as he pulled out the dogs' rations. He flung chunks of frozen fish toward the team, each piece landing with a dull thud on the packed snow as the dogs fell on it like starving wolves.

The fire took slowly, reluctant against the damp kindling, but I coaxed it to life—tiny tongues of flame licking upward, then catching with a soft whoosh. I fed it more bark and split wood until it snapped and spit like it had a voice of its own. I hovered close, letting the warmth seep into my gloves, into the places where fear had lodged like frostbite.

Eli lowered himself onto a pack across the fire from me. The flames licked the darkness, painting his face in restless orange and gold.

"It wasn't just rocks and shadows down there," he said, his voice hushed. "I… I dreamed there were voices. Calling your name."

I felt my chest tighten.

"Dreams are dreams," I said. "You were exhausted. We both were."

"But you… you looked different, Percy, when we got out of that cave. Like something happened to you in there." His eyes flickered toward mine, searching for answers.

I bent forward, feeding another branch into the fire, letting the sparks hiss and whirl.

"Caves do strange things to a man's head. Light bends. Sound echoes. You simply fell asleep, Eli. Whatever you heard was your own mind playing tricks."

He stared at me a moment longer, frowning, but then dropped his gaze to the flames.

Above us, a ragged gap tore open in the clouds, spilling pale light across the drifts. Somewhere beyond those ridges lay the Nenana Valley—and the unfinished tracks we were risking everything to build.

After thirty minutes, I stamped out the fire until only embers glowed in the dark and announced, "Dogs have rested enough. We're moving out."

Eli climbed onto the sled without another word. He gave the reins a flick, and the dogs lunged forward, hauling us once more into the silent, bitter wind—away from Denali, and from the secrets still burning inside me like a buried flame.

*

We rolled into the Nenana River Valley just past midday, runners whispering to a halt while the dogs collapsed into their traces, sides heaving steam. Snow banked high against the supply sheds and lay in frozen waves around the ribbed silhouettes of half-built trestles. Crews hunched at open fires where rails were being thawed; iron pinged and shivered as flame licked frost from the lengths. For all that motion, a taut hush held the camp, like the whole valley was bracing for a blow it already felt coming.

A man broke away from a cluster of men near a freight sledge and came straight at us—stocky, wind-chapped, eyes narrowed beneath the stiff brim of his cap. He looked first at the team, then at our laden sled, weighing purpose before personality.

"You the ones they wired, who were coming up from Talkeetna?" he said—no greeting, just a flat demand for affiliation.

"We are," I answered. "Name's Percy Hope. This is Eli."

The truth was we'd come from Denali, but to these men every northbound traveler was counted as "from Talkeetna"—that was where the wire began, where the freighters staged, where the world south of the range ended.

If the name landed, he gave no sign—just a clipped nod, business swallowing any trace of curiosity.

"Good. Drop your gear where it sits," he said, already turning. "You'd best come see something."

He set off without checking whether we followed. Eli shot me a quick look; then we trailed who I assumed was the foreman, past crates crusted white, past a stack of spike kegs half-buried in drifted snow, into the tight, listening quiet at the center of the yard.

He led Eli and me past sleds stacked with lumber and crates marked for the railway. We rounded a corner and stopped near the powder magazine. Splinters littered the snow like yellow straw, glinting in the cold light. The lock on the dynamite store was dangling uselessly from its iron clasp, sheared through as clean as a blade through bone.

Inside, the shelves gaped empty.

"Gone," the foreman said, his voice flat. "Enough blasting powder to rip a hole clean through this valley. And that's not the worst of it."

He reached into a canvas satchel and pulled out a burlap sack. It rattled as he passed it to me.

I untied the top and peered in. Iron spikes—at least a dozen of them—dull, blackened, and cold to the touch. I pulled one free and rapped it against the runner.

Thunk. No ring. Just a flat, lifeless thud.

I frowned and ran my thumb along the shaft. The metal felt wrong— brittle, almost dusty. A chunk near the head flaked off like dried mud.

Eli leaned in, brow furrowed. "That's not right."

I didn't answer at first. The medallion pressed warm against my chest, and a knowing rose in me, unbidden, specific.

"These aren't hardened," I said slowly. "See this?" I turned the spike so he could see the rough edge. "Impurities in the grain. They poured the cast too fast, probably into a cold mold. The structure's fractured before it ever cooled."

Eli let out a sharp breath. "Holy hell, Percy."

I dropped the spike back in the sack. "These'll shear off under the first hammer strike—or worse, under the weight of a locomotive."

"Jeez," sighed Eli.

"You saw anyone?" I asked.

"Snowstorm wiped out tracks. But at first light, a freight sled was spotted heading south. Three men. No manifests. Didn't stop, despite hail calls."

I turned toward the fire, where a dented ashtray sat on the stove, its contents catching the flicker of orange flame. The room had quieted. The foreman followed my gaze, then stepped forward and knelt.

"This isn't vandals," the foreman said, squatting beside the stove where a spike lay warped in the ashtray like a curled snake. "Nor are they drunks. Someone's organized. Someone with coin."

I stepped closer. "Organized for what?"

"For profit," he said flatly. "Steamship men don't want us reaching the Yukon. Big coal's happy with the mines they've already got. And some of these politicians? They're betting on a different route altogether."

Eli frowned. "You think the sabotage's coming from outside the camps?"

The foreman nodded grimly. "I think someone's getting rich off every day we lose to broken tools and spooked crews."

I turned toward the south, where the trail disappeared into a curtain of trees. The men we were chasing weren't just fleeing—they were executing a plan.

"Then we ride," I said.

South. Toward Talkeetna… or farther. South, where the telegraph wires hummed with secrets, carrying whispers to men in distant cities— men who stood to gain from every delay that kept Alaska's iron rails from pressing north.

I glanced at Eli. He met my eyes, jaw tight, his breath quickening with realization.

I dropped the bent spike into the snow.

"We're heading south," I said. "Whatever's happening, we're going to find out who's behind it."

Eli gave a single nod, already moving toward the sleds. Above us, the pale sun flickered behind rolling clouds, casting shifting shadows across the valley.

And somewhere down that trail, the men who wanted this railroad stopped were already miles ahead of us.

*

We reached Talkeetna beneath a sky bruised with stars, the dogs staggering with exhaustion as we pulled into the yard. Lanterns glimmered between darkened buildings, casting long shadows across snow that crunched underfoot like broken glass.

Before we settled in for the night, I pushed open the door to the telegraph office. The air inside smelled of hot metal and cold ink. I hunched over the narrow counter and scrawled a wire for Frederick Mears, the railway's chief engineer: STOP ALL IRON SHIPMENTS UNTIL VERIFIED. SUSPECT COUNTERFEIT SPIKES.

Only then did we bunk down in a canvas tent pitched behind the office. The stove rattled and hissed, pumping out meager heat while the cold seeped through every seam. Outside, the iced-over Talkeetna River cracked and boomed like distant artillery, echoing off the timbered slopes.

Eli lay curled in his blanket, eyes fluttering as he drifted between sleep and wakefulness. The lines of worry on his face were carved deeper than I'd ever seen.

I reached into my shirt and drew out the medallion, holding it up to the lantern light. The raven etched upon its face caught the flame, wings spread in silent flight. It felt heavy in my palm, as if Magnus himself were leaning over my shoulder, pressing me forward into secrets I still didn't fully understand.

"I'll keep the rails alive," I whispered. "Whatever walks in their shadow."

Outside, in the brittle hush of night, I thought I heard a faint train whistle echoing off the ridges—one long, two short—choked off mid-note like a voice strangled before it could cry out.

The medallion seemed to pulse once, sharp and certain. Urging me onward.

Tomorrow, I'd start searching for the men who'd stolen the blasting powder and swapped good steel for iron that would snap like twigs under a locomotive's weight.

The Percy Hope who'd once thought grit alone could build a railroad was gone. The medallion burned warm against my chest, humming with a quiet power that made words ring truer—or falser—in my ears, and shadows flicker with secrets waiting to be seen.

But even as I marveled at how clearly I could read a man's eyes, or how patterns seemed to rise from chaos like frost blooming on glass, doubt gnawed at me, sharp as teeth against bone.

So far, the medallion hadn't helped me find the widow, or the man who'd driven a knife into her husband's ribs and left him bleeding in the snow. Its strange warmth and flickering pulses hinted at secrets just out of reach, like stars glimpsed through shifting cloud. And if it couldn't solve that—couldn't point my boots in the right direction across this frozen country—I wasn't sure how it would help me find thieves hidden beneath layers of silence and drifted snow, men whose footsteps vanished as quickly as they were made.

A small voice in my chest kept whispering that perhaps I'd dreamed it all—the visions, the currents of fate, the sense that the medallion was more than hammered metal and fading engravings. Maybe I'd slipped into the same deep sleep as Eli, and every word from Magnus was only a fantasy.

Perhaps the only truth was the cold wind cutting my face and the railroad unfurling ahead, a ribbon of iron laid by mortal hands, prone to mortal failures.

But deep down, I knew better. I *knew* what I'd heard, felt the burden of secrets thrumming in my chest. Whatever else the world might doubt, I could not. It had been real. All of it.

Yet even as uncertainty hollowed me out, a sliver of stubborn fire remained. Tomorrow I'd try again. I'd hunt the ones who wanted this railroad bled dry, spike by spike. The men who'd rather bury iron rails under snow than let them become the bridge Magnus showed me beneath Denali's silent stone—a bridge not merely of steel and timber, but of destiny itself.

CHAPTER TWENTY
CUTTER

The sun hadn't yet cleared the spruce tops when Eli and I trudged across Talkeetna's main drag—a single snowy lane hacked through the trees, lined with canvas tents, log cabins, and half-finished timber frames. Smoke curled into the pale sky from a dozen makeshift stovepipes, and the air smelled of wet pine, bacon grease, and the tang of river ice grinding in the current. Somewhere, a dog barked, its voice echoing off rough-hewn walls like a warning bell.

Talkeetna wasn't much yet—not a proper town, but a construction camp that dreamed of permanence. A hand-painted sign nailed to a spruce announced "TALKEETNA TOWN SITE — LOTS FOR SALE," the letters blotchy from weather and wood sap. Beside it, men stood haggling over claims, gesturing with gloved hands, voices puffing steam into the cold.

Survey stakes marked new streets that existed only in a city planner's eye. Behind stacks of lumber, an open tent bore a sign reading *Marlowe's Saloon*, its canvas walls bulging with heat and the sound of a battered piano thumping out a ragtime tune. Across the way, the *Talkeetna Mercantile* kept its goods locked in an iron safe at night— flour, coffee, lamp oil, and the latest gossip about the railroad.

The village throbbed with railroad life: survey crews in wool coats unfurled charts across crates; steam rose from cauldrons where men thawed rails; and in the distance, the skeleton of a bridge took shape over the Talkeetna River, timbers jutting skyward like ribs.

We found the construction site alive with noise and movement. Men swung sledges against rails balanced on trestles of new-cut spruce. Sparks skittered across the snow like fireflies as iron met iron. Yet, despite the noise, an edge of tension hung over the place, taut as a telegraph wire. A man with a wind-burned face and soot streaked across his cheeks was bellowing orders near a row of sleds stacked with crates stamped U.S. GOV'T PROPERTY – RAILROAD SUPPLIES. His eyes were red-rimmed from sleepless nights, and his voice sliced through the clamor of hammers and shouted orders.

He spotted us stepping off the sled and strode over, boots grinding through the frozen crust. His eyes locked onto mine, sharp and measuring, like he was checking me against a name he hadn't quite believed was real.

"So you must be the Wizard of Hope," he said.

I let out a breath and shook my head. "Percy is just fine. That 'wizard' talk's more myth than man."

He took my hand in a grip that could've cracked walnut shells. "Foreman Jessup. I got word you'd be coming. They say you've got a knack for seeing what others miss."

I nodded toward the crates stacked along the siding. "We've seen it already. A whole shipment of bad spikes—brittle, uneven, full of impurities."

Jessup's mouth tightened. "Then take a look at this."

He led us through the half-framed shell of a warehouse, where the cold bit through the gaps in the log walls. A circle of men stood around an open crate, murmuring uneasily. One of them held a spike up to a lantern. Its surface shimmered—dark, almost oily. He tapped it against the crate's rim.

Thunk.

No ring. Just a dull, lifeless clack.

Jessup picked up another and passed it to me. "That sound's been coming up all week."

I turned the spike over in my hand, running my thumb along the shaft. The medallion at my chest stirred with quiet warmth, as if nodding. I didn't need to test it further. I already knew.

"This batch is worthless," I said flatly. "Same casting flaws we saw up north. Rushed pour. Cold molds. The iron never bonded right. Structurally, they're already cracked."

Eli grabbed one from the pile, scraped at it with his knife, then snapped the tip against a rail. A sliver flaked off like charcoal.

"They'll fail under strain," he said. "Guaranteed. This isn't poor quality control. It's sabotage." Jessup spat into the snow. "That's the fourth shipment. And now the crew's spooked. Some of them think the line's cursed."

A shout rang out from down the slope. A man came sprinting up, face pale, voice high.

"Foreman! You need to see this—down by the river!"

Jessup bolted without a word. We followed close behind.

At the edge of the bank, two workers stood over a shallow pit carved into the snow. A tarp was bundled there, stiff with ice.

Jessup knelt and yanked it open.

Inside lay a coil of telegraph wire, hacked clean through in half a dozen places, the ends jagged as if chewed by iron teeth. Beside it, a crate of signal lanterns lay smashed, their glass shattered into glittering shards.

Eli drew in a sharp breath. "They weren't just trying to weaken the line. They meant to cut us blind and silent."

I crouched, picking up one of the severed lengths of cable. The copper gleamed in the weak daylight, cold and sharp against my glove. It felt less like sabotage and more like a warning—a message meant for us as much as the railroad.

Jessup rubbed a trembling hand across his face. "I'm pulling double guards on every powder magazine from here to Curry."

I nodded, understanding the stakes. Curry lay twenty-odd miles south of Talkeetna, a railroad camp and supply hub where crews bunked and dynamite was stacked in timber sheds. If saboteurs hit there, it could cripple the line for months.

He turned to his men. "Spread the word. No one leaves camp without a pass from me. And check every load coming in off the river."

Eli and I followed Jessup back toward the telegraph shack. The men stared as we passed, suspicion swirling in every glance.

Inside, the stove crackled. Jessup dropped onto a bench like the weight of the entire Alaska Range had settled on his shoulders.

"I'll wire Mears," he said.

I shook my head. "Already done. As soon as we saw the first batch of bad spikes. He knows something's wrong."

Jessup looked up slowly, surprise flickering behind the fatigue. "Good. One less thing to chase."

Eli moved toward the stove, rubbing his hands. "Whoever's behind this isn't done."

"I'm not waiting for them to strike again," I said. "They've been through Talkeetna—there'll be a trail. Not in footprints, but in pockets, whispers, and quiet deals. I'll find it. And I'll smoke them out."

Jessup nodded slowly. "Then you'd better start right here. There have been strangers drinking at Marlowe's these past nights. Asking too many questions for men supposedly passing through."

Eli shot me a wary look. "Percy, we're running on no sleep, and you're talking about poking rattlesnakes with a stick."

"I'm not waiting for those snakes to strike first," I said.

Outside, a wind rose, rattling the tin roof like distant gunfire.

I pulled up my collar and headed for Marlowe's. Behind me, Eli fell in step, muttering under his breath.

Past the telegraph shack, the sign for Marlowe's swung on rusty chains. Piano chords leaked through the canvas, mingling with men's laughter and the sharp scent of cheap whiskey. Above a nearby rooftop, a raven wheeled against the pale sky, crying once, a high, rasping call that sliced through the dawn.

And in my chest, the medallion pulsed, fierce and certain.

I ducked through the flap into Marlowe's. The place was crowded, lanterns strung from the rafters, their flames trembling in the draft that swept through every time the door opened. The wooden plank floor was slick with melted snow, mud, and spilled liquor.

A battered upright piano sat in one corner, keys stained yellow, while a wiry man in a red scarf banged out a ragtime tune, his foot stomping time against the boards.

Men hunched over tables scattered with cards and whiskey glasses, voices low, eyes flicking toward strangers with guarded curiosity. A haze of pipe smoke hung under the canvas ceiling, catching the lantern glow like storm clouds lit from within.

Eli nudged my shoulder. "You sure this is wise?"

"Nothing about this is wise," I said. "But it's necessary."

I moved deeper into the room. Heads turned as I passed, the conversations rippling and falling silent in my wake. I felt the medallion pulsing against my chest, each throb like a drum calling me forward.

At the bar stood a man who looked out of place among the rough laborers and freighters. His greatcoat was black wool, cut sharp across the shoulders. His hair was dark and slicked back, and his beard was trimmed to a fine, precise point. He leaned one elbow on the bar as though he owned the room.

He was sipping from a crystal glass when his eyes met mine. A flicker of recognition passed through his gaze, followed by a smile as smooth as silk drawn over a blade.

"Well, well," he said. "If it isn't Percy Hope."

My spine stiffened. His face clawed something loose in my memory—a dark echo from a night drenched in blood and snow.

I stepped closer, eyes locked on his face, his groomed beard, and the narrow, sinewy hands gripping his glass.

I'd seen this beard before and these hands. Seen them glisten red in the lantern light as a knife was wrenched free from a man's ribs.

"I know you," I said, my voice low. "Your face… your hands. Tent City. You're the one who—"

He gave a low chuckle, smooth as oil. "Easy, Hope. Names first."

He set his glass down with delicate care and straightened his fine coat.

"Jabez Cutter," he said. "Though I suspect you already knew that."

My throat felt tight. "Not until now," I said. "But I know what you did."

Cutter tilted his head, considering me like a specimen pinned beneath glass. His eyes were cold, bright as polished steel.

"Careful with accusations," he murmured. "This territory has a way of swallowing men who ask the wrong questions."

Eli hovered behind me, his breath shallow.

"You killed him," I said, voice rising. "The man in Tent City. Left his widow screaming into the night."

Cutter's smile was small and humorless. "If I were you, Hope, I'd be far more worried about what's coming next. For you… and for your precious railroad."

He paused, his gaze flicking toward the shape of the medallion pressing against my shirt.

"And for that little secret you wear so close to you."

Eli shifted uneasily behind me.

I felt a chill run under my collar. "I don't know what you're talking about."

"Oh, but I think you do," Cutter said. He set his glass on the bar and folded his hands. "The widow spoke of you. Told me about that little trinket you stole from her dead husband and now wear so close to your skin. The medallion. With the raven."

The clamor of the saloon faded into a distant rush in my ears. I forced myself to keep my voice level. "She told you wrong."

Cutter's smile widened. "Hope, you and I are both men who understand the power of secrets. You think you're here chasing saboteurs: spikes, powder thefts. But there's a bigger game afoot. One with stakes far beyond a few miles of iron track."

"I'm not interested in games," I said.

Cutter leaned in, his breath warm and sharp with whiskey. "You should be. Because if you don't learn to play, you're going to lose everything—including your railroad."

I narrowed my eyes. "Are you behind the counterfeit spikes?"

Cutter gave an artful shrug. "I'm behind a great many things, Hope. Progress. Expansion. Profit. Sometimes progress requires… obstacles. It's nothing personal. Just business."

"This railroad isn't for sale," I snapped.

"Oh, but everything's for sale," Cutter purred. "Especially up here, where winter and distance strip men down to bone and want." His gaze drifted to the bulge beneath my shirt. "That medallion… I'd like it. Hand it over, and maybe you'll live to see the thaw."

My voice came out rough. "You've been watching me."

"Watching?" Cutter gave a low laugh. "I've been three steps ahead. Harlan Morse thought he could slip the medallion to you in secret."

My pulse thudded like hammer blows. "You killed Morse."

"Do you even know how Harlan came to possess the medallion?"

He inched closer, voice dropping to a venomous hush. "Morse stumbled onto the Tyonek village when he got stranded in a storm. Half-frozen, half-mad. Their medicine man nursed him back, fed him stories about spirits tangled in the earth, about a medallion forged before white men ever set foot here."

Cutter's eyes glittered like shards of ice. "They told him it was a piece of the old world's power, meant to protect the land from men who'd carve it up and sell it for profit. The Tyonek said a name while he lay there burning with fever—Percy Hope. That's how you got tied into this mess."

He gave a short, sharp laugh. "At first, Harlan told me everything. He thought it might be valuable. Thought we could sell it to the highest bidder. But the more he remembered, the more he started believing in the Tyonek's mystical drivel. He claimed he'd seen visions of you standing in the snow, holding the medallion like a shield. Said it was your destiny to keep it safe."

Cutter leaned even closer, his breath sharp with whiskey. "The next night, Harlan packed up and vanished. Slipped away like a thief, planning to find you before I did. He wanted to give you the medallion and wash his hands of the whole business. Poor fool. He thought he could outrun me. Thought he could keep secrets in a country where the snow records every footprint."

He gave me a smile as thin and cruel as wire. "But secrets don't stay buried, Percy. Not here. And now Harlan's gone… and you're all that's left between me and that medallion."

He paused, his eyes glinting with something far more dangerous than mere greed. "You want to hear something curious? All through Talkeetna, I've been catching whispers, soft as snow landing on canvas. The rail workers, the freighters, men hunched around campfires with frost crusting their beards… they talk about a man they call the *Wizard of Hope*. A man who always seems to appear when disaster's breathing down their necks. Who solves problems no one else can. Who plucks impossible answers out of thin air, like a magician pulling silk from his sleeve."

Cutter's low, mirthless laugh scraped the air like a blade. "Your name's Percy Hope. It doesn't take a genius to piece that puzzle together. And now this medallion turns up—an ancient token from the Tyonek, wrapped in talk of prophecy and salvation. So tell me, Wizard…" He tilted his head, his voice dropping into a whisper sharp as a knife's edge. "Is it true? That trinket lets you see things others can't? That it shoves secrets into your skull—blueprints, calculations, solutions to engineering puzzles you've never studied in your life? What kind of power is that? And why the hell should you be the only man to wield it?"

I spat the words at him. "It has nothing to do with you."

Cutter's smile vanished, replaced by cold resolve. "That's where you're wrong. Because if that medallion makes you powerful… I mean to have that power for myself."

For a heartbeat, we stood locked in a silence so taut it felt like a wire ready to snap. The sounds of the saloon roared back into my ears—the clink of glasses, the thud of boots on plank floors, laughter too sharp to be genuine. My breath came shallow, as if the walls themselves were closing in.

He turned and vanished into the crush of men, leaving the smell of sweat and whiskey lingering in his wake.

Eli leaned close, voice shaking. "Hell of a friend you've got there."

"He's no friend," I said, my voice low. "He's the man who put a knife in a man's ribs and left a widow sobbing in the snow."

Eli swallowed. "So what now?"

"Now," I said, watching the canvas flap sway behind Cutter's exit, "we make sure he doesn't get a damn thing he wants."

But as the piano picked up again and conversation washed back in, the unease in my gut only deepened. I felt like I'd stared into a frozen river and glimpsed dark shapes twisting under the ice—unseen, but real enough to drown a man.

Eli and I left Marlowe's as the last glow of daylight drained from the sky. The cold had sharpened, the cold that bites through wool and skin until it presses against bone. Snowflakes danced like sparks in the wind as we cut across the yard toward the telegraph tent.

"That man's dangerous, Percy," Eli said. "You saw how he looked at you. Like he already owns your soul."

"He might think he does," I said.

We were nearly to the tent when I felt it: the hush, sudden and unnatural, as though the wind itself had stopped breathing.

Then boots crunched behind us.

"Don't turn around," a voice growled.

Eli froze, his breath whistling between his teeth.

Two men stepped out from the shadows near a stack of timber, revolvers leveled. Both wore heavy coats, scarves pulled high over their faces, eyes glinting like chips of obsidian in the lantern glow.

"Evening, boys," one of them said, voice mocking. "We'll be relieving you of your valuables."

"Go to hell," Eli spat.

The nearest thug cracked him across the jaw with the butt of his pistol. Eli dropped like a felled spruce, blood streaking the snow.

Rage burned through me. I lunged, but the second man pressed the muzzle of his gun to my temple.

"Ah, ah," he hissed. "Easy, Wizard."

The first man rifled my coat, searching with rough hands until he found the medallion under my shirt. He jerked it free, snapping the chain.

"Got it," he said.

He held it up in the lantern light. The raven glimmered on the tarnished silver, wings flung wide as if ready to tear free from the metal.

"Mr. Cutter sends his regards," the man sneered.

They backed away, guns still trained on me, then vanished into the darkness beyond the stacks of lumber.

I dropped to my knees beside Eli. He stirred, groaning, blood trickling from a split lip.

"You all right?" I rasped.

"Feel like I got kissed by a sledgehammer," he croaked. "Percy… they took it."

"I know." I stared into the shadows where Cutter's men had disappeared. My breath billowed white in the bitter air.

Somewhere, the Talkeetna River groaned and cracked under shifting ice. Above us, the aurora shimmered in pale curtains, green and ghostly.

"They've got the medallion," Eli said. "What now?"

I clenched my fists until my knuckles popped.

"Now," I said, "we get it back."

And somewhere in the darkness, I heard a raven's cry, cold and triumphant, echoing off the frozen timbered hills.

CHAPTER TWENTY-ONE
HELL OF A STORY

We didn't linger long. The cold tore at my coat as Eli and I hurried back to Marlowe's, our boots hammering the frozen boards. Snow swirled around us, thick and relentless, as if trying to shove us back into the dark.

Inside, heat and lamplight spilled over the worn tables and smoky air. Marlowe looked up from behind the bar, a frown deepening the lines on his face.

"You look like you've seen ghosts," he said, voice rough as gravel.

"We've seen worse," I said, stepping closer, breath still ragged. "Cutter's men jumped us outside. Took something I can't afford to lose."

As Marlowe narrowed his eyes, Eli collapsed onto a stool, one hand pressed to his temple. Blood trickled down his cheek.

"Hold still," I muttered. I grabbed a bar towel and a bottle of rye from the counter, dousing the cloth before pressing it to the gash. Eli flinched, jaw tight.

"Just a graze," he said through gritted teeth, though the glaze in his eyes said otherwise.

"Could've been worse," I replied. "Keep pressure on it."

Eli leaned forward, his voice tight. "Where'd they go, Barkeep?"

Before Marlowe could answer, a thick-set man by the stove lifted a hand. Marlowe jerked his chin toward him.

"Jonas here just came in," Marlowe said. "Said he passed Cutter and his boys on the road to the station."

Jonas nodded, brushing snow from his beard. "Four of 'em, moving fast. Packs on their backs. Looked hell-bent on catching the southbound for Anchorage."

I felt a cold knot tighten in my chest. Cutter wasn't running blind—he was getting ahead of us.

And he wasn't wasting a second.

Eli's jaw tightened. "We're going after them."

Marlowe blew out a slow breath. "Blizzard's rolling in. You're courting death, chasing him in this weather."

I held his gaze. "Not chasing him would be worse."

Marlowe squinted at me, eyes sharp. "You carrying iron, Percy?"

I shook my head. "Not tonight."

Marlowe blew out a slow breath. "Then you're a damn fool." He hesitated, as if weighing his options, then reached beneath the bar and drew out a Colt .45. He set it on the counter with deliberate care, the steel catching the lamplight like a flash of lightning.

"You'll want this," he said. "If Cutter's mixed up in it, you'll need more than grit."

I picked up the gun, feeling the cold weight anchor in my palm, heavy with purpose.

"Thanks, Marlowe," I said quietly, as he handed me a worn cartridge belt with six spare rounds nestled in the loops. "We'll settle this."

Marlowe gave a tight nod. "God help you boys."

Eli was already moving for the door. "Come on, Percy. That train's leaving without us."

Marlowe gave a grim nod. "Godspeed. And watch your backs."

And without another word, we plunged back into the storm.

Snow whirled around us as we dashed for the freight yard. Lanterns swung between rows of boxcars and flatbeds stacked high with timbers and bundled rails.

We found a ladder bolted to the side of a half-loaded boxcar and scrambled up, breath puffing white in the freezing air.

The train groaned, its couplings creaking as steel protested the cold. Slowly, it began to roll, wheels clacking over the rails. We braced ourselves as the car swayed, the scent of sawdust and cold iron sharp in the air. Splinters crunched beneath our boots as we moved toward the door, straining to peer out into the storm.

Eli cracked it open, wind shrieking in. "We've got to check each car."

One by one, we crossed between the freight cars, iron platforms rattling underfoot. We passed crates stenciled with "ANCHORAGE SUPPLY," barrels of kerosene, stacks of timber.

The storm howled, swirling snow into every crevice.

In one boxcar, we found sacks of flour. In another, coils of copper wire and crates nailed shut. The lantern light bounced off the iron walls as we kept moving forward.

Then Eli froze, grabbing my arm. Ahead, through the narrow slit of the next door, shadows moved. Voices rose—a bark of laughter, a muttered curse. Cutter and his men were there, clustered in the glow of a swaying lantern.

Eli turned to me, eyes hard. "We found them."

I drew the Colt. The heft of it hit me like a judgment. My heart thundered as we crept forward, the cold biting into my fingers like the edge of something ancient and unforgiving.

Would I actually fire? The question sank into me with the gravity of stone. To pull this trigger meant possibly ending a man's breath— laughter turned to silence, warmth to a cooling body. Was I capable of that? And if I were, what sort of man would remain afterward?

And beneath that doubt, another voice pressed sharper: *Was the medallion worth it?* Worth killing for? Worth staining my hands in blood the way Cutter already had? It was only a piece of silver and stone, yet it had led us here, chasing us across mountains, burying friends in the earth. Was this really its promise—that we all become murderers in its shadow?

Each step felt stolen. The storm screamed around us, wind tearing across the rooftops, but in that pocket of lantern light ahead, the world stilled—three figures, hunched and watchful, weapons slung and breath fogging the air.

One of them turned.

Cutter.

The other two shifted behind him, half-swallowed by lantern glow and swirling snow. But I knew them. Not by name—by gait. The thick-shouldered brute was the one who pressed a revolver to my skull outside the timber stacks, his breath sour and steady while Eli was beaten to the ground beside me. And the other—the way he moved, that loose, slouching swagger—I remembered it from the moment he ripped the medallion from my neck like it meant nothing. Their scarves hid their faces, but I didn't need faces. I knew the sound of their laughter, that smug lilt in *"Mr. Cutter sends his regards."* They hadn't expected us to follow them. But we had. And we'd come back through the storm, not just for revenge, but for what was taken.

And we'd brought the storm with us.

Then everything shattered.

A shot cracked the silence.

Gunfire exploded into the night.

Steel sparked beside my face. I dove left, the Colt clutched tight, breath caught in my throat. Bullets stitched the boxcar wall as Eli surged forward—no hesitation—driving his full weight into the nearest man. They slammed hard against the floor, rolling in a flurry of fists and boots.

I rose, fired once, missed. Another figure came at me from the shadows. We collided. Coal dust rose around us like smoke from some ancient engine, choking, blinding. He swung—I ducked. He clawed for a blade—I answered with a hook that cracked teeth. He staggered back, dazed. For a moment, he teetered at the edge of the boxcar, arms pinwheeling against the snow-laced wind. Then he slipped—his boots lost grip—and he vanished into the white blur below.

No cry. Just the gust and the falling.

Eli roared, elbowed his opponent in the face, and sent him toppling over the edge. For a breath, it felt like we might make it.

Then Cutter turned.

He didn't hesitate. He raised his rifle and fired.

The shot slammed into Eli's chest. The sound wasn't loud—it was final. Eli's body jerked, then folded hard. Blood soaked through his parka, blooming fast, too fast.

"Eli!" I shouted, but the wind tore it from my mouth.

Something inside me snapped.

I charged.

Cutter and I slammed into the coal tender. The cold vanished. The storm dissolved into static. All that remained was motion—raw, blood-bound instinct. He threw a punch—I slipped it, not by chance, but by reflex honed through my experiences in the ring. I answered with two brutal shots—the kind that earned respect or silence. Cutter staggered, struck the steel wall with a thud, dazed but still reaching. His fingers clawed at the medallion at his throat.

I lunged and ripped the chain from his neck. The medallion tumbled into the dust between us, glinting like a fallen star.

We both dove for it. His fingers grazed the edge—then he snapped his hand into the coal bin and flung a fistful of dust into my face. The grit scorched my eyes, grinding under my lids. I staggered back, coughing, blind in a storm of black.

By the time I forced my eyes open, he was already at the open side door—one hand hooked on the frame, boots skidding on the rim of ice. Then he hurled himself into the void, vanishing into the darkness beyond the swaying cars.

For a moment, I thought I heard the thud of boots landing. Or maybe it was just the rails singing under the weight of the train. Either way, I didn't follow. I let the night decide his fate.

Eli was down—and nothing else mattered.

I dropped to my knees, heart hammering, and reached into the coal dust. My fingers closed around the medallion. Cold. Heavy. Waiting.

The roar of the wind and the pounding of the engine were all that remained.

I staggered back across the tender, lungs burning with the cold. Eli lay twisted beside the coal bin, blood steaming where it hit the ice, his face pale and drawn.

"Eli… stay with me." I dropped beside him, breath tearing from my lungs in ragged gasps. Snow clung to his lashes. Blood steamed on the ice.

I yanked open his parka, fingers fumbling with the stiff zipper. The wound was high on his chest—a clean shot, no shrapnel—but the blood poured out, dark and fast. Too fast.

I pressed my scarf to it, hard. "Hold on."

Eli flinched, a grimace twisting his face. "Feels bad," he rasped. "Real bad."

"Don't talk," I said, voice cracking.

He managed a crooked smile. "Too late for that."

His eyes fluttered open, locked on mine—fleeting, lucid. "Hell of a story, huh?"

Tears blurred my vision. The medallion lay slick in my palm, its raven wings catching the flicker of the coal tender light. I'd risked everything for it—followed hunches, ignored warnings, dragged Eli into danger. I thought it was the key to something bigger than any headline.

But now… staring down at the blood pouring from his chest—I was sure it was not worth even a drop of his.

"You're not dying," I whispered. "You hear me? You're not."

CHAPTER TWENTY-TWO
THE FROZEN EARTH

Eli's head rested in my lap, his hair damp with melting snow. His face, once lit with fire and questions, had gone still—the kind of stillness in a face that unmoors everything. I held him as the train swayed and groaned beneath us. The warmth was already leaving him, faster than I could accept.

"You're just a boy," I said, brushing the grime from his brow with a shaking hand.

Of course, there was no answer. Just the distant clatter of wheels on rails and the sharp, sour taste of grief rising in my throat.

"Why?" I asked aloud, voice cracking in the cold. "Why him? Why now?"

He was too young for this. Too full of life. The kind of soul that made others believe again, even when they didn't want to.

I'd known death. I've seen it from both sides.

I'd seen it wear a hundred faces. I'd watched it stalk the wilderness in quiet ways—through bad luck, bad maps, bad timing. But none of it prepared me for this.

This wasn't a reckoning. This was theft.

Eli wasn't like the others. The men in Nome who wagered their lives for gold had seen it coming. And Magnus—hell, Magnus had made his choices long before the sea took him.

But Eli… Eli was still becoming. He hadn't had time to grow into the man he was meant to be. And now here he was, slack in my arms, stiff with blood and ice, his spirit slipping away.

"You weren't supposed to be done," I whispered, brushing his brow with the back of my hand. "Not yet."

I looked past the train walls, past the mountains blurring with snow, past the things of this world. Because I knew there was more. I'd glimpsed it. With the Reverend. With Magnus. In dreams that weren't mine. I'd walked close to that veil, felt its shimmer, its breath. And I knew something lingered on the other side—watching, waiting, listening.

So I closed my eyes.

And I searched.

Not for his body.

For him.

Because if the veil could part for Magnus, it could part for Eli, too.

And I needed him to know I was still listening.

Outside, the mountains blurred behind a sheen of frost and grief. Inside, I counted the rhythm of the rails, hoping they'd carry us to something like peace.

The train hissed to a stop in Portage, brakes steaming in the cold dusk light. I stepped down, my legs numb, my arms aching with more than fatigue. For a moment, I just stood there, Eli's weight still on my shoulder in memory, unwilling to surrender him to the silence.

Two men from the station crew approached, their eyes downcast, hats pulled low. My throat caught, but I managed to lift a hand, motioning them closer. "Help me," I said, the words raw, frayed with a need I couldn't disguise.

They exchanged a glance, then moved to my side. One brought out a length of canvas, stiff with cold, the other a coil of rough twine. Together we knelt beside Eli. My hands shook as we unrolled the fabric, the smell of pitch and dust rising from it, a workman's cloth now pressed into service as a shroud.

"Here," one murmured, holding the edge while I folded it over Eli's shoulder. The other pulled it taut along his legs. We worked in silence, the three of us, folding and binding with a care that felt closer to prayer than labor. Each knot cinched him tighter against the world he was leaving, each pull of twine sealing what I still could not accept.

At last, we lifted him, the canvas whispering as it shifted against itself, and laid him gently across the double-wide plank we'd pressed into service. My grip lingered longer than it should, fingers pressed hard into the cloth, as if I could hold him through it, as if letting go meant losing him twice.

Outside, the sled waited, runners half-buried in drift. The dusk light caught on the canvas as we bore him forward, a pale bundle moving through the hush, heavy with a silence no words could puncture.

We carried him to the sled waiting outside, the runners half-buried in drift. Just a body-shaped burden moving through the hush, stiff with the kind of silence no words could puncture.

I'd paid the musher—too much, probably—but I didn't care. We needed to get back to Hope, and fast.

The dogs pulled steady over the long stretch home. Snow drifted down soft at first, then sharper as the miles wore on. We didn't stop. Just kept moving through the wind and ice, eyes fixed on the trail, my breath rising like ghosts into the trees.

Once, I thought I heard his voice. Just a whisper, threaded in the sled's creak.

Almost home, Percy.

Maybe I imagined it. Maybe not.

When we reached Hope, we turned the sled toward the lower road and made for the back lot of the Hope General Store, where the old storage shed leaned against the trees. Russel came out wiping his hands on a rag, took one look at the canvas bundle in the sled, and said nothing.

"I need a place to keep him," I said. "While I dig."

He didn't flinch. Just nodded once and stepped aside, the way men do when they've already seen too much in their own lives to ask questions they don't need answered.

Still, I felt the words rising, tight in my throat.

"He was shot. Didn't hesitate." I paused, swallowing the grief. "He saved me."

Russel met my eyes. Something passed between us.

"Come," he said, and led the way to the shed.

Together, we lifted Eli inside and laid him gently on stacks of hay bales. The air smelled of old oil and cedar dust.

I stepped back out into the cold and approached the musher still waiting by the sled, his breath rising in quiet plumes. The dogs shifted restlessly, sensing the weight of what they'd carried.

"Thank you," I said, the words dry and half-swallowed, but true. "For getting us here."

He gave a slight nod, eyes unreadable beneath the frost rimmed on his lashes.

Without a word, he stepped onto the runners, gave a soft call, and the team surged forward. Snow kicked up behind them as they cut across the lot, already fading into the falling dusk.

I stood there a moment, listening to the sled runners whisper over the frozen ground until even that was gone. Then I turned back toward the shed, where the silence waited.

I bent close to Eli and whispered, "I'll see to it you're laid right."

Russel was already turning to go. "Mind if I borrow a pick and shovel?"

He nodded toward the corner of the shed. "Take what you need."

I found the tools where they leaned against the wall—handles worn, iron heads dulled by years of use, but strong still. Beside them sat an old lantern, half-filled with kerosene, the glass smudged with soot. I struck a match and lit it, the flame flickering to life like a small promise against the coming dark.

I slung the shovel across my shoulder and gripped the pick by its neck. Hooked the lantern's handle with two fingers and gave Eli one last look.

"I'll make it right," I said. "Best I can."

Then I stepped out into the wind. The door creaked closed behind me, sealing the silence inside. No more words. Just the long walk through town and up the hill, the lantern's glow casting a slow, trembling arc across the snow.

The streets were empty—windows shuttered, chimneys trailing smoke into the dusk like sighs from sleeping houses. Every step felt heavier than the last, not from the weight I carried in my hands, but the one lodged in my chest.

Up the hill, the wind grew stronger. Snow scudded across the ground in ghostly ribbons. My breath rose and fell, loud in my ears, like some old forge bellows worn thin with use.

I chose a spot beside Reverend O'Hara's grave—his weatherworn cross still standing, though the name had faded to a whisper. Eli deserved someone worthy by his side, even in death.

I cleared the drifted snow with my arms, the cold biting through my sleeves, and drove the pick into the frozen earth. It rang like steel on stone—sharp, final. Again. And again.

The hours passed. The sky pressed down in shades of gray and ash. Wind sliced through my coat, through the ache in my shoulders, through whatever numbness grief could not reach. The lantern's light wavered and dimmed, but I kept going. Kept digging.

It wasn't until first light that I returned to the shed. The air hadn't warmed a degree, and every limb ached from digging. Russel was already outside, hitching his horse to the flatbed wagon. He nodded when he saw me—no questions, no words—just the quiet understanding of a man who knew what needed doing.

Eli wrapped in the canvas, the folds stiff. Together, we bent to lift him. His body had gone rigid now, heavy with the stubborn stillness of death. It was not like carrying a man, but more like shouldering a length of timber—awkward, unyielding, too heavy in the wrong places.

Russel gripped him beneath the shoulders while I took hold of his legs. We moved slowly, careful not to jostle him, as though respect might soften the finality already upon him. Step by step, we bore him across the yard and laid him down upon the wagon bed, easing him as if he might feel it still.

The horse stepped slowly up the hill, hooves crunching over frozen earth as the wheels creaked behind. Some in the town watched in silence from behind frosted windows, if they watched at all.

At the graveyard, we turned off the main trail and followed the slope to where the hole waited—rough, narrow, just deep enough. The pick and shovel still lay where I'd dropped them. Frost had crept over the handles like lichen.

We climbed down from the wagon. Russel looked at the grave, then at me.

"You dug that yourself?"

I nodded, flexing my stiff hands. "All night."

He gave a low whistle and shook his head. "Hell of a thing."

We stood on either side and grasped the edges. There was no ceremony, just effort. We lowered him as best we could—slow, careful. Even that was clumsy. The cloth rasped against the frozen dirt as Eli slipped into the earth.

When he reached the bottom, Russel took a step back, head bowed. I stayed a moment longer. Reached into my coat pocket, pulled out a spruce cone I'd picked up without thinking during the long walk to the shed.

I dropped into the narrow grave and straddled Eli's still body, the frozen earth pressing in from all sides. The cold clung to me like a second skin. I reached into the cover and found his hand—rigid, unyielding—and tucked the spruce cone into his palm.

A seed. A symbol. A gesture.

I rested my palm briefly over his and whispered, "You were a good boy, Eli. Better than most. Loyal as they come."

My throat tightened as I looked up at the pale, unfeeling sky. Then, without a word, I climbed out and reached for the shovel.

Russel stood by, hat in hand, as I filled the grave one shovelful at a time. Each clump of soil hit the canvas with a hollow thud. The rhythm became a kind of prayer. Not graceful. Not clean. Just final.

When it was done, I stood there with my breath thick in the air and my heartbeat pounding in my ears. The wind had gone still. Even the trees were quiet.

I gathered the tools in silence. Knocked the frost from the shovel blade. Wiped the pick clean with a fistful of snow. The lantern on the wagon still glowed, faint and trembling behind smoked glass.

Russel looked at me once more, nodded, and without a word climbed up onto the wagon and turned the horse back toward town.

I followed on foot, slow steps over hard ground.

Back at the shed, I hung the lantern on its hook and leaned the tools where I'd found them. Russel had already gone inside. I didn't knock. Some things don't need more words.

Then I walked home.

The streets were hushed. No dogs barking. No boots on the boardwalk. Just the sound of my own steps, fading behind me.

The house was cold. Empty. Still. The kind of stillness that presses into your ribs and stays there. Peggy's scarf still hung by the door. Walter's boots sat crooked near the hearth. They were in San Francisco now, chasing something brighter. I couldn't blame them.

I built a fire that barely touched the cold.

Then poured a cup of two-day-old coffee. Black. Bitter. Sat at the kitchen table, hands wrapped around the mug until they stopped shaking.

And for a long time, I stared at nothing.

But Eli was there—quiet, steady—as if the part of him that had anchored me still hadn't let go.

CHAPTER TWENTY-THREE
REFLECTION

I stayed in Hope longer than I meant to.

The grave settled under snow. A simple mound. No marker yet—just the Reverend's faded cross leaning beside it, the two of them now neighbors in silence. Each morning I walked up there, boots crunching, lantern swinging in the half-light. I didn't speak. Didn't pray. Just stood with the wind and let the cold work its way in.

On the third day, I walked to the general store. Russel was behind the counter, tallying invoices with one hand and holding a chipped mug of tea with the other. He looked up when the bell above the door gave its half-hearted chime.

"Well now," he said, setting his pencil aside. "Thought you might be out at the cemetery."

I nodded, brushing snow from my coat. "I was."

He poured a second mug without a word and slid it toward me across the worn counter.

"You did right by him," he said after a moment. "Hard ground this time of year. Harder still when it's someone you care about."

I wrapped my hands around the mug. "Wasn't enough."

"Never seems to be," he said.

I reached into my coat and pulled out the medallion. The silver was dull in the low light, its raven barely catching the reflection. I set it down between us.

"I think this has something to do with all of it," I said.

Russel squinted at it, then reached for his spectacles. He turned it over in his hand.

"Where'd you come across this?" he asked.

"Next to a man who was murdered. Before the first rail was laid."

Russel turned the medallion in his palm again, the silver dull under the low lantern light. The etched raven caught the edge of the flame just enough to shimmer, as if watching us from another world.

"You think this is just a charm?" he asked.

I shook my head. "No. Not even close."

He looked up.

"I didn't understand it at first," I said. "I found it beside the body of a man—Harlan Morse—in Tent City, stabbed to death. It was half-buried in the mud beside him. Something told me not to leave it."

Russel didn't speak. I pressed on.

"I kept it with me," I said. "Tucked against my chest, like it had always belonged there. And then things began to shift. Not all at once— quiet, like snow settling. Thoughts that weren't mine. Answers to problems I'd never studied.

"I'd look at a failing trestle and know—how to spread the load so it floated on frost instead of sinking, how to cut a channel that wouldn't trigger a slide. It wasn't trial and error. It wasn't logic.

"The knowledge came whole, like someone had buried it in me long ago, and now it was rising up. I wasn't figuring things out. I was remembering something I never learned."

I paused, my thumb tracing the edge of the medallion.

"It was like the thing had unlocked something in me. Something that didn't belong to me… but lived in me all the same."

Russell set the piece down slowly, as if the metal had grown heavier in his hand.

"I never told anyone," I went on. "Didn't want to sound mad. But Morse, the slain man, knew its reputation. He talked too much. And Cutter listened."

I looked down. "After Morse was killed, I saw Cutter at the river, washing blood off his arms like the current could carry it away. He looked up. Saw me. And he knew. He knew I had it, and he's been chasing it ever since."

Russel met my eyes, jaw tight.

"He took it from me. Ambushed us in Talkeetna. I got it back on that freight car—but not before he killed again."

Russel stared at the medallion.

"He's murdered two men for it that I know of," I said. "Morse and Eli. And he's not done."

Russel raised his gaze. "What happened to him?"

"He got away. Leapt from the moving train and vanished into the storm. Like the devil himself disappearing into the white."

"Then this isn't about coin," Russel muttered.

"No," I said. "It's about control. Someone wants this railroad stopped, and they're willing to kill to do it. And whatever this medallion is—whoever made it, whoever it once belonged to—it's tied to the very thing they fear."

Russel rubbed his temple. "You think it's giving you… insight?"

"Call it what you want," I said. "But it's not coincidence. Not when the land swallows whole sections of track. Not when trestles blow a day after they're built. Not when men with no stake in the project show up with explosives and forged iron. This medallion matters. And Cutter isn't working alone."

"What will you do?"

"I want to find him," I said. "I want Cutter to answer for what he did."

Russel leaned back slowly, the old stool creaking beneath him.

"Revenge?" he asked. "That's what you're after?"

I shrugged. "Call it justice."

He studied me for a long moment, then nodded—not in agreement, but in understanding. He set down his mug and folded his hands on the counter.

"You know what I think, Percy?"

I waited.

"I think you've been breathing smoke since the day that boy died. You're carrying something sharp inside you, and if you're not careful, it's going to cut more than just the man you're aiming for."

I looked away.

"You're not wrong to want answers," he said. "Not wrong to want someone to pay. But Cutter's a dead end if you charge in swinging. He's part of something wider, deeper, and angrier than you can handle right now. At the very least, give it time to cool. Give yourself time to cool."

I didn't answer. He pressed on.

"San Francisco?" he guessed. "To Peggy. And your boy?"

I glanced down at the medallion, lying on the counter like a coiled question. The edges were worn now, one side scratched where Cutter's boot had pressed it into the railbed. But the raven remained, etched deep, its wings open wide.

"They need you too, you know," he said, softer now. "Walter's got just one father. Your going off after a killer in the wilderness, won't stitch that wound any tighter."

I ran my thumb along the rim of the medallion. It was cold to the touch, but there was a hum in it—something old and urgent. It had cost too much already. Too many graves. Too many unanswered nights.

"I can't," I said.

"You can," he replied. "You just won't."

"Not yet," I said, eyes still on the raven. "Not until I've found him."

Russel shook his head, but his voice held no anger.

"Then promise me you'll stop before you go too far."

I slid the medallion back into my coat pocket.

"I'll try."

He gave a weary smile. "That's the most I expected."

We stood for a while in the hush of the store, surrounded by cracked ledgers and the scent of pipe smoke and pine soap. Outside, the wind had picked up again.

"I buried a boy," I said quietly. "And I can't bury what comes next until I know the man who did it is in the ground."

Russel nodded, slow and sorrowful.

"Then go carefully, Percy. The ground's cold this time of year. But it still remembers where the graves are."

CHAPTER TWENTY-FOUR
FREDERICK MEARS

The tracks toward Anchorage clattered like a metronome counting down something inevitable. With each mile, Cutter became more myth than man. No sightings. No whispers. Just a smear of sabotage in his wake and a hollow in my chest where Eli's voice used to be.

But this wasn't just about revenge. That word was too clean. Too civilized. What stirred in me now was deeper, darker. I knew Cutter wasn't alone. He wasn't even the point. He was the blade, not the hand.

If anyone could name the hand—or at least feel its shadow—it was Frederick Mears.

Anchorage rose from the frost like a memory half-built. Telegraph wires sang above muddy streets. Laborers hauled timber past bankers in coats stiff with starch. Civilization wore its Sunday best, but the bones underneath were still wild. The Anchorage Hotel stood three stories high, pretending it belonged to Boston or Chicago, though the paint peeled at the corners. It was the kind of place where you didn't lean too hard on the illusion.

They sent me to the second floor. The door to Mears' office stood open, as if it never closed. Maps covered the walls. Drafting tables overflowed with notes, slide rules, half-burned cigars, and the heavy quiet of burdened intention.

Mears stood at the window, arms folded, coat draped over a chair like a soldier off duty. He turned as I entered, blue eyes scanning me with the precision of a surveyor.

"Percy Hope," he said. "Or should I say… the Wizard of Hope."

There was no sarcasm in it. Just weariness and a glint of curiosity. He crossed the room and shook my hand. His grip was firm, dry—like gripping the throttle of a locomotive.

"I've read the dispatches," he said, nodding toward a stack of clippings and reports. "What you did at the Flats—the lateral drag fix— that wasn't just clever. That was instinct bordering on the impossible."

"I pay attention," I said. "And I don't sleep much."

He poured two mugs from a battered percolator. The coffee was dark, hot, and as bitter as truth.

"Matanuska was worse," he continued. "Frost heave had half my engineers blaming the rails. You saw the land. That cribbing solution? Floating rails in permafrost? I've never seen anything like it."

"Just trying not to let anyone die," I said, wrapping my hands around the mug.

"There's talk you've got something more than instinct," Mears said. "Men say you show up before the earth gives out. That you see things."

I didn't answer right away. Just traced a finger along the rim of my cup.

"I see what's there," I said finally.

He leaned forward. "Then you're the only one who does."

We drank in silence. The cast-iron stove ticked as it settled. From below came the faint creak of wagon wheels, the clatter of hooves. Somewhere, someone laughed too loud—and then went quiet again.

"I hear someone's dead," Mears said.

"Eli," I said. "He was just a boy who believed in the work. In what it could mean."

"And now?"

I stared into the cup. "Now I'm not sure what we're building at all."

He didn't speak. Just waited.

So I told him. Not everything. But enough.

"Cutter's men jumped us in Talkeetna," I said. "Knocked Eli down and robbed me."

His brow twitched. "Cutter? Jabez Cutter?"

"You know him?"

"He worked a winter survey on the Susitna route. Short contract. Didn't finish. Walked off over a pay dispute—or so he claimed. But he knew the terrain. Too well."

"I hit Cutter. Thought I'd stopped him. But he threw coal dust in my face and jumped. By the time I could see again, he was gone."

My voice held steady, but my grip around the mug betrayed me.

Mears didn't flinch. He held my gaze, eyes narrowing like a man fitting a final piece into a puzzle he's studied too long.

"Leaps from a moving train after putting a bullet in someone's chest," he said quietly. "That's not panic. That's nerves of steel."

He stepped toward the map wall, jaw working.

"Cutter's name's been floating through my reports for weeks—abandoned posts, missing freight, camp disputes that ignite overnight. Always just out of reach. But now?" He tapped the map between Talkeetna and Hurricane Gulch. "Now I've got a name tied to blood."

Then he leaned back slowly, exhaling through his nose. "Too many men quitting halfway. Too many shipments that never reach shore. Trestles that collapse where they shouldn't. I've been trying to chalk it up to bad luck or green crews. But this isn't chance. It's coordination. And Cutter's not acting alone."

"You think someone wants this railroad to fail?"

"I know it," Mears said. "The forces against us don't wear badges or boots. They wear suits. They sign checks. They own land; they don't want it devalued. They fund competitors. They spread rumors to drive laborers off the job. Some even sit in Washington—waiting for us to fail so they can privatize the remains."

He stood and paced toward the map wall, placing his palm on the line stretching from Seward to Fairbanks.

"This isn't just a railway. It's a stake in the future of Alaska. If it fails—if the land swallows it, or politics dismantles it—it'll be decades before someone tries again. And the ones behind this sabotage? They know it."

I stood and joined him at the map.

"What do you need from me?" I asked.

Mears turned from the map, voice low but firm. "You're a reporter. You've got the ear of readers from Anchorage to San Francisco. But you also walk the rails. You've felt what's happening out there. I don't need the AEC's press office. I need someone who'll put the truth in print— raw and dangerous."

He leaned closer. "This line is under siege, Percy. Not from nature. From men. Men with names and money. And I want those names printed."

I steadied my pencil. "Then give them to me."

He did.

"Start with Clark," Mears said, his voice low and unflinching. "William Andrews Clark. Copper King. Built an empire on smelters and bribes, then bought himself a Senate seat. When his bid to run a private rail line into the Alaskan interior fell apart, he didn't take it lightly. He's been bleeding this project from afar ever since—funneling money through proxies, stirring up opposition, turning men like Cutter into instruments."

I glanced up sharply. "You're saying Cutter works for William Andrews Clark?"

"Cutter's a pawn," Mears said. "A well-paid one. But yes. The sabotage, the threats, the bribes—it all traces back to Clark. The others— Morgan, Guggenheim—they play their part, but Clark's the one pulling strings with a personal grudge."

He turned to the map on the wall and tapped a finger against Montana. "If you want answers, you'll need to go to Butte. That's where his fortune was born, and where the ghosts still whisper. There's a man there—a former foreman, now a drunk. Name's Red Fenley. He knows what Clark did to bury his failures. And if Clark's reaching into Alaska, Red might know how."

I scribbled the names. William Andrews Clark. Butte. Red Fenley.

"You realize I write for Hearst," I said. "William Randolph Hearst dines with men like Clark. Hell, he probably owes him favors. You think he'll run a story that exposes his friends?"

Mears tilted his head, voice low. "You know damn well his papers aren't the only ones in the Union. Plenty of editors would bleed ink for a story like this."

I gave a dry laugh. "I've walked that road before."

He looked at me, waiting.

"Back in 1900, I uncovered Wyatt Earp's shell game with the Nome claims—collusion, fraud, the whole dirty tapestry. Sent it straight to the *San Francisco Examiner.* Hearst killed it. Said it didn't 'suit the tone of the times.'"

Mears grunted. "Not surprised."

"I wasn't about to let it rot. So I sent it to the *San Francisco Call.* They ran it front page."

Mears gave a faint smile. "Then you already know how to do it. Do it again."

"All right," I said. "I'll go to Butte."

Mears extended his hand. "Then go fast, and come back faster. We need your words like we need steel."

We shook. This time it wasn't a formality—it was an oath.

Outside, the snow fell harder, clinging to the windows like ash. I zipped my coat, gathered my notes, and stepped out into the white silence.

Clark's war had reached our frontier.

Now I'd carry the fight to his doorstep.

CAHPTER TWENTY-FIVE
AN OATH

Dawn found me at the ridge above the Arm, driving a nail through frost-bit wood. The cross wobbled until I braced it with my boot and hammered it true. Two boards, plain and unvarnished, joined not as a tribute from friend to friend, but as a reckoning from one who should've kept him safe. I'd carved his name with my blade—*Eli Brandt*—each letter stiff with cold and guilt. He was young, green. Still believed the world could be bent toward good if you pushed hard enough. I should've told him it bites back. But I didn't. And now this—this cross, this ground, was the mark of my silence.

I stood back, breath fogging the morning air, and spoke aloud—not to the trees or the sky, but to him.

"I swear it, Eli," I said, voice low. "I'll follow the line you died for. I'll name the men who bought your silence and broke this land to keep their grip on it. Cutter may have pulled the trigger, but he wasn't holding the purse. William Andrews Clark was. And I'm going to lay it all bare—names, ledgers, lies. By the time I'm through, the whole country will know who profits when the rails bleed."

The spruce creaked overhead, but nothing answered. Didn't need to. The silence had heard me.

I told him what Mears told me—about Butte, about a foreman who once did Clark's dirty work, about the map full of pins that led to the Southlands. I told him that this wasn't the end of his story. That it would begin again in newsprint and ink, not blood. Then I bent down, touched the cold earth once more, and dropped the coal-dark stone I'd carried since that night. A marker for memory. A burden for the soul.

*

I left Hope in the cold, blue hour, before the first light crested the mountains and spilled over Turnagain Arm. Just the hush of snow, the creak of harness leather, and six dogs and a musher pulling me across the frozen flats toward Portage. Each mile felt like a line drawn further from Eli's grave and closer to the man who put him in it. The wind sharpened as we climbed, then eased when the trail bent low again. I watched the mountains slide past, cold and still as judgment.

By the time I reached the Portage depot, the dogs were lathered, and my hands stiff from gripping the sled rails too long. I paid the musher, nodded my thanks, and stepped up onto the platform just as the southbound train hissed its arrival. Smoke curled off the engine like something coiled and waiting. The cars behind it were worn but sturdy— timber-walled and iron-ribbed, built more for hauling ore than men, though this one had been converted for passengers. A change from my previous trips.

Inside, the air was warmer than expected—wood stove near the center, coal-fed and breathing slow. The benches, though hard, were wide enough for two passengers with gear between them, each fitted with iron hooks for hanging coats and packs. The floors were scattered with straw to keep the wet from pooling. A single lantern hung from a roof beam, swaying gently with the motion as the train lurched forward.

A woman sat across from me, maybe forty, bundled in wool. Her boots were cracked but polished, like someone who still cared how she left a place even if she had nowhere to go. Two seats ahead, a pair of miners argued in hushed tones over the weight of something they couldn't afford to ship. One of them held a tin lunch pail with fingers blackened by coal. Near the back, a missionary read aloud from a weathered Bible, more to himself than anyone else, lips moving faster than his eyes. Every so often he looked up, scanning faces for a soul to save, and finding none, returned to the page.

I kept to myself. Back straight against the boards. The train clattered through the Kenai like it meant to outrun winter itself. Steam rose in ragged pulses, trestles groaned beneath us, and the windows fogged with breath and silence. Outside, the land blurred past—spruce and snow and long, frozen rivers slicing between mountains.

No one asked questions.

In Alaska, silence was the only passport that mattered.

Seward came with wind off the water and gulls wheeling above like scraps of thought torn loose from the sea. The harbor reeked of diesel, salt, and the sharp tang of fish guts, the smell curling around crates and rust-stained bollards. Moored just beyond the pier was a black-hulled steamer, broad and low-slung, its smokestacks puffing like a dragon reluctant to wake. Iron plates lined its sides like armor, the gangplank groaning under stevedores' boots as they loaded crates and canvas-wrapped trunks. Ropes hung slack and heavy from her cleats.

She was the kind of vessel that once ferried gold-rush hopefuls and wide-eyed boys from San Francisco north, like Liam and me, eighteen and foolish, chasing a future we hadn't yet named. Now she promised Seattle in a week, maybe ten days, if the wind played fair and no port master slowed her with red tape and bribes.

Inside the harbor office, a coal stove clicked and hissed. The manifest lay open on the counter, neat columns waiting to be filled. I took the pen. Paused. Then wrote Samuel Rothman.

Not an alias. Not this time. The last thing I needed was for word to reach Butte that Percy Hope—the so-called Wizard of Hope—was bound for Montana. Samuel Rothman wouldn't raise eyebrows. Wouldn't turn heads. Just another name scrawled in a harbor ledger.

The clerk didn't ask questions. Just handed me a ticket and turned to the next name in line. I stepped out onto the dock with the paper folded tight in my pocket and my past folded tighter. There was nothing left to do but board.

The SS *Northwestern* carried us out into the Gulf under low cloud and falling light. The coastline slipped away without ceremony. Hills, docks, smokestacks—all of it swallowed in gray.

Below deck, I kept to myself. Claimed a bunk, rolled my coat into a pillow, and watched the shadows stretch along the riveted ceiling. The ship groaned with the weight of old iron and new purpose. A few men snored. One muttered through a fever dream. Somewhere behind the bulkhead, a rat skittered between crates.

I didn't sleep.

Not with the itch between my shoulder blades. The kind you get when someone's watching.

It started the first night.

A man in an oilskin coat leaned too long by the stairwell. Eyes forward, hands tucked tight, like he was waiting for nothing. I passed him once, then again. Both times he didn't blink.

Later, in the mess, another man sat too straight, too still. Gloves that didn't belong on a boat, a posture that spoke to cities, not storms. He read the shipping bulletin without turning a page. His eyes stayed fixed on the same corner of the room—my corner.

They didn't speak. Didn't follow. But they didn't need to. They were placed.

Below us, the ship's engines beat a steady rhythm. We were two days out from Seattle, riding low under rough skies. Meals came at odd hours. Sleep came later. The deck swayed just enough to make men reach for walls. I took to walking the promenade at night, when most were laid flat by motion or rum.

On the third night, near the bow, the weather turned hard. Cold rain swept the deck and the ship bucked west into a heavier sea. I gripped the railing and let it soak through me. That's when he stepped out of the shadows.

"Careful," he said, catching the back of my collar before I lost my footing.

City gloves. Trim coat. Same man from the mess.

"Mr. Rothman," he said evenly. No smile. No real question in it, either.

He tipped his hat and walked off before I could answer.

I didn't follow.

Seattle was ahead. From there, the tracks led to Butte. To men who thought they owned the silence of the West. To ledgers buried deep. And to the name that paid for all of it—Clark.

I'd promised Eli I would speak the names.

Now I had an audience.

CHAPTER TWENTY-SIX
UNION STATION

Seattle rose from the gray, a city braced for war—fog pressed against the harbor, smothering cranes and smokestacks. Shipyard smoke smeared the low sky, and sirens cut in and out without answer.

Posters clung to trolley poles—*Victory Demands Sacrifice*—their corners flapping in the rain. Uniformed boys marched two by two past women selling Liberty Bonds. Most were barely out of school. At thirty-five, I was past the draft board's reach; Walter, at fifteen, was still too young. The war had taken other men's sons, not mine—not yet.

It struck me how different it felt here. Back home, the war was a rumor on the telegraph line, distant as the battlefields themselves. But Seattle wore it openly—on every pole, in every uniform, in the anxious eyes of women scanning the harbor for news. The city carried that knowledge like a pulse, restless and unsettled.

I stepped off the steamer with my collar high and my name hidden in my coat.

Samuel Rothman.

Not a disguise this time. A name reclaimed. Better kept quiet—the fewer who knew the Wizard of Hope had arrived, the safer.

Union Station loomed ahead, crowded and echoing. Iron beams, marble arches, the shuffle of soldiers and mothers clutching telegrams. Light from stained glass painted the floor in fractured reds and blues.

At the counter beneath a dead clock, I bought a one-way to Spokane. Cash. No name. No luggage, only my satchel.

Then, quieter: "What's the transfer time to Missoula? Need to reach Butte quick."

The clerk slid me a timetable. "Spokane before midnight. Missoula by dawn. Butte on the spur a few hours after."

Behind me, a man in regulation coat stamped freight tags. His rhythm faltered when I asked about Missoula. He didn't speak, but I felt him listening.

I pocketed the ticket and turned away—into steam and the smell of iron.

"Headed all the way to Butte?"

The voice came too close. Calm, practiced. A railway inspector. Brass tag on his cap: MORAN.

"Spokane," I said. "Business."

His eyes dipped to the timetable peeking from my coat. "What kind of business?"

For a beat, I weighed it. Too vague, and he'd press. Too specific, and I might trip on details later. I settled in the middle.

"Supplies for the mining camps," I said, steady as I could.

He studied me a moment longer, then tipped his cap. "Safe travels."

The words lingered. He turned, but not before glancing back. Watching too long.

I moved down the platform, away from the chatter of soldiers and polished shoes. The air grew heavier, freight crews shifting crates under steam.

Canvas-wrapped cargo lined the siding. One tag drew my eye: *Mechanical Equipment — Copper Consortium.*

Ordinary enough—until the wind lifted the canvas. Burned into the crate beneath: CFH.

I flipped through my notebook. Weeks ago, circled twice: CFH — Clark Freight Holdings.

William Andrews Clark. The Copper King. A name spoken like a curse in rail camps, and now here in ink, wood, steel.

Mears had warned me—sabotage wasn't winter's fault but deliberate. And here was the proof. Clark wasn't a rumor. He was moving freight under military priority, hiding behind corporate stamps.

This was why Eli was dead.

This was why I came.

A whistle screamed. Rain rattled on the roof. I boarded the Spokane train with Clark's name pounding in my head.

Not a lead anymore. A target.

I found a seat midway down the coach, wedged between a window streaked with rain and a pair of traveling trunks that smelled of damp leather. The car was crowded but hushed—soldiers dozing with their caps tilted low, a mother rocking her child, a salesman fussing with his sample case. No one paid me much mind, which was how I wanted it. I folded my coat tighter across my chest, the timetable still warm in my pocket.

The train lurched forward. I didn't sleep. Couldn't.

I wasn't chasing a story now.

I was hunting one.

The Cascade Range rose like a cathedral of stone and snow, spires of pine cutting shadows against the frost-glazed sky. From my window seat, the world turned colder, narrower. Valleys closed in, peaks sharpened, and the track coiled upward.

I held the medallion in my palm, letting it dangle from its chain like a pendulum over the mysteries I still couldn't solve. It hadn't glowed since Anchorage. Not once. No heat. No pull. Only silence.

Was it bound to that land? To the glaciers and granite veins of the North? Or had its spirit retreated entirely—gone dormant, or worse, dead?

I thought of Sha-e-dah-kla—not a man standing in daylight, but the presence that had come to me in the caves. A voice pressed into the soul like wind moving under ice: *It is not yours,* he'd said, *but it came to you for a reason.*

A reason. Or a warning?

The conductor's voice broke through the hum of steel: "Stampede Tunnel in five."

The mountain loomed ahead, a mouth carved into the belly of stone. Men shifted near the doors, pulling coats tight, watching the black hole grow larger. Then it swallowed us whole.

The world vanished.

Only the tunnel now—cold, wet, echoing with the groan of the past. The air thickened; my ears popped. A low hum threaded beneath the rails, not from the engine.

Then the brakes slammed.

The car pitched forward and locked. Steel screamed. Luggage thumped to the floor. A woman yelped. For a breathless moment, the train just trembled, metal groaning like a wounded beast.

Shouts broke through—sharp, scattered.

Boots pounding ballast.

A voice up the line: "Brake line's ruptured!"

I shoved past a pair of stunned passengers toward the rear platform. Wet steel under my boots, the tunnel's breath cold in my lungs. Lantern light spilled thin along the siding.

That's when I saw them—two shadows dropping from a freight car, hitting the ground at a run. They moved low and fast, vanishing into the dark.

And that's when I knew.

They weren't passengers caught in the panic.

They were here for this.

Something inside me snapped into motion. Not bravery—just the sharp pull of wrongness. The medallion was still silent. The tunnel was closing in like a trap. And the timing… too perfect.

And maybe—just maybe—they were waiting for me.

Was this Cutter's doing? A trap I'd walked into the moment I stepped on this train?

I shoved past the startled faces in my row, boots striking the aisle. The coach door banged hard against the frame as I pulled it open. Steam and cold air tore in. I climbed down the iron steps two at a time, landing heavy on the gravel siding.

They were running.

And I gave chase.

Not out of heroics. Not even anger. But hunger.

I needed to see their faces. I needed to know if this rupture, this moment, was about the medallion… or about me.

The tunnel breathed around me—damp, close, ancient. Footsteps echoed a beat too late, disorienting. The cold bit hard, pulling at my coat. Just ahead—a flash. Shoulder, elbow, the glint of something metallic.

Then they were gone.

I burst from the east portal into snowlight. Spruce stood like sentinels, white-crowned and watching. The fugitives cut into the trees without hesitation, swallowed whole by shadow.

I followed but lost them in thirty paces.

The woods absorbed their trail like water into thirsty roots.

Only a raven called—harsh and sudden. Its cry bounced off the trunks and vanished into silence.

I stood still. Listening.

Nothing.

By the time I returned to the tracks, the crew had patched the brake line. The conductor shook his head, muttering about rock shelves and bad luck. But his eyes said something else entirely—tight with unease, scanning shadows.

We both knew accidents didn't run on timetables.

I climbed back into the car, heart still pounding. My seat was straightened. Neater than I'd left it. Too neat.

Then I saw it.

A slip of paper, barely visible beneath the cushion's edge.

I pulled it free, slow.

A sketch.

The medallion.

Drawn with precision—winged circle, raven's eye, the stone at its center.

Too exact to be imagined.

Beneath it, two words and a signature:

Still watching. — J. C.

I read the initials once. Then again. Folded the paper and slid it into my coat without a sound.

Jabez Cutter's name was hardly a surprise. But it was a signal. Timed. Planted and not meant to startle—meant to inform.

He knew where I was.

The medallion lay cold against my chest. No warmth. No hum. It hadn't stirred since we left Alaska. Whatever force had once pulsed through it was bound to the North.

Out here, it was just metal and silence.

I kept my hand in my pocket, fingers brushing the edge of the note.

Outside, the spruce blurred past like watchers in motion.

The train leaned into the grade. Spokane next. Then Missoula. Then Butte.

Still watching?

Good.

So was I.

So no—this wasn't myth.

Not whispers.

Not shadows.

Cutter was here. Or near enough to leave calling cards.

Near enough to know I'd find them.

The medallion pressed cold to my chest. But it didn't feel sacred anymore. It felt surveilled. Not a gift. A link. Not mine.

I was the one being carried now.

The train groaned forward, slipping out of Stampede's black throat into a white hush of pine and powder. Out the window, I caught them—

two figures moving downslope fast, like smoke with legs, coattails flapping, vanishing into the woods.

I unfolded the note again. Turned it over.

Blank.

But the silence on the back said enough.

I slid it into my coat pocket beside the timetable. Let my hand linger there, knuckles brushing paper, pulse steadying against the chill.

In the glass of the window, my reflection looked older than I remembered. Not by years, but by burden. The crooked nose I earned from too many boxing contests, Peggy always said meant trouble. The eyes that scanned what no one else believed was there.

"Ghosts," I muttered. "They're everywhere, aren't they?"

In tunnels.

In trees.

In the cave where Sha-e-dah-kla breathed through the bedrock and taught me to listen beneath language.

Not all ghosts are dead.

Some are watchers.

Some are messages.

And some—

Some are waiting for you to answer.

The train leaned into the grade.

Spokane. Then Missoula. Then Butte.

Where this quiet game would end, or become something louder.

Let him watch.

I was done blinking.

CHAPTER TWENTY-SEVEN
BUTTE

The Northern Pacific carried me east without incident—Spokane, Missoula—each stop a brief exchange of cold air and new faces. Passengers boarded and disembarked, their boots ringing on the platform boards, their voices folding into the steady pulse of the rails. Seatmates came and went. I offered no more than a spare smile and nod, and my thoughts locked tight against the rattle of the rails.

Still, Peggy and Walter slipped in, unbidden—appearing in the glass, fading, then returning, as if the window were some restless mirror. Walter at nearly fifteen, all shoulders and sharp edges now, a voice deepening into the register of men. He'd said more than once he wanted to be a writer, like his father, though I wasn't sure whether he admired the craft or simply the way it let a man move through the world asking questions no one else dared. I could picture him bent over a notebook at the kitchen table, pen scratching in the lamplight.

Peggy's eyes beside him—sharp as flint when she was angry, soft as dusk when she let it go. She still talked about opening her own women's clothing store, a place that would carry the kind of dresses she swore couldn't be found anywhere nearby. I wondered how far she'd gotten with it. Had she found a space? Was she running the numbers? Or had the bills on the table, and my absence pushed that dream farther to the edge?

When the train rocked into another long stretch of pine and frost, I pulled my notebook from my coat pocket. The motion of the rails made my hand wander, the words staggering slightly across the page, but I kept at it.

Dear Peggy,

I hope this finds you well, and Walter with his nose in a notebook, working on one of his dispatches. Tell him the work matters more than the applause, and that every sentence should earn its place. If he keeps at it, he'll learn that sometimes the truth of a thing hides between the lines, and it's a writer's job to coax it out without scaring it away. Dispatches, stories, articles—it's all the same craft in the end. The form doesn't matter as much as the honesty behind it.

As for you, I keep thinking of that store. I can see it in my mind— the dresses hung neat on their racks, your name painted across the window in a hand as fine as the stitching inside each seam. I picture you moving through the space, straightening a cuff here, adjusting a collar there, greeting women who know they've come to the right place the moment they cross the threshold. I want that to be real for you, Peg. I want you to have something that's yours alone, not just a dream folded away for another season.

I know I've been gone more than I should, and when I am home, I'm not always there in the way you deserve. I've carried this work like a compass, and too often it's pointed me away from you. That's a wrong I intend to set right. When this assignment is over, I want to bring something back—not just the money, but the time we've lost. I want to be the kind of father who's present in his days, and give you the partner who stands beside you, not just in letters like this but in the small hours, in the daily business of living.

If this trip works out the way I need it to, maybe I can put something toward the store—more than a token, enough to set you firmly on your path. I can't promise when I'll be back, or in what shape, but know that I'm thinking of you both. When the road feels long out here, it's your faces I carry with me, steadying me the way the rails steady the train.

Yours, Percy

I paused, tapping the pencil against the margin, knowing there was more I should say but not ready to commit it to paper. I folded the page, slid it into an envelope, and tucked it back into my coat. I'd mail it when I could. For now, the road ahead was a race—Clark at the far end, Cutter somewhere in between, ready to block my path unless I found a way to cut him off first.

It wasn't just reporting anymore; it had become something I couldn't name, a duty that lived deep in my bones. Why else had the medallion been given to me, its warmth guiding my hand in Alaska? But since I'd left, it had gone cold and silent, as if the distance had stripped it of its voice. Still, I could feel the pull of the work.

By the time Butte rose from the valley floor—mounds of mining waste and skeletal towers jutting into a smoke-stained sky—I'd already narrowed my focus to one man: Red Fenley. He'd run with the sort who took on other men's dirty work, and Mears had said if anyone could point me toward the Copper King's role in the Alaska sabotage, it was him.

But hunting Red meant keeping one eye over my shoulder. The note under my seat had told me all I needed—Cutter had been on the train with me. He'd gone to the trouble of sabotaging the brake line just to slip it there: a neat sketch of the raven medallion, two words in his hand—*Still watching.* A stunt like that wasn't just a message; it was a move in the game, letting me know he could reach me anytime, anywhere.

The wheels hadn't even stopped before Butte hit me with a gutful of coal smoke and smelted ore. I stepped onto the platform, letting the crowd close around me while I kept my head moving, eyes never resting. Somewhere in that press of miners and drifters, I caught a glint in the steam—sharp, neat, like the way Cutter kept his beard trimmed to a razor's edge. It was gone in an instant, swallowed by the crowd, but not before it sent a slow crawl up my spine.

Cutter was out there. He wouldn't rush, not after the last time on the run from Talkeetna, when his shot buried itself in Eli. That kind of mistake sticks with a man. It stuck with me, too—and I wasn't about to let him vanish before I evened the score.

I started my sweep at the depot saloons, where the liquor was cheap and the gossip cheaper. Every bartender got the same quiet question about Red Fenley, and every answer came with a shrug or a squint, the kind that said they might know more than they were willing to share.

As I stepped back onto the boardwalk, a figure moved at the far end of the street—too far to make out a face, but standing just long enough before melting into an alley. I told myself it could've been anyone. But I didn't believe it.

From there, I worked my way uphill, following the noise of piano keys and the shouts of barkers to the rougher saloons and brothels. The streets narrowed, climbing between clapboard buildings whose eaves nearly touched. Miners in soot-caked coats shuffled past, their coughs tearing at the cold air. Women in doorway shadows sized me up like they could read the coins in my pocket. I asked after Red anyway—half expecting nothing, but knowing you don't find men like him by sticking to the well-lit streets. Behind me, bootsteps fell in rhythm with my own for half a block before fading.

Boardinghouses came last. Places where the wallpaper peeled in curling strips and the air smelled of boiled cabbage and coal dust. I checked ledgers when I could, talked to proprietors when they'd talk. At one place, as I turned to leave, I caught a flash in the corner of my eye—someone slipping out the side door into the cold. A beard trimmed close. A deliberate pace. Gone before I could follow.

The next building leaned with the wind, its paint long since surrendered to the weather. A lace curtain shifted in the second-floor window as I mounted the steps—someone watching.

A woman in a faded housecoat answered my knock, her hair pinned back in a loose, practical bun, the faint scent of soap and stale tobacco clinging to her. She carried herself with the weary authority of someone who'd seen every kind of trouble pass through her doors.

"You the landlady here?" I asked.

"That's right," she said, eyes narrowing as they measured me up.

"You know a man named Red Fenley?"

Her gaze flicked past me toward the street, as if checking who might be listening. "I might know him," she said after a beat.

I slipped a coin from my pocket and held it out between two fingers. "Where?"

She snatched it, the metal vanishing into her palm like it had always belonged there. "Back parlor. Been keeping to himself all day—too much whiskey, not enough sense." She stepped aside, jerking her chin toward the rear of the building.

I crossed the worn hallway and pushed open the door. A man sat hunched over a cloudy glass, eyes fixed on the table, hands restless. I stood in the doorway a moment, then said his name.

"Red Fenley."

He didn't answer right away. Just took a slow pull from his glass, set it down, and wiped his mouth with the back of his hand. Up close, he looked like a man halfway between a binge and a breakdown—shirt rumpled, collar sagging, the sour scent of whiskey clinging to him. A few days' stubble shadowed a face creased deep around the mouth and eyes, the kind of lines carved by years spent squinting against bad weather and worse odds.

"You are?" he said, voice rough from drink and disuse.

"Someone looking for answers," I replied. "About Alaska. About Clark."

That got me a flicker—just a twitch in the corner of his eye—but it vanished fast. He leaned back, chair creaking.

"Don't know you. Don't want to. And if you've got Clark's name in your mouth, I'm guessing you work for him… or for someone who does."

I stepped inside, letting the door click shut behind me. "If I worked for Clark, I wouldn't be here asking questions. I'd already know the answers."

"Or you're here to see what I'll spill," he said, tilting his head. "Then run back and tell him what I've been saying. That's how men get dead in Butte."

His hand drifted toward the glass again, but it wasn't for the drink— it was a stall, a way to avoid my gaze. I moved closer, lowering my voice.

"I've got no stake in Clark. What I've got is a dead friend and a trail that leads straight to this town."

For a moment, he said nothing, his jaw working like he was chewing over the risk. Then he gave a dry laugh, without humor.

"You think walking in here cold is gonna make me open up to you? No, stranger. That's not how this works. You want something from me, you better come with more than questions."

I slipped a hand into my coat pocket and came out with two folded bills, laying them on the table between us. "Then let's start here," I said.

Red's eyes dropped to the money, then back to me. He didn't touch it. "That all you think I'm worth?"

"It's enough to cover the drink and buy you some silence about this conversation," I said. "What you tell me on top of that depends on how much you want to see Clark's shadow off your back."

He snorted, shaking his head. "Clark's shadow don't come off. Not for me. Not for anyone in this town who's ever taken his coin."

I nudged the bills closer. "Then maybe this buys you the smallest of sins—talking to a man who isn't on his payroll."

Red stared at the money for another long moment, fingers tapping the rim of his glass. Finally, he scooped it up and tucked it into his shirt pocket, leaning forward so close I could smell the whiskey on his breath.

"All right, stranger," he said, voice dropping low. "I'll tell you something. But once I do, you walk out of here and don't look back. Because if Clark gets wind of you asking the wrong questions, you'll be the next body they haul out of a flooded shaft."

The words landed heavy. I'd seen those black, yawning holes before—shafts that swallowed men without a sound, where the water below was as cold and final as the grave. In a place like Butte, a man could vanish underground, and by the time anyone thought to look, all they'd find was his hat floating in the dark.

"What do you know about Clark?" I asked.

Red smirked and leaned back, glass in hand, and let the name roll slow off his tongue.

"Clark. William Andrews Clark. Name alone smells like metal and money. Born in Pennsylvania, made in Montana. He carved his fortune outta the guts of copper country—banks, railroads, newspapers, you name it."

He took a sip, eyes narrowing over the rim. "Man once bought himself a US Senate seat with enough bribes to make even Washington blush. They yanked it from him—'bribery of unprecedented proportions,' they called it. Four years later? He strolled right back in and took another seat, this time just clean enough to pass."

Red set the glass down, leaning forward until his elbows rested on the table. "That's the thing about Clark. Power ain't something he asks for. He takes it. And if he fails, he buries it so deep no one ever digs it back up. That's the man you're after, stranger. And if you think you're the first to come looking, trust me, you ain't."

I let the words settle between us. "So tell me," I said, "what's Clark got to do with the construction of the Alaska Railroad?"

Red's jaw tightened. He glanced toward the door, then back at me, his voice dropping to a rasp. "Some say Clark's reach ends at the state line. Those people don't know Clark. He's got money in veins that run farther than copper—up through the Yukon, down into your gold camps, and straight into men's pockets who don't ask questions."

He rubbed at his stubbled chin, eyes darting again toward the door. "If that railroad gets built, it won't just haul freight—it'll haul power away from Clark. Open the land to new outfits, new money, and cut the rates he's been charging through his steamship lines and copper hauls. That line would make men rich who aren't him, and Clark's not in the habit of sharing. He's the kind who protects what's his by making sure no one else gets a foothold. If the rails stop short, the territory stays bottled up, and Clark keeps the chokehold on what comes in and what goes out. And the thing is—he's not doing it with his own hands. He's got men who can turn a fortune or bury one without Clark ever leaving his office."

The idea sat heavy in my mind. If Clark wanted the railroad stopped, he wouldn't dirty his boots to do it—he'd send someone north who could work in shadows, someone who left nothing behind but trouble. Someone like Cutter.

"You're saying he sent someone north?" I pressed.

Red's gaze locked on mine, unblinking. "I'm saying the trail you're on leads to a man who don't leave tracks. If you keep walking it, you better hope you find him before he decides you're not worth the trouble of keeping alive."

I leaned in a little closer. "You know a man named Jabez Cutter?"

The name seemed to land hard. Red froze, his jaw working slow, eyes slipping toward the door again before finding mine. "Why? You seen him?"

"We've crossed paths," I said.

Red's fingers drummed once on the table, then went still. "If Clark sent Cutter… whatever he's up to, it's serious. And it won't be stopped. Cutter's the kind of man who doesn't take orders so much as he takes opportunities—and Clark lets him, because he gets results."

"What kind of results?"

Red shook his head. "The kind that end with someone in the ground or out of the game. If Cutter's sniffing around, you're already late to whatever play they're making. And if he knows your face…" He let the thought trail off, his meaning clear.

CHAPTER TWENTY-EIGHT
TRAP

The morning light pried through the warped shutters of my room above the Silver Crown Saloon, dragging me back from the thick, smoky haze of the night before. Below me, the clink of glasses and low murmur of early risers drifted up from the bar, while somewhere higher still, the muffled laughter of women from the third-floor rooms threaded through the floorboards.

I sat up slow, my head full of last night's Faro hands, the scent of stale whiskey still clinging to my shirt. Wyatt Earp's lessons had served me well at the card table, though my winnings barely offset the cost of the room and the bourbon I'd used to buy a few conversations.

When I went looking for Red later that morning, he was gone. I crossed the street to the boarding house where I'd first found him. The landlady claimed not to have seen him since last night, though a chambermaid swore she'd heard boots on the back stairs before dawn.

Maybe Red had decided he'd already said too much and slipped out ahead of whatever trouble he'd been courting. Or maybe Cutter had paid him a visit in the dark hours. Either way, he was gone before I could press him on the details—the names, the routes, the proof that could tie Clark's hand to the railroad's troubles. My lead had gone cold.

If Red had stayed, I might have been able to pry open the rest of the story. Now I'd have to find my answers elsewhere. But in Butte, with Cutter somewhere in the wind, that meant keeping one eye on Clark's world and the other over my shoulder.

Anyway, I couldn't waste the day chasing a man who didn't want to be found.

Clark was the hub of this wheel, and the spokes all pointed in his direction. If I couldn't pry the truth out of Red, I'd have to dig it out of the Copper King himself—or at least out of the men who kept his hands clean.

If I were lucky, Clark would be in Butte. From my evening conversations around the Faro tables, I learned that the Copper King—seventy-six now, though still sharp enough to count every penny—kept an office here for when he deigned to look in on his old empire. However, he spent most of his time in New York offices or basking at his Los Angeles estate under the California sun. I doubted that luck and Clark were two things I would find in the same room.

I stepped out into the morning chill, the street still slick from a night rain. Butte was waking—wagons clattering over the ruts, miners filing toward the hoists, the air thick with the mingled scents of coal smoke, damp earth, and ore dust. Somewhere in this city of brick blocks and steel headframes was the place where Clark's name was etched in brass.

The first stop was the business district, where the banks, law offices, and company headquarters loomed over the storefronts like watchtowers. I asked at a tobacconist's counter, then at a bootblack stand. Both pointed me toward the Hennessy Building on Main Street—a grand, six-story block of red brick and pride, with windows polished to a glare and a lobby tiled in black and white. Clark's Montana offices, they said, were on the top floor.

If he were in town, he'd be there. And if not, the men who kept his ledgers and licked his envelopes might be willing to talk—if I could find the right way to loosen their tongues.

I pulled my collar up against the morning chill and joined the slow current of miners and clerks on Main Street. Something in my gut told me Butte wasn't the kind of place where you could walk toward a man like Clark without someone taking notice. I wasn't here to hide. If Clark were in this city, I'd walk straight through the front door of whatever hole he was in and make him answer.

Inside the Hennessy Building, the smell of oiled wood and coal heat wrapped around me. A brass directory board listed the Clark Montana Realty Company at the very top, letters neat and spare as if carved to last longer than the man himself. I took the elevator—a gated cage that rattled like loose teeth—to the sixth floor.

A woman with hair pinned high and a collar starched sharp enough to cut paper looked up from her desk as I stepped into the outer office. Before I could get a word out, she rose.

"Mr. Hope?"

The question caught me off guard. "That's right."

"You're expected."

Expected. The word landed wrong in my gut, but she was already gliding toward a pair of tall oak doors at the far end of the room. She pushed one open and stepped aside, motioning me in.

The office was built to make a man feel smaller than he was—high ceilings, dark paneling, a carpet so thick my boots didn't make a sound. At the far window stood a figure, hands clasped behind his back, staring out over the smoke-stained city.

I took two steps inside, the door closing behind me with a soft, deliberate click.

"Mr. Clark?" I called.

The man turned.

First, I saw the beard—close-cropped, dark against the spill of daylight. Then the eyes, sharp and cold enough to pin me in place. My stomach dropped.

"Cutter," I said.

"Disappointed?" His voice carried the same easy menace I remembered. "I'll try not to take it personal."

I didn't answer. My mind was already working through how he'd known I'd come here—and why.

He stepped closer, a slow, measured prowl. "You've been carrying something that doesn't belong to you, Hope. I'll take it now."

I took a step toward him. "Where's Clark?"

His expression stayed flat, though a trace of amusement tugged at the corner of his mouth. "You really think Senator Clark's got time for a newspaperman chasing ghosts? No, Hope… you get me. And that's the best offer you're going to get today."

Cutter took another step, closing the space between us until the smell of his tobacco clung to the air.

"You've got a habit, Hope. Sticking your nose into other men's business."

"Only when it starts blowing poison down my way," I said. "That railroad belongs to more than just the men who own the shovels. And from what I've been hearing, Clark's got reasons to see it fail. Big ones."

He gave a slow shake of his head, like a teacher humoring a slow pupil. "Senator Clark's got reasons for everything he does. The difference between him and you is that his reasons make him rich. Yours?" He tapped his temple. "Yours gets you killed."

His mouth curled into a sneer. "Just ask Eli—oh, wait. You can't."

The words hit like a fist, but I didn't flinch. "Careful, Cutter."

I let the silence hang a moment, then leaned in, my voice sharp enough to cut through his smirk. "You think you're clever, but you're not. You're just the hand that pulls the trigger. Clark's the one aiming the gun."

His eyes hardened, though he tried to shrug it off. "You're asking questions you don't have the weight to carry."

"Then give me the weight," I snapped. "Tell me why Clark wants the line stopped. Tell me how long you've been dancing on his strings."

That drew the faintest twitch at the corner of his mouth. "Why? So you can scribble it into your little paper? Or play hero for the poor fools in Alaska? Ever think maybe they don't want saving?"

"I think maybe they've never been asked."

That earned a cold chuckle. "You're like a dog worrying a bone, Hope. Trouble is, you haven't noticed the leash around your neck."

"I've noticed," I said, steady as stone. "And I know Clark's the one holding it."

The smirk died. He let the silence stretch, then leaned close, his breath sour with tobacco and menace. "The medallion. Now."

I didn't move. "Not until I see Clark."

His smile vanished altogether. "That's not how this works."

I straightened, meeting his eyes. "Then we're done here."

Cutter's jaw flexed. He raised his voice: "Boys."

The side door opened, and two broad men stepped in, their Colts gleaming in the low light. They spread wide, cutting off any chance of escape.

A sharp pang hit me. My own Colt was back in Hope, forgotten in the rush to leave. The one Marlowe had slid across the counter in Talkeetna—I'd lost that one on the train the night Eli was killed. The emptiness at my hip felt heavier than iron.

Cutter came forward, slow and sure, the air thick with tobacco smoke and gun oil. "You've got grit, Hope. I'll give you that." He stopped inches away, close enough for me to see the red veins in his eyes. "But grit without sense…"

His hand shot out like a striking snake, seizing my shirt. One wrench upward, and the fabric scraped across my ribs. The medallion glinted between us, warm against my chest until his fingers closed around it. He tore it free, the chain snapping with a sound that made my stomach drop.

"…only gets you buried."

His cold stare lingered before he stepped back and jerked his chin. "Take him."

The gunmen pressed steel to my back and herded me out, the heavy door slamming shut behind us. The medallion—my last link to the truth—was gone again, sealed in that room with Cutter and Clark's shadow looming over it all.

They marched me down the hall toward the rattling cage of the elevator. Outside, the night wind cut sharper than I remembered, the city itself seeming changed, as though it knew what I'd lost. But grief wasn't all that burned in me.

As the cold bit deeper, a thought settled in my chest—hard, dangerous, and unshakable:

Cutter might have taken the medallion, but like before, I would take it back.

CHAPTER TWENTY-NINE
CAGED

They didn't march me far—just half a block through the wind, down an alley slick with half-frozen runoff. The brick walls leaned close, muting the clang of wagons on Main Street until all I could hear was the scuff of boots behind me and the faint rattle of a chain in one man's pocket. My stomach was a tight knot, the kind you get when you know you're walking into something you won't walk out of the same way.

A steel door waited at the end of the alley. Two sharp knocks. It opened just enough for a shadow to wave us through.

Inside, the heat hit first—coal-stove heat, heavy and stale, smelling of sweat and wet wool. The light came second, sour and dim through smoke-stained glass high on the wall. We turned toward a staircase tucked against the far wall, its treads worn smooth by years of boots.

The men kept close as we climbed, their presence crowding me in, the steps groaning under the weight. Halfway up, I caught a glimpse through a filthy window: the alley shrinking below, the street beyond it fading into a blur of smoke and wagon ruts. By the time we reached the landing, the cold outside felt a long way off, replaced by a heavier, closer kind of air.

They steered me past stacks of freight crates toward a door in the far corner.

The room beyond was no bigger than a cell—bare walls, a single chair, and a narrow cot with a mattress that looked like it had been dragged out of a mining camp years ago. One grimy window sat behind bars on the outside, more to keep eyes out than to keep me in. A quick glance told me the drop was two stories—enough to break a leg, maybe worse.

"Hold still," the taller one said, his voice flat with authority.

The second man moved in, patting me down with quick, practiced hands. Pencils, my notebook, pocketknife—all dumped on the cot like scraps worth nothing.

Only then did the tall one jerk his chin toward the chair. "Sit."

I lowered myself. The chair creaked like it might give out before I did.

"You stay put," he added, "until you hear otherwise."

The bolt slid home with a finality that tightened the knot in my gut.

I sat still, listening. Somewhere beyond the wall, footsteps shuffled. Further off, a muffled clang—metal striking metal. The warehouse didn't sleep; it breathed and shifted with the work. That meant voices, movement, and maybe—if I kept my head—cover enough to disappear.

I crossed to the barred window. The alley below was patched with dirty snow, no crates stacked high, no ladder in sight. Even if there were, the drop would be a gamble. And I had the feeling my luck was running low.

I leaned my forehead against the cold glass. Cutter had the medallion now. Whatever he thought it was worth, he'd guard it close. Which meant I wasn't just up against his hired muscle—I was up against time.

A sound behind the wall broke my thoughts—two voices, low, moving closer. I caught pieces:

"…taking him tomorrow…"

"…Clark won't wait…"

I strained to hear more, but a door slammed and the words died.

I sat back down, heart ticking in my ears. Wherever they were taking me, it wasn't anywhere I wanted to go.

So I'd have to make my move before then.

*

The warehouse never slept.

Even in the dead hours, the floor trembled with the slow roll of handcarts, the thud of crates hitting the planks, the scrape of something heavy being dragged across the room below. I sat on the edge of the cot, watching the dim light creep along the barred window, listening to the rhythm of the work. I timed the sounds in my head, mapping patterns— the pauses, the gaps—but no plan I could make ended with me outside, not from two stories up with nothing but frozen alley below.

And the medallion—that was the part that gnawed at me.

Not the cold, not the stink of wet wool, not even the bruise from the gunman's shove. It was the hollow weight on my chest where it should have been. I kept replaying the moment Cutter's hand tore it free, the chain snapping against my skin.

Suddenly, the bolt scraped back.

Light spilled into the room as Cutter stepped inside, closing the door behind him. He wasn't in a hurry. He just stood there, rolling the medallion's chain around his fingers. The silver caught glints from the lamp like it was mocking me.

"Funny thing," he said, letting it swing. "I thought this would *do* something. A clue, a hidden latch, a secret worth killing for. But it just sits there. Quiet as a lump." He gave it a sharp look, like it had personally betrayed him. "You've been carrying this like it's the key to the kingdom. Turns out it's nothing but a useless trinket."

I kept my face still. "Then give it back."

That pulled the faintest grin from him. "Oh no. It may be useless, but it's mine now."

He took a step closer. "So tell me, Hope—how did you know what to fix in Alaska? Where to go; who to talk to? You walk into a mess that's been bleeding this railroad dry, and in a moment, you patch the holes. That doesn't happen by accident."

"I pay attention," I said flatly.

He tilted his head. "Which is why you're here. Senator Clark likes men who can see around corners. Likes them even more when they work for him. You join us, you walk out of here. You get coin, protection…

maybe even a visit with your precious medallion. Decline, and you rot in this room until the walls forget your name."

I kept my face still, but my mind was already moving. Working for Clark wasn't in the cards—not in any lifetime I could picture. But saying no now meant sitting in this cell while Cutter decided whether to starve me or shoot me. Saying yes meant one thing: a walk out of here and a straight line—or as straight as a man could get in Butte—to the man I'd come all this way to see.

I gave him a slow, considering look. "You tell the senator I'll listen to his offer."

Something in his eyes shifted—not quite trust, but interest. "Smart man."

Cutter stepped back from the cot and turned toward the door. "Boys!"

The bolt slid open a moment later, and the same two men who escorted me here filled the frame. "Tie him," Cutter said.

One pulled a length of rough hemp from his coat and yanked my hands behind me. The fibers bit into my wrists, and I made a show of not resisting—better they think I'd made my peace with this arrangement.

"Let's move."

They marched me out of the cramped cell, the smell of coal smoke and damp wood swelling in the hallway. We descended the narrow staircase I'd been forced up earlier, the steps groaning under the combined weight of boots and bad intentions.

At the warehouse's rear exit, a gust of winter air slapped my face, sharper than I remembered. We turned into the alley, boots crunching over patches of old snow and grit. I kept my eyes forward, but my mind noted every corner, every shadowed doorway—anything that might matter later.

It was only a short walk before the brick bulk of the Hennessy Building rose ahead, its windows catching the weak daylight like cold mirrors. The same doorway, the same brass-handled door as before. One of the men pushed it open, and the warmth and oiled-wood scent of the lobby wrapped around us.

The elevator cage rattled its way down to meet us. No one spoke on the ride up, the floor numbers ticking by in the dim light until the gate clattered open at the top.

They guided me down the same hall, past the same secretary's desk, straight to those tall oak doors I'd walked through the day before. Cutter didn't knock. He pushed them open and stepped aside, his hand on my shoulder as if to remind me who was doing the leading.

And just like before, the room beyond waited, paneled in dark wood, the carpet swallowing sound, the window framing the smoke-stained city.

Only this time, I wasn't here for Cutter.

I was here for Clark.

CHAPTER THIRTY
CLARK

Senator Clark didn't look up right away.

He sat behind a desk big enough to double as a judge's bench, pen moving across a sheet of cream paper with the measured patience of a man who knew the world could wait on him. His shoulders were square, posture precise, the cuffs of his white shirt gleaming where they peeked from his tailored coat. Behind him, a wall of books rose like a barricade—leather spines in orderly ranks, flanked by the gleam of polished brass fixtures.

When he finally raised his head, the movement was slow, deliberate. His face was a study in controlled authority—thick, swept-back hair gone silver at the edges, a full mustache and beard carefully groomed, framing a mouth set in a line that could tilt toward charm or command at will. Deep-set eyes, sharp and pale, took my measure with the weight of a prospector judging ore, deciding if it was worth the trouble to smelt.

"Mr. Hope," he said, then let the name linger a moment before a faint smile curved his mouth. "Or should I say… Mr. Rothman." His eyes held mine, unblinking. "You made the change on the SS *Northwestern* manifest between Seward and Seattle—thought it might keep your trail cold. It didn't. My men had the passenger list wired to me before you stepped onto the Seattle pier."

Cutter steered me to a chair opposite the desk, one hand gripping the backrest until I lowered myself into it. My wrists were still bound, the rope biting into my skin. Clark's gaze drifted to the hemp, then to Cutter, his brow lifting ever so slightly.

"Unnecessary," he said.

Cutter didn't argue, just leaned down and sawed the rope with a pocketknife. The fibers fell away. I rubbed my wrists, saying nothing.

Clark folded his hands atop the blotter. "You've been busy in Alaska. Too busy for a man who claims to be nothing more than a newspaperman."

"That depends," I said.

"*Mm.* " He leaned back slightly. "And what you see, you fix. Broken supply lines. Idle crews. Labor unrest. Even the most discreet problems have a way of vanishing after you arrive. Almost as if you're—how should I put it?—working from a map no one else has."

I kept my face blank. "Just good instincts."

"Instincts," Clark repeated, as if tasting the word. "You see, I value instincts. In business, in politics, in… more delicate matters." He steepled his fingers. "You have a talent, Mr. Hope. I make a habit of acquiring talent."

He flicked his fingers at Cutter, who reached into his pocket, pulled out the medallion, and handed it over.

"I don't know what this trinket means to you," Clark said, fingering it, "but I assure you, men have killed for less. My question is, does it mean enough for you to listen to what I have to offer?"

I leaned forward slightly. "I'm listening."

He smiled faintly, though it didn't reach his eyes. "Good. Then let's speak plainly. Alaska is rich, but raw. Railroads, mines, ports—it's a feast for those who can stomach the work and survive the competition. You've proven you can do both. I could use a man like you to keep certain ventures… moving smoothly."

"And if I say no?"

"Then you'll leave Butte with nothing but the clothes you walked in with. Assuming you leave at all."

The room was warm, but the air between us carried a thin edge of cold steel. He wasn't bluffing.

I let a beat pass, then another. "I came here to see the man who's been pulling strings from one end of the territory to the other. Now I have. What's your offer?"

Clark's smile widened, this time showing the barest flash of teeth. "I'll tell you over dinner. Cutter will see to the arrangements. You strike me as a man who thinks better with a full plate and a glass in hand."

He stood, signaling the audience was over. Cutter moved toward the desk, his hand darting out to snatch up the medallion. But before he could slip it back into his pocket, Clark's voice cut across the room.

"Give the medallion back to Mr. Hope."

Cutter froze, the chain pooled in his palm. "Sir—"

"You heard me," Clark said, eyes still on me.

With a tight jaw, Cutter set the medallion down on the blotter, the chain landing with a reluctant click. Clark slid it across the desk until it rested within my reach.

"A gesture," he said. "Consider it collateral until our next conversation."

I picked it up, feeling its weight settle back where it belonged.

"Until dinner, Mr. Hope," Clark said.

Cutter opened the door, and I stepped out into the hall.

I'd come to Butte for Clark. Now I had him. The question was whether I'd make it out with more than just a seat at his table.

*

Cutter put me back in the same room, the door bolting shut with a finality I'd already learned not to test. Only this time, the medallion lay heavy in my palm. I turned it over in the dim light, tracing the curve of the raven's wings, the faint nicks along its edge. Warm, yes—but only from being carried close to the skin. Whatever pulse or whisper it once held was gone. No guidance. No stirring. Just the silence of a thing holding its breath.

Clark hadn't returned it out of generosity. That much was clear. It was a move, a piece slid across the board with deliberate intent. A gesture of goodwill meant to soften me, to make me believe we were partners instead of adversaries. He wanted me tethered, convinced that keeping the medallion meant keeping faith with him.

Hours passed in the muffled quiet, broken only by the shuffle of boots in the hall and the occasional groan of a settling beam. I kept the medallion clenched in my fist—not as a gift, not even as a talisman, but as an anchor against the tide he was trying to pull me into. And still, I waited.

When the bolt finally scraped back, Cutter stepped in. "On your feet," he said, his tone all business. "Dinner's waiting."

Dusk was closing in when I was delivered to Clark's mansion. The house sat on a rise above the street, its facade a sweep of stone and stained glass, the tall front doors more suited to a cathedral than a home. The electric glow from the windows pressed back the indigo sky.

Inside, the air was heavy with beeswax, polished wood, and the faint sweetness of some imported bloom I couldn't name. What struck me first was the light—not the flicker of lanterns or the soft gutter of candles, but a brilliance that poured from bulbs fixed into brass sconces and chandeliers. The glow was steady, tireless, without smoke or shadow, as if the house itself had captured daylight and bent it to Clark's will.

In Hope, our nights belonged to kerosene and firelight. Electricity was a rumor, something promised for cities far to the south. To step into this mansion was to step into another age, one where darkness was banished by command. It unsettled me as much as it awed me, this sense that Clark lived not just in wealth, but in a future the rest of us hadn't yet reached.

Every surface gleamed beneath that current-born light—marble busts with their polished brows, the golden banister of a grand staircase spiraling upward like it meant to carry men to heaven. Cutter handed me off to a butler who wore his black coat like armor, then slipped away without a word. "This way, sir."

The dining room was a cathedral to power. Its ceiling soared high enough to house a second story, walls paneled in dark wood that absorbed the glow and sent it back in warm, expensive waves. A table stretched nearly the length of the room, dressed in white linen so sharp it looked cut from ice. Above it, a chandelier blazed with bulbs, each one burning with a calm authority. Even the orchids in the centerpiece seemed touched by that brilliance, their petals shining as if they had bloomed in the heart of some far-off sun.

Clark was already there, standing at the head of the table with a glass in hand. "Mr. Hope," he said, voice smooth but edged with steel. "Welcome. And… my condolences. I understand you were there when that young man was killed."

I kept my expression flat. "I was. His name was Eli."

"A damn shame," Clark said, sounding as if he meant it.

"He didn't deserve what he got," I added.

Clark inclined his head as though agreeing, then gestured toward a seat. "Sit. Eat. We'll talk."

The butler poured wine the color of garnets, and the first course appeared—something French, with a name I couldn't pronounce but a taste that made me suspect Clark's chef knew some form of magic. Clark spoke easily, spinning talk of mining ventures and shipping contracts, never naming names but dropping enough breadcrumbs for a man to follow if he knew where to look.

The oysters came next—plump and briny on the half shell, their chill a sharp contrast to the warmth of the room. I'd eaten them before on the crowded streets of New York, quick and brackish from a vendor's cart, but never like this. Clark ate them with unhurried precision, each shell set neatly back in its bed of crushed ice.

A tureen of soup followed, its steam curling upward between us, the scent rich enough to almost disguise the formality in the air. By the time the roast arrived, I knew two things: Clark didn't intend to let me walk away without owing him something, and he was used to getting what he wanted. The trick would be leaving with more than I'd come for— enough to tie him to the sabotage—without showing him my hand.

Clark raised his glass first, his smile faint but deliberate. "To new acquaintances."

I matched his gesture, the crystal cool in my fingers. "And to the roads they lead us down."

"You've heard, no doubt," Clark said, "about the delays north of Anchorage—equipment shortages. Men are quitting without notice. That sort of thing can ruin a schedule… or make a man very rich."

"Depends which side of the ledger you're on."

"Exactly." His eyes fixed on me. "And, from what I've heard, you've a talent for shifting ledgers."

I shrugged. "I write what's true. Sometimes the truth moves a decimal."

He laughed, more freely this time. "You're wasted on newsprint. A man like you should be shaping events, not chasing them."

"Let me be plain," Clark said. "The Alaska Railroad is more than a line on a map. It's a key. Whoever holds it decides who eats, who freezes, who prospers, and who begs. I intend to hold it. And I think you already know how close I am."

I leaned back, feigning a casual interest. "And if someone were to decide you shouldn't?"

Clark's smile thinned. "Then that someone would be very, very cold before the first snowfall."

For a moment, the only sound was the soft music drifting in from the other room.

"You make a compelling argument," I said finally. "But I've learned not to buy the map until I've walked the ground."

Clark raised his glass again, studying me over the rim. "Then perhaps it's time I showed you the lay of the land."

I clinked my glass to his, thinking of every hidden ravine and deadfall a man could stumble into if he followed the wrong guide.

The last of the plates were cleared, and the butler moved in with coffee poured from a silver pot so polished I could see my face in it. Clark drank his in two slow sips, then rose.

"Come," he said, motioning toward a side door. "Dinner is only half the conversation."

I followed him into a long hallway lit by sconces that spilled warm light over oil paintings in gilded frames. Landscapes of Montana's copper country. Steamships cutting across gray seas. A portrait of Clark himself, younger but already certain of his place in the world.

He led me into a study that could have passed for a museum. Floor-to-ceiling shelves groaned under the weight of books bound in leather so old they smelled faintly of dust and animal hide. In the center, a globe as tall as my chest hung lazily on its axis, oceans mapped in deep blues, continents in faded gold leaf. Clark gave it a casual flick, the world turning under his fingers.

"This is where I do my best thinking," he said. "Deals are made at desks, yes—but they're born in rooms like this."

He moved toward a glass case against the far wall. Inside, artifacts gleamed under a sheen of dustless glass: a nugget of raw copper the size of a fist, its surface greened at the edges; a revolver with an ivory grip, its cylinder resting open as if mid-load; a stack of ledgers bound in green ribbon, each spine marked with dates in neat gold leaf.

His hand brushed a small tray of iron spikes, their heads split and twisted. "Do you remember the batch they uncovered in Talkeetna?" His tone was conversational, almost idle. "The crews said the steel was flawed, poured cold. A tidy explanation. But some failures"—he turned the spike with a fingertip—"arrive at the precise moment they cause the greatest delay. Curious, isn't it?"

The spike clattered back into the tray. He poured amber into my glass, steady as a surveyor's hand. "The world is always divided, Mr. Hope. There are men who act, and there are men who endure the acting of others. The first shape events to their will. The second are left writing explanations after the fact—excuses, really, for why they were too slow to seize the moment."

I kept my glass steady, though the words coiled in my gut. He hadn't admitted a thing, yet the meaning was there, plain enough for anyone willing to look past the smoke. Those spikes hadn't just failed—they had been made to. And if Clark wanted me to know that, it was only to remind me that the line between progress and ruin was thinner than iron.

I accepted the drink, the burn sliding down my throat. "And I assume you're in the first group."

He smiled faintly, the curve of his lips cold as a rail in frost. "I am. The only question is… where do you belong?"

I swirled the glass, watching the light fracture through the liquid. "Belonging's tricky. For instance, a man could own every steamship line running to Alaska, every dock worth landing on… and still see his hold slip away the moment a government railroad cuts into his freight rates."

For the first time, the faintest crease marked his brow—gone as quickly as it came, replaced by a slow, easy smile. But I'd seen it—just a flicker, like a shutter catching the light, before the mask slid back into place.

He tipped his glass toward me as if toasting the observation. "Business is all about winners and losers."

The words settled heavily between us. The fire popped in the grate, the chandelier light trembling across the polished table. At first, it was only a flicker—Eli's boyish grin, eager and uncertain, the way he'd hover close, waiting for a nod or a word of approval. Then came the memory of him on the sled, reins tight in his hands, his voice breaking from youth yet steady enough to guide the dogs across frozen miles. The flicker caught, burning hotter with the stubborn loyalty in his eyes, the unspoken trust that I would see him through.

But what seared deepest was the end—the weight of him crumpling against me, his breath ragged and fading, the warmth draining from his body as I held on, desperate to keep him tethered to this world. I felt his life slip in my arms, felt the stillness that followed, and a hollow ache carved itself into my chest. That boy, with all his searching and half-formed dreams, was gone, and yet his fire remained—lodged inside me, fierce and unrelenting. I had no choice but to carry it forward.

I gripped the arms of my chair until the wood creaked. My voice, when it came, was low but steady, forged in that fire.

"There's one thing more," I said. "Your man Cutter. He put a bullet in Eli. That blood's on your payroll, whether you like it or not."

The words hung between us, heavy as iron. Inwardly, I bit back the rest—because I already knew the truth of it. Clark's empire had been built on more blood than he'd ever care to count.

But if the charge struck him, he gave no sign. Clark's expression stayed smooth, his glass poised midair as though we were trading pleasantries over supper instead of death. Only the faintest tightening at the corner of his mouth betrayed he'd even heard me at all.

"Cutter has his uses," Clark said carefully. "But even useful men can overstep."

"I don't care about his uses," I said. "I want justice."

Clark leaned back, steepling his fingers like a man considering a new investment. "Justice is such a pliable word. You want Cutter dealt with? I can arrange that. Quietly. Permanently. But bargains require balance. You'll keep your pen away from matters best left alone—no articles linking me to sabotage. In return, Cutter is done. Consider it… business as usual."

The phrase struck me like a hammer. Business as usual—revenge reduced to a number on a page, another transaction to be tallied and closed.

Eli's face lingered in my mind—youth unspent, laughter silenced, a boy carried off before he had the chance to become a man. I felt again the slack weight of him in my arms, the last breath rattling against my chest, and the stillness that followed like a stone laid over my heart. Cutter's death—swift, certain, final—tempted me with its cruel simplicity. One life bartered for another. A ledger balanced.

But behind him came Peggy and Walter—her warmth, his boyish grin—lives bound to mine. To resist was not just to invite my own grave, but to leave them abandoned, wife and son with no husband, no father. That thought burned deeper than vengeance ever could.

Clark leaned back, glass in hand, his eyes never wavering. He didn't need to press further. The choice was already choking me.

My hands curled into fists against the arms of the chair. The word never left my mouth, but the decision did. I lowered my gaze, giving him the answer he wanted.

Clark smiled faintly, as if he'd been waiting for this moment all along. He raised his glass in a silent toast, the firelight catching the amber liquid like molten gold. The bargain was struck.

CHAPTER THIRTY-ONE
HOME

The butler showed me out without a word. The mansion's electric glow fell behind me, swallowed by the chill of Butte's streets. I walked quickly, though no one gave chase—Cutter's shadow lingered in my thoughts, sharper than any that might follow me from the house itself.

I had agreed to Clark's terms—or rather, I had not refused them. "Business as usual," he'd called it. The phrase clanged in my skull like a hammer against steel, a rhythm too cold and precise to be mistaken for mercy. Cutter dealt with… *permanently*. But permanence was a word with edges. Did Clark mean a cell, a life cut off from daylight and air? Did he mean exile, Cutter sent scuttling into some dark corner of the world where his name would fade like smoke? Or did he mean a grave— unmarked, unseen, the earth swallowing him as if he had never existed?

And what of me? I walked the streets with Clark's bargain stitched into my very skin. Had I not bartered my own soul for Peggy and Walter's safety? For the fragile thread of family that still bound me, however frayed, to something worth clinging to? In that warm, suffocating study, I had nodded without nodding, spoken without speaking, and in doing so, I felt the faint click of shackles, unseen but no less real.

Eli's face rose in my mind, unbidden. Youth extinguished, laughter stolen, a body cooling in my arms before I had the chance to promise him the world he would never see. Would vengeance be satisfied if Cutter lay dead, struck down by another man's order? Could I accept that as justice—or was it merely the illusion of balance, a debt rearranged on paper but never settled in the heart?

The thought gnawed at me. Perhaps I had not purchased justice at all, but only deferred payment—placed myself in debt to a devil whose ledger ran longer than rail lines, whose ink was blood and silence. Clark's bargains were never even. He took more than he gave, and when he said "permanently," I wondered if he spoke not just of Cutter, but of me.

And so, I made my choice. The railroad would have to wait. To return there now would be to face too many ghosts. The dead could keep their silence; the living could not. Peggy and Walter were in San Francisco, flesh and blood, their letters still folded close to my heart. If I were to salvage anything of myself, it would be through them. I needed to see their faces, to hold fast to the fragile thread of family before it frayed beyond repair. The rails called me westward, not north, and I would answer.

*

The following afternoon, I boarded the Oregon Short Line at Butte's depot. The air was still bitter with copper smelter fumes, smoke hanging low over the gulch like a black veil. I carried no luggage save my satchel and the medallion Clark had pressed back into my palm—a token I could not decide was a gift, a warning, or a leash.

The train jolted forward, carrying me out of the city's clamor and into the wide-backed valleys of southwestern Montana. I leaned against the window, watching the mountains slide past in slow procession, and felt the strange paradox of escape. The rails carried me south past Dillon, then over Monida Pass, where snow lingered on the ridges. Night swallowed the train, and I stretched out in my berth, though rest never came easy.

By morning, the train skirted the Snake River plain, sage and volcanic soil stretching to the horizon. In the dining car, I drank coffee thick as tar while businessmen argued about copper shares. A teenage boy at the next table dropped his fork, and for a moment I saw Walter in his place—freckled and curious, though he had no idea I was on my way west. The thought of Peggy, too, waiting without knowing, stirred a sharper ache in me than any distance. Each mile carried me closer to the life I had left suspended, and to the questions I wasn't sure how to answer once I stood before her again.

At Pocatello, the train shifted onto new tracks, pressing south toward Ogden. The depot there was a storm of movement—soldiers crowding benches, families with trunks, porters darting like ants. I boarded the Southern Pacific express bound west, and with the clang of the bell came a realization colder than the mountain air: Clark hadn't merely spared me—he had armed me, or thought he had, with the very token others believed gave me sight beyond sight.

That puzzle kept me awake across Nevada's wastes. The desert stretched in monotonous rhythm—sage, mirage, dust—broken only by the whistle echoing off hotels in Winnemucca and Elko. At night, I turned the medallion over and over in my hand, its edges catching against my skin like a burr that wouldn't let go. If Clark truly believed it held power, why surrender it? Perhaps it was a test, waiting to see what I'd uncover. Perhaps it was leverage, tying me to a myth he could use when it suited him. Or maybe it was simply mockery, his way of reminding me who controlled the board. *I can give it back and still own you.*

The rails carried me into the Sierra Nevada by the third day, winding through snow sheds and over Donner Pass. Spruce crowded the slopes, streams flashed with meltwater, and the air carried a sharpness that felt like renewal. Beyond the mountains, California opened wide with orchards and green valleys. From Oakland, the ferry bore us across the bay, San Francisco rising through the fog like a vision—masts bristling along the waterfront, the new dome of City Hall gleaming above rebuilt streets.

The ferry nosed into the slip, lines tossed, gangway rattling down to the pier. Passengers pressed forward, eager for the city that rose out of the fog—its domes, spires, and masts tangled together like a promise. I kept to the edge, one hand brushing the outline of the letters in my coat pocket. Peggy's handwriting, Walter's uneven scrawl, and beneath them the return address: 214 Natoma Street, San Francisco, California.

They had no notion I was coming. Walter was a lanky and restless young man beginning to outgrow the letters he had once scrawled in an uneven hand. His words had grown sharper with each page, stitched through with stories of San Francisco—the bustle of Market Street, the clamor of ferries on the bay, the stray dog he swore followed him home from school for a week. Between the lines, I could sense his hunger for more, for life beyond the boundaries his mother tried to hold firm.

Peggy's steadier script tempered Walter's with news of rented rooms and long days. Her letters carried something unspoken—a restlessness of her own. She had written of plans to open a women's clothing store, using her maiden name—*Greenburg's*. The name stirred old memories, for it was not only hers by birth but the sign that once hung above her shop in Nome when we first met. Now she revived it in San Francisco, as if circling back to a part of herself that had never truly been mine to keep. Was it only practicality, a bid for independence in a city that allowed no easy foothold? Or was it a sign of something deeper, a turning I had yet to reckon with? Only ink on paper guided me now— their words, the return address written weeks ago from a home I had yet to find. The city was theirs for the moment, and I would have to seek it out—those narrow streets and shifting quarters where life carried on without me.

I stepped onto the pier with the crowd and pushed into the stream of Market Street. It surged with clanging streetcars, drays rattling over the cobbles, newsboys crying headlines about Europe and the border war with Mexico. The air smelled of salt and coal smoke, mingled with roasting chestnuts from a cart. Tall buildings, still new from the city's rebuilding, loomed above me, their glass and stone gleaming pale through the fog.

I walked east toward the heart of downtown, then turned south into the warren of smaller streets. Natoma lay hidden there, a narrow lane tucked between warehouses and boardinghouses, its buildings leaning close as if to share secrets. Laundry fluttered from second-story lines, and a piano tumbled notes from behind a saloon door. The city's grandeur fell away here, replaced by the hum of tenements and the grit of working families.

I slowed as I neared the number, my heart thudding harder than it had on any stretch of track from Montana to California. The medallion pressed cold against my chest, but in my pocket Peggy's letters burned with warmth. I had crossed mountains and deserts to reach this door, not knowing what welcome I would find—or what truths I would be forced to tell once I did.

CHAPTER THIRTY-TWO
FAMILY

The boardinghouse stood at the corner of a narrow street, its door painted blue but worn pale at the handle. My heart thudded like it had in my past before stepping into a ring. I knocked once, twice, and heard the shuffle of feet on bare wood.

The door opened.

Peggy stood framed in the threshold, apron dusted with flour, a streak of gray in her blonde hair I had not noticed before. For a moment, she only stared, as if I were a figure conjured out of some half-remembered dream. Then her hand flew to her mouth.

"Percy?"

I nodded, but words failed me.

Behind her, Walter appeared, taller than I remembered, his shoulders sloping like a man. His eyes widened, and then he was moving, pushing past his mother, throwing his arms around me with a force that nearly knocked the breath from my chest.

"Pops! You're here!"

The boy I had last seen standing on a pier was now nearly grown, his voice a low timbre, his cheekbones sharper, but his embrace was the same—unrestrained, full of all the love he had not been able to express in his letters.

Peggy found her voice at last. "Why didn't you write you were coming?"

"Because I needed to see you," I said, the words ragged with truth. "Both of you. I couldn't wait for another letter."

She let me in, and the three of us sat in their small kitchen, a kettle whistling low on the stove. It was nothing like the house we had once shared, but it was warm, lived in, theirs.

Walter launched into stories, his words tumbling over themselves—the schoolyard fights he had won, the odd jobs he had picked up along the docks, the characters he had met on the city streets. His energy filled the room, and I watched him with a kind of awe, realizing how much of his life had already slipped past me while I chased rail lines and reckonings.

Peggy listened, her hands folded in her lap, her eyes on me more than on Walter. There was distance there—something unspoken in the set of her jaw, in the way she did not reach for my hand. Yet when Walter leaned against her, she smoothed his hair without thinking, as she always had.

When his stories ebbed, silence pooled between us. I knew it was mine to break.

"I need to tell you what's happened," I began. "Since you left Hope."

And so I did. I told her and Walter of Eli—how he had died in my arms, his laughter cut short by Cutter's bullet. I told them of the sabotage that plagued the railroad, of the men who schemed in shadows to profit from its delay. I told them of the medallion that had once burned with strange life but had gone cold the moment I left the north, as though its power had no claim beyond that wild land.

Peggy's eyes darkened when I spoke Cutter's name, and Walter's fists clenched tight on the table.

"And Clark?" she asked softly.

I looked down at my hands. "I made a bargain with him. Cutter getting his due… in exchange for my silence."

The kettle shrieked then, and Peggy rose to take it off the flame.

Her back was to me when she said, "You've always carried too much on your shoulders, Percy. Always."

I wanted to protest, but Walter spoke first. "Let me help." His voice was steady, older than his years.

I looked at him, my son—lanky, restless, already half a man—and in his words I heard the truth I had been running from. All the justice, all the vengeance, all the bargains—they were dust compared to this. Family.

When Peggy turned back, her eyes were damp, though she tried to hide it. She set the kettle down and met my gaze squarely. For the first time in years, I felt something unbroken between us—frail, perhaps, but alive.

Whatever came next, whatever price Clark's ledger demanded, I knew what mattered now sat in that room: a woman who had once been my compass, a boy who still believed I could be his father.

And for the first time since Eli's death, since the medallion had gone silent, since Clark's cold hand had closed over mine, I felt the faintest spark of hope.

Peggy moved with practiced efficiency, setting bread on the table and ladling stew from a pot that smelled of onions, beef, and barley. It was a humble meal, yet I couldn't remember the last time I'd felt so grateful for a bowl of food.

Walter sat close, still keyed with excitement, peppering me with questions about Alaska. Did the snow already fall heavy in Hope? Were the bears still thick in the hills? Did the train truly climb mountains that no horse could ever manage?

I answered as best I could, letting the sound of his voice wash through me. He had grown into a boy who craved stories, not because he doubted them, but because they tied him to something larger. And though my heart ached for the things I had missed, I felt a thread binding us again—fragile but real.

Peggy's voice broke into my thoughts. "Are you hungry, Percy?"

The question carried more meaning than its words. I'd been eating, but she wasn't asking about food. I hadn't realized how long it had been since anyone had spoken to me with that kind of care—how long since Peggy had looked at me without anger or distance. A wave of emotion rose in my chest, sharp and sudden, and I found myself nodding before I trusted my voice.

She gave a small smile and moved about the kitchen, refilling our cups, adjusting the loaf of bread, her hands steady and sure. Walter passed her the salt without being told. There was a rhythm between them—quiet, familiar, the rhythm of a home I'd been gone from too long. To sit within it again felt like stepping into a room I'd once believed was locked to me forever.

For the first time in months, the tightness in my chest began to ease.

The rest of the meal passed in currents—Walter's eager talk, Peggy's measured silences, my attempt to bridge the time lost between us. It was not perfect. There were shadows at the edge of the table—the questions that had no easy answers. Yet beneath it all, I felt something stir.

Family, I thought. Not as it once was, nor perhaps as I once dreamed it. But here, alive, still within reach. The quiet that filled the room felt less like peace, more like the moment before a blade falls. Peggy stayed at the table, her hand resting on her cup, the lamplight flickering across her eyes. When she finally spoke, it was plain and direct.

"Why are you here, Percy?"

I held her gaze. "I came from Butte."

"That's not what I asked."

The air between us tightened, the quiet pressing in. I drew a breath, heavy as a stone in my chest.

"I needed to see you, Peggy. To speak with you. To know if there was still something worth saving. This family. If I lose that, none of the rest matters."

Her silence was sharper than words, a weight I could barely bear. Walter shifted beside me, his young face tense with questions he didn't yet know how to voice.

At last Peggy said, "You've been gone a long time. And whatever you've carried back with you, it isn't just yours anymore. It touches us, too."

I lowered my eyes. Whatever bargains I'd struck, whatever shadows still followed me, they had crossed this threshold with me tonight.

But so had something else. A chance, however fragile, to be more than the man I had become.

Peggy's expression did not soften; if anything, it sharpened, the lamplight turning her face into something carved, unyielding.

"So you've come back to us muzzled. You've traded your voice for his leash."

I swallowed, the truth tasting of iron. "A devil's pact, yes."

"And left you half a man," she said coldly, her words striking harder than Clark's threats ever had. The air between us tightened, filled with all the years unsaid.

Then, after a pause, her tone shifted—not softening, but deepening, as if some hidden well within her had broken open.

"If Clark bound your pen, then write around the binding. Tell the truth without naming him. Let the world see the shadow he casts without ever speaking his name. You've always known how to strip a lie bare, Percy—use that gift. Do it again. This time, let the silence accuse him."

Her hand, pale in the lamplight, pressed against the table as if anchoring her words to the wood. Her eyes—clear, unwavering—bore into mine. "Don't you see? It was never the railroad alone. It was never just the medallion. It's Walter. It's us. You can't save your family by striking bargains with men like Clark. You save us by refusing to let him own your voice."

The words came like prophecy, cutting through the fog I had carried from Alaska to Butte and back again. I felt them settle into me, heavier than any pact, brighter than any promise.

She leaned closer, her voice lower but burning with conviction. "You stand at a threshold, Percy. Either you keep drifting—Clark's man, a ghost of yourself—or you step fully into the life you were meant for. A father who cannot be bought. A man whose words still carry truth. Do that, and Walter will know what kind of man his father is. Fail, and he'll learn that every man has his price."

Her challenge struck deeper than Clark's threats, deeper than Cutter's violence. This wasn't about railroads or empires anymore. It was about the choice across the table—the family I had lost, the family I still longed to save.

CHAPTER THIRTY-THREE
LOOKING HOPEFUL

The words circled in my mind like gulls above the bay: *Tell the truth without naming him.* Peggy had given me the path, though it was no less perilous than the one I'd already walked. If Clark demanded silence, I would give him shadows. Not lies, not omissions—but the kind of truth that slipped through the cracks, light spilling in where no man's hand could stop it.

I thought of Eli, of the others—men maimed, men buried beneath timber and stone—all for the sake of profit. Their stories would not wear Clark's name, but the pattern would be there for anyone with eyes to see. The shape of the hand behind the curtain, the ledger inked in blood and coin. Perhaps justice would never be clean. Perhaps it never was. But if words were weapons, then my pencil remained sharper than any blade.

Peggy said nothing. Her silence was not absence but presence, heavy as the tide pressing against the pilings down by the wharf. She sat stiffly, hands folded in her lap, knuckles pale against the lamplight. In that small tension—the twist of her fingers, the tight line of her shoulders—I could feel the storm she held back. She had heard speeches from me before, excuses dressed as convictions. But this, this was no performance. The words came raw, stripped of ornament, my chest lay open before her.

Her eyes did not soften. They measured me instead, as though weighing a coin in the palm: the face of the man she had once loved against the man I had become. For years, I had tried to win her with promises, and for years she had watched those promises collapse like rotted timbers under too much weight. Tonight, I did not promise. I confessed. I admitted the shadows I carried and the bargain that had nearly broken me. And in that admission, something shifted.

The lamplight flickered, and in it, I thought I saw her shoulders slacken by the smallest measure. Her gaze, still steady, held mine long enough to make my throat tighten. When she finally spoke, her voice was even, but beneath it I heard the quiver of something fragile, something alive.

"With spring coming," she said, "Walter and I could return with you. To Hope."

The words struck like a hammer to the chest. For a moment, I could not breathe. I had braced myself for refusal, for the cold edge of finality that would leave us scattered in separate worlds. Instead, she had offered me a door—a narrow one, yes, but a door nonetheless—where I had expected only a wall.

Hope. The name tolled in me like a bell. Not just a settlement stitched to the rails, not just a speck on the map, but the promise of a life I had nearly let slip from my hands. Return with you. To Hope. Each word bore the weight of something greater than geography: a family gathered, a marriage salvaged, the chance to stitch torn fabric back together before it frayed beyond repair.

I looked across the table at her, the light setting a steel glint in her eyes, and understood how much it had cost her to speak those words aloud. She was not surrendering. She was risking. Risking her heart, her son's trust, her own battered faith that I could still be the man she once believed in.

The silence stretched long, but it was no longer heavy. It was fragile, like the hush after the first crack of ice in spring, when the river prepares to break free. My pulse drummed in my ears. I wanted to speak, to promise I would not fail her again—but I bit down on the urge. Words had undone us before. Better to let this one moment breathe, unspoiled.

And so I held her gaze, the distance between us narrowing not by declaration but by simple, steady truth. For the first time in years, the chasm felt less like an ending and more like a bridge. I lingered there, in the quiet warmth of that possibility, afraid to move lest the moment fracture.

The room around us seemed to fall away. All that remained was the rhythm of her breath, the faint tremor of my heartbeat, and the fragile promise of a home waiting in Hope.

*

Later, I walked with Walter down to Fisherman's Wharf. The pilings groaned beneath the weight of tide and ice, gulls shrieking overhead. Walter's boots scuffed along beside mine, his pockets stuffed with folded scraps of paper, filled with his thoughts and imagination. He was a lanky boy, all elbows and knees that hadn't yet caught up with his height, his blond hair falling into his eyes whenever the wind caught it. His coat hung loose on his frame, as if he'd grown too quickly for his mother to keep pace with the mending.

"You've been writing," I said.

He nodded, eyes fixed on the horizon. "Not news stories. Not like you. I want to tell about the wilderness—the rivers, the mountains, the things nobody notices but should." He hesitated, then added, "Jack London wrote like that. He's my favorite. The way he makes the wild feel alive—it's what I want to do."

I stopped, watching the earnestness burning in his eyes. "Jack London, you say?"

Walter looked over, puzzled. "You've read him too?"

"I did more than that," I said quietly. "I met him. I knew him. Years ago, when I was a little but older than you, hungry to make my way with words. We became friends. He edited my first novel—*A Summer of Hope.*"

Walter froze, his mouth falling open. "You… you knew Jack London? And he—he worked on your book?"

I nodded, the memory stirring like an ember long banked. "He showed me that words could carry not just stories, but whole worlds. He challenged me, pushed me, the way a river drives a boat forward, whether you're ready or not."

Walter let out a breath that was half laugh, half wonder. His thin shoulders lifted as though the weight of the world had shifted into possibility. "That's incredible. To think you sat with Jack London…"

I laid a hand on his shoulder. The boy was still all bone under his coat, but the fire inside him made him feel sturdier than most men. "Then write, Walter. Write the rivers, the mountains, the wilderness you see. Ink can outlast stone—Jack showed me that. Now I'm showing you."

His grip tightened on the scraps of paper in his pocket as though they'd suddenly turned to treasure. I let the silence rest between us a moment, then added, "We'll be heading back to Hope soon. The railroad runs a good way both north and south from Portage, carving through country most folks will never set eyes on. If your mother would allow it, you could ride with me. See it for yourself. It might give you more stories than you can fit in a dozen notebooks."

Walter's eyes widened, the tide-light flickering across them like the first spark of a fire. "Ride the railroad… with you?"

"Yes," I said, feeling a warmth in my chest I hadn't expected. "There's no better classroom than the wilderness itself. London would have told you the same."

"You've been on the railroad, then?" he asked suddenly, his voice brimming with a mix of disbelief and hunger.

"I have," I answered.

"What was it like?" he pressed, eyes locked on me. "The engines— are they as loud as everyone says? Did you ride all the way into the mountains? Were there bears along the tracks? And the tunnels—did you go through any? How dark was it? Could you hear the timbers creak above you?"

His questions tumbled out in a rush, one tripping over the next, until I laughed and raised a hand to slow him. "Easy, Walter. One at a time."

But he couldn't stop—he was aflame with it. "Did you see the men building it? The bridges over rivers? The places where avalanches fall? What about the workers—were they tough, like the ones in London's stories? Did you ever…" His breath caught. "Did you ever feel like you were part of something no one else would believe unless they saw it themselves?"

I let the sea wind fill the pause before I answered. "Yes," I said at last. "All of that, and more. The engines shake the earth when they pass, like thunder rolling through your bones. I've watched men drive spikes into frozen ground with hands blistered raw, and I've seen them sing while they did it, just to keep the cold from swallowing them whole. I've felt the tunnels close around me, black as the inside of a coffin, then burst out into sunlight so bright it stung my eyes. And I've known the danger—the cliffs that give way, the snow that buries camps, the rivers that rise up to swallow trestles whole."

Walter's mouth had fallen open, the sea spray clinging to his lashes. "And you'll take me there?"

"If your mother allows," I said again, softer this time, though I felt Peggy's presence behind us like a steadying hand. "You'll see it for yourself. Not in a story, not in the pages of a book—but with your own eyes."

He drew in a sharp breath, as if he were already aboard, already hearing the whistle echo through the valleys. The boy he had been only moments before seemed to give way to something larger—an heir not just to my blood, but to the restless calling I had carried all my life.

CHAPTER THIRTY-FOUR
ONE MONTH LATER

We came home to Hope with the sound of gulls in our ears and salt crusted on our coats from the voyage north. A month gone, though it felt longer. Three weeks in San Francisco, a steamship to Seward, the train to Portage, and at last a wagon jolting over rutted roads into the valley where the mountains leaned close.

The town had not changed, not in the ways that mattered. The Hope General Store still greeted customers with a bell that stuck on a half-ring, the dock still shouldered the same tired ropes, fit only for skiffs and rowboats, never the steamers that had to anchor far out in Cook Inlet. Down at the creek, a handful of gold panners still knelt in the shallows, stubborn as ever, coaxing glimmers from the gravel. Patches of snow still clung in the shadows where the sun had not yet found them, reminders that winter's grip was not so far behind. The wind still ran long and low over Turnagain Arm as if carrying a message to mountains farther on.

After the clangor of trains, the stink of coal bunkers, and the press of strangers, the narrowness of Hope soothed us, its familiar rhythm wrapping close, as if it had been waiting all along for our return.

San Francisco had been all noise and appetite, and nowhere more than the *Examiner*. The newsroom roared like a boiler room at full steam—typewriters clattering, presses shaking the floor beneath our boots, copy boys darting like sparrows between desks. The air smelled of ink and sweat and coffee gone bitter on the stove. Every man seemed to have ink on his cuffs, smoke on his breath, and desperation in his voice, as though each sentence might be the one to keep him employed another day.

I took Walter there, let him breathe that heat and racket. He stood straighter than usual, chin lifted, as if posture alone might earn him a place among them. His notebook bulged from his pocket like contraband he didn't quite dare pull out. I caught the hunger in his eyes as he studied the walls plastered with broadsides—war headlines, railroad strikes, scandal sheets—each pinned up like a battle flag.

My editor spotted us from across the room and lumbered over, a square man with a baritone like a struck drum. He flicked his gaze from me to Walter. "This him?"

"This is my son, Walter," I said, pride slipping into my voice before I could check it.

The man grunted—his version of approval—then waved me toward his office. Walter followed at my heel, quiet but alert, eyes raking over the cluttered desks, the sheaves of paper stacked like barricades, the smell of ambition so thick it seemed to stick in your throat.

Inside, the editor wasted no time. "What have you got on the railroad?"

I gave him the bones of it: the frozen ground, the crews hammering spikes until their hands split, the accidents that left men buried in timber and stone. My voice kept to fact, to rhythm, but I trimmed away mention of Copper King Clark, trimmed away the truths that would have scorched the page if I'd let them through.

"Sabotage?" he pressed, eyes narrowing.

"In the air," I said carefully, "but nothing I can print."

The lie tasted of river ice—cold, heavy, and alive against my tongue. I had a name enough to burn a city, but I held it, even as my editor leaned back, dissatisfied. Walter's eyes flicked toward me at the word sabotage, bright and sharp, hungry for more.

The editor tapped his pen against the desk. "Readers don't want smoke, Hope. They want fire. They want names they can spit at over breakfast. You can't sell them shadows."

"I won't give them what I don't have in hand," I replied, steady as I could manage.

He studied me for a beat, then snorted. "Fine. But bring me something solid next time—or don't bring me at all."

We left the office to the clang of typewriters and the shouts of copy boys, the whole room beating like a single restless heart. Walter kept close, his silence as taut as a bowstring until we reached the stairwell. Then, in a rush, the questions came.

"Who would sabotage a railroad? Why? Was it the miners? The company? Is it dangerous to ride? Have you seen it happen?" His eyes searched me as though I carried the whole truth in my pocket, waiting to be unwrapped.

I stopped him on the stairwell, laid a hand on the railing, and turned to face him. "There are men, Walter, who would rather see iron rust than progress roll forward. Some for money, some for power, some because they can't stomach change. But none of that's for the *Examiner*'s front page—not yet."

He frowned, unsatisfied, but I saw the spark there, the way he weighed every word, every omission. For a moment, I saw myself at his age—hungry, restless, desperate to wrestle meaning from the world's chaos.

"Will you ever tell me the whole of it?" he asked.

I held his gaze, the din of the newsroom fading behind us. "When the time's right. And when I do, you'll know what to do with it."

For a time, neither of us spoke. The clamor of typewriters and shouting editors gave way, in memory, to the sound of gulls. By the time our feet found the wharf again, San Francisco's thunder already felt like a dream—a brief flare of heat before the long cool stretch north.

*

The sea carried us after that. The steamship throbbed beneath our boots, decks slick with salt spray, the stacks smearing the sky with coal smoke. Walter lived at the rail, hair blown wild, plying me with questions as the coast unrolled like a chart. He pointed to distant headlands and asked if saboteurs might strike there; to fishing boats, wondering if they too kept

302

secrets; even to the lighthouse beams sweeping the fog, asking if light itself could be trusted. I answered what I could, parried what I must, watching his mind leap like sparks across the water.

Peggy, for her part, kept a quieter vigil. She leaned against the rail not far from Walter, a scarf tied close about her hair, her eyes narrowed against the spray. She smiled at his questions but rarely interrupted, as though letting him gather the world for himself. Yet when his voice ran too fast, she'd lay a hand on his sleeve, a gentle ballast to keep him from tipping too far into his own excitement. Sometimes she caught my gaze over his shoulder, and in that look were both pride and worry—pride for the boy's fire, worry for where it might one day lead him.

At night, bundled against the cold, Walter trailed me along the deck where men smoked and swapped stories, his ears pricked for every scrap of adventure. Peggy stayed closer to the cabin, a book in her lap she scarcely read, glancing up whenever we passed as if to be sure we were still tethered to her. I saw the hunger in Walter—the same hunger that had once carried me from Hope to San Francisco, from youth to the long road of ink and trouble.

The voyage was no mere passage; it was a slow unwinding of city fever, each mile northward a loosening. By the time the Alaskan coast began to lift itself from the horizon, even Walter grew quiet, his questions trailing off into silence as he stared at the endless sweep of mountains. Peggy slipped her arm through mine then, and for a rare moment, all three of us stood together in stillness, listening to the sea as though it might tell us what waited at journey's end.

By the time we boarded the train at Seward, spring had come to Alaska. Rivers boiled with melt, mountains gleamed under their white crowns, and every spruce breathed again. Walter pressed his face to the glass, his breath fogging the pane as though he could will himself closer to the landscape rushing past. He called out what he saw, his voice quick and eager—ridges bristling with spruce, glaciers tumbling like frozen rivers from the heights, the huts of workers standing like scars against the raw earth. Each sight seemed to strike him with the force of revelation.

When the train shrieked around a bend and opened onto a broad valley, Walter let out a cry that drew smiles from the other passengers. "Look, Pops! It's like the mountains are moving with us!" His fingers flew across the pages of his notebook, sketching peaks in rough lines, jotting words in a scrawl that could hardly keep pace with his thoughts. He bounced in his seat whenever the whistle blew, the sound echoing against stone walls and sending ravens skyward.

At Portage, where the train slowed to cross the flats, he craned to see the grand sweep of water shimmering beneath the ice, his eyes wide as though it were the edge of the world itself. I watched him drink it all in, the boy's wonder outpacing even the locomotive's steel drive.

We hired a wagon there and set our faces toward Hope. The road jolted our bones and sent the dust up in clouds, but Walter didn't mind.

His notebook lay open on his knees, already filled with a hundred impressions. He tapped his pencil against the page, thoughtful, then grinned at me.

"It doesn't feel like we're going back," he said, his voice steady with conviction. "It feels like we're beginning."

When at last we stepped through our own door, Peggy moved ahead of us, setting down her satchel as though she had never left. She had baked before we left San Francisco—nothing grand, just a pan of bread carried all the way north, its husky sweetness still clinging to the air of the room. She unwrapped it now, the crust hardened by travel but fragrant, filling the house with something gentler than the sea.

I shrugged off my coat and felt, absurdly, that I had returned a decade older instead of a month. Peggy brushed the flour dust from her hands—hands a little chapped, winter's old proof. When I reached for her, she didn't turn away. I kissed the backs of those hands, then her cheek, and she allowed it—no speeches, no ledgers, just a breath that left her shoulders and did not come back tense. Walter, already nosing through his pack, glanced up and grinned at us, as if the voyage had reset something none of us had the words to name.

*

The next few days were built from small distances, small repairs. I fixed the sticky latch on the back door; she mended a cuff I'd torn. I found I could make her laugh by telling the truth plain, without performance. She poured the kettle and slid my mug across the table without looking, the way she always had, like a ferry sending its one passenger home. At night, with the lamp between us, the light gilded her hair and showed the fine lines around her eyes. I did not pretend not to see them. She caught me looking and tilted her face so the light could do its work. Once, I had loved her for her fire. Now I found I loved her for the embers—steady, useful, warm.

Walter filled the house with paper, as though words were a kind of tide spilling into every corner. He wrote at the table, on the porch rail, on his knees in the yard—each page an earnest struggle with the world, raw and unshaped but alive. I didn't correct so much as keep him company, watching him wrestle his sentences into form. "Find a thing you can touch," I told him. "Start there. The reader will follow your hand." Sometimes his brow knotted, then smoothed again as if a cloud had shifted. We argued gently over verbs—he wanted stride and swagger, the kind Jack London had fed him in *The Call of the Wild* and *White Fang*. I nudged him back toward the plain truth of what he saw. "A gull doesn't 'plunge dagger-like' unless you've seen a dagger do it. Watch it. How does it really move?"

So we watched gulls wheel over the wharf, a fox test the chicken crate, the tide slipping loose and tucking itself back into its sleeve. He tried out "tilts," then crossed it out, then "angles," then added "true." I said nothing, only let the word sit between us, feeling a gladness far too large for the moment.

Some afternoons, we walked down to where Resurrection Creek emptied into the Arm. Once he said, half daring me, "Jack London would've told me to get lost in the woods for a week before writing a word." I smiled. "London would've told you to freeze your feet off and call it research. You don't need frostbite, Walter. You need patience." He bent to trace the tide's fine chevrons in the gravel, sketching them as though they held a secret. "They look like language," he said.

"They are," I answered. "Everything is, if you're willing to translate."

At supper, Peggy listened to Walter's stories, her hands laced, her eyes intent as if she were in church. His words carried more weight than length. One began with the bay's pull making tiny rivers in the flats and ended with a fox's track stitched into the margin. In that line, I heard something that was not mine. It pleased and frightened me equally—the good teachers hope to be outgrown, but dread the moment it begins. When Walter finished, Peggy clapped once, startled by her own sound. "I'm sorry," she laughed. "It surprised me." Walter flushed, grinning, and I reached across the table to smudge ink from his knuckle. "You've got it," I said. "Keep going."

By the month's end, the three of us were whole enough to be ordinary. I mended the handle of her pot and built a shelf for jars in the pantry. I patched Walter's window with oiled paper and promised to replace it with the glass pane I ordered from Russel. We read aloud in the evenings from a spine-sprung *White Fang*. On Sundays, we took our meal to the porch and watched belugas rolling where the light changed.

Walter tried to hide his wonder, then bent over his notebook. His pencil scratched quickly across the page until he pushed it toward me, cheeks flushed. The words were plain, yet they carried the curve of the sea-creatures as if etched in frost:

"They rose like white hills from the dark water, slow and certain, as if the tide itself obeyed their will. Their backs shone like glass beneath the sun, each roll a breathing mountain that broke the silence of the bay. I thought they would vanish, but they circled back, as if to say the sea was theirs and always would be."

One night, he fell asleep in a chair with his pencil still in his hand. I eased it away. Peggy covered him with a blanket and stood with her hand in his hair, not petting, only resting there.

Watching them, I understood that all my grand ideas—justice, myth, what a man owes the truth—mattered because of this and only this.

I banked the stove, blew out the lamp. The house breathed, timbers settling. Outside, the tide took an inch of shore and gave it back. Peggy's foot found mine in the dark. I didn't move it away. Hope held. For that month, it was enough.

And yet, when all had gone still, my thoughts returned to the medallion—silent, waiting. It seemed to breathe with the timbers, to shift with the tide, holding its breath with the night itself, as if listening for an hour not yet come.

CHAPTER THIRTY-FIVE
FAREWELL

The spring of 1916 loosened the ice around Hope, though the mountains still clung to their heavy crowns of white. The thaw brought mud to the streets and the smell of spruce sap on the wind, as if the land itself were stirring awake. Yet for me, there was no rest. Mother's words lingered: *You've been summoned.*

I could not ignore them. The medallion pressed against my chest like a whisper I could not silence, reminding me at every moment that my journey was no longer just about ink and headlines.

Peggy knew it before I spoke a word. She watched me fold my shirts into the satchel, her arms crossed, her expression unreadable.

"So it's true," she said at last. "You're leaving again."

I paused, the weight of her voice heavier than the satchel itself. "I have to, Peg. There's something waiting for me beyond these rails, something I can't turn away from."

Behind her, Walter stood in the doorway, fists balled at his sides. "I'm coming with you," he blurted.

Peggy spun on him. "Absolutely not."

"You promised!" Walter's voice cracked, a boy's fury colliding with a man's determination. "You said I could come when the thaw came. You said it, Pops!"

His words struck me harder than any blow. I made that promise.

"Walter," I said carefully, "the trail I'm walking now isn't fit for you. It's not the rails, or the camps, or even the men—it's something else. Something older and stranger. I can't risk you to it."

I folded another shirt, and beneath it lay the Colt that Marlowe had pressed into my hands back in Talkeetna. I slid it into the satchel among the clothes, its cold weight hidden but not forgotten. The pistol lay there like a secret coiled in the dark, whispering of the dangers waiting ahead.

Walter's face flushed with hurt. "You think I can't handle it. That I'll just slow you down."

Peggy's hand settled on his shoulder. "You're just a boy, Walter. Your place is here. With me."

He jerked away from her touch and stormed out, leaving only the slam of the door behind him.

That night, I hardly slept, listening to the creek rush in the thaw and the silence that pressed between Peggy and me. By morning, the decision was made. I kissed her cheek, lingering on the warmth of her skin, and whispered, "I'll come back."

She gave me nothing in return—not a word, not even a look. Only the knowledge that she had seen this before, and she would not forgive it again.

*

The train to Anchorage hissed and steamed, its black iron bulk crouched like some great beast about to leap. I boarded with my satchel, the whistle shrieking overhead, and found a seat by the window. As the cars lurched forward, the Portage station slipped behind, swallowed by spruce and shadow.

I tried to settle into the rhythm of the rails, but my mind bucked against it. Peggy's silence as I kissed her goodbye wasn't a mystery to me—I knew that silence well. It was the same cold stillness she wore when she once took Walter and left for San Francisco. Back then, I had promised never again, never to abandon her. Yet here I was, breaking that vow with every mile of track that unspooled beneath me.

She was angry; there was no doubt. The stiffness in her shoulders, the way she clutched Walter to her side, told me plain enough. And I deserved every bit of it.

My heart longed to stay in Hope, but the story—the story—was not there. It lay beyond the mountains, tied to forces older than marriage or ink on newsprint. Magnus Vega's shadow, long after death, still curled through Alaska like smoke that refused to dissipate. Sha-e-dah-kla's voice, the Tyonek shaman who once opened my ears to the land, still echoed in me, warning that *the earth remembers.* And always there was the medallion, dormant yet alive in its waiting—a raven etched in silver that seemed to breathe with the tide, a key I scarcely understood.

A fool, perhaps, to chase these threads while Peggy shouldered the burden of keeping our house whole. But even I knew the story wasn't finished in Hope. Something vast was stirring, and I was bound to follow it.

Lost in this tangle of thoughts, I hardly noticed the sway of the car or the dim shuffle of movement nearby—until a shadow fell across me.

I looked up.

Walter.

His cap was pulled low, his satchel clutched to his chest, but the fire in his eyes gave him away. He slid into the seat across from me before I could speak.

"I told you," he said, breathless but defiant. "I'm coming."

For a moment, I only stared. "What in God's name—"

He leaned forward, words tumbling out as if rehearsed. "I climbed into the wagon before you left—hid under the tarp with the crates. When you weren't looking, I slipped off at Portage and snuck onto the train." He patted his pocket, a faint jingle answering. "I've got enough for a ticket."

"Did you leave a note for your mother?" I asked.

Walter blinked, the fire in his eyes dimming a fraction. "No," he said, swallowing. "I didn't... I didn't think of that."

I rubbed my temples, feeling the strain of it all pressing in. Peggy. What must she be thinking at this very moment? Standing in the doorway, realizing her son was gone, her husband vanished again, the two of us run off on rails that stretched into God-knows-what. The thought made my stomach turn.

"You're a fool," I muttered at last, though my voice lacked heat. The truth was clear: the boy was here, and nothing short of throwing him from the train would change it.

Walter's jaw tightened, his eyes lit with the same restless fire that had driven me north all those years ago. I saw not a child but a reflection of myself at that age—stubborn, unyielding, unwilling to be left behind.

I sat back, exhaling sharply. "Anchorage. We'll send a wire to your mother from Anchorage. She needs to know where you are, and she'll have my hide for letting it come to this."

Walter didn't flinch. "So be it. But I'm not turning back."

I shook my head, already calculating. I'd have to put him on the next train south to Portage, maybe find someone I trusted to see him safely back to Hope. It was the only sensible course.

Yet the rails sang beneath us, steady and unyielding, carrying us both toward Anchorage and whatever waited beyond.

*

Anchorage was raw and restless, smoke from cookfires curling over the low roofs of Tent City, the clang of hammers carrying long into the night. The moment we stepped from the train, I led Walter straight to the telegraph office. Inside, the air smelled of oil and damp wood, and the brass key clacked briskly as the operator tapped out my message.

Walter safe. Found me on train. He will stay with me. I'll keep him safe.

314

I handed the slip across the counter and turned away, heart thudding like a man standing before judgment. There would be no undoing this. Peggy would rage when she read it, but her anger was a problem for another day. Turning back now would cost me time I didn't have. Better to take Walter forward, let him learn the world for himself—Jack London style—an education not found in any schoolhouse.

But before I stepped away, the operator called after me.

"Wire come through for you, Mister Hope. Just arrived."

He handed me a folded slip. The words were spare, each one pressed into the paper with urgency:

PROCEED TO HURRICANE GULCH. MEET ME AT SURVEY CAMP. YOUR INSIGHT REQUIRED – F. MEARS

I read it twice, the letters striking harder than the telegraph's brass key. Hurricane Gulch—the engineers' nightmare, the place where the rails threatened to falter. And Mears, of all men, asking for me. The name alone sent me backward in time. The last I'd stood there was with Eli, both of us staring down into that raw wound of the earth, the carved chasm stretching like the mouth of some ancient beast. We had marveled at the sheer audacity of men who believed they could bridge it, and in our awe, there was a kind of reverence—stone, water, and time stacked against the thin will of humanity.

Walter walked beside me as we stepped back into the street, his eyes wide at the clamor of Tent City. He didn't speak, not at first. Then, with a grin that broke through the boy's stubborn scowl, he said, "So I get to stay?"

"You get to stay, for now," I answered. "But be aware that you'll see things, Walter—things that'll scar some men. But they will be yours to carry."

He straightened at that, shoulders squaring as if I'd handed him a uniform.

We reboarded the train, the whistle splitting the night, and as the cars lurched forward, I caught his reflection in the window. No longer sulking, but restless, eager, the way a young wolf scents the trail ahead.

I said nothing more, only watched him observing the world rush past, knowing this journey would shape him as much as it would test me.

The train groaned northward, its iron wheels biting into new-laid rails. Sixty miles of track stretched behind us now, gleaming in the moonlight like a silver vein stitched into the wild.

Another hundred miles had been graded, the earth carved and leveled in anticipation of steel. Crews had cleared right-of-way for more than two hundred miles, hacking spruce and birch down to stumps, and the rock cuts had begun in earnest—blasting stone from the mountainside to carve a passage toward Fairbanks. Even in the darkness, I felt the hum of industry under us, a great machine of men and iron clawing its way north.

About twenty minutes later, Walter dozed off beside me, his head pressed against the rattling window, lips parted in a boy's untroubled sleep. His satchel lay across his knees, one hand draped over it as though it held more than shirts and a knife—it held his claim to manhood.

I envied his ease. My own mind was a restless tide.

Magnus's voice still lingered, that sorrowful warning carried out of the mist: spikes sinking into living flesh, rivers pulsing like wounds. A land bleeding beneath the weight of progress. He had bartered with shadows once, and now his spirit recoiled against the same forces of steel and fire being driven into Alaska's heart.

But then there was Sha-e-dah-kla, whose words bore not accusation but remembrance. He urged me onward, to see the rails not as scars but as bridges—spanning not only rivers but the chasms that divided men from wisdom, fear from freedom. His was a call to proceed, but with reverence.

And beyond them both, a third presence pressed cold against my chest: the medallion. It was no trinket of chance, but the Tyonek's trust, placed in my keeping. Its raven wings seemed to stir faintly with the rhythm of the rails, as if the land itself breathed through it. More than once, it had granted me knowledge when no mortal wit could prevail—insight enough to unravel problems that should have broken men and halted progress. But its gift had a cost. It had marked me, drawn enemies into my path, and brought death to Eli when Cutter hunted it for himself.

Three voices, all contending for my soul: Magnus's grief, Sha-e-dah-kla's counsel, and the medallion's summons—the Tyonek's inheritance, pulsing with their memory and their demand.

And yet a fourth shadow haunted me: Walter's letter. The boy had drawn, without knowing why, the same jagged mark I'd seen in the caves—a circle split by a fracture, three lines beneath. He had never stood in that ice, never traced its frostbitten walls, yet his sketch matched as if copied.

The train pressed on into the night, smoke trailing like a black banner. Each mile carried us deeper into a story older than either of us could grasp. I watched my son's face, still soft with boyhood, and dread curled inside me like a hidden ember.

Was I guiding Walter toward manhood, or toward the same reckoning that Magnus waited to claim? And if the medallion had already chosen him, what power on earth—or beneath it—could turn it aside?

CHAPTER THIRTY-SIX
HURRICANE GULCH

Peggy's face haunted me still—the stiffness in her shoulders, the silence that spoke louder than any words. I had left her once more, and now Walter had slipped from her grasp as well. No apology or wire could mend what she must be feeling, watching both husband and son vanish on the same rails. The guilt pressed hard, yet it was too late for regret. The boy was here beside me, stubborn as I once was, and for our safety, the track ahead demanded my attention.

For beyond the ache of home lay something greater. Mears had called me north, asked for my presence at Hurricane Gulch—the place where the railroad met its most formidable test. A gorge so wide and deep that even seasoned engineers faltered at its edge. They had theodolites—tripod-mounted scopes for measuring horizontal and vertical angles—and tables of figures, but no clear solution. And so, the chief engineer of the Alaska Railroad had sent for me.

The train labored up the grade toward Broad Pass, iron wheels shrieking against the climb, steam drifting in ragged gusts across the mountain wind. The spruce thinned, giving way to a wide sweep of tundra, the white silence stretching out like a shroud.

Broad Pass.

The name alone pressed upon my chest. I had been here before, with Eli at my side. He had shivered at the emptiness, eyes darting to the slopes as if expecting the mountains themselves to close in. *"This place feels wrong,"* he had whispered. *"Like we're standing in the middle of something we're not supposed to see."*

He was right. That night in the cabin, when the wind clawed the roof beams and the stove glowed faintly against the dark, the vision had come. A voice rising from the abyss of my sleep, carrying me west into the ice caves under Denali.

Now, as the train climbed again through that same desolate corridor, the memory of Eli's breath in the cold air and the echo of Magnus's voice pressed close. He was gone, shot in the chest over the medallion, yet Broad Pass reminded me that death would never be enough to silence him.

I closed my eyes, the whistle cutting across the tundra like a blade. *You were right, Eli,* I thought. *We were standing in the middle of something we were not supposed to see. And I fear I am still standing there now.*

By afternoon we reached the survey camp at Hurricane Gulch, where men wrestled with the measure of the impossible. The train carried us as far as the graded line allowed, just beyond Broad Pass, where the rails ended in a jumble of ties and gravel waiting for more steel. From there, Walter and I hired a horse and wagon, joining a teamster who hauled supplies north across the thawing track bed. The road was rough and rutted, cut with pools of meltwater, and more than once the wheels sank to the hubs before the horses strained us free. Each mile was a reminder that steel had not yet conquered this country—it still bowed to mud, frost, and distance.

The approach to the gulch announced itself long before we saw it: the wagon tilted along the blasted cuts, sheer granite crowding us on one side, empty air dropping away on the other. The wind picked up, sharp with the bite of snowmelt, and the earth itself trembled with the river below. Sound carried strangely here—our driver's shouts to the horses broke apart and scattered, as though even words couldn't cross the void ahead. Walter clung to the seat beside me, his silence matching my own as the trail bent toward the edge.

And then it opened.

The gulch yawned beneath us like a wound carved by ice and centuries, half a mile wide and three hundred feet deep. The river at its bottom flashed silver in the weak light, thrashing itself white against hidden boulders, its roar muted only by distance. Sheer granite walls plunged like cleavers into the torrent, their faces black and slick, while spruce clung to impossible ledges with roots twisted like knuckles gripping bone. Down in the throat of it, the wind rose in a constant moan, carrying flecks of ice and spray that stung the skin even at the rim.

Walter stood beside me, pale but alight with a strange fire. His breath caught as he leaned forward, peering into the abyss. "They're going to build a bridge here?"

"They'll have to," I said. "The rails can't climb or turn back. It's forward or nothing."

Surveyors crept across the rim, stringing lines, sighting through brass transits. They muttered of piers, girders, spans, and stresses—words heavy with numbers but light against the scale of the chasm.

Then the medallion stirred.

It thrummed through me like the pluck of a hidden string, a note that lingered in the bones more than the ears. The gulch, the river, the mountains themselves shifted in my sight—not chaos, not threat, but harmony.

Without meaning to, I murmured, "It's already here…"

Walter tugged at my sleeve. "What is, Pops?"

I realized I had spoken aloud, my hand sketching spirals in the air. He followed the motion, squinting at the empty space between spruce and stone.

"It's a pattern," I told him. "Do you see how the trees climb the wall? How each branch turns, never at random, but just so? Even the gulch itself widens by the same measure. It's the same in the curl of a shell on the beach, or the way a flower seeds itself. Nature builds by law, not chance."

Walter blinked, still searching the gulch as if the lines might reveal themselves to him too. "So… if the builders don't follow it—"

"They'll fail," I said quietly. "But if they listen, the bridge is already waiting in the stone and river. All they must do is uncover it."

Shouts rose from the camp below. A knot of engineers crowded around a long table where maps were weighted with stones against the wind. Their arguments carried up the gulch like hammer blows.

"The piers will never anchor!" one man barked. "We'll be throwing steel into the void!"

"It can be done," another retorted. "Shorten the center span and brace the ends against granite!"

"Shorten it," a third growled, "and the girders won't carry the load. Do you want two hundred men plunged into the river?"

Their voices clashed like steel on steel, and for a moment, the bridge seemed no more than a fever dream.

"We need numbers, not guesses!" he barked. "A miscalculation here will cost lives, not just timbers. This is no place for bravado."

I leaned close to Walter. "That's Frederick Mears," I whispered, nodding toward the man at the table. "The railroad's chief engineer. Without him, none of this would be more than lines on paper."

Mears looked up then, scanning the rim, his gaze sweeping over the surveyors and laborers standing idle at the edge. When his eyes locked on mine, a flicker of recognition crossed his face. To my astonishment, he raised his voice across the wind.

"Hope! The Wizard of Hope—come down here!"

Walter tugged at my sleeve, his voice quick and sharp. "The what?"

I said nothing, though the name burned in my ears. My boots crunched on the gravel as I made my way down toward the table. The engineers parted grudgingly, some with skepticism plain in their eyes, others with weariness born of too many failed figures. Mears gestured at the spread of maps, his jaw tight.

"Gentlemen, this is Percy Hope—the Wizard of Hope. You've all heard the name. You all know Placer Flats—the ground gave way, swallowed half the line. He told us how to spread the load and shore the grade, and we saved weeks, if not months. And again in the Matanuska Valley. He was right. Twice now, he's seen what trained eyes could not. That's why he's called the Wizard of Hope. And now we stand at Hurricane Gulch. If he's got something to say, let him speak."

A murmur passed through the engineers, some nodding in recognition, others narrowing their eyes as if weighing whether to trust a newspaperman in their ranks.

But it wasn't their reaction that caught me—it was Walter's.

His mouth had fallen open, his eyes darting between Mears and me. "The Wizard of Hope?" he whispered, the words more question than statement. "They call you that?"

I felt heat rise in my face. The name had trailed me since Placer, but I had never spoken it at home. Never wanted to.

Walter's voice carried a tremor—half wonder, half accusation. "And you never told me?"

"Names are cheap," I muttered, eyes fixed on the map table. "It's the work that matters."

But I could feel him staring at me, his boy's admiration sharpened by something new—the hunger to know *how* I had done it, how I had seen what others could not.

"Gentlemen," I said, steadying my voice. "You're searching for steel to conquer the gulch. But the gulch doesn't need conquering. Look out there—the trees, the river, the granite. Nature has already written the bridge. All we have to do is learn to read it."

One engineer snorted. "Patterns in trees and rivers? We're building in steel, not poetry."

"Even steel fails when it fights the land," I countered. "But if you match its law, the bridge will not only stand—it will belong. Your calculations must follow what the gulch itself dictates. The span can't be forced. It must be proportioned."

A younger surveyor leaned over the map, tapping nervously with his pencil. "Proportioned… by what measure?"

"By the same measure you find in a seashell, or in the curve of your own hand," I said. "A ratio that repeats in storms, in flowers, even in galaxies. It appears in the spiral of pine cones and the unfurling of a fern. It is not ours to invent—it is written already, everywhere."

Across the table, Mears tapped the map with a forefinger. "The golden section," he said, as if naming an old friend. A low murmur rolled through the circle—one man nodding, another already penciling 1.618 in the margin; an older draftsman whispered, "extreme-and-mean," and a younger surveyor, eager, added, "the divine proportion." Slide rules clicked open. Set squares shifted. Figures were struck and recast, spans trimmed and deepened by instinct refined in books—Euclid in the back of their minds, bridge steel under their hands.

As they spoke, the medallion at my chest warmed faintly, its pulse steady and sure. For months beyond Alaska, it had been mute, stripped of its voice, a coldness pressing against my ribs. More than once, I had wondered if it had forsaken me altogether, if its silence was the final word on my part in whatever mystery it carried. I had grown accustomed to the dread of it—carrying what felt like a relic that had turned its back on me.

Only now, back upon this soil, did it breathe again. The warmth was not a surprise—it was a homecoming. A relief so deep I nearly staggered with it. Its current surged through me, not in words but in knowing, carrying the line I should draw as if the gulch itself had whispered it into my bones.

I let my finger sweep the map, drawing the arc from rim to rim, its rise echoing the spruce's turn, its fall answering the bend of the river below. The gesture felt less my own than carried through me, a memory awakening in metal and marrow alike.

Silence fell. Pencils hovered. Then, slowly, they began to sketch the arc where my finger had passed. Numbers followed, hurried whispers of load distribution and stress ratios. The chatter shifted from doubt to calculation, from quarrel to possibility.

One of the younger surveyors straightened, his face pale with astonishment. "By God… the span holds."

Another bent low over the figures, his voice hushed. "The stresses resolve cleaner than any truss we've drawn. No buckling in the girders, no impossible loads. It… it's beautiful."

And there it was—the hush of men confronted with a truth larger than their training. They knew, as I did, that this pattern was not crafted by human ingenuity alone. It was older, deeper, stitched into the marrow of things.

The circle shifted, their arguments drained away, replaced by the quiet urgency of men who sense possibility. Even Mears, iron-eyed and skeptical, stared long at the arc and then out at the gulch itself.

At last he looked back at me. "Wizard of Hope," he said under his breath, as if tasting the name anew. "Perhaps the land has been waiting for you after all."

Walter pressed close against my side, whispering, "Pops… how did you know?"

My hand brushed the medallion beneath my shirt, still warm with its secret tide. I had no answer that would not frighten him—only the certainty that the line had been there long before us, and would remain long after.

*

That night, the camp quieted, though the engineers still bent over their maps by lamplight, scratching figures with a fever I had not seen before.

The gulch had yielded its secret, though none would admit it had passed through me.

Walter and I settled into our tent. He tossed on his blanket, rolling onto his side and then his back, until at last he lit the stub of a candle and pulled his notebook onto his knees.

"What are you drawing?" I asked.

He hunched over the page, tongue caught between his teeth. "Not sure. Just… trying to see what you saw."

I leaned closer. Circles spiraled across the paper, crude at first, then tighter, more certain. He drew the curve of the gulch as he remembered it, then traced lines through the spruce and river below.

"It doesn't look right," he muttered. "Not the way it looked when you traced it."

"It never will on paper," I said softly. "The truth of it isn't on paper. It's in the land itself."

He looked up, the candlelight catching the hunger in his eyes. "But you saw it, Pops. Clear as day. How?"

For a moment, I said nothing. The medallion pressed cold against my chest, heavy with its silence and its demand. I had hidden the truth long enough.

I reached beneath my shirt and drew it out—the raven etched in silver, wings spread wide as if to take flight. It shimmered faintly in the candlelight, as though it drank from the flame. Walter's breath caught.

"This," I said quietly. "This is why they call me the Wizard of Hope. Not because I'm cleverer than the engineers, or because I read the land better than most… but because of this. The medallion. It shows me what others cannot see."

Walter stared, wide-eyed, as I placed it in his hands. His fingers curled around it, hesitant, reverent. He held it as if it were alive.

"It doesn't tell me in words," I continued, watching his face. "It's more like a stirring, a vision that takes shape when I stand in the right place, when the land calls for it. At Placer Flats, when the rails sank, it was the medallion that showed me how to spread the weight across the frost. In the Matanuska, when the permafrost buckled the rails, it gave me the answer again. And now here, at Hurricane Gulch, it woke to show me the bridge."

Walter turned the medallion over in his palm, his eyes reflecting both awe and fear. "It's… beautiful," he whispered. "And it's been with you all this time?"

"All this time," I said. "But it's no simple charm. It carries a burden. Knowledge comes at a cost. Eli died for this little piece of silver."

His gaze flicked up, searching my face. "Yes, you told me."

I hesitated, then forced myself to speak the name. "A man named Cutter killed him because of this." My voice caught, and for a moment the tent seemed to shrink around us, lit only by the candle's thin flame. "That's the kind of shadow this medallion carries. Every time it reveals its gift, it draws danger closer."

Walter swallowed hard, fingers tightening on the chain. He stared at the raven's wings, as though trying to read some hidden script in the metal.

"Walter," I said carefully, "there's something I've been meaning to ask you."

He looked up, wary.

"In the margins of one of the stories you sent me—the dispatch you wrote—you drew a circle. A crooked line cutting through it. And three dashes underneath. Why? Why did you make that mark?"

Walter frowned, the memory tugging at him. "I… don't know. I wasn't thinking about it. My hand just… moved. Like it wanted to draw it." He shook his head, eyes narrowing. "I remember feeling strange— like something was pressing on me, not heavy but… guiding. It didn't feel like it came from me."

The candle sputtered, shadows leaning across the canvas walls.

Walter shivered, lowering his voice. "When I finished, I stared at it and thought… I've seen this before. But I don't know where."

My heart tightened. "You couldn't know," I said. "But I do."

He blinked, waiting.

"I never told you," I said softly. "The first time was in a tent. Frost climbed the canvas and, for a breath, it drew the sign itself—a circle split by a crooked line, three short dashes beneath—then melted away. At Broad Pass, the pull wouldn't let me be; it rose from sleep like a hand on my shoulder, turning me west toward the ice under Denali."

"In the blue ice, I saw it again—no flicker this time, but carved deep into the wall—and I understood it wasn't a charm at all, but a map." The candle flickered, shadows bending across his face. He looked down at the medallion, the silver raven catching and releasing the light.

I reached out, closing his hand gently around it. "That's why we have to be careful, son. This isn't just mine anymore. It's calling to you as well. And I don't yet know if that's a gift… or a curse."

He looked up sharply, as if I had confirmed a secret he already suspected. The candle flickered between us, light dancing on the raven's wings.

"Does it choose who sees?" he asked.

I swallowed hard. "Maybe. Or maybe it just remembers. The Tyonek say the land keeps its truths, waiting for someone willing to bear them. I don't know yet which of us it has chosen."

Walter's grip tightened on the medallion before he handed it back. His eyes shone with something more than boyish wonder—something heavier, like inheritance.

And as I slipped it once more around my neck, dread stirred inside me. The gulch had given up its bridge—but in doing so, it had awakened something in my son.

CHAPTER THIRTY-SEVEN
A WIRE

The camp at Hurricane Gulch quieted by midnight, the engineers remained hunched over their maps, scratching figures with fevered intensity as carbide lamps hissed in the wind. Walter had finally drifted into sleep beside me, his notebook still open, pencil dangling from his hand as though he feared the patterns might slip away if he let go. I envied his rest. My own thoughts churned too violently.

At first light, the sound of hooves broke the silence. A rider appeared at the edge of camp, a lean young man with a courier's satchel slung across his shoulder, dust and spruce needles clinging to his coat. He swung down from the saddle and asked for me by name.

"Percy Hope?"

I stood, wary. "That's me."

He dug into the satchel and produced a folded slip of paper, the Western Union stamp fresh across its corner. "Came through from Anchorage yesterday. They said it was urgent."

My heart thudded as I broke the seal. The message was brief, but the words struck harder than any gale across Broad Pass:

WALTER MUST RETURN HOME AT ONCE. NO ARGUMENT. IF YOU VALUE OUR FAMILY, BRING HIM BACK IMMEDIATELY.

— PEGGY

The letters blurred in my sight. I read it twice, three times, as if repetition might soften their edge. It did not.

Walter stirred, rubbing his eyes against the morning light. "What is it, Pops?"

I hesitated, then handed him the slip. He read it slowly, his lips moving over each word. By the time he reached the end, the boyish defiance was gone from his face. In its place was something quieter, heavier.

"She wants me home," he said.

"She does," I admitted, my voice rough. "And she's right. This isn't the life for you, Walter. Not yet."

He looked out toward the gulch, where the first rays of sun cut across the abyss and lit the surveyors' lines like threads of fire. "But I was helping," he whispered. "I saw it too—the pattern. I wasn't in the way."

"You weren't," I said, resting a hand on his shoulder. "But your mother is not wrong. These gulches, these shadows we walk in—they take men. Eli was barely older than you when it claimed him. You should not carry this burden yet."

"When do we leave?" he asked with a sigh.

"Today," I said. "The sooner we start, the sooner you'll be home."

I glanced once more at the engineers clustered over their maps, at Mears's stern silhouette against the rim of the gulch. They would carry on without me, or perhaps they would summon me again. But Peggy's wire had drawn a line sharper than any surveyor's stake.

The land would have to wait. My family came first.

We set out before noon, the wagon rattling south with the thawed earth sucking at the wheels. Walter sat quietly beside me, the wire from Peggy folded in his pocket, as though he feared it might vanish if he let it go. Each mile toward Broad Pass eased the pressure in my chest, though the country gave no kindness—mud, stone, and wind fought us at every turn.

*

By the next day we reached the pass, where the tracks resumed their climb. A freight train idled there, its iron bulk panting clouds into the frozen air. Within the hour, Walter and I had hauled ourselves aboard. The whistle split the silence, and the cars groaned to life as they lurched ahead.

The train thundered into the night, its iron wheels shrieking against the rails. Lanterns swayed overhead, throwing crooked beams across the freight car, but beyond that trembling light, the corners pooled with shadow. I had grown used to the rhythm of the clatter, the steady pulse of steel and timber beneath us.

That was when the shadows moved.

A figure stepped forward, thin but coiled with menace, as if the dark itself had given him shape. My blood froze before my mind even formed the name. Cutter.

His coat hung in tatters, his face leaner than I remembered, but the fire in his eyes was the same—the fire that had stared back at me when Eli fell.

"Evening, Wizard," he drawled, the words cutting through the roar of the train.

Before I could rise, his hand lashed out with the speed of a striking whip. He seized Walter by the collar and yanked him from the bench. My boy cried out, fists flailing, but Cutter was faster, meaner, forged in violence.

"Let him go!" I roared, lunging forward. My shout vanished into the thunder of the rails.

Cutter's grin widened, wicked and sure. He dragged Walter backward, his boots thudding against the planks, until they reached the sliding freight door. With a sharp jerk, Cutter threw the latch. Metal clanged, and the door shuddered open, blasting the car with a howling wind. The world outside blurred—a trestle bridge stretched across a yawning black ravine, its skeletal beams flickering past in the lantern light.

Walter's eyes found mine, wide with terror. I dove, fingers outstretched, grazing his sleeve. But Cutter wrenched him away, holding him like a shield, like a prize.

"Too late for promises, Hope," he sneered, his voice a knife of triumph.

Then, with a savage heave, he hurled himself and Walter into the night.

The boy's cry split the darkness—then was gone, swallowed by the roar of the wind and the chasm below.

For a moment, I could not move. The night was a blur of wind and shrieking steel, my son's cry echoing in my skull. The lantern swung crazily, throwing jagged light across the empty doorway where they had vanished.

Then my body remembered what my mind refused—I lurched to the opening, clutching the cold edge of the frame, and leaned out into the rushing dark.

Below, the trestle's bones flashed beneath me, the black mouth of the ravine yawning wide, swallowing shadow and sound alike. My breath caught—too far, too sheer, no man could survive that fall. Yet farther back, the land changed. A slope of gravel and spruce-studded ground lifted like a hand cupped against the gulch. It was there they might have landed, there or not at all.

I strained to see through the blur of speed. For an instant, I thought I caught motion—a figure tumbling, another dragging after. Cutter's shape, unmistakable even in chaos, clutching Walter as they crashed through the brush.

My heart seized. Walter lived. He had to.

I pulled back into the car, the gale tearing at my coat, the rails clattering like war drums beneath my feet. My hand found the satchel, and in one motion I pulled the Colt free, strapping the belt tight around my waist. The weight of it settled against me like a vow. Every instinct screamed to hurl myself into the night, to chase my son no matter the cost. But the trestle still stretched below—one slip here and I'd be broken on the rocks, useless to Walter.

So I waited, teeth clenched, knuckles white against the frame, eyes locked on the slope ahead where the land began to flatten, where a leap might not mean certain death. Each second dragged like an eternity, the train thundering on, carrying me farther from the boy I had sworn to protect.

When the ground at last rose to meet the rails, when the ravine's mouth gave way to firmer earth, I did not hesitate.

I leapt.

The air tore the breath from my chest, the earth rushed up hard and unyielding. I hit, rolled, the world exploding into stone, mud, and spruce needles. Pain lanced through my shoulder, but I forced my body to move, staggering upright, vision swimming.

Somewhere ahead, Walter was alive. Somewhere ahead, Cutter still drew breath.

I spat blood into the dirt, my hand finding the medallion at my chest. It pulsed faintly, as if it too had leapt with me, guiding me onward.

I set my jaw, eyes fixed on the broken trail Cutter had carved through the brush.

I would find my son.

And this time, I would kill Cutter myself.

CHAPTER THIRTY-EIGHT
THE HUNT

The forest swallowed me, and for a long, punishing while I let it. I stumbled forward because there was nothing else left in me to do—stone and root and cold air turning my breath to knives, mud and snow gripping my boots like the hands of the drowned. Every step rang through my ribs where I'd met the ground after the leap; every jolt up my spine was a memory of the train thundering away.

Walter. His name became a wound I kept pressing so I wouldn't forget to bleed.

The country between Broad Pass and Curry has no mercy for a man alone. The rail, when you can see it, carves south through gulches and black timber as if a giant had dragged a blade through the land. Ravines open with no warning. Muskeg lies in wait, glossy and innocent until it swallows you to the knee. Snow lingers in the hollows long after spring has decided it is spring, and the wind pours down from the ridges smelling of iron and old ice.

I kept near the railroad but off it. On the ballast you're seen—section men, telegraphers, anyone at a siding—and Cutter knew it. He'd shadow the surveyors' line through the timber instead. So I did the same: moving roughly parallel in the spruce, guided by the grade's poles and stakes, with the whistle and the creosote on the wind telling me the track was still to the west.

I told myself to listen for Walter. I told myself to call his name, to bargain with any god listening, but the first hours gave me nothing—no track, no torn branch, not so much as the echo of a cry. Only the moan of spruce and the dull, animal ache of my body doing the one thing left to it—keep moving.

Guilt kept pace beside me, step for step. Peggy's wire burned in my pocket—*WALTER MUST RETURN HOME AT ONCE...*—as if the words themselves had heat. How would I face her if I failed? How would I shape my mouth around the truth—that I had meant to bring him home and instead had lost him to the very darkness I'd sworn to spare him? I could see her eyes, the way they go still when she's holding back everything she wants to throw. I had promised her the man I am when the world is gentle. Alaska had demanded the other one.

Dawn bled into the sky without warming anything. Spring light in this country returns like a stubborn thought—longer each hour, unwilling to leave, making a theater of your fear. It showed me the bigness of the place, the smallness of me. It showed me nothing of Walter.

Pain had begun to take inventory: my shoulders flared each time I lifted an arm; ribs needled every breath; thighs burned raw from the roll down the slope; palms split where bark had bitten deep. Bruises spread and darkened as the hours stretched—the only proof time was moving.

The first sign wasn't a footprint. It was the woods.

Further in, I found what no train leaves: fresh axe marks, a kicked-over stake stamped CURRY STA 218+40, and a strip of red flag on an alder. All of it pointed south.

Stationing is simple: one station equals 100 feet. 218+40 is 21,840 feet—just over four miles from Curry. That put me about that far out on the line.

Cutter was using the surveyor's path to hide. I followed. The medallion warmed on my chest and pulled the same way the markers did—south.

The forest sharpened. Axe blazes flared like lanterns. The faintest cut of pencil on wood pulled at my eyes. Knowledge not my own poured into me: how a man steps when burdened, where he breaks brush and where he slips past it, the hidden logic of slope and shadow. I was no longer just chasing. I was tracking.

By midday, the thaw ruled the valley. Water sang in every cut, stitching the ground with quicksilver streams. Melt slicked the rock and made a liar of the earth. Yet the medallion steadied me: seek the low ground for crossings, cling to the shoulders of slopes where a man could haul unwilling cargo without losing speed.

Then came the undeniable truth—the heel of a hobnailed boot stamped deep beside a creek, the stagger of a man carrying more than himself, and the faint rope-like drag through moss that no animal could leave.

Walter.

I dropped to my knees, cold biting through the cloth, and touched the mark with two fingers. Nearby, alder bark hung ragged and wet, sap gleaming like tears. Farther on, a bent branch sagged beneath a weight no storm had made. The relief was so fierce it nearly knocked me backward. They were here, just ahead of me, walking south toward Curry.

The medallion pulsed once more, urging me forward.

I rose too fast and the world tilted; I steadied myself on a spruce, tasted iron, and forced my feet to remember how to move.

Peggy's face would not leave me. The morning I left, the way she stood in the doorway with her arms folded tight, as if that could keep me from going. *You can't keep drinking danger like medicine,* she'd said once. And here I was, a man made of bruises and promises, hunting the worst of my failures through a forest that would be happy to claim me.

At the creek, spring's fury blocked the way, the current thrashing against stone. Upstream, a gravel bar kept its story: boot prints pressed sharp into the wet stones, edges still clean where water hadn't yet worn them away. Someone had crossed here not long ago. I splashed through, the water biting me to the hip, and came out with legs that felt more stubborn than strong.

The sun should have dipped. It refused. Spring in Alaska stretches the day on a rack until it forgets what night is. The light turned the rails— far off to my right—into a dull, silver wound. Shadows shrank; my failures had nowhere to hide. I wanted darkness if only to let me pretend. Instead, the land gave me more day.

I slipped in muskeg, and it had me to my knees in a heartbeat. Panic ran its nails up my throat. I tore free with a roar that startled birds from the spruce, the muck letting go with the sound of something hungry and disappointed. The effort lit my ribs on fire. I bent double, gasping, and for a few bad breaths I believed what the wilderness wanted me to believe—that I was broken enough to quit.

My hand found the medallion beneath my shirt.

It was warm. Its quiet pulse spread through my chest like a rhythm I could fall in step with. No words. No promises. Just forward.

Toward evening, clouds tore open and the land went strange with gold. Light pooled in the cuts and bled along the ridge-edges; every spruce shadow pretended to be a man at first glance. That was when I found the first true sign of my boy: a lock of blond hair snagged on a low spruce branch, sun-shot and sticky with pitch. I pinched it between thumb and forefinger and felt something in me lift and harden at once. Walter had fought. He was still fighting.

I climbed a low ridge, lungs scraping, legs stuttering under me. From there, the valley unfurled—a long, bruised body of timber and rock and water. Far ahead, where the trees thinned toward a bend, two figures stitched across the ground. Small at first, only the suggestion of movement. Then I could see the gait: one dragging, one resisting. The taller frame hunched as if the burden had grown teeth.

Cutter. And my son.

Relief and fury did not take turns; they arrived together, a flash and a burn. I pressed myself against the bark and closed my eyes because the sight hurt worse than any bruise. I opened them again before it could turn to cowardice. They were too far to call to; the wind would make sure my voice didn't find the right ears. Too far to rush without losing them in the folds of the land. But the hunt was no longer blind.

"Hold fast," I said into the air, and if the world has a memory, I want it to remember that vow.

The sun slouched lower and then stopped trying. I moved again because to stand still hurt worse. Muskeg became mirrors; the half-light made sky and ground trade faces. I slid, swore, hauled myself up by spruce that shed needles into my collar. My shoulder sang; my ribs kept time.

By near-midnight, the world went quiet enough that I could hear the blood in my ears. The animals had decided to let the land keep its secrets. Even the wind spoke in a thin voice. Exhaustion began making me offers—*sit here a minute, just until the trembling stops; close your eyes and see him as a baby again, that's easier than seeing him now; Peggy will forgive you if you lie well enough; lie well enough and you can live*—and I argued with it like a drunk with a priest.

The medallion pulsed again. Not louder; closer. It tethered me to the one truth that mattered—the trail was true.

I pressed on until the edges of things went soft and the center of the world was Walter's name. I don't know how long that was. Time is a poor instrument out here. The sky stayed a bruised blue-yellow that refused to quit. I stayed a bruised man who couldn't either.

At last, when my legs shook without my permission and the ground had started to tilt under me when it wasn't tilting at all, I gave the land my weight and slid down the trunk of a black spruce. The bark bit new lines into my palms; the pain was clean, and I was grateful for it.

Peggy's face came back—the softness she keeps hidden, the steel she doesn't. *Bring him home.* She had not asked; she had commanded. If I returned without him, there would be no story I could tell that would put light back in her eyes. If I didn't return at all, Alaska would be the one to explain my failure to her, and Alaska has never been gentle with its truths.

"I'm coming," I said, to the boy, to the woman I'd failed, to the land that was testing which one of us deserved to keep him. "I'm coming."

The light did not darken. It only thinned, like a vow whispered instead of shouted.

I let my eyes close—not sleep, only a shutter pulled against the sting—and felt the medallion warm my sternum in tiny heartbeats. When I opened them again, the world had shifted hardly at all: same ghost-light, same lonely rails glinting far off, same wind combing the spruce as if the trees had hair. Somewhere ahead, two figures threaded the belly of the valley.

I stood, made an inventory of my hurts, and accepted the balance still owing. Then I moved south toward Curry, following the shy mathematics of survey stakes and the unkind honesty of wire, into a day that would not end until it ended with Cutter in the ground.

The hunt had narrowed. Fear walked with me. So did love. Only one of them knew the way.

The lock of Walter's hair burned in my pocket like a coal as I moved downslope. Voices leaked through the spruce—Cutter's low and easy, Walter's shorter, ragged breaths. I dropped to a knee at the edge of a muskeg and watched the ground darken with evening. My fists wanted the old boxer's answer—the ring, the bell, the step-and-slip—but the sound in my head wasn't a bell. It was the train, clattering through Talkeetna, and Eli folding to the floorboards when my Colt spoke last.

I wrenched the gun from its shroud, the metal biting colder than the storm itself, colder than the graves I carried in memory. My hands moved as if they belonged to another—checking the cylinder, thumb brushing the hammer—rituals born of desperation, not habit. The weapon was no longer just steel and powder; it was judgment, waiting to be cast. If fate demanded a sacrifice tonight, let it be mine. Better my blood than Walter's.

I rose.

I stepped out from the trees, the Colt heavy in my grip, gleaming in the thin light.

"Cutter." My voice cut through the night like a shot. "Let him go."

He spun, eyes widening for the briefest beat before twisting into a sneer. With a savage tug he hauled Walter forward, the boy lurching to keep his feet, a shield between us. Cutter's laugh cracked the silence, harsh and mocking.

"Well, well," he drawled, baring his teeth. "The Wizard finally shows his teeth."

Walter's voice broke, defiant even in fear. "Pops—don't listen to him!"

"Quiet, boy," Cutter snarled, digging his fingers into Walter's collar. "Your old man put us here. He's the reason you're gasping."

"Walk him out," I said, Colt steady. "This ends between you and me."

Cutter's grin went knife-thin. "Clark don't pay me for your blood. He pays for silence. And this"—he shook Walter like a rag—"is quiet that don't come cheap."

Walter spat dirt, glaring up. "I'm not afraid of you."

That steadied me. My son hadn't broken. Not yet.

Cutter shoved him aside and yanked his pistol free. Walter hit the ground hard, scrambling on his knees.

"Run, Walter!" I roared.

The world shrank to the black eye of his gun and the weight of mine.

We fired almost together.

Cutter's bullet ripped bark from the spruce by my ear. My round caught him high in the chest, spinning him sideways. He staggered but didn't fall—snarled and leveled again, blood on his teeth.

"Pops!" Walter's scream cut through.

We circled in the brush, smoke stinging the air, guns cracking in bursts. Cutter laughed between shots, each grin wider than the last.

"Still writing, Hope?" he spat. "Print this."

His slug grazed my sleeve, burning a line of fire down my arm. I steadied, squeezed. My shot tore his bicep. His pistol dropped, but he kicked it up with his boot and caught it, grinning like a beast.

Walter shouted, voice high and desperate. "Don't let him win!"

Cutter swung toward him and fired wild—one shot whining off a telegraph pole, the other kicking dirt inches from Walter's boots.

"You missed!" Walter screamed, voice cracking.

I answered with two shots. One clipped Cutter's shoulder, the other punched through his thigh. He stumbled but drove forward, teeth bared, eyes bright with madness.

The Colt's cylinder was near empty. I thumbed back the hammer— one round left. He saw it.

With a roar, Cutter hurled himself at me. His pistol slipped from his grip as he crashed in, and the ground went out from under us.

We hit the needles hard. The Colt jarred loose and vanished in the brush. Cutter jumped on top of me, hips heavy, weight pinning my breath. His fists fell blind and brutal; elbows and knees hunted ribs and throat. He fought dirty—head-butts, teeth flashing, a hand grinding at my windpipe.

The boxer in me woke the way a bruise wakes. I shelled up—chin tucked, forearms tight—letting knuckles scrape bone instead of jaw. I caught his wrist, jammed my forearm across his throat, and gave him the kind of shots you throw in a clinch: short, mean, all elbow and shoulder. No canvas, no crowd—just an inch of space and will.

I trapped his arm to my chest, planted a heel, and bridged hard. We rocked; needles flew. He clawed for balance. I slid a knee between us, a wedge of bone, and hammer-fisted his ear. He snarled, drove his head into my cheek, split my lip. Blood filled my mouth.

Through the ringing came Walter's voice, thin and torn: "Pops! Please—get up!"

I heaved, slipped his grip, and got a knee under me. Cutter crashed back in, clubbing my ear; the world went watery. His free hand dove for his belt. I saw it then—the bone-handled knife. He yanked it clear, the point hunting me.

I caught his wrist and wrenched it down. Steel scraped my ribs. We locked there, breath to breath, both hands on the knife—his to drive, mine to stop. He bucked, cursing, trying to free the blade. I cinched his arm to my chest and ground the hilt sideways, inch by inch, turning it back toward him.

His eyes widened, fury giving way to fear.

"Tell Clark," I rasped, breath raw, "he picked the wrong man's silence."

The knife slid home.

Cutter stiffened, fought a heartbeat more, then went slack. His breath rattled once—then nothing.

I rolled him off, gasping, blood hot in my throat. Walter crawled to me, face streaked, eyes wide but unbroken. I pulled him close, my arms trembling as much as his.

It was over. For now.

But as Curry's whistle echoed across the valley, I knew Clark's reach stretched farther than Cutter's grave.

CHAPTER THIRTY-NINE
HOME

The brakes shrieked as we slid into Portage, steel on steel. Steam shouldered across the platform and drowned the depot in a gray veil. Beside me, Walter sat rigid—too still for a boy—Peggy's telegram folded to the hardness of coin in his pocket, the paper creased where his thumb kept finding it.

A wagon waited beyond the platform, wheels buried to the hub in thawed mud. The driver tipped his cap and moved to load our bags.

"Hope," I told him.

He grunted, snapped the reins, and the wagon lurched south along Turnagain Arm, the tide pouring silver to our right, black spruce ribbing the hills to our left.

I tried to speak—once, then again—picking at the silence like a scab. But he only stared through the wagon boards, jaw set, eyes gone distant, just as he had on the train from Curry to Portage. Each time I pressed, he shook his head, the answer lodged too deep to rise.

So we rode on in the rattle of wheels and the groan of harness, the tide rushing beside us, the words unsaid weighing more than the baggage piled at our feet.

By the time Hope's rooftops rose out of the trees, the tightness in my chest wasn't dust to be brushed aside. Peggy would be waiting—not for a headline, but for an accounting no words could soften.

She stood on the porch with lamplight behind her, arms folded, chin high. A few strands of hair had shaken loose and caught the wind like wire, but nothing in her face was soft. Walter climbed down first. He faltered, then took the steps. I followed, each footfall heavier than the last.

Her eyes moved from our son to me and back again. Relief flickered—and the heat behind it. She said nothing.

Walter's lip trembled, and then the dam broke. He clutched his mother, burying his face against her, sobs tearing through him in great shuddering waves. When he lifted his head, his wet eyes searched mine. I gave the smallest nod.

"He pulled me off the train, Mama," Walter choked out, words thin at first, then stronger. "In the freight car. He slid the door, and the wind came in. We jumped out."

Walter clung to her sleeve, eyes wild and wet. The words tumbled out between sobs.

"I was… I was sitting with Pops in the freight car when—when this man came out of nowhere." He hiccupped, breath ragged. "Before I could think, his hand was on my collar. He yanked me off the bench so hard my feet kicked air. I tried to fight him—I swung, I clawed—but he was too fast, too mean."

Peggy's arms tightened around him. "Oh my God…"

Walter shivered, pressing his face to her shoulder before forcing the words out. "He dragged me backward until we hit the freight door. I heard the latch crash open, and then—the wind, Mama. It roared in like a storm." His shoulders heaved. "The train was on a trestle, black space under us, beams flashing by. Pops lunged—he almost had me—but the man pulled me away like I was nothing. He grinned at Pops… and then he jumped. He took me with him."

Peggy gasped, her knuckles white against the fabric of his shirt.

I found my voice, low and rough. "Cutter," I said. "It was Cutter."

Walter sobbed hard into her, then pushed on. "We hit the ground—gravel, cinders, brush—I thought my ribs were broken. My mouth filled with dust. He never let go. He hauled me up by the scruff and shoved me forward. He said…" His voice cracked, fell to a whisper. "He said I was security."

Her eyes shot to mine, blazing. I bit my lower lip.

Walter's breath rattled as he went on. "He dragged me through the spruce. I stumbled, I fell—he yanked me back to my feet every time. And every step, I told myself, Pops was behind us. I couldn't hear him, couldn't see him, but I knew. Even when he pressed a knife against my back, even when he told me to keep quiet or die…" He broke, shoulders shaking, his voice a thread. "I knew Pops was coming."

I drew a breath. "He took Walter to get to me," I said before she could speak. "Not for ransom—leverage. To flush me into the open and prove Clark's reach."

She looked at Walter, mapping him with her hands—shoulders, cheekbones, the small hurts boys collect when men make war around them. Then she lifted her gaze and fixed it on me.

"You kept Clark's name out," she said, even as a whetted blade. "And still our boy was nearly killed. So what did your silence buy us?"

"Not a thing," I said.

She held my eyes a beat longer, measuring cost against salvage, what was spent against what was saved. Walter leaned into her.

"You promised me this wouldn't touch us," she said—not loud, but with a steadiness that cut cleaner than anger. "You promised."

I had no answer. I opened my hands so she could see they were empty. Whatever defense I might've had thinned to breath and stayed there. I took the truth she laid on me, nodded once, and kept my silence while the tide whispered and our boy pressed closer to her side.

Peggy drew Walter in, her thumb brushing the ridge of a bruise as though she could erase it, as though love alone could shield him from the world I had brought to our door.

Walter pulled free, his young voice trembling but firm. "He saved me, Mama. Cutter would've killed us both if not for Pops."

His eyes darted between us, wide with memory. "I saw it... the knife in Cutter's hand. He was stronger, bigger. I thought—" His voice cracked, but he pushed on. "But Pops didn't let go. They were locked together, the blade shaking between them. Cutter's face—he was laughing, like he already won. Then..." Walter swallowed hard, shoulders stiffening. "Then Pops turned it. I watched Cutter's eyes change when the steel went in. He fought, but Pop held on until he fell. I thought they'd both die, right there in the dirt."

Peggy froze, staring at him as though she barely recognized her boy. His voice was older now, stripped of its childhood ease, carrying something weightier that would never leave him. She reached up and brushed the hair from his brow before kissing him hard, as if to anchor him back to her.

When she looked back at me, her eyes were wet but unyielding.

"This cannot follow us home. Do you hear me? Whatever war you're fighting out there, it ends now."

I gave a single nod. She was right. Clark's name would never pass my lips, nor find its way onto a page. For a newspaperman, that silence cut deepest—the truth denied not only to speech but to ink itself. The attempted sabotage of the Alaska Railway would remain buried, the story unwritten, the evidence locked away.

It was a painful consequence, but to keep Peggy and Walter safe, I had no choice. Yet I knew the truth had a way of working itself loose, like frost heaving stone from the earth.

"I love you. Both of you," I said at last. "And I'll protect you. That's all that matters now."

Peggy gathered Walter close. I stepped onto the porch beside them, the weight of the town pressing from the darkened streets, neighbors' eyes flickering behind curtains. We stood together, a family bound by blood and mercy, fragile as thawing ice.

Hope lay before us—its name more a question than a promise.

CHAPTER FORTY
A SIGN

The storm had pressed against our home for days, wind clawing down from the mountains with a fury that rattled shutters and made the stove groan like an old beast. Snow clung to the windows in thick layers, a white blindness that turned the world beyond into silence.

Two years I had been home, trying to forget. I chopped wood until my blisters opened and my hands bled. But silence has its own voice, and in the long nights of winter, it gnawed at me, whispering what I had left undone.

I tried to write. God help me, I did. Page after page, the story of the railroad spilled onto my desk in fits and fragments. I wrote of the men who swung hammers until their hands split, of the trestles that climbed over gulches like spider webs of steel, of the mountains that loomed indifferent, and the rivers that roared with spring thaw.

But I could not stop there. To tell it plain, I had to write of the dangers too—the winters that turned breath to ice in the lungs, when frostbitten fingers froze to the very tools they gripped. The winds that cut like knives across the open flats, toppling tents, scattering rations, and leaving men to dig themselves out of drifts taller than their shoulders.

I wrote of sickness that came without warning—scurvy hollowing cheeks, pneumonia filling lungs, fevers that spread through camps like wildfire. I wrote of men who collapsed on the grade, too weak to rise, their graves marked only by the frozen earth that swallowed them.

And the heights—the trestles strung across canyons so deep a man could feel the drop pulling at him even as he lay belly-flat across the beams. One slip, one misstep on ice-slick timber, and he was gone, swallowed by the white roar of river or the black silence of rock below.

I tried to give them the truth—or at least the truth my lie would allow. A story carved not only in iron and timber, but in blood, frost, and silence.

But the silence pressed in between the lines. How could I write of Tent City without naming the murder that was more than whiskey and knives, without admitting what Mears had warned me—that the railroad was as much war with men as with granite and ice? I remembered his words: *The truth is a dangerous thing. It's a blade, Percy. Handle it without caution, or you'll bleed more than ink.*

I tried to shape the story of the rails of telling how we found the counterfeit spikes, brittle as chalk, or the blasting caps hidden in crates like seeds of disaster, yet could not name their cause. I kept my pencil steady, but my hand burned with the knowledge that sabotage lived not only in the wilderness, but in the very camps where men laid down steel.

I could not name the man behind it. I could not write Clark's name—the Copper King whose grudge turned labor into graves. To put him on the page would be to invite his shadow into my home, to place Peggy and Walter beneath his gaze. That price I would not pay.

So I wrote around it. I wrote of progress, of triumph pressed into wilderness, of men's sweat binding mountains with iron. But in the margins of my drafts—the ones no editor would see—I scrawled the rest: that every rail carried not just the weight of trains, but of secrets buried in silence. That I was building a story of half-truths, while the land itself remembered all.

I kept those pages folded in my desk drawer, locked away from sight. Peggy knew better than to ask. Walter was curious, but dared not disobey. Every time the wind shook the shutters, I imagined the land itself clawing at the walls, demanding its story back.

It was Walter who broke that silence. He pressed his nose to the frost-blurred window, breath clouding the glass. Then, sharp with wonder, he cried: "Pops—look! There's a mark!"

I crossed the room, half expecting some random pattern, the branching of ice, or the swirls of a draft. But when I bent beside him, my blood ran cold.

Etched clear in the frost was no idle design but a symbol: a circle split by a crooked line, and beneath it three short dashes, stark and deliberate, like steps cut into darkness.

Peggy came up behind us, her knitting abandoned, eyes narrowing as she took in the windowpane. Her voice was low, steady, but edged with unease.

"Walter," she asked, "is that the same one you drew?"

Walter nodded, his breath fogging the glass. "Yes. The same. Exactly the same."

Then he turned to me, eyes wide, hungry for meaning. "What does it mean, Pops?"

Now, etched on the window of my own home, I understood. Magnus was calling me back. His tortured soul had not found rest. He was bound still, and he would not release me until I faced him once more.

"It's a calling," I said at last, my voice rough. "Magnus is not done with me."

Peggy's eyes narrowed, her face pale in the lamplight. "Oh no. You promised, Percy. You promised to leave those shadows behind."

"This promise isn't mine to keep," I answered. "Magnus's soul is trapped, and the land won't let us rest until his burden is lifted. If I turn away now, the railroad itself could be cursed by what binds him. He warned me—*the iron road is not salvation, but a net, a cage.* Every spike we drive is another chain forged. And worse—he said I am the one forging it. If his soul isn't set free, then when the last rail is laid, the road will belong to them, not us. And by then it will be too late to turn back."

The stove cracked, sparks leaping into the air. And for the first time since Curry, heat seared through the medallion at my chest, throbbing in time with my pulse.

Magnus's voice rose in the silence, not with words, but with the same heavy ache I had felt in the caves—a cry unfinished, a life not yet loosed.

"We should all go," Walter said suddenly, his hand pressed against the frost-mark. His eyes shone with the same inevitability I felt burning in my chest. "We all see it, Pops. The sign is for us too."

Peggy drew in a sharp breath. For a long moment she said nothing, her gaze shifting between the window, Walter, and me. I saw the war in her eyes—fear and resolve locked in battle. Then her jaw set.

"He's right," she said, her voice steady now. "It's time. No more guessing, no more shadows. It's time I see what you see, Percy. We'll face it together."

I forbid it outright. "No way," I insisted. "This isn't a storybook trial we can outlast with grit. It's a death march. You'd be gambling your lives, Peggy—Walter's life. I won't allow it."

Peggy's chair scraped back, her eyes blazing in the lamplight. "And what do you call this life we're living now?" she demanded. "Two winters locked away in this cabin, watching you fade into silence, carrying a burden you refuse to share? That's not living, Percy—it's waiting to die. If we stay here, we wither. I might as well throw myself into the Arm tonight and take you both with me, because this"—she swept a trembling hand around the cabin—"this is already killing us."

I flinched at her words, at the steel beneath them. "Better this than dragging you into the mountain's grave."

Her gaze didn't falter. "You're wrong. Survival isn't measured in heartbeats, Percy. It's measured in what binds us. If you go alone, you'll be lost to us whether you return or not. But if we go together, even if the mountain swallows us whole, we'll still be a family—bound in this life or the next. That's the only survival worth fighting for."

Walter's voice broke the silence. "She's right, Pops. We can't hide forever. Let us see what you see. Let us stand beside you." His hand found Peggy's, steady despite the fear in his eyes.

I tried to speak—to shield them from Magnus's warnings—but the frost rattled the panes, and the medallion seared through my chest. The silence of two years pressed down until it cracked.

At last, I bowed my head. My voice was low, hollowed out. "So be it. Magnus calls, and the mountain waits. But know this—getting there alone is half the trial. The railroad only carries us so far. From Broad Pass, the wilderness begins. We'll need a musher with dogs strong enough to haul us through the white silence, past gulches that split the land like open graves, and into the shadow of Denali itself.

"And worse still, we must find a musher willing to wait. The caves are not hours, but days of ice and darkness. If our musher loses his nerve—if he turns back before we emerge—the mountain will claim us whole. No rescue will come. We'll die entombed in the ice, like Magnus before us."

Peggy's grip tightened around Walter's hand. "Then that's what we face. Because I'd rather die seeing what you see, than live blind to the truth you carry alone."

The lamp hissed, shadows trembling as I laid my hand over theirs. Heat and frost mingled at my skin, the medallion thrumming like a second heart.

"Then hear it," I whispered. "Whatever comes, we go together. Whatever comes, we face it together. This life or the next, nothing shall divide us."

The frost's symbol blurred, dissolving into the pane, but its imprint sank deeper than ice. Magnus had marked us. And now, so had we.

CHAPTER FORTY-ONE
THE RETURN

The train clattered north, its whistle echoing across the snowbound valleys. I sat opposite Peggy, her gaze pressed to the window, watching the Alaskan frontier unspool like a painted scroll. She had seen this country before, yet from the warmth of the railcar it struck her differently—forests buried in white silence, rivers locked under glass, mountains rising like walls at the world's end. From the safety of polished wood and coal-fed heat, she could almost imagine it was beautiful instead of merciless.

Walter barely kept his seat. He chattered of dog teams and sled trails, of racing the wind with only the three of us, behind a musher, and the stars overhead. His voice carried a brightness that felt almost foreign after so many months in Hope's cabin, a brightness I feared Denali might extinguish.

By midday the clouds tore open, and the mountain showed itself. Denali stood like no other peak, a throne of ice and sunlight, impossibly high, impossibly near, as if all the land tilted upward to bow before it. Peggy caught her breath. Walter pressed his nose to the glass.

The train shuddered as it slowed, iron wheels squealing against the rails. Outside, the spruce thinned to tundra, a vast, wind-swept openness where the land seemed scraped bare by ancient hands. Broad Pass stretched before us—flat in its middle, yet ringed by ridges rising sharp and silent, the kind of place where weather could turn in an instant and swallow a man whole. I had crossed it with Eli, and the memory clung to me like frostbite. Now, stepping from the comfort of the train, I felt the same pull, the same foreboding silence.

The musher was waiting, a stocky man wrapped in furs, his beard stiff with ice. He gave us a single nod, no more greeting than that, and set about checking the traces. His team of huskies stood lean and restless, their coats mottled gray and white, breath rising in quick, sharp plumes. Their eyes, bright as lantern glass, flicked to us with an energy that made Walter's grin stretch wide.

The musher grunted, motioning us onto the sled—Peggy and Walter first, tucked into furs at the front, and I crouched behind them. When he barked the command, the dogs surged forward with a power that nearly threw me off balance.

We skimmed across the tundra, the sled runners hissing against the snow. The wind cut sharp and clean, carrying the bite of spruce smoke from some far-off camp, then nothing but the scent of cold itself. Gulches yawned beneath us, bridged by narrow sweeps of snow-packed ground, and frozen rivers cracked faintly under the dogs' weight as they raced across. The horizon tilted, and Denali swelled larger with every mile, until it no longer seemed a mountain at all but the edge of the world itself, waiting to receive us.

Peggy held Walter tight, her face half-hidden in her scarf, though I caught the awe in her eyes whenever the sled crested a rise and the vastness opened before us. Walter whooped into the wind, his voice swallowed by the silence as quickly as it left him.

And me—I kept my hand pressed against the medallion through my coat, each beat against my chest reminding me that this was no mere journey north. We were being carried toward something older, deeper, waiting in the shadow of Denali.

The sled flew across the tundra as the day stretched and waned. At first, the sun hung high, casting sharp blue shadows on the snow, but slowly the light began to shift—gold bleeding into rose, then fading toward violet. The long shadows of the dogs pulled out before us, lengthening with every mile. My breath froze in my beard, and Peggy's cheeks burned red above her scarf, though she never once complained. Walter's laughter carried on the wind until even he grew quiet, lulled by the steady rhythm of the team and the immensity of the land.

By late afternoon, the cold deepened, the world sharpening into edges of ice and shadow. We passed frozen rivers that groaned beneath us, gulches that dropped away sudden and black, ridges where the mountain's weight seemed to press the very air thinner. The musher said little, only hissed sharp commands, his voice cutting through the wind.

At last, the sun slipped behind Denali itself, and the sky surrendered to indigo. Stars pierced the dark one by one until the heavens were a blaze of fire, and the aurora unfurled like a green veil drifting across the night. The sled slowed, the dogs' tongues lolling, their flanks steaming in the moonlight.

By the time we reached the caves, night had fallen clear and sharp. The walls of ice caught the starlight as though the earth itself glowed from within. We built a fire at the mouth of the first cavern, its glow licking the frozen walls, but beyond the opening stretched only blue darkness.

I told the musher to wait, no matter how long. He only nodded, his face lost in shadow, as though the mountain's will was no concern of his.

We entered the first cavern—the Cave of the Body, its turquoise vault catching our lamplight. Green veins pulsed faintly through the walls, like rivers seen through ice.

Walter's gloved hand brushed the wall, his breath quick in wonder. He tilted his head back, and his voice echoed thinly, "It feels alive," the sound bouncing from curve to curve until it came back to him in a ghostly whisper. A soft drip somewhere in the shadows joined the rhythm of his breath, each drop exploding against the floor like a bead of glass.

Peggy shivered, though her chin was set with resolve. The air here was sharp, metallic, almost sweet—the taste of snow caught before it touched earth. Each breath burned her nostrils and settled cold as stone in her lungs. She hugged her arms tight, her wool sleeves stiff with frost, and tried to ignore the way her knees quivered—not just from fear, but from the ache of standing in such damp chill. "It's never the same, is it?"

she murmured, hearing the hollow creak of the cavern, as if the walls were shifting minutely around us. She noticed how the ceiling glistened with icicles suspended like knives, the faintest vibration enough to send them crashing down. The cave was not a sanctuary but a waiting threat, fragile and merciless.

Walter's excitement carried him closer to the chamber's center. His boots crunched lightly on a film of frost, each step crisp as broken glass. He leaned close to the ice, nose almost pressed to it, and sniffed. "It smells clean," he said, not knowing another word for it—the absence of smoke, of sweat, of earth. It was the smell of nothingness, pure and unbroken, and it filled him with a dizzy exhilaration.

The air grew heavier as we lingered, the silence broken only by the creak of unseen pressure, the slow groan of the ice adjusting somewhere deep within. The sound was not loud, but it carried a force that pressed into the bones, reminding us that the cavern was alive, and that it could shift or seal at its own whim.

The cold sank into us like teeth. My gloves stiffened, Walter's cheeks flushed raw, and Peggy's breath feathered into the lamplight, curling like smoke only to vanish instantly. The cave seemed to breathe with us, our own warmth swallowed into its lungs.

The tunnel coiled like lightning trapped in ice, throwing back our every sound in distorted echoes. More than once, I could have sworn Magnus's voice whispered my name from the walls. The cold thickened, pressing into my chest until each breath felt like inhaling shards of glass.

At last, the passage widened, spilling us into the second cavern—the Cave of the Mind. Its walls bent and forked like frozen lightning, angles collapsing in upon themselves. The air was heavier here, close and smothering. Peggy's lamp began to falter in her hand. I tried to steady her, but the same leaden weight pressed against my limbs.

Her voice broke the hush, thin but insistent. "Is this where we'll find him?" she asked, her gaze sweeping the jagged angles of the chamber. "The soul of Magnus—trapped somewhere in this maze of thought?"

I shook my head, forcing the words past the heaviness pressing on my chest. "No. Not here. This is only the Mind. His spirit waits deeper—in the third cavern. That's where Magnus lingers."

Walter's eyes darted upward, the lamplight trembling in his hand. "How far are we under the mountain now? It feels like miles. Like the whole peak's pressing down on us." His voice cracked, echoing strangely, as though the mountain itself repeated his fear.

Peggy bit down hard, steadied by the answer even as her knees trembled. "Then we keep on. We'll face him where he waits."

I wanted to reassure them further, but the air thickened with every heartbeat. I remembered Eli folding to the ground in this very place, eyes glazed, lost to a sleep no shaking could break. Now Peggy swayed beside me, her strength unraveling as if the cave itself were drawing it away.

Walter clutched her sleeve, whispering, "Don't fall, Ma. Don't leave me here."

My knees buckled moments later, the medallion burning against my chest before the dark pulled me under.

The last thing I saw was Walter, still standing. His eyes were wide, fixed on the tunnel ahead that led deeper, toward Du Yahaayí—the Cave of the Soul.

CHAPTER FORTY-TWO
WALTER

"Pops. Pops, wake up!"

The words reached me first as a murmur, then as a sharp tug, dragging me back from the black. My eyes blinked open to Walter's face hovering above mine, his cheeks flushed, his eyes wide with both fear and determination. His hands gripped my shoulders, shaking hard enough to rattle my teeth.

The cavern swam into focus. My lamp guttered low, throwing weak arcs of light across the angular walls. For a moment, I didn't know where I was.

Peggy stirred beside me, groaning, her breath fogging into the chill. She rubbed her eyes, confusion etched across her features. "What happened? Did we fall asleep?"

Walter sat back on his heels, the lamplight haloing his hair. "Not just sleep," he said, voice tight. "The cave made you both stop. Like it was pulling you down." He glanced at the medallion in his hand. "I took this from you, Pops. I thought maybe it would protect me."

Peggy sat upright at that, her hand darting to her throat. "Walter—"

"I only borrowed it!" he said quickly, holding up his hands. "I felt it burn, like it wanted me. I remembered the drawing I made that was again etched in frost on our window back in Hope."

He glanced toward the tunnel's dark mouth, his voice lowering. "You said it was a map, so I followed it. And it brought me to the next cave—the Cave of the Soul."

Peggy's breath caught. She pulled Walter closer, searching his face as if to measure the truth. "And you went inside?"

My stomach clenched. *"Du Yahaayí."*

Walter nodded, his eyes darting between us.

Walter's voice trembled, but he forced himself to go on.

"I stepped into the chamber, and it was like the mountain swallowed me whole. The lamplight didn't just fade—it was eaten. I couldn't hear my own footsteps. My breath felt stolen out of me. Then… then it came."

Walter's fingers twisted. "Not a voice. More like a thought that pushed itself into my head. Heavy. Sad. It said my name, Pops. It *knew* me. I wanted to run, but I couldn't. The whole place was holding me still."

Peggy drew him closer, but he kept speaking, his words spilling out in a rush.

Walter's hands trembled as he spoke, but his voice carried a strange, steady current beneath the fear.

"When I stepped inside, it wasn't just dark—it was like the world ended there. The mountain swallowed every sound, every breath. And then… I felt it. Not a voice, but a pulse in my chest, like someone pressing their hand into me. It said my name. Clear as anything. *Walter.*"

Peggy's fingers clutched his sleeve, but he shook his head, eyes locked on mine. "Pops—it wasn't calling for you. It never was. It was waiting for me."

He opened his palm, and the raven medallion lay on his palm, catching the lamplight in quick flashes. "This. You thought it was yours, Pops. You carried it, fought with it, and almost died with it. But Magnus said you were only keeping it safe. He called you its guardian—just the one to hold it until the time was right. It was meant for me all along."

The words pressed into me like frost against bone. My throat tightened, but Walter kept going, his voice rising with something close to awe.

"When I held it, it burned again—but not to hurt me. To wake me up. It opened the cave. And Magnus was there, not in body, but in the air, in my head. He told me why he couldn't leave. The bargain he made bound him here, chained him to Denali and the sins he carried. He said you tried to free him, Pops—you spoke to him once, gave him hope— but it wasn't enough. You're too close to him. Too much alike. The chains needed someone new. Someone unbound."

He swallowed hard, glancing between us. "Me."

Silence hung like ice around us, only the hiss of the lamp filling it. Walter's face was pale, but his eyes blazed.

"Magnus said the railroad will never stand until he's gone. The mountain fights it because his spirit is still buried in the ice, tangled in its memory. But when I touched the medallion and spoke his name, the chains broke. I felt it—like the whole cave sighed. He was pulled upward, Pops. Gone. Not into the dark, but into light. I know it. He moved on."

Walter's shoulders sagged, the effort of the telling spilling out of him. Then, softer, almost to himself: "He said the railroad's salvation isn't in steel or spikes—it's in the soul that carries it forward. He said that was me. And now that he's gone… the rails will hold."

He fell silent, the medallion now cold and gleaming in his hand, no longer a curse, but a key finally turned.

For a long moment, none of us spoke. The only sound was the hiss of the lamp and the faint drip of water echoing down the stone throat of the cave.

Peggy was the first to move. She drew Walter against her chest, her hand splayed over his hair as though to shield him from the very power of his own words. But her voice was steady, fierce even, when she said, "Then it was always meant to be you. The mountain chose you. Not to punish, but to free."

I couldn't breathe. My whole life—the fights, the bargains, the near-deaths under ice and stone—all of it had led me here, only to find out I was never the one. My throat worked against the silence. "I thought…" My voice cracked, and I started again. "I thought I carried this for a reason. That Magnus bound himself to me, that I was the one meant to undo him."

Walter lifted his head, eyes sharp and solemn beyond his years. "You were, Pops. But not to finish it. To keep it safe for me. Magnus said so. You were the keeper. I'm the key."

The words cut and healed in the same breath. Keeper. Not chosen. A custodian of something bigger than myself, bigger than any man. My chest ached with the truth of it.

Peggy's gaze met mine, and I saw the storm in her eyes—the fear, the pride, the unbearable knowing that our boy had stepped into something neither of us could touch. "Percy," she whispered, "you carried it as far as you could. Now it's Walter's turn."

The mountain seemed to lean in at her words, the air shifting around us, lighter, freer. For the first time in years, I didn't feel Magnus pressing against me. The silence was clean, no longer haunted.

Walter reached for my hand, pressing the medallion into my palm. "It's not leaving us, Pops. It's ours. But it listens to me now."

I curled my fingers around it, the silver cool and alive against my skin, and looked at my son. Seventeen years old, and yet carrying the fate of rails and mountains, of spirits and salvation. Pride swelled against my fear, a tide I could not hold back.

"You've done what I never could," I said, my voice breaking on the words. "You freed him. And now, maybe, Alaska will let us finish what we started."

Peggy drew us both in then, our three shadows merging on the cave wall, the medallion glinting between us like a fourth presence—no longer a burden, but a bond.

CHAPTER FORTY-THREE
THE GOLDEN SPIKE

I stood with Peggy and Walter at the edge of the crowd, my heart beating as though it belonged to the rails themselves. Four years had passed since our encounter in the ice caves, and still the memory clung like frost. Sha-e-dah-kla's warnings, Magnus's restless spirit, and the medallion's searing weight—they had never left me.

Walter was no longer the boy who had followed me into the frozen chambers with wide eyes and trembling hands. He stood taller now, shoulders squared, his jaw set with the resolve of a man. The medallion that once burned my chest now hung against his. Its wisdom had yet to reveal itself to him, as it had to me, but I knew the time would come. For now, it lent him something else—an unmistakable confidence, a steadiness that set him apart from the boy he had been.

But time had not been idle. We had been spared the cruel tide of the Spanish Flu. From the winter of 1918 through 1919, as it swept through the railroad camps and Native villages—stealing whole families, leaving camps silent save for the wind—Hope lay tucked against the Kenai, protected as if the mountains themselves had drawn a shield around us. Word came in grim reports: coffins stacked in Anchorage, tents emptied overnight, riverside villages gone quiet.

The outbreak struck hardest near Anchorage and the Matanuska Valley. Entire crews perished in a matter of weeks, leaving survey stakes abandoned in the snow, steam engines idle, and camps gutted of their men. Rail work, so close to triumph, staggered and nearly collapsed under the crush of sickness.

I wrote what I could of it, my words carried south, printed in papers desperate for news. In my prose, I could not soften the truth: it was a battlefield without trenches, without rifles, without uniforms. The enemy was invisible, yet more merciless than any foe of flesh and blood. It struck without warning, tore through lungs like fire through tinder, and left behind rows of the dead as though the camps themselves had been shelled. Nurses fell beside their patients, fathers beside their sons.

And yet, by some providence, we endured, untouched. Hope's isolation, its distance from the main line, became our salvation. We watched the storm from the mountains, grieving for those lost but grateful for the strange mercy that spared us.

Beyond Alaska, the world itself was shifting. The Great War had ended in 1918, leaving Europe scarred and mourning, and though its thunder had felt far away, its shadow touched even here. Men who might have come north to work the rails had marched instead across fields in France. The influenza followed in the war's wake, riding the same ships that carried soldiers home. It struck our camps and villages with a cruelty no bullet could match. Yet, by some quirk of fate, Hope remained a refuge, our little town spared while the rest of the world staggered to its knees.

I looked at Walter—tall and steady at my side—and felt the truth of it even more keenly. In another place, in another life, he would have been wearing a uniform instead of the medallion. He might have been swallowed by mud and trenches an ocean away, claimed by a war that ended just as the plague began. Instead, he stood here in Alaska, alive, his path unwritten, his burden only just beginning.

Now, standing in Nenana beneath a clear July sky, the air trembled with the sound of thousands gathered to see history hammered into iron. The town had never held so many souls before—railroad men in patched wool coats, Native families who had walked for days along the riverbanks, dignitaries in stiff collars, and ordinary settlers who wanted to say they had seen the moment when steel finally bound Alaska from sea to interior.

Among them stood the men whose hands, visions, and tempers had shaped this line. Frederick Mears stood tall, the crowd parting slightly around him, sensing the authority he carried. Beside him, Thomas Riggs spoke in sharp gestures, as though even here, amid ceremony, he could not stop himself from calculating grades and reroutes. Not far off, Otto Ohlson leaned back, arms folded, eyes cool and practical. His mind was not on speeches but on timetables, on the relentless arithmetic of profit and loss. And in the shade of a timber post, John Ballaine watched with something like resignation and pride, the dreamer who had once nearly ruined himself trying to carve this same line north. His ghostly presence seemed to bind the past to this present triumph.

And at the center, surrounded by his retinue, President Warren G. Harding lifted the ceremonial mallet. His face looked worn by the journey north, but resolute—this was not just a spike for Alaska, but for the nation. Cameras clicked, bands blared, the crowd pressed closer.

The spike gleamed in the northern sun, not pure gold but plated—a symbol, not substance. Yet when Harding lifted the hammer and brought it down, it rang louder than iron, carrying the spirit of every mile between Seward and Fairbanks. It was meant as a promise: that Alaska's wilderness could be bound in steel, that its riches would flow south as surely as the rivers to the sea.

I felt Peggy's hand slip into mine, Walter's shoulder press against me, and yet my eyes searched the crowd for a figure I knew would not be there. William Andrews Clark. Copper King. Saboteur. He would never show his face at Nenana. He had spent years and fortunes trying to bleed this project dry, hiding behind men like Cutter, turning labor unrest and collapsed trestles into weapons. Mears had spoken his name to me once in confidence, the secret I had carried like a burning coal in my pocket. I had never dared put it in print. I hadn't needed to.

Because the truth was here now, plain as steel: the line was finished. Every mile of track, every blasted cut, every coffin lowered into frozen ground bore silent witness to his war against us. And yet here stood the living, thousands strong, gathered to cheer the golden spike.

Harding brought the mallet down. The spike rang like a bell across the valley. The crowd roared. And in that peal, I heard the final note of Clark's defeat. He could sulk in his Montana mansion, tally his copper profits, and curse the line that refused to die. But it was done. The Alaska Railroad was complete.

And then the world shifted.

The cheering crowd thinned to whispers, their faces fading like breath on glass. The spike shimmered as though molten. A shadow crossed me, though no cloud moved across the sun.

And there he was.

Sha-e-dah-kla stood before me, as real as the rails beneath my boots. His shoulders were cloaked in a heavy coat of raven feathers that shifted with a life of their own, black gloss catching glints of unseen fire. His face was carved deep with lines like riverstone, ageless and immovable, yet his eyes churned like storms. When he spoke, his voice carried the timbre of dry wind through cedar—brittle, solemn, and vast as the land itself.

"You see now, Percy," he said, though none around us seemed to hear. "The line is not only iron—it is memory, binding the living and the dead. Magnus has crossed, but his burden lives in you, and in the boy. Look—already the medallion has chosen."

I turned, and my breath caught. The silver disc that had once seared my chest now glinted at Walter's throat, alive in the sunlight. For an instant, its polished surface flickered with a dark sheen—like raven feathers stirred by unseen wings. Walter stood tall, chin lifted, no longer a boy but one marked for a path only he could walk.

Sha-e-dah-kla's voice deepened, rumbling like thunder over stone:

"What men call an ending is for him a beginning. The spike binds the rails, but the medallion binds memory. It answers his heart now, and through him remembrance will outlive iron and fire. Guard him, Percy— for though the track is finished, the true journey has only begun."

Peggy's hand clenched mine, her gaze fixed on the president, yet I felt the tremor in her grip. Walter looked up at me, and in his eyes was no fear—only knowing.

Then the vision dissolved. The cheers swelled again, the crowd alive with triumph. But I stood frozen, my pulse hammering with the certainty that while the railroad was complete, Walter's task had only just begun.

EPILOGUE
RAILS OF HOPE

San Francisco Examiner

Sunday, July 29, 1923

RAILS OF HOPE

By Percy Hope, Special Correspondent for the San Francisco Examiner

Hope, Alaska

They call it complete. From the tidewater at Seward to the banks of the Tanana, steel now binds Alaska into one long breath. The golden spike has been driven, its ring echoing across valleys that once knew only silence. With it, a dream long dismissed as impossible has taken root in iron.

I have walked nearly every mile of this line. I have seen men swing picks into frozen ground that curled steel like fiddle-strings overnight. I have heard the thunder of dynamite shattering gulches and granite cliffs. I have stood by scaffolds that buckled into rivers roaring with ice and watched coffins lowered into permafrost where the line demanded its toll. Yet always, the hammer rang again. Always the spike was lifted anew. Always the whistle of progress summoned men onward.

A RAILROAD OF EXTREMES

The Alaska Railroad began at Seward, where spruce forests bent in the sea wind. From there, it climbed into the Kenai Peninsula, winding through Moose Pass and carving a precarious course northward.

At the Susitna, engineers drove girders into frozen riverbeds, building a bridge upon winter's gift of ice. In Broad Pass, graders contended with avalanches that buried whole crews in silence deeper than any cathedral. From the coalfields of Matanuska came the very fuel that stoked the engines—coal wrested from the mountains by men whose lungs grew as black as the ore they mined.

Anchorage, once no more than a sprawl of tents, shanties, and sawdust streets, rose on the shoulders of this enterprise into permanence. It is today a city of order, its frame buildings, warehouses, and depots testifying to the will of the rails. From there, the line pressed north, crossing muskeg, forest, and tundra until, at last, it reached Fairbanks, fastening a frontier town to the coast by steel.

THE HUMAN COST

It is easy to praise the names of presidents and governors, but the true credit belongs to the laborers: Norwegian tie hacks whose axes sang through the forests, Irish dynamiters who blasted open rock faces, Alaska Natives who hauled freight across ice trails, Black cooks who kept men alive in camps, and nameless thousands whose cracked hands, frostbitten cheeks, and hollow stomachs testify to the price of progress.

I spoke with a Swede named Anders, who told me, *"It's madness—but a holy madness. We build what no one else dares."*

An Inupiat freighter, Nanuk, said, *"It is not the cold that breaks men. It is the silence. The whistle will be a comfort. It means we are not alone anymore."*

Yet even their resilience was tested by storms far beyond the frontier. World War I pulled men away from the line, sending them across the globe to fight in Europe's trenches. And scarcely had the war ended when the Spanish Flu arrived, sweeping through camps with ruthless speed. Coffins stacked in Anchorage, Native villages were emptied overnight, and the work faltered beneath grief as heavy as the snows.

OBSTACLES AND SABOTAGE

The land itself fought us—permafrost that devoured rail, floods that swept away bridges, winds that tore tents into ribbons. And there were darker forces still: men who profited from Alaska's isolation, who whispered rumors, tampered with supplies, and, in the dead of night, pulled spikes or weakened trestles.

It was in such moments that I was branded the Wizard of Hope. I never sought the title, but when frost-heaved track was steadied with cribbing, or when schemes of sabotage were countered by vigilance and quick repair, the men began to believe I had answers. I had none but stubbornness and the conviction that this line must be finished.

THE GOLDEN SPIKE

And now it is done. At Nenana, before a crowd thousands strong, President Warren G. Harding raised the mallet. When the golden spike rang home, hats flew skyward, and cheers rolled across the valley.

It was triumph, but also remembrance: of every man buried in permafrost, every family left waiting, every child who would never hear their father's whistle home.

What none of us could know was that this triumph would also be among the president's last. Just weeks later, Harding collapsed on his western tour and was gone. That he gave his strength to Alaska in his final days lends this spike a deeper echo—part victory, part elegy.

A FUTURE IN IRON

Now the whistle runs the length of the Territory. Farmers will send grain to tidewater. Miners will ship coal and ore to market. Families will travel not by weeks of sled but by hours of rail.

For me, it is also personal. My son, Walter, was but thirteen when I first reported from this line. He stands taller now, nearly a man. He will inherit not only the steel that lies across this land, but the possibilities it opens: education, livelihood, a future where journeys are measured not in weeks of peril, but in the steady hours between whistle-stops.

THE LAND REMEMBERS

Yet I will not pretend this is the end of the story. Steel is never permanent. Alaska remembers every trespass. Winds from Denali, muskeg that swallows iron whole, rivers that grind against their banks— these will test what men have built.

Still, for this day, the Alaska Railroad stands. Complete. Defiant. Alive.

And so I say to you, reader—as I did when the first rail was struck at Seward eight years ago: come with me. Hear the whistle cut through the northern air. Listen to the song of steel echo across a land both wounded and healed by its making.

The Alaska Railroad is no longer a dream. It is a memory forged in iron, a triumph born of sacrifice, and a promise carried into tomorrow.

THE END

About the Author

Neil Perry Gordon approaches storytelling as more than a craft—it is his passion and purpose, a means to explore the extraordinary and bring it within reach. Through his writing, he masterfully intertwines the threads of history, metaphysics, and speculative inquiry, crafting immersive narratives that uncover hidden truths and resonate deeply on a human level.

With over a dozen published novels—including the widely acclaimed *The Wizard of Hope: The Alaskan Adventures of Percy Hope*—Neil has dedicated himself to creating stories that inspire reflection, wonder, and a deeper understanding of life's mysteries. His work spans historical fiction and metaphysical fantasy, blending meticulous research with visionary imagination.

Neil's storytelling is rooted in a reverence for the power of narrative to connect, uplift, and transform. His novels are rich tapestries where history, myth, and "what if" possibilities converge—inviting readers to explore alternate realities and the untapped potential of human existence.

For Neil, writing is an act of discovery. Each book becomes a living canvas upon which he explores the interplay between the seen and unseen, the temporal and eternal. His prose carries both intellectual rigor and emotional grace, weaving tales that are as spiritually resonant as they are vividly human.

Whether delving into the depths of consciousness, posing speculative questions that expand perception, or illuminating the sacred threads that bind past and present, Neil's stories invite readers to encounter the world anew. They are a feast for the mind and spirit—narratives that linger long after the final page has been turned.